HEAVY IS THE CROWN

GOTHIC GROVE
BOOK 2

JA GEORGE

Formatting by: Mads at Breathless Lit (@breathlesslitpa)
Kindle Formatting: JA George (@PNWwritingWitch)
Original Edits by: Paisley Prophit
Revisional Edits: Bre with Mythica Edits (@mythicaedits or
mythicaedits.com)
Cover Design By: Sam (damnfinesam.com)

READING ORDER

Venomous Love: A Gothic Grove Halloween Novella (This book does not have to be read prior to the rest of the series and is only available via author)

Gothic Grove
Heavy is the Crown
The Demons they Forged: A Gothic Grove Novella
Ruined Kingdom (coming Jan 2025)
Untilted Book Four (coming spring 2025)

When I set out to rework Gothic Grove I had not intended to do Heavy is the Crown. Honestly once this book was done I truly did not want to go back through it. Shadow and Drago are near and dear to my heart in a beautifully painful way. So even when I have annotated this book its been really hard for me to reread.

So I want to give a very big thank you to my new editor and good friend Bre, Mythica Edits, who was with me every step of the way. Even at 2am as we were both awake with kiddos and chatting.

Love you lots my friend!

And a shout out to Writhe Pole Dance Studio because without you I wouldn't have found her!

And future characters would not have found their inner goddess that's for sure.

sexual activities, nor should it be used to reflect healthy rela-
tionships.

If you are interested in gaining education around the
kink community and exploration of kinks here are some
resources:

Authentic Kink by Princess Kali
Wild Side of Sex by Midor

**This is a dark romance. If you do not like
darkness, do not proceed. This is the last warning. Again, this book is darker than its
predecessor.**

If you encounter errors in the book OR have other triggers
you feel should be added, please reach out to the author, not
Amazon. Author email: authorjageorge@gmail.com

It is important to note I use some language that is not
translated until the very end of the story, and this is
purposeful.

Author Note

This book was a lot more personal for me to write. Shadow's character took on a lot of my own personal healing journey, and as such, I'm very protective over him and his healing arc. Not everyone will have the same experiences with substance and self-harm. If you are someone who believes in abstinence-based models of recovery, particularly with substance use, you might struggle with his healing. Harm reduction does not work for everyone. Nor does it work for everyone through every stage of life.

If you are having suicidal thoughts or need support for your mental health please take care of you above all else.

Crisis Line: 866-427-4747

PLAYLIST

Apple Music Playlist
"bad guy" – Vitamin String Quartet
"In the End" – Linkin Park
"Clint Eastwood" – Gorillaz
"Cobra (Rock Remix) [feat. Spirit Box]" – Megan Thee
Stallion
"You've Created a Monster" – Bohnes
"I Can't Stop" – Flux Pavilion
"Gold Dust (Flux Pavilion Remix)" – DJ Fresh
"Mermaids" – Florence and the Machine
"From the Inside" – Linkin Park
"Labour" – Paris Paloma
"She Will Be Loved" – Vitamin String Quartet
"It Had To Be You" – Tommee Profitt
"SACRIFICE" – In This Moment
"I Hate Everything About You" – Three Days Grace
"I'm OK" – Christina Aguilera
"Eat Your Young" – Hozier
"Rumors" – NEFFEX
"Gold (Stupid Love)" – ILLENIUM

"Something To Hide" – Grandson
"STILL NUMB" – Ryan Oaks
"Somewhere I Belong" – Linkin Park
"Lovely" – Tommee Profitt and Fleurie
"Don't Blame Me" – Taylor Swift
"despicable" – Grandson
"Just Pretend" – Bad Omens
"I Love You, I'm Trying" – Grandson
"The One That Got Away" – The Civil Wars
"Half God Half Devil" – In This Moment
"ARMY OF ME" – In This Moment
"The Beautiful & Damned" – G-Eazy
"Judith" – A Perfect Circle
"Down With The Sickness (feat. Ai Mori)" – Violet
Orlandi
"Tell Mama" – The Civil Wars
"Let It Go (with Lø Spirit)" – Chandler Leighton
"Godly" – Tommee Profitt and Vo Williams
"Land Of Darkness" – Rated R and CELO
"Miracle" – Bad Omens
"THE DEATH OF PEACE OF MIND" – Bad Omens
"Closer" – Nine Inch Nails
"Gasoline" – Halsey
"SWEET DREAMS" – HANZO
"Promises (Skrillex and Nero Remix)" – Nero
"Movement" – Hozier
"Exile" – Taylor Swift
"Dangerous Hands" – Austin Giorgio
"I Walk the Line" – Halsey
"The Grey" – Bad Omens
"The Fighter" – In This Moment
"FATE BRINGER" – In This Moment
"I Would Die for You" – In This Moment

"How Villains Are Made" – Madalen Duke
"California Dreamin'" – Sia
"Wicked (feat. Royal and the Serpent)" – Tommee Profitt
"Shadowboxer" – Fiona Apple
"The Tradition" – Halsey
"Iris" – Tommee Profitt and Ruelle
"Shattered Dreams (feat. VE)" – Hidden Citizens
"(I Just) Died In Your Arms Tonight" – Hidden Citizens
"The Devil Wears a Suit and Tie" – Colter Wall
"Me and the Devil" – Soap&Skin
"Voices" – Hidden Citizens
"This Is Where It Ends" – Hidden Citizens
"Don't Speak" – Hidden Citizens
"Paint It Black" – Hidden Citizens
"Bigger Than the Whole Sky" – Taylor Swift
"marjorie" – Taylor Swift

Dedications

To the people out there who sought refuge in sharp objects
and substances, you are worthy of healing.
To my husband, for always being my person and helping me
get through this book without even realizing it.
And to my healers of the world who sit in the darkness with
people and don't judge them, I see you.

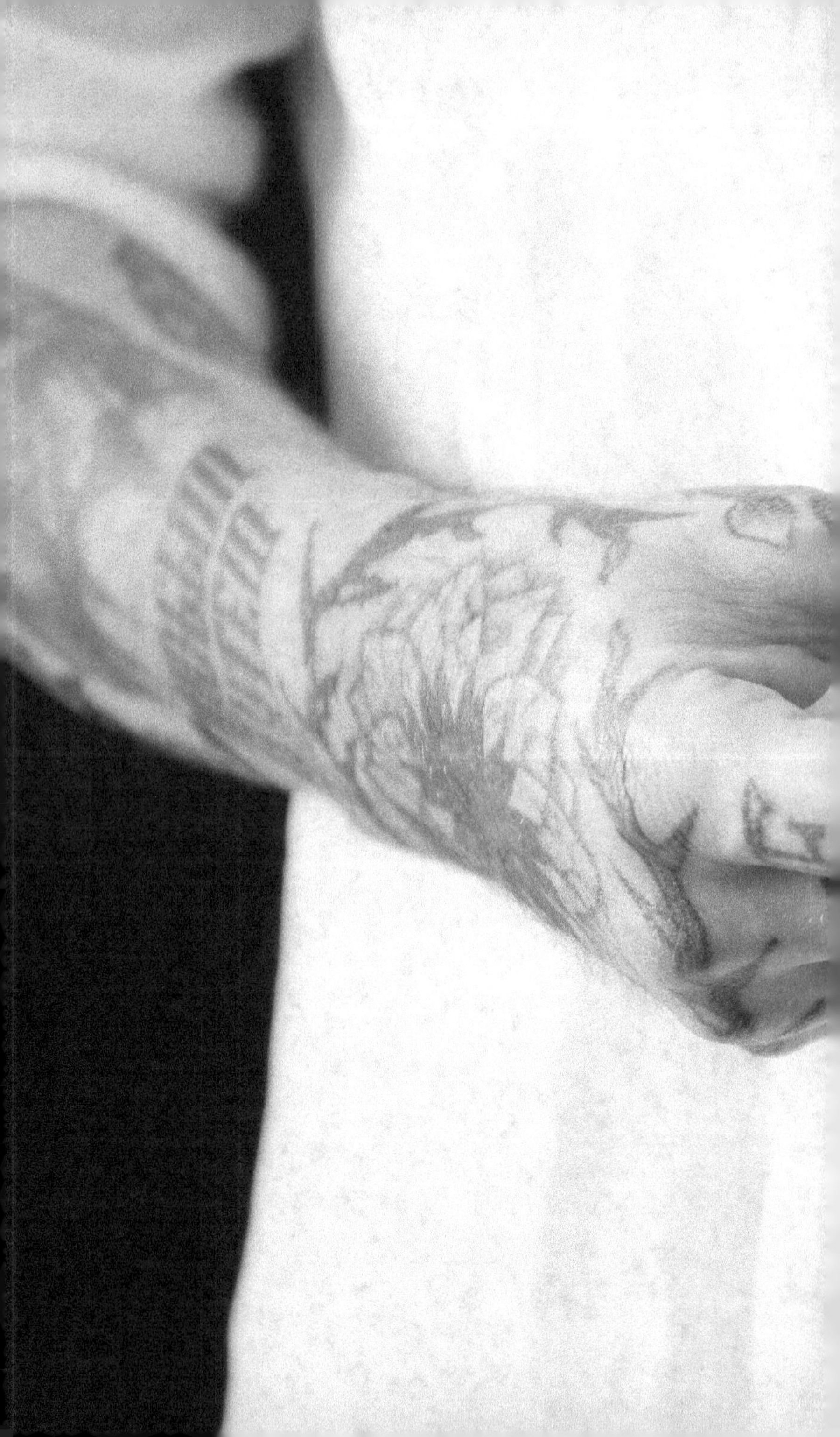

PART ONE

A brief history
This portion occurs prior to the events in Gothic
Grove

ONE

A dragon's first shift is the most volatile.
The pain of allowing your two parts to merge is beyond
comprehension,
but once the two are merged, you will know peace as you
never have before.
— Rosewood Family Journal

SHADOW (SIXTEEN YEARS **old**)

They say when you shift the first time, it's euphoric. The merging of you and your dragon counterpart makes you complete. Maybe it is euphoric for your average shifter. But I've known nothing but fear since it awoke in my mind. The raw power of it has terrified me from the very moment we first became aware of each other, and as soon as I started feeling the shift coming, I tried to deny it. Tried to pretend I wasn't changing.

But you can only deny reality for so long . . .

The world slams back into me as my body shifts down,

scales dissolving back to skin, wings pulling into my spine with bone-crushing pain, as my massive body pushes back inward, trying to fit into a space that cannot accommodate it. *This is it. This is how I die. Being ripped apart by the shift.* But as quickly as those words race through my brain, the pain ceases and my body belongs to me again. Naked and shaking, I blink rapidly as I try to come to terms with what just happened.

Silence greets me just for a moment before I hear screams and racing feet through the hallway. My heart drops into my stomach as I go to shove my shaking hands through my hair only to stop and see them shining with red. Dread pools deep within and bile rises into my throat. Disoriented, I step forward but slip on something warm, and the scent of blood slams into me. My eyes snag on my worst nightmare. My mother's body is lying under me, her blood fanning out around us.

"No," I choke out. "No, no, no!" I cry, a sob wrenched from my chest. I let myself drop to the ground, hands shaking as they hover over her.

This wasn't us, my dragon roars, but I can see the truth in front of me. The undeniable truth.

I try desperately to push my mother's blood back into her wounds. The ragged claw marks across her chest pulse in time with her fading heartbeat. "Mom, no! Please! Oh, gods, no, no, no." My tears are blurring my vision, causing the world around me to appear as if through a kaleidoscope.

A cool hand braces my face, the touch so familiar to me. "It's okay, my love. Please stop. This is okay." Her voice is soothing. "You must calm down and listen to me, dear one." I try my best to breathe in her steady voice, but my body is still shaking. Tears are still cascading down my face. "Promise me you won't let your father know who you are.

Promise me, Shadow. He can never see your dragon. He can never know how powerful you are."

"I promise! Mom, just please stay with me." The only person in my life who loves me is slipping through my fingers.

"I love you." Her broken voice turns cold as her hand slips away from my own. The world seems to dim around me as I watch her life get sucked into the underworld, as though if I watch long enough I could actually see the reaper beckoning her soul forth.

Time loses all meaning until I can no longer tell just how long I've been kneeling in the, now cold, pool of blood that has seeped free of her.

More screams echo outside, the sounds of my fathers' men shouting orders drawing me out of my haze.

On shaking legs I stand and back away from my mothers lifeless body, the warmth she was exuding now gone leaving nothing but icy, fridged pain in its wake. My feet drag me through the halls, the sounds from outside luring me towards them like a sailor following the siren's song.

I find myself standing at the back door, the French doors flung open, and glass shattered in brilliant fractals over the deck. I blink rapidly against the sudden brightness compared to the dark halls. When I'm finally able to take it in, the horror that grips me is unparalleled.

As if a volcano erupted, pools of lava gather around, and beyond that lies the smoldering remains of the field. It's my fault. It's my fucking fault. I killed her with my shift. I did this. I couldn't control myself, couldn't control *it*.

NO! This wasn't us. This is not our fault; my dragon roars back.

Agony rips through my body, shattering my heart and

shredding my soul. A scream tears itself from my throat as that grief that was hidden beneath the ice within my soul breaks free and rips into my heart. I am lost to it as I see the remains of people scattered throughout the yard, the smell of charred flesh now penetrating my senses. Whoever these humans were is unidentifiable now because I killed them. My dragon killed them.

We did not fucking do this My dragon roars.

Worthless. Pathetic. Weak. Murderer. The words repeat over and over in my mind, until I feel hands pulling me away, and when a fist connects with my jaw, the world blessedly blinks out.

I wake up in a sterile-looking room. A wooden desk and a small twin bed the only furniture. The walls a blinding white, the scent of fresh paint covering something else that I can't identify. When I turn toward the window, I'm not shocked to find bars on it. It resembles a prison cell. Which is fitting. I killed her. I deserve this.

It's the first time I shove my dragon deep into a cage, ignoring how he roars and thrashes against me.

It's the first day I find escape in pain . . .

And the first time I understand how good it feels to atone through my own flesh and blood.

———

SHADOW (EIGHTEEN YEARS **old**)

Bonus

My father looks me over from top to bottom, the sneer on his lips barely contained as his eyes snag on the scars that litter my arms. Normally I wear long sleeves if I'm forced to be in his presence but today, in a rare act of defiance, I've worn a t-shirt. Forcing him to look at the mess of a son that I am. Forcing his new family to see what type of world they are marrying into.

"You couldn't have covered up your weakness?" He growls.

I shrug, raising the cigarette to my lips and taking a long drag before blowing the smoke out towards him. It's funny he's so concerned with my scars considering how many he's given me across my back. All the spots easily hidden where the Dragon Lord has taken it upon himself to release his wrath upon his son. "You will behave." He snipes, stepping in closer and gripping my face. His eyes glow golden as his dragon challenges me. My own thrashing against the bars of the cage I keep him in.

Worthless dragon, the old man would never stand a chance against us if you allowed yourself to claim your true power. He hisses.

I hold perfectly still, ignoring the challenge and holding back my power. Upholding the promise I made to my mother as her blood stained my hands and soul.

The butler clears his throat, his black shoes squeaking on the polished marble floor as he approaches us. "Sir, your fiancé and her son have arrived."

My father rips the cigarette from me and crushes it under his foot before releasing my face and taking a deep breath. When he exhales, I see the carefully constructed mask he wears for all but me and when he turns towards our servant, I can imagine the perfectly painted smile he has now plastered over his face.

My eyes snag just beyond as the front door swings wide open and the most beautiful man I've ever seen walks in.

"Shadow," my father beckons me forward. "Meet your new brother. Drago."

Mine.

SHADOW (TWENTY YEARS **old**)
("bad guy" – Vitamin String Quartet)

I watch as my father parades his new wife around the massive party. Shifters, vampires, and witches have all come out to see the marriage between Julien Rosewood and Penelope Cadence. The Dragon Lord with his pretty bride. Even Alexi Helvig is here, the Vampire Lord himself. He's currently drinking champagne that looks suspiciously red. His date is a slender witch her long dark hair hanging in a curtain partially obscuring her face. She seems to be tolerating him, only allowing him to touch her when she deems it necessary, otherwise the disgust on her face is barely hidden.

They fashion themselves lords, but they only keep power through fear and through surrounding themselves with lesser beings. I grit my teeth against the voice of my dragon, even if he speaks the truth from deep in his cage. *But we are not lesser beings. We would be a true lord.* He's never quieted down, always loud from his cage.

"Shut up," I mutter aloud, taking a huge gulp of the champagne in my hand. The liquid costs more money than this house is worth, and I'm drinking it like it's fucking water to keep his voice at bay.

My father does another sweep around the dance floor, cutting off my line of sight of the vampire. His new bride, my new stepmother, seems to be enjoying herself, a smile painted across a perfectly made-up face. Only someone versed in abuse would see through that look. You can't even tell she has a black eye or that she is favoring the right side of her ribcage. I watch as he twirls her through the dance, ever the doting husband. My stomach rolls with unease. It's not that I don't like Penelope—she is actually quite kind to me, which makes it worse that she is marrying into this shit show. No one should be subjected to the hellish life we've been living since my mother died.

Since I killed her. Since I woke to her blood coating my hands. Because I'm a murderer. Weak. Weak. WEAK.

We are not weak; you are choosing weakness. I can taste the smoke on my tongue as he fumes in his cage. Ever since my new stepbrother moved in, my dragon has been growing louder. Most days, I try desperately to ignore him, but right now, he's too loud, and I can almost feel him rolling under my skin. The champagne isn't working.

"You're looking awfully uncomfortable standing there." The deep voice pulls me from the degradation going on in my head. Drago stepping out of the darkness. As usual, he looks perfectly put together, and my mouth goes dry as I look him over. At some point, he removed the bowtie, so his tattoos now peek out from the unbuttoned white shirt. The memory of seeing him shirtless the other night shoots to my dick.

He smells delicious. I bet he would taste like sin across our tongue. My dragon rubs up against his cage like a cat in heat.

My eyes track his tattooed hand, each finger decorated in silver rings, as he raises his glass to his full lips. *Just imagine what those fingers could do.* I choke on my own drink at the image that flashes across my mind, courtesy of the slutty reptile in my brain.

He raises an eyebrow at me, and I curse my body for having a reaction to him. Curse my dragon for making me want him. Curse him for giving me a taste of what it would be like to be able to choose a life with him.

"What do you want, Drago?" I manage to ask when I've caught my breath.

He steps directly in front of me, and his proximity makes my dragon go feral in his cage. He likes how Drago smells, and quite frankly, I can't argue. The eucalyptus scent washes over me with a hint of citrus right underneath. It makes my mouth water. It's why I've avoided Drago ever since he moved in. Or tried to. Aside from that fateful day when he dropped to his knees in front of me. The way his mouth felt still haunts my dreams. A shiver goes down my spine as I try to push the want away. We got lucky that time, to not get caught, but I doubt we would get lucky again. And I don't need to add that to the list of things my father punishes me for. I can only imagine what fucking my stepbrother would earn me in punishment.

"I can't say hi to my new stepbrother?" His eyes track over my body. My own tux is still in perfect order. Not a wrinkle on it.

*Fuck, imagine what it would feel like to have him fuck us. His mouth was perfect; imagine that cock of his*I curse my dragon as my cock gets even harder.

Drago's nostrils flare and he steps in closer, eyes widening. He opens his mouth to speak, when over his shoulder, I see the glare of my father, dark eyes burrowing into me. They offer up a promise of violence. Not just toward me, but toward Drago as well. My dragon growls low, rage moving through us like the lava that is our fire.

The urge to protect Drago at all costs is what makes me step back, putting distance between us. "Leave me alone, Drago. I have no interest in talking to you." The lie is bitter on my tongue, but for once, my dragon is in alignment with me, agreeing that we must protect him. One, two, three steps and I'm turning on my heel, fleeing the party and my bastard father.

———

DRAGO

The house is quiet as I meander through the darkened halls, the party all but over, save for the few stragglers who are still too fucked up to figure out how to leave. My mother has long since gone to bed with her piece-of-shit husband. While I should be heading out to do my own nefarious deeds, I find I can't escape the idea of Shadow. It slithers restlessly through my veins, the need to see him, to touch him. I'm proud of myself for not following him when he ran from me this evening, because if there is one thing I love, it's catching prey.

However, I'm not an idiot—the moment I turned around and saw his father glaring in our direction, I knew why he had fled. *When we kill him, I hope we skin him slowly before we let our flames eat him*, my dragon rumbles. I smile at the thought.

I hadn't needed to follow my mother here. However, something had tugged at me and urged me to follow her. So, I did. Only to figure out what a piece of shit her new husband is. I had heard of Julien in passing, all dragons have, but I had never had dealings with him directly. If I had, he would have been dead long ago. Now, I find myself in a peculiar position. One that, if played right, could gain me power over the city. Julien may be an alpha, but I answer to a higher god—not that he knows that. Not that anyone knows that.

The path to my obsession is dark, the hallway lights extinguished. But I don't need my eyes right now. I'm not even to his door yet and I can already smell him. It's wafting down the hallway like a siren's call, luring me to a demise I don't care to avoid. My mind flashes back to the last time I did this. His cock in my mouth was unexpected, to be honest, but now that I've tasted him, I need more. I need to find out what it's like to be inside him.

I don't pause at his door; I just push it open. The light is dim, barely enough to see around the room, but his eyes are wide open, luminous in the darkened atmosphere. His whiskey eyes don't show any shock at seeing me . . . in fact, they show such a variety of emotion, it's hard for me to track them all. But the one they land on looks like the cat who got caught with the canary. My hand rubs absently at my chest as I step over the threshold and let the door click shut behind me, then flip the lock. I step closer to him and take in his form. He's shirtless with a thin blanket over his lower half. It does nothing to hide his cock standing at attention.

"And what were you doing?" I purr, stopping directly at the end of his bed.

His dark hair falls into his eyes, cheeks blushing red. "Nothing. Why are you in my room?"

"Tsk, tsk. I asked you a question." I allow myself to sit on the tiny bed, the twin mattress barely able to fit him alone, much less two of us. I lean forward slightly, invading his space even more. "It looks to me like you were about to be very naughty and fuck your own hand."

His body is tense, every muscle poised to run. If he runs, I won't be able to control myself, I'll take him right here. Slowly, I pull the thin blanket off his body, causing his hard cock to bob when the material pulls free, exposing him fully. A bead of precum has already formed. I swipe my finger over it and pop it into my mouth, never allowing my eyes to leave his.

"Who were you thinking of?" I grab his length and slowly work my hand up and down. His muscles are still impossibly tense, his breathing heavy.

"Fuck," he hisses as I twist and pull at a torturously slow pace.

"Yes, I would like to do that. I would like to bury my cock in your tight ass and hear you scream my name." I lean forward and lick up his shaft, taking his head into my mouth. His hips jerk upward, but I pull off him. "But to get any of that, tell me who you were thinking of."

"I was thinking of some random girl at the party. Fucking her," he growls.

I lunge forward, my eyes blazing and fist now circling his neck. "Tell me again how you were thinking of some cunt and not me." I squeeze as I straddle him and grind down hard on his length. "Tell me how you weren't thinking about your cock in my mouth." I lean down close and allow my pierced tongue to flick out against his cheek as I lick upward.

A deep, throaty growl emanates from him as he tries to push up with his hips. "Fuck off, Drago."

I lean back, still holding his throat, and smile at the image laid out before me. "Fuck, my hand looks good around you. You want this to stop? You say, 'red,' got it?" He nods, but I shake my head. "I want to hear it."

For a moment, I think he'll say no, that he won't agree to play, but then he says the most beautiful words: "Yes, sir."

TWO

SHADOW

6 Months Later

The air is stagnant around me, hot and sticky with the scent of my own sweat, blood, and piss. I'm not sure how long I've been down here in my little cage. All I know is, my father has used some fucking witch magic to keep me from healing. Even without showing my dragon, I still have the ability to heal rapidly, which caused great offense to him after he spent hours taking his whip to me. Hence the sickly sweet-smelling potion that is currently dripping down the chains attached to my arms.

Out of my less-swollen eye, I can see the flickering lights above me, why does every room like this have flickering lights? Can't they fix this shit? The thought pulls a chuckle from me that burns my cracked ribs, causing me to wince.

I'm ninety percent sure my father has forgotten about me at this point; it feels like days have passed since he's been down here. But maybe it's only been a few hours. All I know is, my whole body burns and aches. The iron chains around my wrists bite down hard with no give, keeping my arms extended at an awful angle above my head.

The only thing that has kept me sane has been the memory of Drago. The memory of his hands moving over my body, his teeth nipping at my tender areas, his wicked tongue spilling beautiful promises into my ears, and that thick cock of his bringing me so much pleasure. At first, it was purely physical, but somewhere along the way, it became more. Stolen moments in the evenings turned into hours of talking, whether in person or over text, until we seemed to be in constant communication. At least until I got dragged here.

Fuck, I hope he isn't worried.

My father, the bastard that he is, seems to know something is going on between us. He sends Drago out of the house whenever he brings me here, which makes me wonder how he has managed to get him out of the house for this long. Surely, at this point, Drago has to have returned home, right?

Unless it really has only been a few hours. Time is a mindfuck down here. Before Drago, I had no desire to mark the passage of time, but now? Now, I count the minutes to get back to him. He's awoken something in me that has made me feel something other than despair and hatred for myself. Now that I've had a taste of it, I don't want to go a day without it.

I twist my head around, trying to relieve the pressure on my shoulders, but it only manages to show me how stiff I've become. My attention is pulled from my misery by the door behind me creaking open. An involuntary flinch pushes through me that rattles the chains holding me to the bar across the ceiling.

"I'm going to fucking kill him." Drago's voice echoes through the room.

My chest cracks open when I see him move into my view, watch his eyes catalog every single cut and bruise on my body. The promise of swift retribution is painted across his beautiful face. He reaches up and snaps the chains in one swift movement, deftly catching my body before I hit the ground. He cradles me to his chest, which feels impressive given my height, as he moves us out the door. My eyes snag on the dead guard next to the door and a sick satisfaction pushes through me.

"I'm never leaving you alone here again," he promises.

And even if it's selfish and dangerous, I let him make that promise and pray he keeps it.

He does.

. . . for a while

―――

SHADOW

Bonus

The snow-covered ground crunches loudly under my boots, the sound echoing out over the quiet lakefront property. The morning air smells like frost and balsam with a hint of smoke on the horizon. Pulling up short in front of the a-frame cabin I draw a long drag of the Eufori into my mouth before allowing the red smoke to color the space in front of me. The drug providing some relief to the wounds my father had inflicted upon me.

The image of Drago pulling me from that hell hole is still burned in my head. How he managed to not only do that but also get us to this place is beyond me. My father never lets me out of my cage.

And what will be the price you pay for this escapade?

"You gonna come in or tempt the air to freeze you solid?" Drago's rich voice moves over me like warm honey, pulling me from the depressing thought. He stands against the door, arms crossed over his very toned chest. He looks relaxed in flannel sweats and a v-neck black t-shirt that shows his tattoos peaking out. His normally well-kept blonde hair is ruffled as if he just woke up.

My mouth waters. Drago is beautiful, and the smirk he gives me tells me he knows exactly what he's doing.

Flicking the end of the joint out, I shove my other hand deep into my pocket and walk up the path towards the house. From here I can see a Christmas tree set up, its twinkling lights glowing in the window. Even when my mother was alive, we never celebrated the solstice as a family. Sure, they threw parties, but it was all for show. My stomach twists uncomfortably for a moment, *what am I doing here?*

As if sensing my nerves Drago clears the last few steps and pulls me into his body. "Rakkaani." He breathes against my neck. His nose dragging up and down as if he could mark me. I wish he would. I wish he would claim me. The thought is intrusive and unwanted. Drago would never claim me, why would he? I'm not worth that.

But what if we were?

Shut up, go back to your cage.

"Let's get inside." He pulls away, frowning a bit before grasping my hand and dragging me through the door. We've never spoken about my dragon, but he knows. He has never asked me, aside from that first day, why I refuse to shift but I often catch him looking at me when I have these internal arguments.

As soon as I'm inside Drago slams the cold out. The warmth of the fire washing over me and chasing the chill away. The interior of the cabin causes me to let out a small laugh before trying to reign it in.

"Yeah yeah, laugh all you want." He chuckles, still dragging me deeper into the home. "I didn't decorate this place, my mom did."

I grasp for words but come up short because everywhere I look is covered in bears. Even the couch is buffalo print with small black bears dotting it. The lamps are trees with bears. The walls have framed photos of bears. Statues of the fluffy creatures are on every surface. Even the mugs hanging on the wall are bears.

"It's uh… cozy." I say, because what the fuck else do you say to this monstrosity?

He lets out a warm laugh before dropping my hand and heading towards the kitchen. "My mother gifted this place to me and I haven't had the heart to change it. Even if these bears are atrocious." He explains.

I only nod, not understanding the sentiment because I've done everything to destroy any and all reminders of my mother. I push away the thoughts that threaten to consume me, and return my focus-to Drago.My body misses him despite him only being a few feet away and I rub at my chest absentmindedly. With his back to me I allow my eyes to roam over every inch of his beautiful body. A hunger pooling deep within me.

"Keep eye fucking me like that and I won't be able to give you the romantic night I had planned." He turns back to me holding, you guessed it, two mugs covered in bears. The one he hands me is red with a black bear's body as the handle. The scent of caramel and whiskey flood my nose.

"The drink is to warm you up until after dinner," he leans in close, planting a whisper

of a kiss across my lips. "After that I'll be the one warming your body."

I let out a moan as my eyes flutter. He hasn't touched me since he rescued me and I've felt as if I was dying. My body needing him like oxygen. It's both terrifying and exhilarating. Because when he decides to leave, and he will, it will break me in a way that no one has ever done.

He pulls back and sits down on the bear covered monstrosity of a couch, those powerful legs spread wide as he keeps his eyes locked on me. I shift nervously on my feet, so out of place in an environment that is so clearly a home. It hits me hard in the heart, I've never had a real home. Never experienced this comfort or security.

"Rakkaani?"

That word. The one he keeps calling me. It haunts me in my dreams. "What does that mean?" I ask before drinking down a gulp of the warm liquid in my hands.

"It means my beloved. Because that's what you are to me."

I recoil at the same time my heart jumps into my throat. "I'm not that special." I mutter the words that I can't help believing tumbling out because I'm not special. I'm a fuck up who killed my mom and on the best of days is only alive because I'm too scared to end it. I blink, suddenly feeling the tears that have started to form without permission.

He doesn't say anything, only sets his mug down on the side table and comes towards me. Grasping my face, he pulls me into a kiss that claims my very soul and sets it aflame. It's the kind of kiss that you could die from and be at peace with it so long as the kiss didn't end.

When he starts to pull back a whimper is exorcized

from chest at the loss of contact. Drago only chuckles before dropping to his knees in front of me. My cock hardens immediately as I take in the man, I'm desperately falling for, assuming a position he's only done once before.

"I don't get on my knees for anyone," he says as he slowly pulls down the waistband of my sweats, my cock springing free. "But for you? I'll worship at the altar of your feet for the rest of my life if you'll allow it." When his mouth sucks me in I cry out and grab his hair with both hands.

"Oh fuck oh fuck." I cry out as he expertly bobs up and down my length, his tongue swirling in just the right spot. I'm so lost in the feeling of his warm mouth that I don't notice him move one hand to my balls. When I feel his warm fingers and cool rings start to play with them I can barely hold back.

When I start to feel myself get close, he pulls off my cock eliciting a snarl from my throat that has him up and to his feet with supernatural speed. "Tsk tsk. I may go to my knees for you but I'm in charge." He growls, gripping my throat. He guides me to the couch, pushing me down so my cock stands up tall.

"I need you." I whimper.

He smiles softly before pulling his shirt over his head and pushing his pants down. "Shirt off." He commands, lazily stroking his pierced cock and gods help me I've never moved so fast. When I'm finally naked he straddles me. Reaching over to the side table and grabbing a bottle of lube he squirts a generous amount on our cocks before wrapping his fist around both and starting to pump.

My head falls back, mouth open. "Oh gods you feel good. So. Fucking good. Please don't stop."

"I need you to show me how good you are, don't cum until I say you can." He growls, picking up speed with hand.

The feeling is maddening and I devolve into mindless babble as he fucks us into his hand. Each time I think I'm going to cum he pulls himself back. When he finally does allow his hot release to splash across me I greedily swipe my fingers through it, desperate to get a taste.

"Ah who's my good little slut? You're cleaning up without me even asking. Such a good, good boy." The praises sends me spiraling dangerously close to the edge.

"Please Drago. Please let me cum I need it." Tears stream down my face as he sucks the tip of my cock into his mouth only to pull back off.

"Fuck you look good like this." "Like what?" I ask.

He smirks, "Like you are my perfect slut, and you belong to me. Now cum down my throat." When he puts his mouth over me again, I can't hold back as I fuck his face with a feral energy, I didn't know I possessed.

"Oh fuck. I'm gonna cum!" I scream as my release barrels into me with the force of a tsunami. Drago swallows down everything I pump into his throat before he slowly starts to pull off, my limp cock slipping free of him.

He groans as he catches some of my release with his finger, "You taste so gods damn good. I could feast on you morning, noon and night and never grow tired of it."

Pushing up he lays his head on my lap, nuzzling my naked thigh in a display of intimacy that's rare for him. Closing my eyes I allow myself to bask in the feeling, because despite everything I want. Love. I just don't deserve it.

When his fingers graze the raised scars on my thighs I tense. My body coiling to flee. "When was the last time?"

I don't have to ask what he means.

"A few days ago." I mutter. Shame burning brightly in me.

"Why?" The question is said delicately and somehow infused with a warmth that gives me the courage to explain.

"When I killed my mother, that was the first time I did it. It was punishment, I didn't want to die, I just didn't think I deserved to go unharmed. The next time I did it was to control my rage so I didn't hurt someone else again," I pause. Struggling to explain why I carve into myself, why I enjoy it while also resenting it. He's quiet, giving me space to talk and still gently tracing up and down my leg. "Fuck, it's so many things to me now. Some days it's the only thing I can control, some it's punishment, others it's because I crave seeing the marks and feeling the pull of them healing."

My hand gently plays with his hair, keeping me grounded and providing comfort as I expose my vulnerability to him. Deep within me my dragon lifts his head, curiously peaking out. It's the calmest I have ever felt him.

"Why did we come here?"

Drago lets out a long sigh before lifting his head to look at me. "Because after I pulled you from that place, I couldn't stay there a moment longer without killing your father. Or ripping the house to shreds."

"But why? I'm nothing."

He grips my chin hard, not allowing me to turn away. "You are everything, and if you let me I would burn your nightmares away so you never suffered again." His blue eyes are fierce but when they flash gold an ancient part of me wakes up and for a brief moment I allow myself to picture a life where I'm happy and with him.

————

DRAGO

Hearing Shadow talk about his self harm gutted me at the same time my heart soared that he was willing to open up. It's the most he's ever talked to me about anything this vulnerable. My dragon huffs out approval and is demanding we keep him here, where he is safe. It's hard to disagree as I glance down at his peaceful sleeping form.

Curled up against my body with his leg intertwined between mine he looks so calm, so at peace. Soft, classical Christmas music plays through the small speakers. Outside the snow began falling a few hours ago, the fresh blanket creating our own personal snow globe. One I wish we never had to leave.

We could stay.

But if we do we'll be hunted down.

Shadow shifts slightly, nuzzling into me even closer a sound of contentment whooshing from him. My eyes start to droop shut, despite my best efforts and sleep claims me.

———

I WAKE to the feeling of a warm mouth around my cock.

"Oh fuckkkk." I groan as Shadow's tongue teases my piercings. He isn't hurrying, instead seems to be leisurely sucking and licking driving me absolutely mad. Gripping his hair I pull his mouth from me, his eyes glazed with arousal as they meet mine. "I want to fuck you." I demand. He bites his lower lip and nods enthusiastically at the idea. Rapidly I flip him onto his back, his thick cock jutting up with precum dripping down the tip. Reaching across our bodies I grab the bottle of lube discarded last night and drip some down my cock before working it root to tip with my hand.

Leaning forward I spread his toned legs wide, adding more lube to my two fingers, and start probing his tight entrance.

"Just fuck me." Shadow demands. I arch an eyebrow, but he doesn't back down, and instead impales himself on my two fingers. I don't miss the wince at the intrusion.

"That was very naughty." I growl, removing my fingers quickly. "You know the rules, I'm in charge. Not you." I nudge the head of my cock to his entrance before pushing in. "You're lucky I just want this tight ass." He cries out as I slowly push in and out of him, torturing him with the slow pace. "You, however, will not be so lucky to get to cum now. Because only good boys get to finish, and you are not a good boy."

My pace increases as I lose myself to the feel of him, his tight hole squeezing me with just the right pressure as I piston my hips forward and back. "Pleasseee Drago. Fucking hell, please." He cries out. His cock looks painfully hard and his hands are fists on the sheets to keep from gripping it.

Reaching down I grab his thick length, jerking him in time to my thrusts. "Is this what you want?"

"Yes! Oh god yes!" He cries.

I smile at him before resuming stroking him. "I didn't know I was your god. But I do love when you worship at my feet." My cock starts to twitch as I feel my orgasm nearing. "I'm going to fill up this tight little hole and if you take it real good I'll let you finish. Okay?"

His agreement is nothing but incoherent begging as I unleash myself on him. "Oh shit, fuck you take me so good. Fucking hell, I'm going to cum. Going to fill you up in this tight little hole." My hand that is still holding his cock moves faster, sliding over his soft flesh over and over again. "Cum with me Shadow, fuck. Cum now."

He cries out, throwing his head back as he paints his stomach while I release deep within him. The room filled with cries of ecstasy as we allow ourselves to be taken away by the pleasure. When the last of us is spent my body collapses on top of his, our sweat sticking to each other. He offers me a smile and I allow my lips to meet that smile in a delicate kiss.

A kiss that turns from delicate to something. . . else. As if we both realize that when I pull out of him the world will return and our bubble will burst. We both pour all our feelings into it, everything we cannot say out loud yet is spoken within that kiss. And when both of us become hard again we spend longer slowly fucking, in an intense vulnerable way. An unhurried exploration of each other.

SHADOW

Drago cleans us up methodically after our morning tryst, my ass still painfully sore from his thick cock and his cum still dripping from me. I'm a mess and I love it. But even that can't keep my mind here because I know the clock is ticking and it's about to strike midnight. We can't stay here forever, we have to go back. But something shifted that last time we had sex. It's as if we knew when we walk out this door nothing will be the same.

"We could leave." The words are out of my mouth before I can stop them. He goes deathly still, turning towards me ever so slowly. "Leave?"

I nod, "run away. We could be happy. Don't you think?"

In the months I've been with Drago I have never seen him look as terrified as he does now. No, not terrified. . .

Unsure? Uneasy? Whatever it is, it's foreign and not what I want to see post asking him to leave. "Never mind." I mumble immediately embarrassed, my cheeks flaming.

"Fuck, Rakkaani. It's not that I don't want to. But we can't leave. I can't leave."

I nod, no longer wanting to be involved in this conversation. Already starting to look for an escape plan so I can smoke. I'm moving towards the front door before I can stop to think, those stupid bears judging the tears that are welling up.

Dragos hand grips my wrist, attempting to pull me back but I yank my arm free.

"Shadow, wait. Please. Let me explain." But no amount of begging is going to stop me from fleeing because he confirmed exactly what I've always known. I'm not worth it. I just wish I had learned that before I started looking at him as my home.

The snow bites into me as I rush down the steps, opening a portal rapidly. Drago only steps behind me. "I promise someday we'll go!" He yells. "I'll get you out."

I pause for a moment at the portal edge, turning to face him. "Happy Solstice, Drago. Thank you for last night, if nothing else it was the first time I slept peacefully in years."

He stands looking at me as if he wants to say more but instead just says, "Happy Solstice, Rakkaani."

———

SHADOW (TWO YEARS **later - twenty-two years old)**

("In the End" – Linkin Park)

The stone floor under me is stained and cracked, pieces of rock chipping up more and more each time I'm down here. Overhead, the light flickers and buzz like a swarm of bees, causing a migraine to start creeping in. My wrists ache from the shackles I've had around them for the last few days, and my tongue feels like sandpaper from the lack of water. The air around me smells like sweat and mold, guaranteeing that even if I had been fed, I would have puked it up at this point.

My father stands over me, heaving with exertion. His massive body has lost some of its muscle over the years, but he's no less powerful. Sweat beads on his upper lip and drips down his forehead. The displeasure and annoyance are evident on his face as he takes a drag of his cigarette. My body shakes with exhaustion from my father trying to force my transformation, his alpha magic ripping into me over and over again. The brutal beast under his skin refuses to take no for an answer, and it's been a long time since I've endured this type of treatment. Ever since Drago found me, he's kept me out of my father's reaches. Until today.

"I should have known you would be a worthless piece of shit. Thank God, I have your stepbrother, or my empire would be doomed." He kicks me in the stomach and my body curls in on itself against the pain.

Normally, by my age, I would be shifting all the time, but I've held back. He believes I have no power, that my dragon is too weak to come forth. But the truth is, I have far too much. The promise I made to my mother haunts me in these moments. Like a wailing ghost, it sits and mocks me as I take the abuse over and over again. My love for my mother has turned bitter at this point, her memory a curse because of this damn promise.

My dragon is angry, his feral rage always riding me, never giving me a moment's rest. Now, he is so volatile that I have no hope of control when he is finally unleashed.

You let him control us, we could kill. Its voice is always so loud in my head that it now blurs with my own inner dialogue. I don't know where his emotions start and mine end. We are an inferno of contempt and hostility.

My father drops his cigarette on me, the end burning into my skin. I want to rage or cry or fight, anything really, but my mother's voice moves through my head again, reminding me of that fucking promise. He leans down and grabs my chin, forcing my eyes up.

Please don't flash gold, I beg.

You're fucking weak. Let us out. Let us show him who we truly are, he counters. My dragon rattles his cage. If my father learns how powerful I am, he'll either kill me or force me into his service for the rest of my life. While his dragon is powerful, he's getting old and needs someone like me to help him maintain his rule. Dragons have a long, painful history of being forced into servitude, and while Hell no longer buys and enslaves us, my father still holds relics from that time that would make controlling me easy. *Keep it together. Drago will come. Just keep it together. Think about that night in the cabin.*

He leans down, his putrid breath across my face. "You think your little boyfriend is coming to rescue you?" Shock must move over my face because my father's lips shift into an evil grin. "Yeah, I'm not as dumb as you two think I am. You corrupted him, ruined him. You are an infection in this house that needs to be purged."

He snaps his fingers, and the scent of a vampire invades my nostrils. Renewed energy pulses through me as I whirl around, but two men are already grabbing my arms and roughly hoisting my exhausted body off the ground. "You'll be Alexi's problem now."

"What?" I ask, fighting against the two immortals holding me. "What do you mean?"

He pulls another cigarette out and lights it, taking a deep drag before blowing it out in my face. My father's dark eyes peer into mine. His head is shaved, but if it weren't, we would have the same black hair. "You have your mother's eyes," he says, like a curse. "You should have died that day."

Don't react. Don't react. I bite the inside of my cheek to focus on the physical pain over the emotional pain. Because I can't argue with him. It really should have been me who died that day, or any day following.

"Drago!" he yells abruptly.

My stepbrother meanders out of the shadows, his white hair gleaming in the light. Even in this dingy cell, he looks beautiful. My chest pulls toward him. He looks over at me, emotion briefly flashing in his eyes before a mask of indifference slips back on. My mind flashes to our stolen moments together. Sweat-slicked bodies. Moans of pleasure. The feeling of Drago's pierced cock in me. Moments of gentleness as he held me and let me break apart. Those stolen moments have kept me alive through this hell for the past two years. And I've let myself fall for him. Despite everything, I let my heart fall for him.

"What?" His flat voice conveys no emotion. Utter boredom smooths his face. But I can see the slight clench of his fist, the only tell that he is angry.

My father turns to him but motions toward me with a hand. "Shadow is leaving. I've made a deal with Alexi Helvig. All he wanted was a shifter to use for some experiments. As Shadow has shown no ability to shift, he'll be going. It's all he's good for. In exchange, he will leave our empire alone."

Worthless. No one will ever love you. This time, I know

it's my voice saying those things, my own demon, not my dragon. He is sitting quietly in his home, seething.

I bite hard into my cheek again. The tang of blood floods my mouth.

Drago frowns, those blue eyes of his narrowing. "You sold your own son?"

I catch his gaze and hope he can see in my eyes that I am begging him to do something. His own blue eyes flare briefly. He might not know why I'm hiding my power, but I thought he would be my ally in this. I thought he felt something for me. Those eyes lock on mine for only a second longer before they shift back to my father.

"He is no longer my son," my father says. It doesn't matter that I hate my father, it still cuts me deep when he utters those words. And the very small part of me that was holding out hope is extinguished.

I watch my father move away, his back toward me. Drago looks at me, panic flashing over his face, followed by cold rage and back to boredom. All in the span of a moment that I would have missed, had I not been watching him. The word please pushes to my tongue, but I can't seem to beg him to save me. Can't seem to make my mouth open.

Because I deserve this. I deserve whatever fate Alexi has in store for me. Drago knows this, and that's why he won't move to help me. That's why I won't beg for help.

I don't even realize I have been pulling against the two vampires holding me until the fight leaves my body and I go limp, dangling between the two supernaturals. Despite the feeling of my heart breaking into a thousand pieces, I keep my eyes trained on Drago, a grounding force in this maelstrom. When another vampire moves in behind us, Drago's eyes flare with fear and it almost sounds like he yells out my name, but then my neck is pushed roughly to the side and a glint of metal is the only warning I get before I feel the pinch of the needle entering me.

Immediately, my world tunnels and my body starts to feel fuzzy. When my captors drop me back to the ground, I don't feel it. With my last reserve of energy, I think I call for Drago, but my mouth feels wrong.

My vision swims, but I don't miss Drago suddenly by my side, his hands black. A thud echoes to my right, and I drag my check along the ground to turn my head. I come face to face with one of the vampires that was holding me. Black veins run up and down his flesh and blood drips from his eyes and mouth. Screams echo through the cavern. No, not screams. A single scream.

Drago, yelling my name.

I force my head to turn back over, and I can see my father's men holding tightly onto Drago as he struggles against them. He manages to drop one with that magic in his hands, but the fallen henchman is quickly replaced. My eyelids blink slower. I'm losing the battle against whatever drugs they forced into me. In my last moment of consciousness, I see my father slam a needle into Drago, subduing him. And in that moment, my whole world falls apart.

THREE

The royal family of Hell have guarded their magic for as long
as the covens have existed.
They alone hold the power to open or close the gates of Hell.
As with all things, this power should be harnessed for the
good of the coven.
—Mori Family Grimoire

AVA

("Clint Eastwood" – Gorillaz)
The warm night air moves through the open window, bringing with it the scent of the jasmine flowers outside, which slowly replaces the musty, old smell of the house we are in. The soft lap of the lake can be heard just under the low music Jackson is playing. A wood-paneled wall supports my weight as I watch my brother take a long drag off the red cigarette. He holds the hit in so long, it begs the question of how powerful his lungs are. The crimson smoke curls around his face, obscuring it. My head feels fuzzy just from standing in the smoke-filled room; a soft haze floats over my body, making me feel disconnected and pliant.

I fidget nervously with my sweatshirt. This is the first time I've actually been invited to hang out with my brother and his friends, not just snuck myself into their gathering. The prince of Hell has always been allowed to go out, or at least, the guards and our parents look the other way. But the princess? I am supposed to appear chaste, and if my mother had her way, I would be locked up in my room until she married me off to some noble.

Arcanna is lounging with her long legs up against the wall while she lays with her hair spread out in a halo around her head. Her hair so dark it seems to eat the light around her. Every now and again her eyes track towards my brother, lingering on his bare chest with a hunger before she jerks them away. Lately her gaze has lingered longer and longer, and I often find her sneaking out of his room when Oisin isn't around.

As if summoned, the door to the room opens and my brother's boyfriend meanders in, his bare chest exposed, and his sweats hung low on his hips. His black hair is pulled up in a half bun, showing the ragged scar that cuts through his eye. My brother smiles warmly at him, pushing up to stand and moving toward him. When Oisin enters the rest of the world disappears for Jackson.

Oisin grabs the back of my brother's golden neck and pulls his mouth into a long kiss. When they pull back, Oisin exhales smoke, and a smile steals across his face. I avert my eyes when my brother bites his lip. Arcanna watches them, a frown pulled onto her lips before she schools her face into neutrality.

Not for the first time I wonder if Oisin never came around would Arcanna be the one stealing smoke from his kiss?

"Ava!" Oisin's rich voice pulls me from the thoughts.

"Finally got to come hang out with us?" He pushes past Jax and sweeps me into his arms, his warm body pressing into me and flooding my head with his rich scent of tobacco and leather. When he finally puts me down, I watch his red eye trace over the oversized sweatshirt and bare legs. Disgust coursing through me at the way he lingers.

Jackson comes up behind Oisin and swings his arm around Oisin's shoulders, his silver eyes glazed over and blonde hair disheveled. "I figured she was old enough now." He shrugs, nipping playfully at Oisin's neck.

"You guys are the worst," Arcanna says. She flips over and pushes her long onyx hair over her shoulder as she stands. Despite the drugs, her hazel eyes are much clearer than my brother's, or even Oisin's. Her leggings cling to her muscular legs and the tiny slip of exposed stomach hints at defined abs. "You treat Ava like she's a fucking child, Jax. She's barely younger than you."

"You might be the only one who remembers that, Arcanna," I mutter.

She passes me a bottle of beer as the boys move to sit down on the long couch. I take a long sip of it and smile at her appreciatively. She is who I want to be. She doesn't back down, doesn't take shit from my brother or Oisin, and most importantly, she has her future wide open for her. No expectations placed on her at her birth.

"It's not like I haven't been following you guys for this long anyway." I pull myself from the safety of my wall and sit cross-legged on the old carpet. This place was once beautiful, a testament of how my father felt for my mother. He built her the lake house when he was courting her, and if she can be believed when she's drinking, they spent years being blissfully in love here. Until they weren't. Now, the old house sits abandoned beside a lake that no one dares come to anymore. The houses here were built before Hell was what it is now, before the glittering spectacle of clubs and slot machines took over. It was a simpler time. Probably boring as fuck, too.

Everyone thinks this is what I want. A simple life. All because I haven't fallen into the narrative of the party girl, not like my brother now. His reputation of being a playboy party prince is all over Hell. He's at a different club every weekend with Oisin and Arcanna in tow.He wasn't always into those things, but now with Oisin it seems all he wants to do is party and race, losing the image of perfect prince like a snake sheds their skin.

I've managed to go in with them a small handful of times, but Jax makes sure no one actually sees me. I am not even sure they know what I want. That sitting by the lake getting high sounds awful and I would much rather be at a club drowning in music and dancing. This? This is what Jackson used to love, before Oisin.

I'm pulled back into the conversation by a loud barking laugh from my brother. The room has grown even hazier since I let my mind wander. I watch as Jax lets Oisin drape himself across his lap, and a small pit grows in my stomach. I want to feel someone's hands on me. I want to be able to lose myself in my friends. I want to not feel like I'm fucking suffocating.

("COBRA (ROCK REMIX) [FEAT. SPIRIT BOX]" – **Megan Thee Stallion**)

Jackson inviting me to hang out with them has emboldened me to make choices some might say are poor, or risky. That taste of freedom was like a hit of Eufori straight to my veins, though, and I can't resist looking for that high again. Which is how I currently find myself wearing skintight black leather pants, high boots, and a tight leather jacket as I sit atop my brother's black Ducati with the visor of the helmet securely down to hide my silver eyes and blonde hair.

Hell's street races are legendary. Not just because of the type of cars that race but because of how dangerous they are. Hundreds of people race in a single evening, but not that many make it back over the finish line. It's also the only time people can race the future king of Hell. At least once a week, Jax, Oisin, and Arcanna are here, joining in on one or two of the races. Jax either races his bike, which thankfully, he conveniently left at home tonight, or his all-matte-black Subaru STI. Even from here, I can see him leaning against the driver's side door smoking his cigarette and laughing. Oisin stands near him sipping a beer. He never races, only rides along with Jax or watches from the side.

Arcanna's red Dodge Demon is parked next to Jax, but I can't spot her anywhere. Both have already participated this evening and now preside over the rest of the races. My brother looks happy, peaceful. He looks normal. The green-eyed monster that is jealousy floods my brain, and I suddenly hate my brother for getting to have this life. Regardless of how misplaced that anger is, it's still there. The rational side of me knows it's my parents who did this, not him. But the rational side has taken a backseat tonight, and that draw of freedom burns thick in my veins, which is why when I hear the call for the bikes to line up, I don't second guess, following a few others over to the starting line that is dangerously close to my brother.

("You've Created a Monster" – Bohnes)

Arguably, the bike races are the most dangerous, most

likely for me to end up dead on the side of the road. Cars offer some protection. Bikes don't. Which is why I try to push the bike into the center of the pack, to obscure his view of the bike he will surely recognize for as long as possible.

"Let's get ready, riders!" the man at the front yells as two women in bikinis walk forward. Their job is always the same, to signal the start of the race. As if seeing half-naked women will really get the racers ready to go. I grip the handlebars hard and feel sweat starting to drip down my back. I glance nervously over to my brother, who is still distracted, and see Arcanna has appeared next to her car.

"Fuck," I breathe under my helmet as she looks directly at me, her eyes narrowing briefly before they flare wide with recognition. "Shit, shit, shit."

She pushes toward my brother, and I see her yell his name and point toward me. His silver eyes swing to me at the exact moment the signal to go sounds. He pushes off his car, his magic gathering around him. I fumble with the bike but manage to take off, the air filled with the scent of exhaust. A glance in my side mirror shows him now standing in the middle of the road, looking absolutely furious with me.

If I survive this race, I may not survive my brother.

FOUR

Two years later

DRAGO

"Drago!" Shadow's slurred voice and hand reaching for me snaps my resolve to play the long game against Julien. I manage to kill one vampire and two of Julien's people before he stabs me from behind with some sedating drug. It's the only way he's able to subdue me. My body drops down and I can see the tears coming from Shadow as he watches me fail to save him. I watch as the remaining vampires drag my mate away from me. My world starting to dim, the drugs pulling me under. But before they do, I make a vow with myself that I will slaughter them all.

The punch impacts my left side, directly into my ribs. I grunt, pain flaring, and stagger back, until I feel the cool metal of the chain-link fence hit my exposed skin. My mind is abruptly pulled from the memory. Jeers from the crowd come roaring into my awareness as I heave in a breath, expanding those freshly broken ribs courtesy of the shifter in front of me. The wolf, a former member of the Primal Knights MC, looks smug as he spits blood onto the dirty floor of the ring.

Somewhere in the crowd, my stepfather is watching, taking bets on the outcome of the fight. Two long years, I've been his little puppet, helping him build his kingdom. Two long years, he has been stuck in that fucking prison. Every time I hear a story about his dragon, my heart breaks thinking of what he is being put through. Sometimes, I regret trying to save him that day because it ultimately put me on Julien's radar, revealing that I was not loyal to him. It put my mother on his radar. But my mother is gone now, and all bets are off.

His time will come. We will rip his heart out with our bare hands. He's grown soft. Lazy. His dragon is barely awake now. He's lost his power, my dragon rumbles, sleepy and slow from the drugs they give us to keep from shifting while we fight. Otherwise, no one would step in the ring with me. A smile ghosts my lips. They think having my dragon and magic locked away means I'm less dangerous, but I'm still the most powerful person here.

The wolf in front of me rushes forward, our small break over. The sound of the bell ringing and screams of the crowd now loud in my ears. The ring is nothing but a chain-link fence placed in a circle on old wrestling mats, the venue itself an old warehouse that should have been condemned long ago—half its roof is rotting away. But every

Thursday, the fights are held here. And every Thursday, I win. According to my stepfather, I should lose this fight tonight. He bet against my undefeated streak. But I'm not losing tonight, no. The king is going to be toppled, and tonight is the start of it. I've spent my years planning and building my own empire, all for this moment.

It's time to bring my mate home. Even if I have to burn this whole gods forsaken city to the ground and drag his body through the ashes, I'm bringing him home.

———

AVA

("I Can't Stop" – Flux Pavilion)

The party sounds cascade around me, a symphony of chaos. The air is thick with the scents of chlorine and alcohol, wafting up from the pool deck into the giant mansion. Every window is thrown open, every door unlocked and beckoning partygoers. The air vibrates with the bass coming from the speakers; a live DJ presides over the dance floor. Standing back from it all, I observe and sip from my drink.

"Ava!" I hear bellowed from across the room, and I see Ophelia and her boyfriend, Nyx, wave as they make their way over. The smile across her face as she spots me is undeniable. The crowd parts immediately, giving space for Nyx. While she is in a swimsuit with a small wrap around it, Nyx is dressed in all black, per usual. She's the closet thing I have to a friend that I can call my own, despite having met her through my brother. The moment she makes it to my corner, she wraps me in a soft hug, her curves pressing into me. Her long curly hair has the scent of jasmine.

"Hey," I say timidly. "I didn't realize you guys would be

here." Subtext to Nyx, do not tell my fucking brother I'm here. His dark gaze pins me with a look that says he knows exactly what I want but isn't guaranteeing I'll get it.

Ophelia offers a wide grin, her freckles popping out on her makeup-free face. "Us?! We didn't know you'd be here! Is Jax here?" She looks out over the dance floor. "Or Arcanna?"

I take a long sip of my drink, avoiding eye contact with Nyx.

"Deva. I think she's here alone," he says into her ear.

She frowns over at me. "Did you sneak out?" Ophelia was raised in a small town, so unlike the capital; in a lot of ways, her life was no different than mine has been. She was kept in a gilded cage until she broke free with Nyx at her side.

I give a noncommittal shrug, taking another healthy gulp of the alcohol in my hand. The taste is a little too sweet for me, but I need the liquid courage. Ever since that street race, I've done whatever I can to get out and away. The need for independence is an addiction that I can't kick. And my brother's need to protect me is something he can't kick.

"I won!" I scream, ripping my helmet off. My body still vibrating with adrenaline, heart pounding and hands shaking as I make my way toward my brother, a giant smile plastered on my face. His face, however, shows nothing but rage.

"And how the fuck do you think you won?" he growls.

I frown. "By racing."

Arcanna grimaces behind him, and Oisin just shakes his head in disappointment.

"You are naive as fuck, Ava," Jackson says.

Jax had used his magic, along with Oisin and Arcanna,

to make sure I survived the race. It was the last time I ever felt free. I'm still bitter about it.

Ophelia grabs my hand and pulls me into the crowd with a wide smile painted on her face. "Oh, we have to go dance!" I'm pretty sure that behind her, Nyx curses but allows her to drag me out into the middle of the sweaty bodies.

("Gold Dust (Flux Pavilion Remix)" – DJ Fresh)

I'm unsure of myself standing with her, this confident woman who drops her hips and throws her hands in the air. She moves with such self-assuredness, I'm envious of that. Envious of her ability to be so carefree, even with her responsibilities. Nyx moves in behind her, and I watch his hands loop around her waist. I attempt to mimic her movements, but I feel dumb, awkward. I start to say I'm going to head back to my spot, but she wraps her hand around my wrist, pulling me into her body.

"Just copy me!" she yells into my ear and places my hands on her hips, the feeling strangely intimate, given Nyx's hands are right there as well. "Stop thinking!" she says over the music.

Yeah, Ava. Stop thinking. This is why you snuck out.

Taking a deep breath, I close my eyes and lose myself to the music and the feel of her body pressed into mine.

Hours seem to pass while we go from dance floor to bar and back. By the end, the room is twirling, and my sides hurt from laughing so hard. After an eternity, I signal that I'm heading to the bathroom and slowly make my way out of the crowd. When I turn and look back at my friends, I can see Nyx locked onto Ophelia's mouth, his hands creeping under that wrap over her bikini bottoms. I'm envious of what they have. I want that desperately.

It's because of that desperation, and the alcohol, that when I see the blonde-haired boy waiting in line for the bathroom, I don't think twice about disappearing into a back bedroom with him.

———

("MERMAIDS" – **Florence and the Machine**)

One would think sneaking into the royal palace would be much more difficult. But as my heels sink into the wet grass, I come to the chilling realization that my father only cares about us getting out. Or more accurately, me. His coveted little prize, his untouchable princess. The amount of dodging and weaving I had to do to get out could have given the best assassin a run for their money, but coming back, I barely have to hide myself as I move toward the side of the massive home. Covered by old shrubs, this door is known to very few. In fact, I would bet my soul that there are only four of us who know of its existence, none of which being my parents or any of the guards they employ.

I'm sure Jax regrets the day I figured this out. I snort. My older brother and his friends discovered it when we were younger. And being who I am, I followed them in and out many times. When he finally discovered me, he was furious. It took Oisin and Arcanna to calm him down. After that, we spent so many summer nights going in and out together. But that ended when I turned sixteen. Gone were the days when Jackson saw me as his little sister. Since then, he only sees me as the princess of Hell.

Pushing the ivy aside, I shove my weight into the oak barrier, my body screaming, until the door finally gives way and opens into a dimly light hallway of marble. The scent of stale air washes over me before it's pulled out into the night sky. I will my magic up, a small flame of blue appearing in my hand as I shove the door closed behind me. Cobwebs litter the space and the flame I've created casts an eerie glow. The urge to run pushes through my bones, as if I'm being watched. I take a deep breath, refusing to race down the hall like I did as a child.

"I'm a grown woman. Princess of Hell. I will not run from imaginary ghosts," I mutter, my words slurring slightly still. But my feet move at a quicker rate through the twisting space. I ascend higher and higher, until I can finally see a small strip of light penetrating the inky black air. A relieved whoosh leaves my lungs as I press my ear to the door. This would always be the tricky part—coming out of a coat closet like I'm walking out of Narnia does not look normal. After a few moments of silence, I twist the knob and step in.

When Jax and his friends first discovered this, they used it so much that my mother's fur coats she kept in here began to show their secrets. With each pass by, more of the outside world would collect on them. After one particularly bad moment when Mother had a guard gut a maid in front of us for "neglecting" her precious coats, we decided something had to change. So, they slowly but surely replaced them with our own coats, putting her precious jackets in the hall closet closer to her room.

Jax's scent of smoke and evergreens washes over me as his green canvas jacket brushes my face.

Pausing one more time to listen, I step into the massive hallway just inside our front door. Bending down, I slip my ruined heels off my feet and sigh internally when my bare soles land on the cool white marble. With the alcohol rapidly leaving my system, I wince every time I move; the space between my thighs is tender. The hangover threatening to push inward is starting to fuel the shame and regret

I feel for what happened earlier. I bite the inside of my cheek as I try to avoid making a sound, my steps wobbly. Waking up my parents won't happen—Mother drinks herself to sleep every night, and my father probably isn't even home yet. But my brother? Jackson can't know I snuck out and can't know what happened. Getting past his room will be the hardest part of the night.

"And what did the cat drag in?" I cringe at the sound of my brother's boyfriend's voice. I turn slightly and see Oisin step out from the kitchen, his shirtless body silhouetted against the lights still blazing in the opposite room.

Recently, Oisin has started to pay less attention to him and more attention to me. It initially didn't bother me, but now, the scrutiny makes my stomach curdle and my skin tingle unpleasantly.

His face flares with concern when he sees me stumble and wince as I try to turn toward the stairs that will lead me to my room. "Jesus, Ava, what happened?" Rushing forward, he attempts to steady me.

"It's nothing," I say, steeling myself against the tears that want to pour down my face. I will not cry in front of him. Safety is an illusion in Hell, and no one, especially not Oisin, will get my tears.

"You're clearly drunk," he growls. Pulling me into the light, he takes note of the small skirt and even smaller top I'm wearing. His eyes track over my smeared make up and messed-up hair. The whole picture finally clicks for him. "Are you really that stupid? I hope it was a good fuck, because you won't be leaving this place again."

The statement hits me hard. I shake my head, cheeks flooding with the heat of embarrassment. "Please don't tell Jackson." Learning what happened would only reinforce the idea that I shouldn't be allowed out alone. His fingers tighten on me. "Oisin, ow! Let me go." Arcanna's voice meanders through my alcohol addled brain, her cryptic warning that Oisin has changed. . . that Jax has changed.

As if summoned Arcanna steps into the hallway. "Ossy,I thought you were coming—" She comes to a full stop when she sees me standing there, Oisin's hands on my body, my panicked expression. Her storm blue eyes narrow in on the hold he has on my hips before they sweep back up to my face.

He drops his hands, pushing away from me quickly. "She's fucking drunk. Went out and got laid finally." His voice is laced with a cruelty that has my eyes stinging.

My body suddenly starts to shake, the adrenaline crashing out of me now that Arcanna is here. Three years older than me, she has always felt like the older sister I always wanted. "P-p-pl-lease, you can't tell Jax," I say through chattering teeth.

Her slender body pushes Oisin aside, her long black hair brushing against my arm. "If you don't want to tell Jackson, we won't." She glances behind at Oisin. "Will we?"

"Don't tell Jackson what?" my brother's voice floods the kitchen. I don't bother turning to face him as I watch Oisin track his movements behind me, and Arcanna cringes a little. My brother's golden frame comes into view as he plants a kiss on his lover's cheek. The two couldn't be more opposite. Jackson, the model surfer boy with his blonde hair and golden skin. Oisin with his shaggy black hair and a jagged scar cutting through his left eye. Since Oisin appeared I can't remember when the three weren't together.

When Jax finally turns to look at me, his face becomes livid as he takes in my appearance. No doubt, the scent of alcohol is pouring out of me as I start sweating under his scrutiny. Darkness descends upon the kitchen. In the distance, thunder rumbles. My brother's face goes grave, his eyes shifting to black. The scent of a storm floods the kitchen around us.

Arcanna and Oisin wisely step to the side, though even from this angle, I can see Arcanna frowning at my brother, her brows pulled tight.

"What did you do?" The question hangs heavy in the air. A line has been drawn. Regardless of my answer, I know I'll never leave this house unguarded again. I know tomorrow, if I check that passage, it'll be sealed shut.

"Jax . . ." Arcanna starts, but he shakes his head, cutting her off with a look that would make anyone else shrink back. But not her. She grinds her teeth and levels him with a glare.

"No. I told her not to go. So, she gets to live with the knowledge that I've slaughtered the person who touched her." His anger wraps around us in the kitchen.

"Fuck you, Jax. It's not wrong that I want to live my life a little!" I grind my teeth down, anger pulsing through my body. "You have everything you could want, freedom, friends that get to stay with you here, a life. I have nothing. I've never even had a boyfriend! I wanted a normal fucking night!"

"You're a spoiled brat. You have a duty to this family, and you jeopardized that by going out—alone, I might add— tonight. If someone hears you've been whoring around, that could damage all of us." The poisonous words drip into the thick air around us.

A gasp emits from Arcanna. "Jackson, you fucking ass," she mutters.

Jackson holds my stare before his face softens. "Look, Ava—" he starts.

Tears spring to my eyes, and I can't hold them back.

"No." I take a deep breath. "You've changed Jackson. Something is wrong with you. You are no better than Mother or Father at this point. So, stop pretending you care about me as a sister. You've made it clear what I am to you now." Spinning on my heel, I race out of the hallway as quickly as I can, Jackson yelling after me that it's for my own good to stay guarded. To stay home.

And sure, maybe it would seem that way to him. Or anyone.

But the prince of Hell will never understand what it feels like to be the princess. From the outside, I look like I live a beautiful life. But once you get in close, you realize it's nothing, but a gilded cage meant to hold me until my father decides what he wants from me. My virginity and my body are the only usefulness I have for this kingdom.

It's in this moment that I know my decision to put my needs first was correct, to no longer allow others to control my story and push their agenda. Even if it means I have to leave my home, I'm fucking creating my own story. I steel my back and drop the clothes I was wearing, no longer cowering in my own skin, and step into the piping-hot shower. The steam billows up around me as I allow my new resolve to soak in.

SHADOW

("From the Inside" – Linkin Park)

I see the warehouse burning through my dragon's eyes. The wharf is completely engulfed in flames and thick smoke. The heat alone is enough to melt the structures that haven't yet fallen to the streams of lava that pour from my mouth. The witches are scrambling to put the fire out, but their water magic is doing nothing against the anarchy I've caused. The oranges and reds stand out vividly against the backdrop of the dark city of Gothic Grove.

My dragon still feels annoyed at the collar we wear, but he enjoys the freedom Alexi allows. Enjoys the pandemonium and death we unleash every time we are allowed out of the aviary, he keeps us in. Screams echo out into the inky night as I launch into the air, my black-and-gold body swooping over the witches like the physical manifestation of a plague sent to kill them. And maybe that's what I am, at this point.

My massive body comes to land in front of a group of witches fleeing the scene. Their faces covered in soot, some already crying, the tracks easily seen. Others are preparing to fight, determination shining on their faces. I shift down into my human form, my dragon slipping away. "Do not make me kill you," I grind out. My fists are wreathed in flame and a portal opens behind me, the massive stone prison that Alexi runs directly on the other side. I see one witch step backward, as if to run, but I send out my flames around us. No one is escaping with their life.

Vampires file out of the opening and grab the witches quickly; despite their magic, these witches are not powerful enough to take on this many vampires. As the last woman is shoved through, the vampire turns toward me. "Alexi says to leave no other survivors." I don't say anything, don't acknowledge the command or the feeling that it gives me to think of killing the remaining witches and shifters.

My flames drop as the vampire steps back through my portal. My skin crawls as I crack my neck and prepare to feed the other beast that lives within me. One that is scarier than my dragon, because it's not a supernatural creature. It's just my own personal lust for death and destruction.

I allow a partial shift, my eyes golden, claws and teeth coming out. I look at my bare arms and the scars that decorate them. Tonight, I'll be adding more, one for every person whose blood quenches the need here. I take a deep breath and lose myself to the blood lust.

FIVE

*Should the king decide to wed either of his children,
we must not allow that magic to go to anyone other than our
coven.
We have the ability to harness it, should we gain access to
one of them.
–Mori Family Grimoire*

AVA

One Month Later
("Labor" – Paris Paloma)

My eyes gaze out over the crowd collected in our home. The receiving room is a large, open, marble-floored area with giant columns supporting it. Banquet tables line the outer edges of the room and servers move about offering drinks to the people who have joined us. People of all genders mingle within, dressed as if they are going to a club. But instead of access to a club, they've all managed to secure a coveted spot to see my father yell at his advisors.

"This is unacceptable! How have these people stayed hidden so long? Find them!"

My father's advisors shake in fear before his rage. The Order of Infernal Sin has been a thorn in his side for as long as I can remember; recently, however, they've become bold in their quest to remove him from his throne.

"Y-Your Grace," an elderly advisor stammers, a sheen of sweat making his gray hair stick to his forehead. "The Order has gotten larger; we are doing everything we can—"

A wave of my father's power moves through the room, and screams erupt as the man in front of him bursts into a bloody mess on the floor. Nervous laughter and gasps erupt from the crowd. My stomach rolls.

"Find The Order! Eradicate them!" he seethes to his remaining advisors. They utter promises I know will only result in more death. If they could have found The Order, they would have. I glance toward my father, sitting on his gaudy throne with my mother directly to his right. Jackson sits just to the left of him, while I'm planted firmly off to the side, not in line with the other chairs but set off alone next to the window, where sunlight can leak in like a mockery of heavenly rays.

A pretty little package, the perfect picture of obedience. Tonight, my mother has me dressed in a tight bodice that is the color of blood, the lace whirls moving from the corset into the flowing skirts that match in color. My blonde hair is pulled up high in a tight updo that is making my head pound, but the thick makeup on my face doesn't allow me to rub at my temples. As much as I love to party, I have no interest in going to the party that will follow this. I want nothing more than to take my hair down and wipe the makeup off my face.

I shift my gaze to my brother, who is dressed comfortably, his dark linen shirt and pants exposing his muscled body. His golden skin is so at odds with my own alabaster white. The running joke between him and his friends is, I'm not his shadow, I'm his ghost. It's been a month since he found me in the foyer, a month of tension dripping through our world; a month of avoiding one another. My only companion, Arcanna, offers me a small smile when I catch her gaze.

I let my gaze wander back to Jackson in time to see him offer a smile to Oisin, who is seated with Arcanna toward the front of the dais my family sits on. Oisin's dark features brighten when he sees my brother's smile. He attempts to offer one to Arcanna too, but it falters briefly, like someone tripping and regaining their footing. Arcanna, however, keeps her face oddly blank. I had heard her arguing with Jackson the other evening, but she had refused to share what it was about, waving a dismissive hand in front of her face as she took a long drink of wine.

My guess? She was calling him out for how he's changed. How he's let Oisin change him. It's clear as day now that I'm not with them regularly. Oisin has a hold on my brother. I had always assumed that Arcanna would be added to their duo but not anymore. Now I just pray that Jackson gets free of his odd influence.

I look back to Oisin, and a strange look passes over his face when our eyes lock, but it quickly winks out and he returns his gaze to my brother. I've done my best to avoid him since that night, but every look leaves an unsettling feeling in my stomach.

"Lady Ornate," my father's booming voice echoes out, and Arcanna's mother comes forward. Her long periwinkle skirt brushes the floor, and when she bends forward in a curtsy, her breasts can be seen peeking through the lace turtleneck under the corset she wears. Her hair is thick and dark as night, just like Arcannas, but her eyes hold none of the warmth that our friend's normally do.

"Your Grace," she purrs as she stands up. My mother lifts an eyebrow at the suggestive tone she has. My mother's jealous streak is legendary. While she may not want to fuck my father, she sure as shit doesn't want anyone else doing it either.

My father clears his throat, but it's my mother who jumps in. "Lady Ornate, my lovely. You have been a true gem in our kingdom." My mother's voice, to anyone else, sounds sweet, but I can tell the Lady knows my mother is anything but sweet. "You have delivered both my children, as well as helped many others in their labors. However, we cannot be greedy; we must share you. I'm sorry to see you go, but the kingdom needs a healer such as you. It would be selfish to keep you."

Panic and confusion start to show on Lady Ornate's face as she takes in my mother's words. Her frantic gaze shoots from my father back to the queen.

"Effective immediately, you'll be traveling to the forest of the priestesses, where you'll help teach them your ways." What my mother is really saying is, you are being exiled, and you will be lucky if you make it there alive.

"But your Grace—" she starts. My mother holds her slim hand up, silencing Lady Ornate before two guards move up on either side of her. My father doesn't move, even though the woman he's been sleeping with the past month keeps trying to garner his attention. When it's clear my father isn't going to help her, she schools her expression and nods, her face holding nothing but venomous contempt for my family. Whirling, she exits the room with her head held high and doesn't even bother to look back at her daughter.

Arcanna keeps her face clear of emotion as she watches her mother be escorted out.

"Arcanna, dear, you are, of course, welcome to stay here," my mother coos.

Arcanna offers a smile. "Thank you, Your Grace." She pushes her thick hair off her shoulder, still avoiding Jackson's gaze. She wears loose pants that almost appear to be a skirt, and a tight wrap covers her torso, leaving her arms bare. Tattoos cover her exposed areas.

"Is that all?" My father grumbles. He's losing his patience. He wants to get on with the party.

My mother huffs in announce. "The king and queen of Divinity will be here in a few days. We need to make this place ready for their arrival. Rhea will remain here, with us, until you both marry."

A split second later, Jackson shoots up out of his chair. "Absolutely not!"

"Sit. Down." My father hisses, rage turning his face red.

My brother balls his fists up as he takes in a few breaths. Oisin, for his part, looks oddly smug as he watches it all unfold. Odd for someone who claims to love the prince. But what do I know of love?

———

AVA (Bonus)
1 Week Later

"Dead?" Arcanna gasps. "All of them?"

The world feels dark as my mother delivers the news that the ones we gain our power from, the ones who help us every full moon, are all gone.

"They went in and slaughtered the whole gods damn group." Her anger shows only by the flare of her nostrils as she continues to report the devastation until I'm lost in it. Without the priestesses, or a mate, Jackson and I will have no ability to recharge our magic. Each use will slip our life-force away until it eventually kills us. In one swift move The Order has destroyed us.

"Come Ava, we must get you into your party dress." I tentatively reach and grab the offered appendage. I glance at Arcanna who still seems lost to what my mother had been saying.

"We aren't still having this ball now?" I say tentatively.

She scoffs. "Of course we are. Why ever would we not? Just because a bunch of forest hippies got themselves killed, we will still do our duty to show up and look unbothered."

I almost shake my head at her cold words, but I know my mother well enough to understand that would end with her palm across my face, regardless of Arcanna being here. "Very well but I'm already dressed." Gesturing to the red dress she had directed me to put on only moments ago. Moments before she threw this bomb into the room.

Her lips pull tight in annoyance as she shakes her head, "No, I'm thinking white. This color simply won't do for the occasion."

———

("SHE WILL BE LOVED" – **Vitamin String Quartet, Bridgerton Soundtrack)**

The ballroom is decorated in shades of crimson and deep golds. The walls are covered with silken tapestries that ripple in the wisteria-scented breeze creeping through the open archway windows. They look like ghosts trying to break free of chains holding them captive. Candlelight flickers just behind them, giving the illusion even more credence. They barely illuminate the corridors leading to the ballroom, allowing intimate corners where guests can embrace their inner deviance.

My feet are bare on the cool marble floors, adorned with golden chains intricately woven over the tops of them and connecting to golden cuffs on my ankles. The sheer white skirt I wear brushes the ground, and my legs peek out through slits up both sides. I smile politely at people as I make my way through the room, my long blonde hair sweeping my bare shoulders. When I sip the champagne in my hand, I can feel the diadem on my forehead move slightly, the diamond in the center moving with it. It matches the choker around my neck, affixed with even more glittering jewels. My mother has overdone herself this evening.

Appearance means everything to her. Just the thought of what she wants from me in this outfit makes me grip my glass so tightly, I worry I'll snap the slender stem. She has made it clear what her expectations for both of us are in regard to marriage. I am to remain pure, and Jackson is to avoid knocking someone up and making the kingdom, aka her, look bad. Sweat trickles down my chest, and I can't help but count down the moments until I can flee this place. I cannot remain their obedient puppet.

I just have to wait for the king and queen of Divinity to return to their home, I can hitch a ride in their entourage. Not that they know the princess of Hell will be going with them. Nope, I'll be hiding until they pass the gates to Gothic Grove. Once there, I will leave and use my magic to gain access to the city. The risk of using it now greater than before but worth it. If it means freedom, I will trade every-thing for it.

My father's booming voice can be heard over the band

playing some string melody. His mood feels far to jovial given the news we've received. "Ava!" he yells, pulling me from my thoughts, his voice slurred as it booms over the room. It's only because of years of experience hiding my reactions that I don't wince. He's standing talking with a larger man with dark hair, someone whom I've never seen in the palace.

I gracefully pad over to him, careful to keep my body straight and my movements delicate. "Yes, Father?" Ever the demure princess, I keep my tone low and my gaze at his feet.

My father, however, grabs me roughly and drags me closer to him, squeezing my upper arm in a vice grip that I know will leave bruises tomorrow. My hair snags in his grip and pulls. A hiss escapes my mouth before I can hold it back, earning me a small shake. A reminder to keep my mouth shut. My father has never hit me, but he's never been loving either. Sometimes, I think the only reason he doesn't get physical is because of Jackson. He still views my father as a good man, and therefore, my father can control him better. I like to think if Jackson knew, truly knew, how our father treats me, he'd put a stop to it.

The dark-haired man laughs. "Ah, it's hard to break them, isn't it? She is a beauty, though; it pains me that we could not form an alliance through our children. My son would have given her powerful children."

When I look at the man, his leering gaze burns into my body.

My father chuckles, but the sound sends chills down my spine. "Ah, you mean your stepson? I heard you sold your flesh and blood to Alexi. And how disappointed you must have been to learn just how powerful he ended up being, and you gave him over to a vampire." The man goes red in the face. "You'll forgive me, Julien, if I didn't want to bind our family to someone who couldn't even read his own son's power level."

("It Had To Be You" – Tommee Profitt)

"There is still time for our houses to be joined; my stepson would produce a fine heir with her." They speak as if I'm not even present. "Or even myself, I have not been wed in a long time."

Panic starts to crawl up my throat, a thickness that I can't swallow back. My tongue refuses to help me form words to ask the questions I have.

"She's already been purchased. You are too late, dragon," my father says.

My reality bottoms out for a moment, the room slowing to a halt before it all speeds back up with alarming clarity. "Excuse me, what are you talking about?" I finally manage to get out, eyes tracking between my father and Julien.

The dark-haired man addresses me first. "Daddy didn't tell you? You are bought and paid for. I missed out on one hell of an opportunity."

My stomach rolls, the champagne I consumed threatening to come up. "What have you done?" I breathe out, horror worming its way into my body like a parasite as I stare up at my father.

No emotions play across his face, no warmth or love, as he says, "I did what has been done for centuries. Your body, your womb. They have been for sale since you were born. You will produce powerful heirs and serve this realm." He glances at the massive clock next to the throne he and my mother normally sit atop. "Why do you think you're dressed as you are? Tonight is your wedding."

I want to vomit. My body shakes head to toe. Wrenching myself free of his grip, I turn and flee, shoving myself through the crowd as quickly as I can. People shout when I knock into them, and I hear glass breaking as I hit a server with a tray. But none of that matters, all that matters is escape. I bolt up the grand staircase, my pace never slowing until I run headfirst into my bedroom door. I fumble with the knob, nearly in a panic before it unlatches, and I push myself in, slamming the door behind me.

Sobs heave through my chest as I try to get control of my breathing. Try to calm down. *Run. I need to run. I can't wait for my original plan.*

I rip the jewels from my body and hastily remove my dress, then I pull on dark leggings and my brother's sweat-shirt. The sound of knocking on my door has me pausing, but when I hear my mother's voice, I throw myself toward my window and haul up the dark backpack hidden below it for this moment. I wrench the window open but pause as an idea barge into my head. Doubling back, I grab the discarded jewels and shove them deep into the zippered pocket with the stack of money I've been squirreling away. The straps of my pack loop around my chest as I secure the one thing that will keep me alive outside of Hell.

"Ava, stop being dramatic. You come out this instant and return to the party. I will not have you ruining this," my mother yells.

But I don't stop. I keep moving until I've hoisted myself up and over my balcony climbing down into the grass, and racing toward the garage that holds my brother's cars and bikes and send up a silent thank-you that the door is unlocked. For a moment, I'm immobilized by the idea that Jackson will have no idea why I fled, that I won't be able to say goodbye to him. And then an equally terrifying thought slams into me—what if Jackson knew what tonight was? His words from the that night slam into me, spurring the fear forward.

Taking a deep breath, I swing my leg over the massive piece of machinery, my tiny body barely able to support its weight. I only have precious moments before my mother realizes I'm not in my bedroom and sends the guards to find me. Turning the key, I feel the engine rumble to life beneath me, and before I can second-guess myself, I speed off into the inky night toward my freedom. Toward a life that will be one of my own choosing.

———

ONE MONTH **Later (Bonus)**

Thunder rolls in the distance and the rain offers up a soft lullaby through my open window. Or it would. If I didn't have the pesky raven cawing in my ear.

"Go away," I groan. Rolling over in the lumpy bed I want to cry when I see the digital clock reads 3:34am. "I've been asleep for 30 minutes you insufferable bird." The beast caws again, this time landing on my pillow and pulling at my hair with its slender beak. I pull the covers firmly over my face, "Samhain I swear to all that is unholy I will lock you out in this storm!"

The bird, my familiar, caws again in protest before I hear the flap of his wings. The fussy creature found me the moment I crossed into Gothic Grove. Perched on a tree outside the gate he fluttered down to my shoulder and immediately gave me a peck on the ear that was hard enough to draw blood. As if he was angry, I had made him wait. And for the month I've been here his attitude hasn't improved.

Another caw and Samhain lands back onto my covered

body. I let out a frustrated sigh and uncover myself, fully sitting up. "What?" I ask, hands open. "I fed you already and I'm exhausted. Please let me sleep." The shift at the bar had been busy and my feet still ache from the heels I had danced in. Tonight, had been my first night as a dancer instead of bartender and my body felt it. By the time I had dragged myself out to my bike I was ready to sell my soul to be in my bed.

I watch as he takes to the air again, this time his dark body landing next to the front door. He cocks her head to the side. Listening. I frown, wincing as I scoot up on my knees and stare at my door. The creak is bearably audible before I'm throwing myself out of the bed as the vampires burst through the door.

SIX

Dragons are difficult to kill.
Not impossible.
— Rosewood Family Journal

DRAGO

3 Months Later

Nothing about this moment feels as satisfying as it should. Shadow's father, my stepfather, lies in a bloody mess at my feet. His body is not even cold yet. The crimson liquid pools from him, staining the white marble floor he lies on, along with the front of my white shirt. While I wanted him dead, I wanted to be the one to do it. We are hard creatures to kill, harder than wolf shifters. But we are not immortal. Blessed with long life, yes, but not immortal.

My palm opens to expose the bullet that had been lodge in him, the bullet from Hell. "Who did you piss off Julien?" I mutter looking back down at him.

The compound is buzzing with activity now, my men searching down whoever did this while also taking out anyone who isn't loyal to me. The old dragon was not well loved, so it's only a small group who remained loyal to him. He ruled through fear; I rule through loyalty. And it seems, in the end, my way has won.

"Sir." I glance away from the body, looking up toward one of my men. "We couldn't locate anyone. We searched the rooftops and all buildings in range, nothing was found."

"And his men?"

"They are in the courtyard, sir."

I step over his body, stuffing my hands into my pockets, and meander out toward the courtyard. The large doors are already flung open and the thick, humid air of Gothic Grove pushes into the cooler room. In the distance, thunder rumbles, and the wind slowly picks up.

Kai stands in front of the small group of Julien's loyal people while my other guards circle them. He stands slightly shorter than my six-foot frame, his bulky muscles barely contained in the black suit he wears. His luminous yellow eyes stand out sharply below thick black hair that's cut short against his scalp.

"Ready for your command." His voice is scratchy, as if he has smoked his whole life. If I weren't already mated, I would enjoy hearing that voice moan out in pleasure.

I pull my hands from my pockets and slowly roll up the sleeves to my button-down. "You all made a decision long ago to serve only Julien." I walk a little closer to the group, my magic now shimmering beneath my skin. "You stood by as he tortured his son." Black veins start to appear on my hands. "You allowed your prince to be taken by vampires." Those veins now spread up my arms, my hands wholly black. The scent of fear washes over me as the wind sweeps through the courtyard. "And you have made no effort to retrieve him from those vampires. The very vampires who have worked tirelessly to destroy this city."

("SACRIFICE" – In This Moment)

"Shadow was worthless, he deserved to be sold off." The man has barely gotten the words out before I have my hand on his throat, hauling him up and allowing my death magic to seep into him slowly. He thrashes and screams as his internal organs wither and melt, his blood boiling. I make sure it's slow. Make sure he feels the agony that I have had to endure while knowing my mate is imprisoned.

I look at the other twenty or so remaining traitors, noting the various levels of fear plastered on their faces. It occurs to me that since I've kept my magic contained, none of them understand who, or what, they are dealing with. "I think you people forgot what I am." I release the body of the man, and he hits the ground, blood oozing from his eyes. "Because I have spent the last few years not truly showing myself, you believe me weak. Believe I am the same type of dragon Julien was."

My dragon pushes to the surface, and I know my eyes are now golden. I allow him to begin taking control. "I am nothing like Julien." I can hear a man uttering a prayer, as if that will save him as my face starts to shift into the skeletal beast. Slowly, I turn my head until my eyes lock onto him. "You are praying to gods that won't hear you. You should pray to the one standing in front of you."

When my dragon bursts forth, I take great satisfaction in the mind-numbing terror those twenty or so men feel as they take in my form. And then I unleash my black fire across the group and watch their bodies writhe in pain, their souls being torn apart as they are ravaged by my magic.

Once the last man is dead, I shift back into my human form. Kai stands impassive, as if he didn't just watch a giant skeletal dragon shred the humans shifters into a mess of charred remains and body parts that now litter the open yard.

I walk past him, my mood dark and determined. "Let's bring Shadow home."

SHADOW

("I Hate Everything About You" – Three Days Grace)

Everything hurts. It's been a week since Ciaran got me out, and my body and mind are struggling to adjust. My dragon is furious at me, locked deep in his cage again. Always scratching at the lock, demanding he be let back out. But I can't do it, I can't let him do whatever he wants. Not when Ciaran risked so much to get me out. No, not risked. He gave so much. He made a deal with his father, one he refuses to tell me about, but I can guess based on his haunted expression when he comes home each night.

Home.

I don't think I've ever had a home, not until now. That physical space where you feel safe never existed for me. Drago was as close to a home as I got until this moment, and I haven't seen him in years. My heart aches at the thought of my stepbrother. I miss him. Despite him leaving me alone all this time, I still fucking miss him. And I hate myself for that. Hate him for making me fall for him and then abandoning me. *And where is he now? You've been out a week, and he hasn't bothered to show up?*

I roll over on the wood floor, looking out over the skyline across the river. My skin crawls anytime I get into the soft bed Ciaran purchased for me. The sheets, a silky gray material, feel slimy on my skin. So, every night, I find myself pulling the weighted comforter off the bed and laying myself on the cedar floor to watch the storms break over the city.

"Ciaran gets you a bed, and yet, I still find you on the floor." The voice burrows into me like a splinter, the sound both soothing and painful. I don't turn my body over, but Drago's presence fills the room from ceiling to floor. An overwhelming and suffocating feeling. I see his feet come into view and allow my eyes to trace up his body as I roll onto my back. The moment my gaze lands on his face, my breath wooshes out of me.

"You've grown up." My voice comes out rough.

He cocks an eyebrow, slowly rolling up the sleeves of his white button-down. More tattoos adorn him, if possible. His fingers, hands, arms, chest all appear to have some type of whirl of ink. His white hair is longer, and his body . . . fuck, his body looks stronger than I remember. My cock rallies to life in my shorts as I remember the feel of him. His eyes rake over me, snagging on each and every scar he can see on my bare chest and arms. They linger on the tally marks that decorate my arms.

Silence settles loudly around us as his gaze burns into me. I slowly sit up, and the weighted blanket falls with a thud to the side as I scoot back, giving him space to sit on my hard bed. He folds himself down, until both our backs lean against the actual bed as we look out the darkened window.

"You have too," he says quietly.

I shiver at his voice. "I've what?"

Turning, he looks me head-on again, those blue eyes blazing and flashing to gold. "Grown up."

"I didn't have a choice."

A moment passes before, "Neither did I."

Silence once again encroaches into the room until it's broken apart by the deep rumble of thunder and a deluge of rain opening from the sky above, filling the room with the echoing sounds of the sky unleashing herself. The wind moving through the open window drags Drago's scent into my nostrils, and I can't fight back the groan as my eyes close. The war between how much I still want him and how angry I am at him rages inside.

When I finally open them, it's to his golden ones blazing in the dark. I'm not sure who moves first, but suddenly, my mouth collides with his, his tongue sweeping into mine. We both groan as he fists my hair, and we lose ourselves in the kiss. Our bodies tangle as he pushes me to the floor, pressing his erection against my own and grinding down.

"Fuck." He pulls off my mouth, extending a whimper from me, and circles my throat with his hand. "I've missed you, Rakkaani, so much." He dives back in, claiming my mouth in a kiss that could shatter the world and remake it all at once. Time loses all meaning, and suddenly, I'm aware of my shorts being slipped off. "Look at me." Drago's command makes my dragon purr in his cage, and I open my eyes again to take him in as he leans back and slowly unbuttons his shirt, exposing his defined chest. His pants are next, and I think I might die when his cock bobs free and I take in the four barbells pierced down his shaft.

His hand slowly pumps his hardened cock, taking care over the piercings. The smile that spreads across his face is wicked as he pushes two fingers of his other hand into my mouth. My tongue swirls around his fingers, coating them in saliva before he pulls them out and inches down to probe my entrance. My cock jerks at the feel of one finger pushing against the tight ring of muscles. A groan leaves my body as my head falls back at the delicious intrusion, the pain and pleasure mixing together.

"I need you," I moan. "I don't care if I'm ready or not. I need you now," I demand. It's been so fucking long since I've felt anything other than pain and anger that now I feel parched. Like I've been standing in a desert, and he is my first drink of water. I need to feel him inside me. Need to feel pleasure alongside the pain.

He pushes another finger inside me, giving no warning before he starts to curl them on that little node. "You don't get to make demands, Rakkaani, did you forget that? I'll decide when you get me."

I cry out as his mouth is suddenly on my cock, his tongue swirling over the head and down the shaft. The world is lost to my pleasure. Each time my orgasm is about to crest, he pulls back, until I'm a sobbing mess begging to cum. When he pulls his mouth all the way off my cock, I hear the click of a cap and feel coolness spread down my cheeks.

"I don't need that," I pant.

He growls low. "I'm not fucking you without lube."

I feel his head push at the tight opening. I don't know how to tell him I need pain now. How does one explain to their lover, they need to hurt now to feel good? The burn of his cock breaching me makes me arch up off the floor, and when that first piercing follows into me, I think I've gone to heaven.

"You are taking me so fucking good; I wish you could see this. Fuck, your ass is tight."

I open my eyes and almost cum from the look on Drago's face as he watches his dick disappear inside of me. When he finally bottoms out, I hold my breath, waiting to see his next move. His golden eyes finally lock onto my own.

"Going to fuck you now," he says as he begins thrusting. "Going to claim you like I should have. Because you're mine. Mine to fucking claim, no one else."

"Fuck yes," I moan over and over until what he said finally hits me. Claim. The word settles into my core, into the space in my chest that's been empty until this moment. "Wait," I start, but Drago keeps going, a relentless pace being set that makes it near impossible to get the next word out. "Red," I whisper.

Everything stops, his powerful body stilling above mine, that word hitting pause to the delirious pleasure I was feeling. His chest is heaving, but he sits back and slowly pulls his hard cock from me. "What is it, Rakkaani?"

"You just said you were going to claim me . . ." And it's all I have to say to see the devastating truth on his face. Because you don't claim someone you are fucking. You claim a mate. The truth of it settles like dust over me.

I told you, my dragon growls. *He is ours.*

"You knew . . ." I start but can't finish. Because he knew I was his mate and fucking left me in that prison to rot. My heart shatters. He didn't want me. I wasn't good enough for him.

He wants us! Don't be an idiot! But I ignore my dragon, pushing away and forcing space between us.

"Fuck, Shadow. I'm sorry. You don't understand. I couldn't get you out yet, I didn't have what I have now. Had I known how long it would take, I would have done things differently. And that fucking collar made it even harder." I can see how broken he is, the desperation in those eyes, but I can't find it in myself to forgive him.

So, against every fiber of my being, I look him dead in the eyes and say, "Leave."

SEVEN

Three months after freedom from prison

DRAGO

"I'm telling you right now, Drago, he won't survive much longer." Ciaran's concern coils under my skin in an uncomfortable way as he talks about my mate. He huffs out a breath and braces his arms against my desk. "He's going to end up killing himself."

Everything had gone to shit when trying to get Shadow out. In the end, it had been Ciaran who managed it, not me. It's why it took so long for me to see him, the shame I felt— the shame I still feel—for failing him is a parasite in me. It's feeding on me every day, getting bigger and bigger. Some-day, it'll consume me completely.

"You knew . . . " The pain in Shadow's face slices me deep, the force of it almost physically pushing me backward. I could see it in his eyes, the realization that he will never forgive me.

My chest aches as I see his pain in my head again. It's been three months since he demanded I leave. I have avoided forcing my way into his life, instead giving him space to heal after that moment. He's right to be angry with me; as much as he'll never forgive me, I know I'll never forgive myself, either. "So, what do you want me to do, Ciaran? He won't speak to me."

"So, make him," Ciaran growls. "I can't worry about him bleeding out or overdosing while I'm out. I've done everything in my power, but I can't get through."

I rake my hand down my face, the rings dragging over my skin. "I'll move him in here."

But Ciaran shakes his head. "He stays with me, but you are going to go be with him when I'm not."

"You want me to babysit?" I growl. Despite the words tasting bitter in my mouth, my dragon prowls below me, angry that we've let it get this far.

"No, I want you to take care of your fucking mate, Drago." My eyes widen a fraction of an inch, barely a tell, but Ciaran smirks. "Yeah, I'm not an idiot. I know who you two are to each other. So, go take care of him." Ciaran spins around and storms back into the club from my office. The sounds briefly penetrate the room before the door shuts and blocks out the noises again. Ciaran has been on edge lately, and it makes me wonder, not for the first time in our history, what my friend is up to.

I shoot back the amber liquid left in my glass before gathering my shadows around me and stepping into them. Darkness clouds my vision for a moment before I'm stepping into Ciaran and Shadow's penthouse. The spacious main room is dark, the only thing illuminating it are the occasional flashes of lightning over the skyline of Gothic Grove. A perpetual storm presides over the city now that the original families are being killed off. Fucking Alexi Helvig. I have my suspicions as to what his motivations are, but I've kept them to myself thus far. It's Ciaran's battle, not mine.

Mine is currently somewhere in this penthouse.

Walking through the darkened living room, I follow the slight tug in my chest toward a back bedroom. At the end of the long hallway, the door is shut. Faint sounds of music escape under it, but no light shines from the crack. Something in me is recoiling at the idea of opening the door. A deep unsettling fear creeps into my bones like poison. When I'm only a few steps away, the scent of blood hits my nostrils and my body locks up. I am simultaneously paralyzed with fear yet mobilized by the need to see if I am too late.

———

SHADOW

("I'm OK" – Christina Aguilera)

It's hard to describe what being a burden feels like to someone who has never felt it. Never had to experience the chest-tightening, heart-crushing feeling that you are failing the people who mean the most to you. It's a feeling I wouldn't wish on my worst enemy because it's one that spirals deeper and deeper until eventually, you can't feel anything but that guilt. The dark feeling takes on a life of its own with claws and teeth that rip you apart, eat you alive. My skin is crawling, and I desperately want to carve a piece out to relieve myself, to punish myself. After all, if I hurt myself, pay the price the guilt demands, I can't hurt anyone else. Right?

That's what I tell myself as my handshakes holding the razor blade. It's for my own good. I deserve this. Beads of sweat break out across my forehead. Being high was so much easier. Being alive hurts. I can't get past the crushing guilt that I'm a burden. That I hurt everyone around me. My anger at my own failures wraps around me like armor, keeping others safer by pushing them away from me. It's the rattle of a snake's tail to warn people before it strikes.

The first slice beads up and I feel the calm take over. The numbness that's different from drugs but no less power-ful. It brings a sense of peace as I watch myself bleed, knowing that I'm giving payment to the guilt that demands such a heavy price. Another slice, and I can pretend that I'll have this feeling forever.

Another.

And another.

One more.

I can almost pretend I won't feel guilty after this, that I won't feel bad. That this, too, won't turn into another badge I'll have to wear that shows how inadequate I am. How unworthy I am of being loved. I hate these thoughts, hate how they have infested my brain. Deep down, I know that it's all a lie my demons have created in my head, but fighting the demons is so exhausting, and honestly, I'm just too fucking tired.

DRAGO FINDS me on the bathroom floor sometime later. Time has no meaning at this point. He cleans me up without a word. Maybe that's worse. I would rather him yell and rage at me. His acceptance of my faults makes me feel even more worthless. The pity in his eyes makes me want to pick up the razor again. On the surface, I hate Ciaran for telling him what has been happening, but I suppose I understand, deep down. I know he can't keep looking after me while I'm like this, not after the deal he was forced to make to get me out. It's my fault so many others are suffering, because he had to agree to whatever Alexi asked of him.

He has an empire to topple, a father to kill, and I am just a constant reminder of a deal gone bad. Or, at least, that's what the voices keep saying in my head.

The first few times he found me high, he was fine, but when he found me bleeding, he threatened to call Drago. So, it's not a shock Drago has finally shown up. Now, Drago will be trapped in this cage with me. Yes, this home is lovely and far more comfortable than the aviary Alexi kept me in, but it's still a cage. Still a place I'm trapped in, while those demons chew away at my sanity.

Drago sits down next to me, looping his hand through mine. "I won't leave you, Rakkaani. I'll be here no matter what."

His words, meant to comfort me, only fuel the guilt I hold onto. And the touch that is meant to keep me grounded only pushes me further away.

———

"YOU DON'T HAVE to keep coming back here, Shadow," Ciaran says for the hundredth time, it feels like. Since finding out that Drago knew we were mates and the last time he picked me up after my breakdown, I've banished him from the penthouse. Again. Drago's only statement was, he will find a way to make amends and that I have a home at his penthouse, should I need it. He even left a key for me, despite knowing I can get in regardless. A symbolic reminder that I always have a home with him.

Ciaran didn't argue when I told him my stepbrother was no longer welcome here, but he continues to argue against me returning to the prison to work with him. Truth be told, I don't know why I can't walk away, everything in me should be screaming to leave that place behind, but there is a pull in my chest that won't stop, and when I think of never returning, it physically hurts.

I swipe my hand through my hair, forgetting that I shaved it down. The short ends feeling odd between my fingers. "I get it, it seems weird, but something in me refuses to let me leave that place." I pause and look him over. "And you need help taking down your father."

He snorts. "I don't need help." But I can see it, the exhaustion that is creeping in on him. A darkness that has slowly taken over my friend and seems to be weighing him down. He cannot continue to bring innocents to his father and expect his soul to remain intact. Which, maybe, is the key difference between us. I lost my soul long ago; now, all that's left is a rotting wound where it should reside.

"Ciaran, I can't stay here. I'll lose my mind." He looks me over, his blonde hair braided back and sides shaved, showing off the runes tattooed delicately on his skull. He looks like he wants to keep arguing, but when he goes to open his mouth again, he just shakes his head.

"Fine," he relents. "You can help, but Shadow . . ." He pauses, uncertainty in his face. "I can't lose you. I can't do this all on my own, so if the prison becomes too much, you tell me. I would rather have you here and safe."

My body sags in relief. That space in my chest loosening just a bit. I nod my head; despite knowing I'll never tell him if I'm struggling.

Maybe you're just excited to go back to a space that could kill you. My dragon may have said it, but it wasn't far off from my own thoughts. I may not be actively trying to die, but I have no issue allowing it to happen, should the time come.

Ciaran moves toward me, backing me into the wall. Flashes of Drago move through my mind, when he's crowded into me before. "That wasn't convincing enough. You do anything stupid, Shadow, I will drag you back from the afterlife myself. Or if I even get a hint of you doing something risky, I will pull you so fast and have Drago lock you up until we can get you help."

My eyes narrow. "You wouldn't dare."

"Fucking try me," he snarls.

"You don't control death," I snap.

He laughs, the sound of it hollow as he pushes away from me and walks toward the windows. "You have no idea what I control, or who I know," he mutters. "Believe me, Shadow, I won't let you die."

The words hold such a finality that I cannot argue against them. So, I simply stay quiet while my friend looks over his city.

EIGHT

Alexi Helvig has been taking witches from the streets.
More and more disappear, yet it is unclear why he broke the
treaty.
Even after we gave him the Carmine witch.
— Mori Family Grimoire

AVA

Two hundred and thirty-six hours, that is how long I've been in this fucking box of a room. Nine whole days. I've kept track by scratching into the walls with a rock. I can't be sure how long I was in the other one; I didn't think to keep track until too much time had passed. Until I had already started to forget what the feel of Samhain's feathers felt like, and the smell of my small apartment.

I don't want to make the same mistake by forgetting to track now, even if it is depressing as fuck.

To be fair, it's a nicer room than the one I was previously housed in. This one has a mattress with only a handful of stains and a wool blanket. At one point, the scratchy piece of material was green, but the stains on it have turned it a brown color that if looked at too long appears vomit toned. This box also has a window, though bars cover it. The one before was just a concrete cage, no mattress or blanket or view. And it's the view that has kept me grounded, that grove of trees calling to me endlessly. On the nights I can't keep the tears at bay, I stare longingly at those evergreens. The scent of those trees and just beyond provides a soothing balm to my soul.

I've heard mention that a beast used to live in the grove, in a cage made of steel and iron and bone. I have never seen the great creature, but I have dreams of one coming to rescue me. Molten lava pours from its mouth as it burns away the bars that keep me here. Its great roar shatters the stone walls, and its teeth rip apart my captors. We fly away, its great black wings lifting us far from this place. Some-times, a skeletal beast joins us.

It's laughable that I'm dreaming of a beast to take me away, given the powers I hold on my own. I have been tempted to tap into that great well of power I hold, but once I do, there will be no mistaking who I am. Or what I am. And I cannot allow that to happen. Despite hating Hell, I can't risk my brother. Despite Hell being, well, Hell, there are good people there. My people, and I won't allow them to suffer because of my decision to run away. So, instead, I daydream of being rescued by great winged beasts.

Letting out a long sigh, I drag myself away from my daydream. If my brother could see me now, he would hardly believe how far I've fallen. My heart stutters a bit thinking about him, a deep ache settling in my chest. I miss him. Despite knowing he was so similar to my father in the end, I can't help but miss him. We have the same dirty blonde hair and deep silver eyes that mark us as royalty. When I was first brought here, I worried my eyes would give me away, but no one seems to have any idea what they mean.

Dropping down into the bed, I go to pull the scratchy blanket over me when the door to my box swings open. I don't flinch. I have never flinched, and I refuse to start now. I stare at the vampire who has barged in, my eyebrow raised in question. His cheeks flush red in anger at my obvious disregard for him. This guard in particular hates that he can't inspire fear into me. Something none of these assholes have learned yet is it takes a lot to intimidate the princess of Hell. They can torture me and feed on me, but they can't break me. I won't let them.

I have had years of training to withstand various forms of torture. They aren't reinventing the wheel in this prison.

"Hello, Gerald. To what do I owe the pleasure?" I ask, kicking my legs out in front of me on the bed, the picture of relaxation despite my tense muscles. Muscles that are screaming to flee out the door he's left open. Magic that is screaming to be unleashed.

He smiles wickedly. "I'm hungry."

I try my best to give him a look of boredom, to quell the fear cropping up in me. "They've already fed from me today." It's a rule Alexi put into place: you can only feed so much from us on this level.

"You think anyone will care if another whore of a witch ends up dead?" Advancing on me, he reaches down and grabs my hair at the roots, pulling me upward. I don't make a peep, despite the pain; they want my screams. I just keep staring at him. I can see the anger brewing and know what's coming before his fist connects with my cheek. Blood pools at the corner of my mouth as he drops my body back down on the dirty stone floor. Past him, I see the still open door, light streaming in like a beacon of hope.

Leaning down, he gets close to my face. "No one will give a shit. Just because you are in a nicer cage doesn't make you any more important."

I attempt to scramble for the open door, but the vampire is too quick, and he yanks my body back against his. I thrash against the hold, but the moment I feel how it excites him, I stop. Anger and rage pour through my veins. My power flickers just below the surface, and I bite down hard on my lip to keep it under control.

"Mmm, you smell good. I may keep you alive for a while. Maybe I'll even give you my blood, slowly break you," he breathes into my ear.

The scent of his breath has me swallowing back bile, but I manage to turn my face to the side and gulp in fresh air. "You have no idea where I came from if you think you can break me," I growl out, then throw my head back, smashing it into his nose. His hold breaks, and I lurch forward again, but he grabs hold of my legs just as my outstretched arm touches the open doorway. He pulls me back and flings me around so I'm no longer facing the only path of escape.

I let out a loud scream of frustration as he wrestles my body into submission. My mind races—is killing him worth exposing who and what I am? But before I make that decision, the weight lifts off my body, and a strange gurgling noise erupts behind me. Turning my head slightly, I see the tattooed fist through the chest of the vampire just before it pulls back out and the guard drops dead. Behind him stands the most beautiful man I've ever seen. My heart sings at the sight of him. His dark hair is short but messy. Tattoos cover every part of him, including one across his face. His eyes are a deep whiskey color, and the moment they lock onto mine, a feeling of peace overwhelms me. I know he's the one I've been waiting for when the word "home" shifts through my mind.

———

SHADOW

("Eat Your Young" – Hozier)

I wipe my bloodied hand on my jeans as I look down at the corpse of the vampire at my feet. "Fuck. This is going to be a pain in the ass to explain," I grumble. I had heard the voice of a woman arguing with the very dead guard at my feet, heard a fire in that voice that made my dragon wake up. And he rarely wakes up these days. Curiosity got the better of me, and when I saw him pinning her down, the rage that consumed me had no hope of being contained. Just like I can't contain how good the blood on my hand feels right now. Or that it is making my cock ridiculously hard.

A tiny squeak has me glancing from his body. Pulling my focus away from the blood.

Two silver eyes lock onto mine as they peer through a mess of blonde hair that's matted and dirty.

I'm struck by her beauty immediately. "I'm not going to hurt you," I say, trying to make myself less intimidating. My dragon rolls its eyes from deep in its cage. The first engagement he's had with me in a long time. It's unsettling and mildly annoying.

Her eyes narrow. "And I should trust you, why?" Her voice sends shivers down my spine.

"I guess because I just ripped this person's heart out." Shrugging, I crouch down to her level. "Isn't that enough?"

She lets out a laugh, the sound beautiful and wild in a place that holds no beauty. It lights up my tattered soul in a way that I've never experienced, better than any high. I know in this moment I would follow her to the ends of the earth if she commanded it, if for no other reason than to chase that feeling and to hear that laugh again.

When she moves to push herself back, her scent fills the air. Lilac fields envelop the room, like a warm spring day, despite the rank smell of this place. All I can sense is her. The instant it hits me, I feel the leash I have on my dragon strain, his essence fully awake now. I close my eyes for a moment to regain some type of control. Even covered in filth, she makes my mouth water and heart beat out of my chest. My teeth shift, elongating into their dragon form.

Before I can shove him back, my dragon pushes outward, taking control of my body for a moment. She lets out a gasp as I push her against the wall, my massive body crowding in on her small one. I burrow into her neck, inhaling her scent deeply, a low rumble building in my chest.

Pulling back, I lock eyes with her again, then flick my gaze down to watch her lips part. She drags her bottom one between her teeth. "Name?" My voice is a deep growl, more animal than human now.

"Ava," she practically whimpers, her voice soft in the space around us.

"Mmm. Ava." I let the name roll around on my tongue.

"Who are you?" she asks tentatively. I'm aware I'm still crowding her, my arms bracketing her body. Her silver eyes are wide, and if it weren't for the change in her breathing and the way her pupils have blown out, I would think she was afraid. But that's not fear I smell.

I smile wickedly. "I'm the monster in the dark."

I crash my mouth into hers and instantly moan at the taste and feel. It only takes a moment before she yields to me and allows my tongue to sweep in. She grips my shirt and pulls herself closer, hunger pulsing through those actions. Her breasts press against my chest, that thin shirt doing nothing to hide her hardening nipples. I roughly palm her breast, earning me a gasp that gives way to a long moan. I huff out a laugh against her lips.

Pulling back, I push up the flimsy shirt before covering her soft mounds with my mouth and ravishing her with my tongue. She moans out louder, and for a moment, I worry someone will hear us, but I can't seem to stop myself. Can't stop my dragon. A desperation claws at me to find out what she tastes like, what she'll feel like when I push my cock into her. Dropping down onto my knees, I begin to pull down the shorts she's in, when her hand grips my hair, pulling my eyes to her face.

"I like you on your knees," she purrs as she leans down to eye level. "Every princess should have a monster willing to bend the knee just for her. Willing to worship her as she deserves." She licks up the side of my face before standing back up and spreading her legs slightly.

The confidence in her voice makes my eyes roll back in my head, the little resolve I was still pretending to have snapping. I rip off her shorts, and my mouth waters at the sight of her pussy. "Fuck, you smell good," I mutter, my voice husky. "I bet if I touch you, you'll be soaking wet. Dripping, all for me." My fingers trail up the inside of her thigh, then back down her leg. The red blood still painting them stands out brightly against her unnaturally pale skin. She lets out an inpatient groan, her fingers tightening in my hair.

"Stop playing with me. Eat my pussy like a good boy," she demands. My cock hardens to a painful level. My dragon preens at the idea of fucking her right here.

The first taste on my tongue as I push through her silky folds has me ready to build temples and worship at the altar of her cunt. And as I move up and swirl around her clit, I'm certain I could die a happy man in this moment. She grinds into my face as I lap at her wetness. I push one finger in and marvel at how tight she is. I continue my slow assault on her tiny bundle of nerves and feel her pussy flooding around my finger as I pump it in and out.

"Oh, fuck, yes, that feels so good," she cries out. "Just like that. You're going to make me cum!" She continues to ride my face, her arousal dripping down my arm now. "Oh, God!" she screams.

I can feel her pulsing around my finger, squeezing it as she pours herself over me. I drink her up greedily, like a man desperate for water. When she is just coming back down, I pull my finger out and push her onto the shit mattress. Working my pants off quickly, I notch my hard dick to her center.

"My name is Shadow, but I'll be your god tonight," I say, and I push my thick cock into her, giving her no time to adjust. Looking down at her, I see discomfort lying on top of the arousal. "Shit," I mutter. Reality crashes around me as I regain control from my dragon.

As I move to pull out of her, she wraps her legs around me, holding me hostage. "If you even think about stopping, I will fucking kill you." She pushes her hips up, impaling herself fully on my hard cock. She breathes in and out deeply as she adjusts to my massive size. Panic starts to claw its way into my chest as I realize she's hurting, but the little hellion under me refuses to allow me to back away. "Fuck me. Now," she demands, rolling her hips.

My body moves without permission, just a puppet willing to obey its master. I push my hand down and circle her clit with my fingers, and her body loosens under me until we are both writhing in pleasure. Her moans fill the dark space around us with a bright light and evaporate my control once more as I become more beast than man. A tether of that light stretches between us, attaching to a space in my chest that has felt so cold and alone.

"Mine," I bark. "You are mine." I latch onto her neck, teeth scratching the skin. The deep ache pulsing in my chest, the push to sink my teeth into her, is overwhelming.

"Yes. Make me yours. Yes, Shadow." My name on her lips as that breathy prayer is my undoing. I feel my canines extend, my mouth partially shifting. My dragon forces my jaw to close around her neck, biting down to put our mark on her. The taste of her floral blood invades my mouth. I rip my teeth out and see the savage mark marring her neck in a messy fashion. It gives me, and my dragon, great satisfaction to know that'll scar.

Just like that, I'm pushed over the edge, my climax flooding me with such intense pleasure, the only thing I'm aware of is her body. Rope after rope of my release fills her as she finds her own. She's panting out my name repeatedly as we ride the waves together. Nothing matters other than the feeling of being inside her, the taste of her blood, and the sound of my name on her lips. I don't care that we are in the place that shattered my already dark soul and remade me into the demon I am today. Don't care those two feet away is the rotting body of the guard I just killed for daring to put his hands on her. Don't care that I've only just met her.

She's mine. Now and forever.

This stranger whom I've claimed, for better or worse, for the rest of our lives.

NINE

Power belongs to those who take it.
And we will take it back.
— Mori Family Grimoire

A few weeks later . . .

SHADOW

"Why won't you look at me?" Ava pleads. Her voice sounds so broken, so unlike her. "You haven't looked at me, much less touched me, in so long. But you keep coming here. It's fucking torture, Shadow." Tears well in her silver eyes. I back myself into the wall, arms crossed, desperate to keep distance from her. The savage claiming mark on her neck is a beacon to remind me why I need to stay away. Every time since that first claiming that I've touched her, I've barely been able to hold back completing the bond. It's why I stopped.

The weeks have not been kind to either of us. We look strung out, the incomplete bond riding us into the ground. I know it's my fault. I should stop coming here to see her, but

I can't seem to give it up. Can I die from this? Can she? Because fuck, it feels like we might.

"I can't, Ava. Just, please, eat the food." I push the meal forward with the toe of my boot. "It was a mistake." The words burn as they leave my mouth. My dragon thrashes against me inside that cage he's locked up tight in.

It's not a mistake! You are being a fool! He seethes.

We'll hurt her; I snap back at him.

I can almost taste the smoke my dragon is breathing deep within. *No. We won't. And if you ever stopped for a moment, you'd realize we never hurt our mother, either.*

Grabbing the food, she throws it at me, narrowly missing my head. Angry tears stream down her face. I'm thankful for the distraction, because it pulls me from that dangerous line of thought my dragon keeps pushing at me. This fucking narrative that we didn't kill our mother.

"Fuck your food," she growls. "I know what this is, Shadow." She points to the bite mark on her neck. "You claimed me." She pushes forward and comes to a stand directly in front of me, her hands grabbing onto my crossed forearms. Her anger softens, and that feels worse. "Shadow, please. You claimed me. I want you. Want this. I know you feel it, the connection we have, or you wouldn't have bitten me. I've dreamed of you every night, that grove of trees out there, the only thing that's kept me sane during the darkest parts of my life here. I knew you would be the one to take me away from here. It's why I let you take me, because I understood our connection on some level already. You're my mate. Please don't deny this."

Everything in me stills at the confession. Words clog my throat, emotions start to suffocate me as they press into my chest. Panic clouds my vision, and I shove away from her at the same time my arms want to reach out and hold her close to me. The mention of my old home rips my mind to shreds as I relive the terror and horror of being in that aviary. What's almost worse is the look of utter devastation on her face when I go back toward the door.

"This was a mistake." It isn't lost on me that I'm doing the exact same thing to her that Drago did to me.

The tears finally leave Ava's eyes, her thin body collapsing to the ground as silent sobs wrack her frame. "Just get me out, at least. If you don't want me, fine. But get me out." Her arms fold tightly around her body as she asks to be saved over and over again. I'm at war with myself as I watch her break apart, because I want nothing more than to scoop her up and ease her suffering, but I know where that will go, so instead, I force my body to leave the small cell. Leaving my mate broken on a cold floor.

I have been selfish. I've kept her here so I could see her whenever I wanted. The reality of it hits me square in the stomach, knocking the wind from my lungs. I've allowed her to suffer for the simple fact that I know once she is out of the prison, I'll never see her again.

A plan starts to form in my head. If I cannot mate her, at the very least, I can save her from that hellhole.

Even if it demands the steepest price yet.

MY PORTAL OPENS into our penthouse. Ciaran looks over at me from where he lounges on our gray couch off to the side. I barely stop to tell him to go check on Ava as I race to my room. I slam my door, the motion making me feel like a teenager pissed at his parents. My movements are jerky as I'm assaulted by emotions and thoughts that I would rather avoid, my hands shaking as I grab the Eufori off my nightstand.

The anxiety is a living beast, devouring me from the inside out. The thought of keeping Ava in my life is just as distressing as not. Both thoughts are parasites, chewing away at the little sanity I hold. My throat feels too tight to breathe properly, as if the anxiety is trying to suffocate me. A slow, painful death. One that I will get to relive over and over again because I'll never be free of Ava and therefore never free of this anxiety.

The Eufori finally lights and the crimson smoke worms its way into the quicksand taking up residence in my chest. The relief is almost instant, the darkness locked back behind a cloudy piece of glass only one crack away from allowing me to sink into the depth of that agony. But not today. Today, the glass holds and keeps the quicksand locked away. Just another predator waiting to be unleashed when I'm least expecting it.

"What is going on?" Ciaran pushes through the door, ignoring that I had closed it. His tone makes it worse. I don't deserve his worry, or the empathy currently plastered across his face. I deserve to suffer, particularly after what I just did to my mate. *But you won't even allow yourself to feel, you just escape into the drug. If you truly wished to suffer, you would stay sober. You would feel all those things.* "Shadow?"

Ciaran pulls me from the spiral. Pulls me from where those dark thoughts will go next. A reminder of how lovely it feels to bleed.

Taking a deep inhale, I finally speak my shame: "I fucked up."

———

AVA

It feels like an eternity since Shadow fled from me, denying our bond, and I feel like crawling out of my skin. Everything in me is begging to be in his arms again, but I can't leave this cell. He is my obsession, an addiction, and when I don't get a hit of my drug, I feel like I'm going to lose it. Until last week, he had become a constant in my life since the day he killed that guard. I never asked what happened to the vampire, but since that day, no one has dared come near me. I see vampires pass me by, disdain clear on their faces, but no one enters my cell.

Shadow.

The man who has taken over my body and soul. The man who owns me completely but won't finish what he started. The claiming mark on my throat pulses with the need to be finished, yet he won't do it. I let out a long sigh as I lie on the shit mattress. He may have friends in high places, but I'm still stuck here. Still waiting to be freed.

It's the soft footsteps that pull my attention toward the doorway. It's late in the evening, a generally calmer time in the prison as vampires head out into the city to get their kicks at the local nightclubs. So, hearing someone in my hallway causes me to frown. Sitting up, I press my back against the wall and watch my door. The key pushes into the old lock, and I see a blonde head in the light as the door opens. A massive Viking-looking man moves in, and for a moment, my heart stutters in fear because he emanates power similar to my home. Those blue eyes of his widen just a fraction when he meets my silver ones.

"Ciaran," he says by way of greeting. As if that name should mean something to me.

I raise my eyebrow at him. "Ava," I respond. "Do you speak in full sentences, Viking?"

He chuckles darkly. Moving into the room, he shuts the door behind himself, leaving us with only the light from the sliver of moon that hangs just outside the window.

I kick my legs back out in front of me, an attempt to look at ease despite the continued discomfort that my body is in. Either from being in these conditions so long or being away from Shadow, it's unknown. "What can I do for you?"

He assesses me, my already small frame even smaller now that the guards have decided I'm not worth feeding regularly, given they can't seem to touch me. Shadow had been bringing me food, but given I haven't seen him in a while, it means I haven't eaten either. Though it's not like I was even eating before that. Ciaran frowns. I can tell he doesn't like what he sees."Shadow sent me."

Fear and anxiety lance through me, the mark on my neck practically burning. "What happened?! Is he okay? Where is he?" My questions come out lightning fast. I'm practically tripping over my tongue.

"He's fine, but the wrong people were bound to notice him being around you too often."

My stomach bottoms out. "And who would those people be?"

He crosses his massive arms across his chest, those eyes still searching over me. "My father, for one."

Fuck. "Ah. So, you're Alexi's son I've heard so much about." My back stays propped up against the cool stone wall of my prison, but my hands fiddle nervously with the frayed edges of the moldy blanket.

Ciaran lets out a long sigh. "My father is a piece of shit. I try to avoid being like him at every turn, but alas, sometimes you have to be a villain." His eyes shine bright for a moment, as if he truly regrets what he just said, but just as quickly, the emotion is gone. "You're almost free, Ava.

Shadow just wants to make sure you'll be safe when you leave, that's all."

I feel my eyes narrow. "Anywhere is safer than here. Why couldn't he come himself?"

Ciaran holds up his hands in surrender. "I'm not here to fight, just deliver the message. And you would be surprised what's safe and what isn't in Gothic Grove now."

"So, he sent you? I feel like this is below you, Ciaran." I try to laugh, but the thought of escape feels like a fever dream, and I don't dare to hope it'll work.

Ciaran shrugs. "Shadow is my brother. I would do anything for him. And you . . . I was curious about you." He turns to head back to the door. "I'll get you some more food but know that he's working as hard as he can to free you. We both are."

He's out and gone before I can say anything. The oddity of the interaction begins settling in my chest. Ciaran Helvig radiated power, and not just vampire power. No, he smelled of witch and something akin to home. But if he was from Hell, he would have said something. Right? The question bounces around in my head. I wasn't hidden from people, so most know who the royal family is, and the silver eyes I have are only a mark of royalty.

I sit against the cool wall for what feels like eternity before finally lying down. The stupid wool blanket is still barely hanging onto life as I cover my body with it. Just as my eyes close, I hear the door open again.

"That wa—" The words turn to dust in my mouth as I see three large vampires enter the room. I can't catch their movements fast enough, and suddenly, they are on me. Holding me down to the mattress as I thrash.

"Alexi wants Shadow to know he'll never be free of this place. Tell him this is his fault," one breathes into my face.

True fear lances through me as the third one, the one not holding me down, brandishes a knife. In a sweeping arc, he cuts open my stomach. A scream erupts from my mouth as I feel my warm blood spill out across my skin. The three laugh as I try desperately to press my hands to the giant wound, to stop the blood from pouring out. My vision goes in and out, their forms hazy as they move out of the room. I try to grab for my magic, a desperate attempt, but the blood is leaving too fast.

"Fuck, fuck, fuck," I cry.

I hear someone come into the room, the sound of their boots echoing in my ears. My vision blacks out, and I swing my arm up in a lazy attempt to fend off another attack. Panic forges a path through my chest as darkness surrounds me. Open your eyes, Ava. Come on, open them up. Despite the heaviness of them, I manage to force my eyes to open for a moment longer, to look my attacker in the face before they kill me. But familiar blue eyes meet mine.

Ciaran.

He's the last thing I see before I pass out.

———

SOMETHING IS TUGGING ON ME—NO, not something, someone. I can hear my name being called in the distance and feel hands tugging at my body as if they are trying to pull me up. I think it should hurt to be moving like this, but my body is numb. That can't be good. I hear my name called again, and I try to open my eyes, but I can't.

"She needs blood," I hear a voice say. No, I hear Ciaran say. That's Ciaran's voice now next to me.

A low growl has my body vibrating, the mark on my neck pulsing with need. Shadow.

"If we don't do this, she'll die." Ciaran again.

Something warm is shoved into my mouth, and the metallic taste of blood surges into me. Renewed strength moves through my body. Magic swirls within me. My eyes crack open a little, and I can see Shadow's eyes on mine, relief blazing through them.

"Hold on, Rakkaani, just hold on." He cradles me in his arms, and we are stepping through a portal.

TEN

DRAGO

The sound of someone banging on my front door pulls me from my already shaky sleep. The clock next to the bed blinks 2 a.m. I let out a long groan. I only just fell asleep. Some assholes thought they could deal their own drugs on my turf followed by another getting handsy with one of the waitresses. Their bodies are now decomposing with the rest of the trash that was taken out. My knuckles are still cracked open from the fights, despite my fast healing. Normally, I allow my men to handle it, but my skin has been crawling lately, my dragon antsy to be released. So, I sated him with what he craves most: death.

The sound comes again, and I let my power move through me as I stand and head toward the front door. The black veins forming from my hands up my forearms twist and curl like snakes against my skin. I feel my eyes narrow as I near the door, a frown forming. This house, unlike my penthouse, isn't known by people. It's my own private oasis away from the city, on a bluff overlooking the bay. Only one person would know of this place, and no way in hell would he show up here.

"Gods damn it, Drago. Open the fuck up!"

The voice stuns me for a moment before it has me moving quicker. My bare feet are almost sliding out from under me on my marble floor. As I rip the metal door open, moonlight cascades over the late-night intruder.

Ciaran Helvig stands tense, his blonde hair down in wavy locks, uncharacteristically messy for him. His eyes are a stormy blue but seem to flash red as he takes in his surroundings. Blood is splattered across his face, that ancient sword gripped tightly in his right hand.

"Wha—" I'm cut off in my questioning as he steps aside, and my stepbrother comes into view holding a wisp of a girl in his arms.

Shadow shoves past us into my home, his arm grazing my bare chest as he pushes by, his black boots leaving bloody prints across the white marble. My nostrils flare at his scent, and a trace of something else right under it . . .

Lilacs.

I take another deep breath and feel my dragon coming out of its slumber, now nuzzling against my death magic. Ciaran pushes in last. I glance outside before shutting the door firmly, sliding the lock into place, and checking the magical wards. All still intact.

She needs help." Shadow's panicked tone has me frowning. From this angle, I can see she has a deep wound across her belly. Blood oozes from it rapidly. He pulls back from laying her on the couch, and I realize now that

Shadow is also covered in blood, the dark night having obscured it originally, but with the light of my living room on him, I can see it splattered over his dark clothing.

I rush to him, ignoring the fact that I'm half-naked, and grip his arm tightly. "Are you okay, Rakkaani?" He tenses at the name and rips his arm from my grasp as if I've burned him. My chest cracks a little at the loss of connection.

"I'm fine." His voice is flat. "She's not." He draws my attention back down to the girl, whose face is unnaturally pale, her long blonde hair hanging limp around it. She's beautiful, despite the filth covering her. A rumble sounds deep in my chest, the sound unmistakable in the quiet of the room. Ciaran lets out a cough, purposefully distracting me from the girl on my couch. My attention snaps to him.

"We need your help, Drago. She needs your help," he says. "She needs a place that's safe to heal." His voice is calm but firm, but his body betrays him as anything but calm. His muscles are taut over his body, ready to spring into action.

Once Shadow was free I began helping Ciaran get witches out of his father's prison. They have the option to either remain in Gothic Grove working for me, or I ferry them out with money and a new identity. Most choose to leave. The few that have stayed have remained under my protection in my club, the only place Alexi doesn't dare go. Injured witches, however, tend to go to The Motel, where Ferra helps tend to them before getting them out of the city.

"What's so special about this one?" I ask, crossing my arms over my chest. I'm at war with my own body, part of me desperate to wrap the girl in my arms while the other wants to get as far away as possible. Shadow's eyes flare as he finally takes in my lack of a shirt, and I smirk. His whiskey eyes trace my form, longing flashing over his face before he schools it again. But not before I catch him pull his bottom lip between his teeth. The movement sends shivers down my spine.

"She's mine," he growls, his eyes flashing golden briefly before he regains control. I involuntarily step back, yielding space between us.

"Yours?" I whisper. Both fascination and hurt burn into my chest like a brand. My dragon seems stunned into submission as it takes the small girl in.

He steps into my space, eyes blazing golden again, his control barely holding. "Mine," he repeats. My heart beats once, twice, and then shatters completely as the words sink into my very core.

I move to push him out of my space, to turn and demand they remove the girl from my home. But Ciaran steps between us. His eyes are stormy as they take in the situation, take in the pain that I'm sure is clear as day on my face. The pain I'm desperate to hide from Shadow.

"Ava is important. We had already planned to bring her here, but I'm sorry to drop her when she's as injured as she is." He pinches the bridge of his nose, his level of exhaustion evident on his face. "She's had my blood, so she'll heal, but slowly. We can stay the night to help you look after her, but after that, we need to return to the prison. My father will wonder where we've been."

Pulling a deep breath into my chest and schooling my face, I turn and watch the struggle move over my stepbrother's face; I can see he cares for this girl. Cares for her on a level that makes my heart twist painfully in my chest. It's all I can do not to rub at the pain. I had hoped one day he would look at me like that, but after everything, Shadow refuses to forgive me. Refuses to listen to my side of the story of when his father sold him. And honestly, I'm not sure I can blame him. Not when I blame myself for letting him get dragged off in the first place.

Pain turns to something dark and twisty. Jealousy. That green poison moves under my skin as I glare down at the girl who has the affections of the person who should be my mate. She shifts a little so her head falls to the side, exposing her neck. I suck in a hiss when I see the claiming mark stamped on the juncture of shoulder and neck and snap my eyes to Shadow.

"You claimed her?" The words leave my mouth in a whoosh of unimaginable pain. He says nothing, only stares me down with those whiskey eyes. "How? How is that possible?" I take a step toward him, but he backs away. The distance between us might as well be a canyon.

"She's mine. My dragon and I chose her." His voice rumbles low, but it feels like he is screaming at me.

My mate chose another, and the devastation feels insurmountable.

After a moment of biting back my emotions, I finally speak. "She can stay here until she's stable. After that, I want her out. I'm not in the business of taking in strays," I say, ignoring how the statement tastes on my tongue. Ignoring how Shadow looks at me like I truly am the monster he's painted me as in his head. But my whole body is vibrating with excruciating pain, thinking my mate chose another.

To deny the mate bond is a death sentence in the end.

Ciaran claps his hand on my bare shoulder, squeezing. "Thank you." He moves past me toward the guest room at the back of the house, leaving me and Shadow alone with the brutalized girl. An array of emotions swim through me as I hold the eyes of the man I love.

"Shadow . . ." I begin, but he shakes his head, before kneeling next to her. "Shadow, please listen to me."

"No." The word is commanding. Harsh.

My heart fractures even more, but I turn and head back to my bedroom. I refuse to allow him to see the tears about to fall. Because in the end, I really did fail him, and I don't deserve his comfort.

———

THE NEXT MORNING, I find Shadow in the same place I left him, holding silent vigil over the sleeping girl. Her hair hangs limply around her thin face, but her breathing seems less labored. Fresh blood marks her pale lips, and the scent floods my nostrils.

"I gave her more blood; she'll be okay," Ciaran says as he licks the blood off his wrist.

Nodding, I burrow deeper into the black hoodie I pulled on above the flannel pajama pants I spent the night tossing and turning in. Sleep evaded me all night, knowing Shadow was only in the other room, so close to me. It was a special kind of torture to know he was with some random girl instead of in bed next to me.

I don't say anything as I grab two coffee mugs, fill them both, and hand one off to Ciaran. My hair falls into my eyes from beneath the hood as I take a long drink of the hot beverage.

Ciaran takes a sip out of his coffee mug as he looks out at the gray morning through the bay windows next to us. They look out over the port, where ships move to and fro. Seagulls can be heard through the glass panes. I love this home. Being able to see the port while having the forest behind me brings peace that

I don't get from being in the city. When I built this place, I built it for us. But now, it's a reminder of what I'll never have. This mystery girl has poisoned it without even being aware.

Silence overtakes the room, heavy and foreboding as I watch Shadow fuss over the girl, pulling the blanket up and over her chest before moving her hair off her forehead. The gesture is so tender.

He takes one last look at her before he stands up from his spot and shoots a death glare at me. "If she dies, I will kill you. Consequences be damned." And then he's stepping through a portal, leaving Ciaran and me alone. Looking down at the girl, I let out a long sigh, fist clenched tightly inside the pocket of my hoodie as I try to rein in my emotions.

Ciaran doesn't move to follow Shadow. He turns to me instead. "He loves you," he says. "He just can't get out of his own damn way."

I shrug. "It's my own fault, Ciaran. I let him down."

He scoffs and shakes his head. "You didn't let him down, his father did. You have always been fighting for him, even if he had no idea." He pauses for a moment, his gaze traveling down to the woman. "Keep her safe. I don't want her leaving here."

His tone causes some red flags to raise in my head, and I frown. "Is she a prisoner?"

He doesn't say anything for a long moment, just walks to the sink and places his coffee cup in it. "She's not a prisoner, but she's . . . different, and I don't want her slipping away."

The way he says it makes my dragon rumble to life, my magic swirling in my veins for a moment as if drawn to protect her. The feeling confuses me to my very core.

Ciaran smirks. As if he sees everything. He waves at me before stepping through the portal.

The room returns to silence, the only sound the light breathing of the tiny female buried under the blankets. I'm not sure how long I stand looking at the spot where the portal was, the spot my mate left from, but it's long enough that the girl suddenly regains consciousness, her arms flailing out around her before she looks over at me, her silver eyes locking onto my blue ones.

Fuck me. Silver eyes.

AVA

When I open my eyes, I'm met with the face of the second most beautiful man I've ever seen. Two crystal-blue eyes peek out from under a dark hood, blonde hair hanging in front of them in wisps. My heart hammers in my chest as the memories of my attack come rushing back, my mind trying to piece together how I ended up here. And where exactly here is. I attempt to push up but wince as my stomach pulls.

"You shouldn't move. Ciaran gave you as much blood as he could, but you are still healing." The voice of the stranger shoots to my chest in a strange way before dropping to my core. His stare is intense and seems to shift from loathing to longing in quick succession.

"Who are you?" My voice is hoarse and scratchy. "Where am I?"

He scowls before stalking off, and I look around, confused at his reaction to simple questions. "What the fuck is going on?" I mutter as I attempt to push up again.

"Here." A glass of water is thrust in front of my face,

causing me to fall back into my pillow on the couch. "You're at my house. Ciaran and my stepbrother brought you here last night after you were presumably attacked."

He pauses, indicating for me to drink the water. I roll my eyes but take a sip of the cool liquid anyway, and I can't help moaning at the taste and feel. The stranger's eyes flash with hunger so rapidly that I second-guess having seen it. "My name is Drago."

"I'm Ava."

His eyes trace over me, making me self-conscious of how dirty I am. "Ava," he repeats back to me, and my name rolling off his tongue sounds like a promise of things to come. "You probably want to shower. It's through the hallway on the left." It's all he says before turning his back to me and heading to the kitchen. A dismissal if I've ever seen one.

Letting out a long sigh, I manage to stand, but when I hit my feet and attempt to take a step, blinding pain shoots through me, causing me to cry out and collapse back against the couch, arms around my stomach.

Cool, strong hands covered in tattoos suddenly grip me. "Fuck," Drago curses. "You are going to hurt yourself. You have to be fucking careful."

His anger sparks my own. "You are an asshole. I didn't ask to be left here. As soon as I'm healed, I'll be out."

"You aren't going anywhere," he growls before lifting me into his arms, earning a squeak from me.

"What do you mean?" I yell, ready for an argument, but it's cut short as he sets me on the countertop of his bathroom and rips off his shirt, exposing his beautiful body. My mouth waters as I take him in, my anger dissolving into a puddle of arousal. Words fail me when he pulls those flannel pajama pants off, exposing the outline of his thick length under black boxer briefs.

He turns his back to me, apparently oblivious of the effect he is having on my body and turns on the giant walk-in shower. "Can you undress, or do you need help?" he asks, still facing away.

I clear my throat. "Uh, you want me to get undressed with you? A complete stranger?"

His soft chuckle sends a fresh wave of arousal through me, and I squirm, cursing my body for betraying me in this moment. "I can promise you; I have no interest in you that way."

The words are a bucket of cold water on my body, causing my face to flush. Of course, he doesn't. I'm covered in filth, and Shadow probably told him how we hooked up. I begin wrestling with my clothing, but each time I go to pull my thin tank top up, I cringe.

"Jesus, let me help." In quick movements, his hands skate over my sides as he gently pulls the material over me. I bless the fabric when it covers my face because I know I am blushing deeply by the way it burns. When the top is finally over me, my eyes refocus on him as he gently lifts me up, then sets my bare feet on the warm marble floors. Slowly, with the grace of someone much smaller than he is, he kneels in front of me. His hands trace up my thighs in a movement that has the arousal back in full force. He pauses, nostrils flaring and eyes shooting up to me. His glowing, golden eyes.

"What are you?" I whisper. But even as I say it, I know in my gut what he is. I know what golden eyes mean—anyone from Hell does.

His lips kick up into a small smirk before he rips my

pants down and stands up quickly. "Come on, let's get you clean."

When he leads me into the shower, my body begins to move automatically, and when the hot water hits me, the moan that comes from me is pornographic. Closing my eyes, I allow it to cascade down my body and run it through my long hair with my hands.

"Oh, fuck, this feels good," I say, pleasure drawing out the words. When I finally open my eyes, I see Drago is pushed against the counter, his hands gripping the countertop so tightly that I worry he'll crack it. His gaze, still golden, is burning me alive. His cock is no longer soft but rigid and straining against those cotton briefs. For a moment, I think he is going to do something crazy like fuck me against this wall, but the heat dissolves to sadness, followed by anger, and instead of pushing to join me, he storms from the room.

*We learned that Hell killed off the most powerful dragon
lines.
Death dragons were thought to be extinct.
Until we discovered one still alive.
—Carmine Family Grimoire*

AVA

The book in my hands falls into my lap just as my head
bobs down, waking me, and I jerk back up. "Fuck."

I swipe my eyes in a desperate attempt to push the
tiredness away. I have no reason to be tired; I don't do
anything. I've done nothing for the past few weeks as I've
healed since my rescue. I sit here, day after day, frozen and
unsure what my next move is. Sure, I'm still healing a bit,
but the biggest thing is trying to figure out what my life will
look like now. Before Alexi snatched me, I'd had a small
apartment and a part-time job as a bartender and dancer at
a local shifter club. I had been dating one of the waitresses.

Well, we had been fucking. Dating is a loose term. My life hadn't been grand, I suppose, but it had been mine. It had been a short time of self-discovery, and I had loved it. But it doesn't feel like I can go back to that life now.

Drago tolerates me here. He isn't outright hostile, but he also isn't warm and welcoming, either. He generally avoids me now that I'm healed, but every so often, I catch him giving me that same heated stare he had in the bathroom that day. It's been confusing, honestly. One minute, I think he might kill me, and the next, he looks like he wants to fuck me. Despite all that, the idea of leaving this place has my entire being rallying against the thought.

I know a huge part of me is hesitant to leave Drago's because it's my only tie to Shadow. If I leave, that'll be the end of it. Even knowing Shadow has no interest in me, despite the claiming mark on my neck, I still have hope he will change his mind. It's pathetic, really.

The scent of eucalyptus suddenly floods the room, and I don't have to turn to see that Drago has meandered in. When he clears his throat, I angle myself toward him. Hair still wet from the shower, the blonde strands hanging in pieces in front of his blue eyes, he finishes buttoning up his dress shirt. As I watch his fingers move, my mouth waters and my pussy clenches at the thought of how it would feel to have those fingers inside me.

He looks me over, my unwashed hair, pajamas I have been in for gods know how long, and my makeup-less face. His body tenses at whatever he sees, and for a moment, I worry he'll kick me out right this very second. But in the next, concern washes through those brilliant eyes. "What are your plans?" His voice vibrates my core, and I shut my eyes briefly against the sensation.

"This." I gesture to where I'm seated, book now properly in my hands. "And looking for a job, I don't have anything left, so I'll need to start somewhere. I used to bartend and dance before I was taken. I could try to get something like that."

A low growl emits from him. "You aren't fucking dancing somewhere."

Curious, I cock my head at that and watch him take a deep breath.

He frowns. "You don't need to leave. You can stay here as long as you want."

I let out a small laugh. "Look, Drago, I know you don't want me here. I get it. I really do. I've invaded your space. I just need a little more time to figure it out and I'll be gone. You won't have to deal with me again."

"Ava, come with me to work tonight." The way he says my name should be illegal, given I'm his stepbrother's unwanted mate. I open my mouth, but he holds up his hand, halting whatever he thinks I'm about to say.

I blink, once, twice, and then allow my face to form a confused frown. "To your club?" It isn't lost on me that Drago owns Club Eufori and what that means. That place is notorious, and I have always wanted to see the inside of it. This is the first time he's suggested I go with him to work.

"Yes. If you like it, you can come work for me." He says it so simply. "Now, go get dressed for tonight. I'll wait for you. You'll find some clothes in your closet."

My mouth goes dry, and I weigh my options. If it were any other club, I would balk at the idea, given the risk of someone from my home being there, but his club? It might be the safest place for me. And the idea of sitting alone for another night sounds like utter torture. So, I give him a small smile and scramble to my feet, running toward my room.

Drago
("Rumors" – NEFFEX)

Shooting a text to Kai, I let him know I'll be running behind and that Ava is coming with me tonight. She's like a ghost in my home, haunting every portion of it and reminding me that Shadow chose her over me. What's potentially even worse is the strange obsession I've developed for her. I find myself watching her damn near all the time, hidden in the dark so she doesn't catch me. Work has been my only escape, and now I'm letting her invade that space as well.

Seeing her tonight, she looked so broken, and when she talked about leaving, my dragon damn near tore from my skin to keep her here. So, I did the only thing I could think of: offered her a job. Against my better judgment.

A throat clearing has me turning, and I swear to all the gods, my mouth dries up and my cock hardens immediately. Ava stands with long pink hair braided into some mohawk style down the center of her head. "You changed your hair?"

She nods. "I wanted something different. I've been blonde my whole life. I needed a change."

It's on the tip of my tongue to ask her exactly how she did it, but I get the distinct impression that she doesn't trust me enough to be honest. "I like it," I respond simply.

A blush creeps up her cheeks. She's applied smoky eyeshadow and a dark lipstick that pops against her pale skin. Golden heels wrap around her slender calves, exposed by two slits in her black skirt that go all the way up to the top of her thighs. The high waistband covers her scar and stops just below the band of black lace that wraps her breasts.

I stare at her, my gaze traveling all over her body, gobbling it up and storing it in my memory for later. When I finally land on those silver eyes, they are heated, and I have to remind myself to stay put on the other side of the room. "You look beautiful." The words spill from my lips before I can control myself.

She smiles wide. "Thanks. It's been so long since I've done this. It feels good."

Indeed, she looks completely different from the girl who was just sitting on the chair. She looks fucking radiant, and I'm regretting my choice to bring her to the club.

We'll kill anyone who touches her, my dragon rumbles.

She's not ours, I remind him. But he says nothing. Only growls, low and deep.

I drag my hand down my face, trying desperately to disagree with him but also knowing if someone does touch her, I won't have control.

"We going?"

I open my eyes and realize she's crossed the room, her body now positioned directly in front of mine. Her lilac scent invades my nostrils, and by the slight surprise in her eyes, no doubt she just saw my dragon peek through. He's like a cat in heat, the way he is demanding to be let free. My skin feels like it's too tight, and my cock is now so hard, I'm fairly certain it's going to rip through my pants. It's confusing as hell. So, I simply nod and whirl around, trying to avoid the awkward situation of getting a hard-on for my mate's mate. Jesus, could this get any more complicated?

Yeah. She could be both of ours, my dragon replies.

Fuck.

———

AVA

Bonus

The evening had been spectacular, a whirl of everything I needed to recharge my soul. Until someone grabbed my wrist and Drago ripped his throat out. The display of violence shouldn't have turned me on and yet my pussy had practically wept with need when the blood splattered over my face.

He had said nothing to me, nostrils flaring, gathering me into his arms and ushering me out of the club. But nothing could have hidden the hard ridge of his cock pressing into my back in the elevator. My body had lit up like a gods damn solstice tree and I had practically rubbed myself over him until he shoved me into the bathroom with nothing but a grunt.

Now, standing at the sink I nibble on my lip weighing the pros and cons of fleeing the bathroom in the towel currently clutched to my chest. Everything in me is screaming to find him, climb him like a tree and let him feast from my pussy. Everything except the small part of me that is still holding out hope for Shadow.

Pressing my forehead into the door I close my eyes to avoid looking at the mark on my neck. The ravaged patch of skin left behind when he started to claim me.

Imagine what it would look like to have a matching set?

The traitorous internal monologue deep within makes my nipples pebble as I think of Dragos teeth sinking into the other side of my neck, of his cock filling me. . . . "Fuccckkk." I huff out. The ache between my thighs grows and I allow my hand to trail downward sweeping over my bare pussy. I hiss when I touch my clit, the nub oversensitive and needing release.

I press down into a circular motion, rubbing soft at first before pressing harder and sweeping down to my opening. My fingers are a poor substitute for the cock I want but they still pull a soft moan from me. The sound echoes against the tile walls but my body feels too far gone to care. I keep alternating between circling my clit and fucking myself. The frustration mounts as I feel myself edging towards orgasm and I finally allow the towel to drop to my feet so I can massage my breast with my free hand.

I allow myself to imagine it's Drago's hand cupping me and tweaking my nipple, while Shadow's fingers plunge deep within. I imagine the feel of Drago's hard cock pressing into me from behind as he urges me forward, urges me to cum on Shadows fingers. It's that visual that has me letting out a desperate wail as I cum on my own hand. The sound loud enough that I know Drago will have heard it if he is anywhere in the penthouse yet I don't give a shit. Not while I'm still panting against this door.

DRAGO (DARKNESS- FATE)

Standing on the other side of the bathroom door and listening to Ava cum snaps the restraint and crumbles any of the walls I've attempted to maintain. When she finally opens the door and her scent hits me my dragon rises up to the surface and a low growl pulls deep from within.

I'm dragging her into my body without thought. Her lips part and cheeks flush even rosier as I raise her fingers to my lips and wrap my tongue around them. My eyes roll back in my head as her arousal floods my taste buds. "Mine," I say once I've licked them clean, "You're cum is mine. Your cunt is mine. You. Are. Mine." I don't let her argue before I'm slamming my mouth into hers. She hesitates only for a moment before she yields to me.

"Fuck yes." She pants out between our desperate,

hungry kisses. Her hands grip my shirt allowing her towel to drop before I'm lifting her into the air and her bare cunt is pressed against my shirt. Her tiny hands fist my hair as I walk us into the living room.

When I dump her down onto the couch her legs splay open giving me an unobstructed view of exactly what I want, no need, to devour. When my eyes finally trail up to her face I drop to my knees, landing between those beautifully splayed legs. Leaning in I allow my tongue to trace up her thigh before it lands on her pussy.

"Oh gods!" Ava cries as I circle and suck. Her fingers once again finding purchase in my hair. "Yessss." She hisses out.

"Mine. I'm not giving you up Ava, not now that I've had a taste." I growl, more dragon than human. "I could fucking live on the taste of your cum on my tongue."

I get lost in the taste and feel of her that I don't notice she's reached her peak until she rips my mouth off her cunt. "Fuck me now." She demands.

I raise my eyebrow at her, swiping her arousal from my bottom lip with my thumb. "Who are you to give me demands?"

She lets out a long laugh, head thrown back. "I'm your fucking queen."

No truer words have ever been spoken.

TWELVE

DRAGO

My breath puffs out in front of my face, the heat forming small clouds in the cool morning air. My hands are tucked into the long black jacket I have on over the suit I pulled on this morning, not to stay warm—no, my dragon does that for me—but to appear relaxed. And it is in appearance only. Every part of me is on edge as I wait for the portal in front of me to open. I want nothing more than to be back in bed with Ava. To have my cock buried in her warm cunt. But since that beautiful evening two months ago she's refused to fuck me.

Two months of knowing she might be Shadow's but she's also mine and two months of her refusing to fuck me until Shadow is with us. The longer she goes unmated, the longer we go unmated, the more I see her losing herself.

My stepbrother, the stubborn asshole, has refused to visit and my last conversation with Ciaran revealed he could offer no support. Not with his father finally finishing off the Original Witch families. Their ancestral lands now sit smoldering in ruin.

Shadow not visiting has taken its toll on her. Physically, she's fully healed, though the scar across her stomach remains. But emotionally, she is someplace darker. She seems alive at the club, but as soon as we are home, the light winks out of those silver eyes. Having watched Shadow lose himself to his own mind, I know the signs, and I'll be damned if both my mates succumb to their depression.

Mates. Plural. It still baffles me how I managed to gain two mates. Of course, there's lore around dragons with multiple mates, but nothing documented that I could find. Part of me wonders if it has more to do with Ava's ancestry than our dragons. The suffering we have all experienced feels entirely unnecessary and maybe this is the gods way of drawing our worlds together, atoning for the past trauma.

The wind picks up slightly, blowing a few hairs into my face. I take another breath, drawing the chilled air deep into my lungs before something shimmers in front of me.

The old brick archway leading into Gothic Grove's cemetery suddenly opens, a cobblestone road and a brilliant amber sky coming into view. The scent of sulfur washes over me as I see two people step through.

"Where is my sister?" It's not hard to identify this man as Ava's brother. Even if they didn't have the exact same silver eyes, their overall looks are nearly identical. His chiseled jaw and disheveled dirty-blonde hair are striking against those silver eyes. His leather jacket fits snugly against his muscular body, and I don't have to touch it to know it's used for racing.

The portal behind the two men shuts in a whirl, and we are left standing back in the cool morning.

"You must be Jackson," I say, keeping my voice level and unhurried.

The other man steps forward. "He asked you a question." His face is pulled into a sneer, making the jagged scar that runs from his hairline to his jaw more pronounced. It passes directly through his left eye, which is fully white. The other is dark red. His black hair hangs down past his eyes, almost shielding the scar from view. My dragon immediately dislikes him, finding the scent coming off him rancid.

Untrustworthy, he growls.

I narrow my eyes before disregarding him entirely to face Ava's brother. "This was a courtesy call—remember that prince." I spit his title at him like a curse. "Call off your dog; we are here to have a conversation."

"Excuse me?" The dark-haired man steps forward aggressively, his power starting to gather around us, insidious and oily in the air. "Do you know who I am?"

My patience snaps, and I pull my right hand out of my pocket, the dark veins appearing. "Do you know who I am?" My skeletal wings flare out behind me, and my eyes glow gold. His own eyes flare with a hint of fear. "Now, let the grownups talk."

He moves to step forward, but Jackson grabs his arm. "Oisin." His voice holds a clear command in it.

Oisin jerks his arm free of the prince, his eyes never leaving me.

Jackson crosses his arms, seemingly unbothered by

Oisin. "Alright, dragon, you have me. Now, will you tell me where my sister is?" he asks.

I glance toward Oisin again. The man reeks of dishonesty. His eyes shift between us, an anxious energy that is beyond protecting his prince emanating from him. He's on edge, like someone waiting for their next fix of Eufori.

He is keeping a secret. He is hiding something. Do not tell him anything.

I can't argue with my dragon. Even I can see he is off.

"I'll answer your questions when you send your puppy away." The statement has the desired effect, and rage coats the man's face, redness bursting into his skin at the audacity I must have to demand he leave. It says enough that he assumes he deserves to know what the prince knows.

Spit sputters from his mouth. "How dare you! I'm not leaving the prince here with you!" he growls. But I keep my eyes on Jackson, who I hope is smart enough to understand his sister's safety is more important.

"Oisin, go back to the palace," Jackson says. His eyes never leave mine.

A smile creeps over my face. Oisin's rage turns feral, and for a moment, I worry he'll lash out, but it's not at me that he's glaring. It's at Jackson's back. This will be very inconvenient if I have to kill this person to save Ava's brother. The portal opens again, and Jackson turns to look at Oisin, whose face suddenly becomes passive. "I'll be along soon."

Without any other option, Oisin walks backward and disappears back into Hell.

Once the portal closes, Jackson addresses me again. "Well, you have me alone. Now, will you answer my questions?"

I nod. "Thank you. All I ask now is you do not breathe a word to that man about what we talk about today."

Jackson frowns. "Oisin wouldn't betray me."

I snort and shake my head. "Your sister is important to me, and I won't risk her safety. So, you'll excuse me if I don't take your word for it."

His silver eyes narrow toward me as he cocks his head, the wind dancing strands of that blonde hair around his face. "And who the fuck is my sister to you?"

"My mate."

———

AVA

I'm not sure when it first started, but at some point, between fucking Drago and realizing exactly what we all are to one another and discovering they are dragons, I've slipped into a dark hole that I can't seem to crawl out of. It's as if I spent so long just trying to survive, now that I feel safe, I'm feeling everything that I kept at bay. The only time I feel somewhat normal is when I'm working. I know Drago worries; he's constantly fussing over me. Part of me thinks it's fueled by guilt that Shadow refuses to see me.

Drago and I have spent hours talking since that first night, and he's shared every secret he has, which is how I find myself in the position that I'm in. My own secret of who I am eating me alive.

My stomach is in knots as I look between the step siblings. Yin and yang. Drago with his light hair and eyes, and Shadow with his dark hair and eyes. The other two thirds of my soul that I can't seem to have. I have been going back and forth in my head for days on if I should tell them who I am. But as I've healed, my anxiety has worsened, the walls closing in around me the longer I'm in the open. Drago thinks I'm scared of the prison, that Alexi will take me back. But it's not him I'm afraid of.

As crazy as it sounds, I was relatively safe in the prison. No one was going to find me and drag me back home. But here? In the open? My brother or one of his friends could easily scent me out now. It's a fear I hadn't known prior to being taken, but one that seems to be poisoning my every moment now.

"You dragged me here, what do you want?" Shadow's voice cuts like a blade, and I don't have to look up to know the low growl I heard came from Drago in warning. He's gotten increasingly more protective of me. I don't know what he said to get Shadow here, but I won't lie and say I'm not happy to have him near me.

I close my eyes, taking in a long, deep breath, before I open them and take in both of the men in front of me. "I need you both to know who I am." Neither say anything, so I take another breath, hoping to steady my racing heart.

"Go on, Ava, it's okay," Drago says, his voice uncharacteristically soft.

"I'm not from Gothic Grove. I left my home a while ago."

"So?" Shadow snaps.

"Jesus, Rakkaani, let her speak," Drago says.

"Don't fucking call me that," Shadow snarls back. Pain flashes across Drago's face.

"I'm from Hell!" I blurt out, desperate to stop the altercation between them. The two turn and zero in on me. The only sound that can be heard is the wind outside.

"Why would that matter?" Shadow asks. "I mean, it's not unheard of for people to cross over."

I close my eyes for a second, hyping myself up to drop

the biggest part of the story. The part that I fear will have them running from me, given what they are. The long history between dragons and Hell is bloody and brutal. Particularly with the royal families. "I left Hell because my father is the king. My brother is the prince. Which would make me the princess."

Silence descends for a moment, laying over us like a thick blanket. Shadow blinks once, twice, before he lets out a laugh and shoves his hands through his hair. Drago, however, stays oddly silent, unexpectedly calm after my revelations.

"So, is this your goodbye?" Shadow asks as he paces back and forth.

"What?" Genuine confusion pings through me.

"You're obviously leaving," Shadow says, tossing the words at my feet. "Why would a royal stay here? You're done slumming it with us? Got your fill of fucking around, now you can go home to daddy?"

Drago growls low, "Careful."

I don't hide the hurt, the pain physically cutting through my heart. "I left because my father sold me off. I wasn't going to marry someone I had never met who only wanted to use me as a fucking mare to breed children for him, all to gain more power." I pause as the emotions I've kept bottled up threaten to spill over. "In Hell, the royals are the most powerful. We have the ability to open and close the gates to Gothic Grove, among other things. But it comes at a price. The magic, while strong, isn't indefinite. Our priestesses perform a ceremony that replenishes our magic every full moon. Without that, if we use too much, we die. I knew when I left it would be a risk, that I might never be able to use my magic or die because I used too much."

"Well, that's fucking ridiculous," Drago says, stalking off to pour himself something to drink.

I shrug. "It was put in place so no royal would be able to take the power with them and use it against Hell."

But Shadow continues to look at me, head tilting. "So, the only way to maintain your magic is a ceremony in Hell?"

Nerves rattle my bones as I look at both. This was the part I was dreading, for Shadow's sake. "If a royal were to find their fated mate they would be able to replenish and share magic. Whatever magic the mate possessed so would the royal. It would be better, and more sustainable, than the magic our priestesses pass to us."

"So, that's why you want to mate," Shadow growls.

"What?! No!" I yell, rushing toward him, arms outstretched. But he's moving toward the door too quickly, and Drago wraps his arms around my waist.

"Let him go for now," he whispers. "He doesn't mean it; we know you aren't here to use us."

Tears cascade down my cheeks anyway as I watch Shadow flee, and then I turn and break apart into Drago's chest.

A Princess and Her Dragons

Events occur directly after Gothic Grove ends.

THIRTEEN

Having premonitions may seem like a great power, but it is in fact a curse.
To see the world in fragments of what could be is a heavy weight to bear.
A lonely weight to bear.
— Carmine Family Grimoire

AVA

One Month Left of the Deal

I blink to clear the dust from my eyes as rapidly as I can before another explosion echoes from my left, sending me tumbling to the dry, cracked ground below my feet. My breath is knocked from me as I land hard on my back. Above me, the crimson sky of Hell is crackling with lightning. Panic edges into my chest, a viselike grip on my lungs that I'm fighting desperately. I roll, pushing myself up onto my feet as I take in the world around me.

People's screams echo in my ears as they flee the destruc-

tion. My eyes track the now wide-open streets for my mates. The bond in my chest is pulsing faintly. I start to follow that pulse, slowly at first but steadily picking up speed until I'm in a dead sprint across what was once the city landscape of the capital of Hell. The place where I grew up. Black smoke clogs the air the closer I get to where the fighting seems to be. Buildings and structures have been knocked down and lie smoldering, blocking my view of what lay on the other side.

Quickly, I begin to climb, something akin to dread starting to pull at me.

Turn back. Turn back, a voice begs me in my head, but I can't. I must keep following the faint tug on the bond.

My hands slip on the hot metal, pain lancing through them as they are cut open. Higher and higher, I climb the mountain of twisted metal until I'm finally at the top. Closing my eyes, I take a breath and hoist myself over. When I open them, my stomach drops and my chest cracks open.

"No." The word lurches out of me in a desperate plea. "No, no, no, no," I chant. An ancient prayer sent to gods that no longer listen.

Before me lies what was once my home. Now, it's a mess of smoldering remains. But that's not what drops me to my knees, not what rips a grief-stricken scream from my lungs. It's my mates' bodies on the ground in front of me. Drago's skeletal dragon smoldering atop Shadow's dragon. As if Drago shielded him to their very last breath, and it cost him his life.

I'm unaware of my body moving, but suddenly, I'm standing before them, my hands searching for life. Blood pools under their broken forms, my feet now covered in it. My own blood mixes with theirs on my hands as I sob into the cold forms of my mates. The faint pulse of the bond is no longer there. I feel only a vast pit of emptiness where it should be. A chasm that is going to swallow me whole any moment.

"Wake up, wake up!" I scream. "Please! You can't leave me here!" The tears pour freely down my face in uncontrolled rivers. Nothing else matters as I beat my fist against Shadow's large chest, before moving to shake Drago by his broken wing, the bones now bent in odd directions.

Something pulls my attention to the left, and I spy my brother's broken body, thick arrows protruding from his chest. I rush to his side and lean my head down, hoping to feel even a small huff of breath. But his chest stays still. His body is brutalized from the battle. His once beautiful wings are cracked, the feathers long gone and the bones protruding at unnatural angles.

I stand slowly, scanning the area for anyone else. A little way off, I see an Elker standing over Kallen's mate, his stomach ripped open. Kallen sits on her knees not far off, her eyes milky white as the Elker feasts on her fear. His end was fast, but hers will be drawn out for centuries. It's what makes the Elkers so terrifying: they can keep you suspended in time as they slowly eat away at your soul. The pain is excruciating; no one ever comes back from that. Her Hellbeasts are scattered in pieces around them, their bodies torn into shreds that make it impossible to come back.

The gore turns my stomach, and I retch up bile onto the ground. When the last heave ends, I straighten back up and find I am not alone, after all. Having seemingly appeared from thin air, Astrea stands stiffly, her once green eyes dulled to black. Her body is splattered with blood and gore. Ciaran stands next to her, his swords dripping with blood. His eyes hold a strange vacancy like Astrea's, as if neither are seeing this reality. I go to move toward them, but the collars around their throats give me pause. As if just now noticing me,

Astrea cocks her head, almost mechanically, her face devoid of all emotion. In slow motion, she unfolds her power, aiming it at the gates that lead to Gothic Grove. Horror pushes through me as I realize her intent.

"Astrea! No!" I shout.

I hit the bedroom floor hard, which knocks me into wakefulness like a fist. Reality slowly pieces itself back together as the vision unhooks itself from my brain. Sweat clings to my skin and my face is wet from tears. Slowly, I work through my grounding, finding and identifying things in the room based on my senses. Based on this reality.

Carpet under my back. Samhain's soft flutter of feathers. Drago's eucalyptus scent. The small cracks in the ceiling.

I repeat them over and over until I know I'm solidly out of the vision and back here.

I sit up and grab my phone. The digital screen reads out 1:00 a.m. A groan escapes me at the realization I've only had an hour of sleep. That vision has been invading my mind anytime I'm alone. Like a poison, it's been seeping into me and sucking away any hope I have. We've already been here for two months, and nothing has changed, nothing has altered the course of that dark future. It's still looming in front of us, and this isn't the first time I've been left wondering if I'm doing the right thing by not sharing it with everyone.

"Ava?" Shadow's voice pulls me from the dark thoughts. Glancing up, I see him standing in the doorway to the bedroom, wreathed in light from the hallway outside. "Why are you on the floor?" Concern and suspicion lace his tone.

"Just a nightmare." I wave dismissively, hoping he doesn't notice how pale I am, or the sheen of sweat. I beg my legs to hold strong as I push myself up, but my body ignores my plea, and when I waver, I'm caught by two strong hands.

"This is more than a nightmare," he says, his voice far from tender or understanding. "What did you see?"

I push away from his arms, forcing myself to walk toward the shower and away from Shadow before I break and tell him everything, confess the darkness invading my mind. "It was nothing, Shadow. I'm fine."

He doesn't argue, doesn't say anything or even come after me, but I feel those eyes burning into my back as I shut the bathroom door on him.

———

("SOMETHING TO HIDE" – **Grandson**)

The lights of The Playground pulse in time with the music vibrating through the air. From my perch atop Drago's lap on the main stage, I can see the bar is bustling with activity, people moving in and out of the VIP hallway in steady droves, and high up on the second floor, the majority of the windows are occupied by various pairings. The window closest to me has a woman bound in silk wraps, her legs spread wide as a man eats her like she's his last meal. Her head is thrown back in rapture. Another man moves up behind the one between her legs but doesn't move to touch them; he just watches as he casually strokes his hardened length.

We have been spending most of our time in Club Eufori, but tonight, Drago and I came to my club instead. He seems to have sensed my anxiety, a claustrophobia that has been slowly drowning me every day since that vision came up again. Shadow has been avoiding us like the plague —we enter a room, and he leaves. Very rarely do I see him, and when I do, he isn't sober. The room he crashes in has a permanent aroma of Eufori, the sweet, spicy smell of the drug now burned into my core memories. I thought he would have broken down by now, but given it's already been two months, I'm starting to lose hope in him mating us.

"Where did you go, Rakkaani?" Drago whispers in my ear. He brings me back into the moment, and I smile, my gaze refocusing on the pleasure being displayed in front of us.

Drago's rough voice caresses the shell of my ear as he pulls me back against his body. His thick length presses into my back. "You're making it very difficult not to touch. Not to have you cuming all over my fingers in front of everyone here." His tattooed hand roughly squeezes my bare thigh, silver rings digging into my milky skin. I bite my lip hard, desperate to avoid the moan threatening to breach my mouth. The idea of everyone here seeing that has me squirming on his lap and ready to beg.

He chuckles before wrapping my long fishtail braid around the fist of his other hand, then he pulls me back, nose tracing the length of my neck as he breathes in my scent. My legs spread a little wider in response, the edge of the white throne chair I'm sitting on digging into them now. As owner of the club, I have a long history of sitting here and observing my court. Since moving in with Drago, he's been joining me over the past couple of months, but tonight is the first night he's made any indication he wants to play with me here.

Or play at all.

Drago has done a frustratingly excellent job of keeping his distance, given Shadow is still refusing us. My vibrator needs to be charged every day, at this point. I have no qualms not hiding what I'm doing, either—if I'm going to suffer, so will they. It's been a long two months.

His fingers trace my leg, each pass getting closer and closer to the apex of my thighs. If the lighting were brighter, people would see the wet stain on the white panties I'm wearing. "You've been very naughty, Ava." He plants a kiss on my bare shoulder. "I heard you this morning, stuffing your tight cunt with a poor substitute for my cock." His fingers sweep over my center, and I whimper at the light touch, pussy clenching, desperate to be filled. "Such a little slut for it."

My body feels like it's on fire, sweat dripping down my temple as I strain not to combust on his lap. Nothing else matters at this moment, my focus only on the way his hands feel pressed against my body and that empty space in my chest pulsing with need. The entire club dims around us, as if we are the only two here, yet I'm hyperaware when he spreads my thighs wide, cupping my pussy possessively as he dips into my soaked undergarment.

"Fuck," he growls. "You are so wet for me. Or are you wet because of all the people salivating at the sight of you?" He pushes one finger into me, and my hips buck as the heel of his hand presses against that tight bundle of nerves. He releases my hair and drops his hand to my neck, bracketing it and squeezing lightly. A moan squeaks out of me in a breathless whoosh. "Such a tease. Fuck, the sounds you make."

"Drago . . ." I finally manage to get his name out of my mouth, barely containing the need and desperation behind it. His name is a plea on my lips. It's a prayer that I hope he answers.

He pushes another finger into me and slowly pumps in and out, those silver rings brushing my sensitive skin. He nips at the side of my neck before licking directly over the claiming mark left by Shadow all those years ago. The feeling sends a pulse through me and my core tightens, desperate for release.

"All these people are so hungry for you, Rakkaani, they want a taste of what is mine," he says. "Look at how turned on they are just by me fingering your tight cunt."

I didn't realize my eyes had closed, and I blink them open in a daze. We've gathered an audience, people sitting in chairs watching as they sip on drinks, eyes hooded with desire. But it's the ones who are so obviously aroused that push me over, make me want to cum, make me ready to fucking beg. I watch as a shifter in front of us takes his cock out, his knot evident at the base, and begins stroking himself as he zeroes in on Drago's fingers in me.

A whimper escapes me as I roll my hips, desperate for him to move faster, but he keeps up the lazy pace he's set. "Fuck, I want to cum in your tight little pussy so badly. Fill you up, fucking mark you." His fingers start to thrust harder and faster, until I'm bouncing on his hand, head now thrown back on his shoulder.

"Oh, shit, I'm going to cum," I cry. Drago doesn't stop me as I fall over the edge, my release dripping down into his lap. I fuck his fingers hard until the very last waves of my orgasm fall away. He allows me to slump against his body as he slowly pulls his fingers out, and I follow with my eyes as he brings them to his mouth and licks them clean.

His eyes roll back in his head at the taste. "Next time, I want you cuming on my tongue," he whispers, his voice full of promise. I capture his mouth in a deep kiss and taste myself lingering on his lips as the promise of what could be dances over our bodies. Sadness encroaches, however, with the realization that we may never bond like we should because our hearts also belong to Shadow. I pull back off him, a sad smile sweeping over my face, and see the same feelings displayed in his eyes.

I go to open my mouth, to say something, anything really, to try and ease our shared pain, but his blue eyes sweep over my head, his face turning neutral and distant in a blink. I whip my head around to see what has captured his attention and see none other than Ciaran, arms crossed and leaning against the dark wall. My mind involuntarily flashes back to that vision, and I have to force myself not to shiver in fear.

I unwind myself from Drago's lap, and he stands up behind me. "What is he doing here?" I ask, turning to look up at him.

But Drago doesn't answer, he only kisses me on the forehead, shoves his hands into his pockets, and disappears into the slowly dispersing crowd of voyeurs.

FOURTEEN

To share a vision of the future is taking a calculated risk.
The future is always uncertain, and if one were to share what
they've seen with others in an attempt to change the course of
their vision, they could doom them to a worse future.
— *Carmine Family Grimoire*

SHADOW
("STILL NUMB" – Ryan Oaks)

The music pulses in my head as I stand at the bar. The strobe lights flashing over the dance floor briefly illuminates the writhing bodies. The smell of sweat hangs like a heavy fog over the room. Right under that scent is arousal, followed by vomit. On top of it all is the thick red haze of Eufori. This was a dumb idea, Drago keeping us here for three months. Ava agreed for us out of necessity, but I know the motivation behind it. They thought the longer I was with them, the easier it would be to finally get me to cave.

The first month was bad but tolerable, the second

month a little worse. With one month left, I'm crawling out of my skin.

One month left. I can make it one month, and then I will never see them again. Even thinking that makes my stomach twist and my chest tighten. It makes my dragon grumble angrily at me.

This has been a living nightmare. Being stuck with two people I cannot be with is like bathing in acid every day. And having to be at this club nightly makes my skin crawl. My stepbrother thrives as the king of this dark empire. He is the Hades of the realm, Ava his Persephone. Even in her own club, Ava is a bright light in this city. There isn't a citizen in Gothic Grove who doesn't love her. Now that she is here most nights, the club is even more popular. The two of them can be seen sitting on Drago's private balcony almost nightly, where she perches on his lap, and I watch, almost hypnotized, as he traces his fingers over her skin. Up and down. Up and down.

They are the royalty of this city.

And I'm their dirty little secret.

I can't remember how I got to the bar on the main floor, but the girl next to me continues to pet my arm. I don't care to listen to her shrill voice trying to keep my attention. The fact that it can get to me over the music makes my brain short-circuit, a frown pulling at my lips. All I want is another shot and another hit; it's the only way I can stand being here. Otherwise, why would I have left the bedroom I've been staying in? With no one home, it's the only time I can relax. I don't have to smell them or hear them. They haven't fucked, but you can smell the need in the air, and it kills me.

Hearing Ava every night through the walls is a special kind of torture. She's made it no secret what she's doing at night. My cock rallies at the thought of her sweet sounds as she cums, at the thought of feeling that against my tongue or cock.

"Oh, my God, you are, like, so hot." The girl hanging on me cuts through the haze of my thoughts again, and the daydream breaks apart around me. Looking down at her, I can see she's wearing a tight black dress with her tits pushed up toward her chin. She's got her lips painted bright red and her hair pulled off to the side in an elaborate braid. Objectively, she's attractive. I'm sure every other person in here wants her attention, but her focus is on me.

"Mhmm," I reply before slamming back the clear liquid in the shot glass in front of me, then lift my hand up to signal for another. I look back at her as she lights up the Eufori in her hand. Taking a deep drag into her mouth, she pulls the joint from her lips and cocks her eyebrow at me. I don't hesitate, I slam my mouth into hers, pulling the drug from her to me, as though I'm pulling her soul from her body. My mind swims, my body instantly relaxing as the Eufori moves through my veins. It takes me a moment to realize she hasn't pulled away and she's still kissing me.

Her taste is wrong, and her hands feel like tiny claws poking at me in a way that has my skin crawling. I clumsily extract myself from her, and the pout on her lips is prominent as she unlatches from my body.

"Let's go someplace more private," she says, trying her best to look seductive. For a moment, a small voice in my head tells me what a terrible idea this is, that it will only hurt me, and them. But I refuse to start listening to that voice now and instead fully commit to my poor choices. Maybe this will finally push them over the edge.

My dragon growls at me, muttering something like, *fucking idiot.*

"Sure, baby. I know just the place," I think I say, but honestly, my speech is slurring, so who knows. She seems to get the hint, though, because she takes my hand and follows me through the dense crowd toward the employee-only hallway. The bouncer frowns at me as I pass, before lifting a phone to his ear. I'm sure he's calling Drago.

"Uh, are we allowed to be in here?" she says as I pull her into Drago's personal room.

I know for a fact he doesn't use this place, not since he found Ava, but before that, he used it to entertain his guests. Even entertained me, once. I can still remember the taste of his cum down my throat, the feel of his fingers pumping in and out of me until I let my release paint my stomach. I quickly shake the memory out of my brain and dig my fingers into my palms hard enough to ground me back to the moment.

The dark room is lined with couches that are deep red. The walls are covered in embossed black wallpaper, the whirling designs almost like camouflage. It smells like Eufori, but right under that is Drago's eucalyptus scent. My dragon flares to life for a moment, but I push him away. Push away the pang in my chest that has me wincing.

I realize, after a moment, I haven't answered her question, and she is sending off nervous energy. "Yeah, it's my stepbrother's club. I can do what I want," I say before I can think better of it and shut the door behind us.

Her eyes are wide as I brush past her toward the couches. "Holy shit, you're related to Drago?"

I sit down on the couch, arms spread wide and let out a chuckle. "I mean, my father fucked his mother, so sure." I'm annoyed that she keeps talking. "Now, did we come here to talk, or are you going to put that mouth to better use?" With Drago and Ava, I submit, but with anyone else? I would rather die than give them power over me. I snap my fingers and point to the floor.

She smiles wide, her pupils blown out. I can smell her pussy from here, but my cock is still soft. I've tried many times to lose myself in both men and women, but it always ends the same. I belong to them.

The drugs and pain may own my body.

Ava and Drago own my soul.

———

DRAGO

Sitting in one of the VIP booths of the roped-off section, I sip the cool, amber liquid from the tumbler in front of me. The burn is lighting up my throat in a way that allows me to find some pleasure in the pain. I keep my arm slung back over the edge of the dark leather couch, my white button-up half undone and sleeves rolled up. The scent of Ava is still strong on my fingers.

"How is he?" Ciaran asks, his voice pulling me from the memory of how her tight cunt felt. The two months that have passed since our last interaction feel like a lifetime at this point. His eyes have grown harder, a cold edge surrounding them. Something is off . . . his scent is changing. It reminds me of long ago, before he pulled Shadow from that aviary.

I shrug. "About as good as can be expected. I honestly thought he would give in by now, but he's just grown more stubborn. He avoids us on the best days, and the worst days, he is high as shit, sulking around." I pinch the bridge of my nose. "I don't know what to do."

Ciaran takes a sip of his drink, his blue eyes looking out over the crowd at The Playground. "Shadow doesn't believe he is good enough for anyone. My fucking father didn't help matters. He fed into the narrative that he is a monster, that he's dangerous." I nod as Ciaran talks, my heart clenching at all my mate has been through. "And when he found out about the deal I made to get him out, fuck . . . I don't think he's ever forgiven himself for that."

"You did what you had to. Alexi never would have released him, and with that damn collar on, you didn't have an option," I remind him.

He snorts, taking a long drink of his beer before continuing. "I know that. But he doesn't. All he sees is the supposed pain he's caused others. Not the love we have for him."

My cell phone vibrates in my pocket, pulling my attention from Ciaran. "Fuck," I mutter when I see Kai's name flash across the screen. "Yes?" My voice is clipped with annoyance.

"It's Shadow."

"Motherfucker," I curse. "I'll be right there."

Ciaran looks at me in question.

"I have to go. It seems my mate took up the old idea of 'the mice will play if the cat is away.'" I push to stand, buttoning my suit jacket again.

"Drago, he's going to try his hardest to push you away, particularly now with only a month left. He'll do anything he can just to hurt you so that you'll walk away," he says. "Don't let him."

I only nod. "Make sure Ava knows I left, but don't tell her why. I'll be back for her in a while." I pause before walking away. "Are you okay?"

He lets out a dark laugh. "No, Drago. I'm far from okay. But my issues can't be solved as quickly as yours can."

A frown twists my face. "I'll call you. We'll talk."

He nods, holding his glass up in response, gaze tracking back out to the crowd.

————

AVA

I walk back up toward the VIP booth I know Drago and Ciaran are sitting at, having just checked in with my staff after changing my destroyed panties and slipping on a flowing pair of harem pants, the black material loose against my legs but gathered tightly at my ankles. As I pull the curtain back, I see Ciaran looking out over the crowd, but Drago is nowhere to be found.

"He got called back," Ciaran says. "He said to wait for him here."

I flop down on the chair next to him, causing Drago's scent to bloom off the material. It tugs at me, and I rub my chest. "You mean Shadow did something, and he's cleaning it up before I get back?"

Ciaran raises his eyebrow at me, and I shrug. "I'm not dumb. I know Drago plays damage control for Shadow, so I don't see anything."

"We do what we have to for our mates." His words send a chill through me, and I look up to find his eyes are a deep storm.

"What's going on, Ciaran?" I ask, tucking my feet up under me on the seat. My skin pebbles with goosebumps, not from a chill but in anticipation of his next words. Because something is going on.

He stays quiet for a long while, and I almost think he isn't going to answer, until he finally lets out a long breath. "Astrea's magic is a lot. Being tied to it. I don't know how she doesn't get pulled under by it."

"Because of you," I reply automatically. "Because you tether her."

He shakes his head. "I shouldn't have been the tether. I shouldn't have access to her magic like this." I frown at the statement, but he keeps going. "Regardless, I don't know how to help her. Which is why I'm here."

"I can't help, I don't know anything about the Harbinger magic, or at least, I don't know enough to be helpful."

"That's why he called me," a voice from behind me says.

I whip my head around to spy Kallen standing in the entrance to my lounge. Her skin is soft and milky, that long white hair flowing down her back. The soft curve of her stomach shows between the dark sports bra she is wearing and the tight leather pants that hug her full hips and ass. Flanking her is a giant redheaded man, his hair pulled back in a thick bun and his beard trimmed. On her other side is a Hispanic male, his mismatched blue and green eyes standing out brightly against his tanned skin. He traces over me, his gaze far too perceptive for my liking. Both men are wearing leather cuts signifying they are from an MC, but the logo is blocked from view.

Kallen smiles and walks forward, the action not reassuring. As both men move forward with her, I see their logo appear. Primal Knights MC. Drago is going to fucking lose it. I glance at Ciaran, whose reaction is calm as he takes in the two shifters in front of us.

"Hello, little *princesa*," the one purrs, his accent thick on his tongue. I stiffen slightly, my body coiling inward. He makes no indication that he notices my movements, the stillness of his gaze unnerving. "*Estás muy lejos de casa.*"

Kallen smacks the man in the chest with the back of her hand. "Dios, leave her. We are here for Ciaran." She looks at me, a strange understanding passing between us. Two people who have seen a devastating future and are keeping it from those around us. "Ava has enough she'll need to face without your bullshit."

Ciaran stands up, setting his drink down and looking toward me. "Thank you for the drink. Tell Drago I'll call him." He looks back to the three others. "Let's go get this over with. I'm not looking forward to how angry Astrea will be about this."

Kallen's eyes widen in feral delight, as if the knowledge that Astrea will be angry is the best news she's heard all day then she creates a portal. The man she called Dios looks me over once more before stepping through, close on the heels of Ciaran. Next, the giant redhead goes, giving a subtle nod of his head toward me before he too disappears, leaving only me and Kallen in the lounge.

She looks me over, eyes narrowing. "We need your magic if we are going to win this."

"I know," I say simply.

She crosses her arms. "So, what are you doing about it?"

A growl slips from me. "Everything I can."

She shakes her head and mutters something that sounds an awful lot like, "Stupid dragons," before she too leaves the VIP lounge through the portal of her creation. Once her body disappears through, it swiftly shuts, leaving me alone with my thoughts and fears.

———

DRAGO

Walking into my club, I follow the pulse in my chest toward the back rooms. Shadow's scent hits me full force in the darkened hallway. Security stands next to one of the closed doors, and my heart cracks a little knowing exactly what I'm about to find. The grimace on my man's face confirms it. Pushing open the door, I see Shadow, barely conscious, his hand wrapped around a blonde's head as she tries desperately to get him hard. As I step into the room, I allow the darkness to cloak me for a moment, just to watch. My chest heaves at the pain emanating from my mate. It almost matches my own.

I know the second Shadow is aware of me because his eyes flare open and lock on mine, despite the cover of darkness. Stepping out of the alcove of shadows, I snap my fingers, and security enters behind me. The girl is yanked off his half-hard dick with a shout. I don't bother addressing her as she is dragged from the room. Instead, I keep my eyes on Shadow, on his own looking unfocused as they take me in.

"Did you have a reason for stopping that?" he slurs.

Crossing my arms, I look him up and down. "Yeah. I didn't want her self-esteem being ruined over the fact that there was no way she was ever going to get you hard." I lean in a little. "Because we all know the only way that dick is getting hard is by one of us."

Shadow lets out a sad grunt as he fumbles to push his dick back in his pants, the movement difficult given how fucked up he is. Another wave of misery washes over me, but whether it's his or mine is unclear.

Security comes back in just as he gives up the fight and slumps over, passing out with his cock still out of his tight jeans. "The girl was seen out. She wasn't happy."

Pinching the bridge of my nose, I shrug. "I couldn't care less." I push my white hair back just for strands of it to fall back in my eyes. The urge to punish him for being reckless pushes through me until I have to clench and unclench my fist to manage it. When he's asleep, Shadow exposes his vulnerability, the deep unhappiness seeping out of him in uncontrolled waves that will drown me if I let them. "Have Kai close down tonight. I'll be gone the rest of the evening."

My man grunts a response and moves out of the room.

My people are loyal to a fault. Most of them have been with me since the beginning, and the rest were brought in by Ciaran; a couple of the girls that work the floor were even rescued from Alexi. It's a safe place, and their loyalty buys my protection in a city that offers little. Particularly in recent years. With the shifter packs at war, the witches being hunted down and slaughtered, and Alexi having run the vampire community into the ground, Gothic Grove is a dangerous place. It's the type of place where law does not exist, and sin is the only currency recognized.

Bending down, I hoist Shadow up onto my shoulders— and find noticeable weight loss now that I'm holding him. Ava has been worried about his lack of food, but I didn't realize how much of an issue it's really become. "When you sober up, I'm going to shovel a steak into your fucking mouth," I growl. It's as though he thinks if he allows himself to waste away, we won't miss him. His passive suicidality shows up in new ways daily.

Walking out of the room, I head toward the elevator that will bring me up to the penthouse where I live. I own the whole building, but when I saw the view from the top floor, I created a penthouse and claimed it as my own.

The elevator dings, and I stumble into the foyer, sending up thanks to the gods that Ava is being occupied by Ciaran now. It's not like I can hide how bad he is from her; she sees it daily. However, seeing a girl sucking his cock will add far more stress and hurt in a way that I'm not sure she'd come back from right now.

I push through into my bedroom; the windows are open to the Gothic Grove skyline. The cool air is trying to give way to summer heat, humidity slowly seeping in. The sunshine will avoid the city in its entirety, summer hardly able to breach. It's as if it can't cut through the never-ending dark haze that spread across Gothic Grove after the original families were murdered. As though, in their death, they laid a curse over the city.

Lightning crackles off in the distance, illuminating my bedroom. I picked this as my bedroom when I moved in because of the view, but it is small. I pull back the cool gray sheets and lower Shadow onto the bed. He groans quietly as I shift him around so I can pull his shirt over his head and shimmy his pants off. Despite the weight loss, Shadow's body is still beautiful. The need to claim him cuts into me. My dragon huffs his annoyance, but consent is important to me, which I remind the beast. Shadow being passed out is not how I want to lay our claiming mark onto him. So, instead, I let my eyes rake over his naked body and try to memorize every tattoo and scar before I turn and leave the room.

FIFTEEN

He is showing magic.
I fear that when this is all over, I will not be the mother I had hoped I'd be.
— Personal entry of Kara Carmine in the Carmine Family Grimoire

SHADOW

My mother's voice enters my dark room. "Shadow? My love?" Her concern bleeds into me as I shake in the corner of my closet, cold sweat beading across my sixteen-year-old body. "Where are you?" she asks. I must make a noise because in a moment, the closet is flooded with light and her scent invades the space. Looking up through blurry eyes, I can see the concern on her face.

She reaches for me, but I press myself further back from her. "I'm sick," I try to say, but my voice is weak. "Don't touch me." It cracks on the command, but she doesn't stop, and her cool skin touches my face.

"*When did you start feeling sick, my sweet one?*" Her *voice maintains that calm tone.*

"*This-s-s mornin-n-ning,*" I *stutter as more shivers wrack my body. When I woke up, it felt like a mild flu, but by midday, I was positive I was dying. Certain that this was the end, despite knowing killing a dragon shifter is damn near impossible. My mouth tastes like ash and no matter how much water I have tried to drink, I keep throwing it up, and no matter what I do, that ash taste stays.*

My mother bends down, her slim face coming further into view. Her black hair is swept up into a bun atop her head. She is so thin these days, too thin. Her frame looks easy to break, and I worry endlessly about her. My father is a piece of shit, and someday, I will stand up to him for putting his hands on her, for making her so sick.

Gathering my lanky body into her arms, she hugs me tight. "Your dragon is coming," she whispers. "It won't be long now until you meet him."

My body shakes. I can't help but feel like she isn't happy. As if sensing my worry, she looks down at me, taking my face between her hands. "Whatever happens, you mustn't let your father know how strong you are. How powerful you are. He cannot know it. Promise me you'll keep it from him?"

"*I promise, Mom.*"

The dream hurts my head and my heart. I want to escape it, but I can't avoid her in my sleep. I try to open my eyes, drawn to the scents of Ava and Drago washing over me, but they are far too heavy. I give up the fight and let sleep take me back.

———

THE DREAMS that invaded my mind overnight have left me even more tired, if that's possible. I shift my body slightly, feeling cool satin against my naked back, and bite back a groan at the hangover currently trying to crack my head open. I blink a few times, slowly bringing the dark room into focus. A light from behind a cracked door is the only thing providing illumination. Not that I need it—now that my dragon has ripped apart its cage, my eyesight is unmatched. He smiles at me, satisfaction at my inability to rebuild his smoldering cage evident on his face.

Just below my chest, I can feel my beast rumbling as I look over at the small form curled next to me. Ava lies in a mess of pink curls, her red lips open as she lets out a relaxed breath. A small smile creeps across my face at the tiny ball she's curled herself into. It's a rare smile these days. I often wonder if Drago sees it as well: when Ava isn't "on," she's pulled in on herself. Distant until she notices someone paying attention and that switch goes back up. Something is going on with her, and my dragon is furious that we don't know what it is.

For a moment, I let myself imagine lying back down with her, pulling her close to my body and relaxing. My dragon huffs approval at the idea, and I start to move to pull her in, but then she shifts, and her shirt raises up so that jagged scar is in view. The illusion shatters, just like that, and that voice in my head laughs viciously as it reminds me that scar is my fault. Her pain is my fault. And I don't deserve to have any peace. So, I carefully slip out of the bed, my mouth tasting of ash as I hold back my dragon and move into the bathroom.

My stepbrother's bathroom greets me with bright lights and the smell of eucalyptus. I squint as my eyes adjust. The shower is rounded and open to the room, and two shower heads attached to the ceiling allow a constant stream of rain, no matter where you step, to pour down on top of you. Tile flows from the shower out onto the bathroom floor, the surface warm under my feet. Pulling off my black boxer briefs, I step in and turn the water as hot as it'll go. Standing under the deluge, I allow it to burn tracks down my tattoo-covered body, my black hair a heavy curtain in front of my eyes as I brace both arms against the wall.

"Funny, how despite being a dragon with flame affinity, you still turn pink under water."

I don't turn to face Drago, just keep my focus on the water running down me, shutting my eyes tight against the pull deep within anytime he gets near me.

"I take it you dragged me here last night?" I ask. Even the sound of my own voice, still rough from sleep, makes my head pound.

"Someone had to; that poor girl was working way too hard just to be disappointed in the end," he says, a quiet laugh following.

I feel him step toward me, and despite there still being distance between us, I feel crowded. Caged in.

"What do you want, Drago?" My voice is barely steady, and I know if he gets any closer, I'll crumble.

("Somewhere I Belong" – Linkin Park)

"You know what I want," he says in a husky voice, taking another step toward me. Without even turning around, I know he's at arm's length from my naked body. His scent invades the space around me. Another step, and his hand is a ghost on my back, forcing me to turn and face him. His eyes are glowing, his own dragon shimmering just beneath the surface. His white hair is hanging loose around his face, tiny water droplets collecting on the strands. His eyes are hungry, and I know if I were to look down, I would see his hard cock jutting out from his tattooed body.

"I'm tired," I whisper, the confession slipping past my lips before I can hold it back. The truth is, I'm exhausted. Fighting for so long, holding this anger for so long, has leeched all my energy. I don't know if I'll survive much longer. Maybe, had I not been forced to live with them for this long, I could have limped through life as I was, but fighting the overwhelming urge to mate has taken what small reserve of energy I had. I'm barely eating, I think the only reason I still have muscle on my body is from my dragon. Sleep exists only from drugs or alcohol. The ghosts of the past don't haunt a house, they haunt me. Follow me.

His eyes flash to something I can't place, but he pulls my head into his, bringing our foreheads to touch. The feeling of him instantly calms me. My breath loosens and my chest relaxes, as if this is the first time I can actually breathe. A shudder escapes me. I allow myself to soak it in, just for now, allow myself to rest against him.

"So let us help. Let us take some of this. You don't have to keep fighting this alone, Rakkaani," he says. "Aren't you tired of running?" I shudder as he grabs my hips, pulling my body into his. My dragon hums out in approval as he holds me, not a single part of my body free of his touch.

Take the help, my dragon growls.

A tear slips from my eye, followed by another, until I'm sobbing and he's holding me tightly. I feel my legs give out, and I drop to the black tile of the shower floor. Drago follows me down, offering soothing noises and promises that he shouldn't be making. My soul cracks open and a tidal wave of regret and fear and shame pushes through as I break apart in his arms. All the things I've held back, kept with my dragon in its cage, swirl around me.

I'm worthless. And weak. And I'm not worth the worry they keep putting on me.

"Shut up, shut up!" I yell at those inner voices. "Leave me the fuck alone!" Viciously, I clutch at my own arms, raking my hands down my skin, desperate to dig out the demons. Drago pulls at my arms, banding himself around my massive body, until I'm in his lap with my back pressed to his chest. Small droplets of blood start to appear on my arms, where my claws must have come through. Even the sight of something normally soothing doesn't make me feel any better.

"Rakkaani, you aren't what those voices say. It's not your fault. None of it is your fault, or your dragon's," Drago says over my begging for those voices to leave me alone. I desperately want to believe him, but years of listening to those demons can't just be undone in a single moment. I can feel my breath quickening, feel my pulse rapidly beating out of control, and panic sets in again. I can't lose control. Losing control means hurting the people I love. And I can't hurt anyone else.

Drago must notice because I feel his lips press to my neck, his nose dragging up as he breathes me in. His hands, having kept me from hurting myself, start to loosen and he traces my tattoo lines up my arms, smearing the blood I drew as he goes. At some point, his touch moves from soothing to erotic. I feel his cock harden against my back, and I let out a moan. He lets a hand move up and grip my dark hair before pulling my head back so he can have better access to my neck.

"Please," I whimper.

DRAGO

Hearing Shadow's broken voice beg me snaps any restraint I was holding onto. The difference between Shadow and myself? I love my dragon. I love when he comes out to play. Like a switch flipping, my dragon surges to the forefront, and I'm no longer in charge. We had two different upbringings. I had the chance to get to know that other part of me, without fear of it being used against me. My mother was many things before she was sold to Shadow's father, but she wasn't abusive. She encouraged me to get to know my dragon and taught me that we are an extension of each other. Shadow didn't have that.

My hand shoots out and grabs his hard cock, drawing a gasp from him as I sweep my thumb over the weeping tip. The shower spray is still falling on us, mist swirling and filling the room, obscuring us from the outside world. As if nothing else matters outside this space, outside of our need for one another.

"What do you need, Shadow? Do you need to cum in my mouth? Hmm?" I squeeze him a little harder. "Or do you need me to use you? Fill your ass up until it's dripping out of you?"

"Use me," he groans. "Please." The sound of his voice is thick with need as he begs.

I push him forward onto his hands and knees before spreading his cheeks and licking his tight hole. I groan at his taste, my own cock barely under control as I feel those muscles spasm around my tongue. Time loses all meaning as I indulge in my favorite meal.

Shadow begs me as I keep licking him, my hands tight on his hips.

I pull off and ask, "You want my cock?" before working my finger into his tight channel, my spit easing the passage, and he bucks forward, a long moan sounding off in the room. I pump in and out before adding another one, scissoring them as I work his hole open.

"Fuck me. Please, I need to feel you."

A wicked smile spreads over my face as I reach up and grab the coconut oil I keep in the shower. Palming a generous amount, I coat my dick with it first before sliding my fingers inside of him again. When I'm certain he's well covered, I notch my dick to his entrance and slowly push. The head of my dick barely fits, his muscles first tightening up at the intrusion. A loud crack echoes through the room as my hand finds his ass. "Relax," I hiss. "Take me like a good boy, just like I know you can." His body shudders under my touch as I keep pushing in. A whimpering mixture of pain and pleasure echoes out of him. A satisfying noise that makes my cock harden even more. "Tell me, Shadow, have you missed my cock? Missed my Jacob's ladder?"

"Yes. Oh, God, I've missed it so much," he cries out, panting in desperation. I smile fiendishly as I watch in utter fascination as one, two, three, four barbells push into him until I'm fully seated. I pause to take a moment to breathe, to keep in control and not lose it all at the feel of him.

"Fuck," he breathes out. "Oh, my God. You feel so fucking good."

Slowly, I pull out and push back in. With each thrust, I feel the resistance give way a little more until I'm certain he's ready. "I'm going to fuck you now, Rakkaani, I'm going to pump you so full of my cum that it will be dripping out of you all day. And then I'm going to claim you because I'm fucking tired of this bullshit." He squirms under me, but I grab his hips and pick up my pace until the shower is filled with the sounds of my balls slapping him and our combined groans. "And you will not be cuming until I say you can, do you understand?"

Shadow lets out a long moan as I continue the relentless pace but doesn't say anything. "Answer me," I demand as I dig my hands into his hips so hard, I know it will leave bruising from my fingers.

"Yes. Fuck, yes, I understand." He pushes back into me, trying to get me deeper into him. "Bite me. Breed me. Making me fucking bleed, God. Just don't fucking stop. I'm yours."

I nip at his shoulder. "Good. Because you might be calling for god now, but in the end, it's going to be my name you scream." I lean closer to his ear, allowing my dragon to show through my voice. The rasp takes on an animalistic quality. "And if I ever find your cock is in a mouth that's not my own or Ava's, I'll rip their throat out and fuck you on top of their bloody corpse to remind you who you belong to."

"Yes. I'm yours. I'm yours. Take me, Drago, please, please, please," he begs. I thrust forward, my hips hitting his wet skin. The shower still pouring over us in a cascade of heat.

"That's it. Fuck, you take me so fucking good," I moan. "I wish you could see how well my cock looks slipping into you." The visual is intoxicating as I watch myself disappear in and out of him. My claws extend out, and I trace them down his back. Blood pools in the marks I leave before I lean down and lick it up. He spasms around me, a long shout leaving his mouth as he sinks deeper into the pain and pleasure I'm giving him.

He's lost in whimpers as I pump in and out. Giving himself fully to me, he holds perfectly still while I fuck myself into his body, the sounds of our exchange drowning in the shower.

When his body starts to push back into me, I know he's barely holding onto himself. "You sound so sweet. Do you want to cum for me?" I ask as I keep up the relentless pace I've set.

"Fuck, yes, I do. Please let me. Please, Drago. I want to cum while you are inside me." His begging is my undoing.

"Grab your cock and show me how you use it when I'm not here. When you think about your mates. When you think about me fucking your ass while you eat Ava's pussy." He lets out a low groan as he grabs his hard dick and begins savagely stroking himself, his other arm holding his body weight. The muscles and veins popping forward make me groan at his beauty.

"Oh, God, I'm going to cum! Drago, I can't stop," he cries.

"That's it, baby, let go," I urge him. I feel the moment he starts pulsing, his ass tightening around me. I grab his hair, yanking him up before digging my teeth into the side of his neck. My own release barrels into me as I taste his blood on my tongue, my dragon pushing forward and out toward him. The connection forms between us as the last few ropes of my own release spill into him.

Mate.

The word pulses through me, my dragon's deep grumble vibrating out of my chest in pleasure. Like a cat curling around its owner's leg, I can feel him rubbing against Shadow's savage dragon.

For a moment, there is absolute peace in our joining. Both dragons are content and happy. Shadow's own emotions pulse down the bond, an atypical array of calm feelings. It overtakes me in a cascade of warmth.

At least until the spell breaks.

And the feeling of happiness coming from him begins turning sour.

"You don't know what you've done. This was a mistake," he cries, his voice broken. His admission cuts me in half, and it takes everything in me to cut off the pain he's causing from radiating down the bond. He scrambles away from me, out of the mist of the hot shower, pulling himself off my cock. His back still covered in my scratches and my cum still leaking from him, his broken form grips the counter tightly.

Leaving the shower and grabbing a towel, I cross my arms. "You're mine. Just like Ava is." His panic claws at the freshly made bond. I can tell his own dragon simmers beneath his skin, calling out to bite me, to complete the bond. "It's not your fault she died." While I've long suspected someone targeted Shadow through his mother it's a mystery, I've never been able to solve. But deep down I know, my dragon knows, he did not kill his mother.

He whirls on me, his eyes flashing a brilliant gold. "Don't you fucking talk about her, you don't know what you're saying." His body vibrates with the strain of holding himself back.

My heart aches, my chest cleaved in two, as I feel him slipping further and further away, so I do the only thing I can think of and bare the side of my neck to him. "Please," I say.

His eyes widen. This might be the first time he's ever heard me say please. And only the third time I've submitted to him, since that first time in his bedroom and then the cabin all those years ago. I stay still as he makes his decision.

"Ava?" he whispers. His cracking voice is gutting me.

"She's fine with this. It'll be easier if we are together first. My dragon will help yours." I know him well enough to know he's terrified of hurting her, and I know Ava well enough to say she won't give a shit that we bonded first. She might care that she missed watching it, but she'll understand. "Please, Rakkaani."

He takes a step toward me, and another, his teeth elongating and his eyes golden. I close my eyes in anticipation, but instead of his teeth meeting my neck, he shoves past me, fleeing the room like a Hellbeast has given chase. I hear the door slam from the bedroom, the sound breaking me. My fist lashes out into the mirror. The glass shatters around me, a visual representation of how my chest feels right now after watching my mate reject me.

SIXTEEN

While our power is great,
it would be wise to align with The Order.
They can give us access to unimaginable power.
With Kara's son, we have an in.
— Mori Family Grimoire

AVA

("Lovely" – Tommee Profitt and Fleurie)

I grimace as the haze of sleep slowly departs my brain. My mouth is sticky and dry from crawling into bed so late. And maybe from having a little too much to drink after Ciaran had left with Kallen and her men. Seeing her had driven my anxiety to new heights, made the vision feel that much more real. After I had gotten good and fucked up, I had attempted to sleep it off in my own home below the club, but Drago had returned for me and dragged me back here. To the place that provides relief to my anxious mind but also spurs it forward. The dichotomy of it is exhausting.

I reach out to the side and find the bed already cool. The bathroom door is ajar, and I can hear the shower running. I move to stand up, then halt as I hear the low moans of two unmistakable voices echoing out of the bathroom. Shadow and Drago. I smile to myself and lie back, stretching out my body as the noises send jolts of arousal through me, straight to my core. It's a nice way to cover up the stiffness that has seeped into my joints and the tightness of my muscles. My body has not recovered from helping Astrea and Ciaran, not that I would tell Drago that. Or Shadow, if he actually stuck around long enough for us to talk.

My magic, while powerful, is weakening the longer I go without replenishing it. Not for the first time, I send out a curse to my ancestors. Not for the first time, my mind floats back to Jax. I wonder if his magic is fairing any better. After the priestess massacre by The Order there is only one option for either of us. Completing our mate bond. And while I happen to have two, only one is willing.

With the future barreling toward us like a train, I can't help but wonder if we will survive this. Everyone talks about wanting to see the future, but no one understands the implications of it. It's not as if I'm watching a movie play out in my mind; it's fragmented pieces of a timeline that may or may not come to pass. Like looking at yourself through shards of a broken mirror, everything changes depending on the way you look at it.

The bathroom door slams open, and I startle fully upward to see Shadow storm out. His scent washes over me as he flees, pausing only to grab his pants and a shirt before he exits the room. For a moment, I debate going after him, but the shattering of glass in the bathroom has me vaulting out of bed and running toward the sound, away from the retreating form of my other mate.

Entering the space, I see Drago's half-naked body silhouetted by the lights as he braces himself against his dark countertop, his white hair a curtain around his face. He leans over the sink, blood dripping from the knuckles of his raised fist into the basin. Pieces of the now shattered mirror are scattered over the black tile in the steam-filled bathroom, the scent of sex heavy in the air.

"Do you want to talk about it?" When he turns to look at me, I see his eyes flash gold, pain evident on his face, before he schools his features. My own chest pulls tight, and I know sadness flares over my face as I fully take in his form.

Dried on Drago's lips is blood.

"Oh, Drago," I say quietly and move over, careful to avoid cutting my bare feet on the sprinkled glass and wrap my arms around his massive body.

He lets out a long sigh and wraps his uninjured arm around me, pulling me closer. "I shouldn't have done it; I knew he wasn't ready. I knew he was saying yes to sex, not mating." My heart breaks even more when I hear the pain woven into his voice. "He needed to escape, and I took advantage of the moment."

I peer up into his eyes, the blue swimming with emotion, and take his face in my hands. "You didn't take advantage of anyone. He wanted you. And like it or not, the bond will help him. He's just too stubborn to realize it," I say gently. My heart warms at the idea of their bond, the bond that will keep them tethered.

He grabs me around the waist, hoisting me onto the counter as he turns on the faucet to start washing his cut hand. While the wounds are already healing, he still takes care to pull the glass from them and wash the blood away. For a moment, I'm mesmerized by the ripped flesh of his knuckles, the ghost of my vision pulling at me. I shake it off and focus on the red washing down the drain to ground myself back into the present. *You don't know how this will end; you don't have the full picture. Panicking isn't helping. You saw a future, not the only one. We might all make it through this.*

"The moment my teeth were in him, and I tasted him, I thought . . . fuck, I don't know. But he's so fucking afraid," he speaks. "You can taste the fear in him. It's bitter and acidic."

My feet swing back and forth, a nervous habit of being unable to remain still. The cool granite countertop rubs against my bare thighs. "He's spent a very long time blaming himself for his mother's death. And you know what his father was like, he didn't allow Shadow to believe he was worthy of love. Ciaran may have rescued him from the physical cage Alexi put him in, but Shadow has been in an emotional one for far longer." I grab my pink hair and twist it up into a bun, wincing at the slight pull of my shoulder muscles. "We need to give him time."

He catches my eyes, and his stare has my heart skipping a beat with its intensity. "And how much longer do you have, Ava?"

I roll my eyes in a desperate attempt not to show the truth. "I'm fine."

But Drago growls low, his dragon pushing forward. "I want the truth. How bad is it?"

My body tenses as the command ripples through me, and I fight it as long as I can before the words are inevitably pulled from me. "If I don't replenish, I'll die next time." The moment I say the words, the spell breaks, and my hand whips out and slaps him across the face. "Don't you fucking use your compulsion on me, you asshole." I try to hop down from the counter, but he grips my forearms hard. I let out a feral hiss at the contact. "We made a promise long ago about that power. Don't start breaking it now," I growl.

"You have to go home if he won't bond." His voice is dangerously low. It's at this moment I regret ever sharing knowledge of my magic with him and even more so regret not sharing more about The Order and the way they wiped out the priestesses. I know when it comes down to it, he will do what he feels is necessary to protect me; he just doesn't have the full picture.

"Absolutely not," I say. "And if you command me, I will get Astrea to have her snakes fucking eat you."

He chuckles a bit, as if I'm joking, before his face goes grave again. "What if we just completed it?"

I groan, my whole body responding, the space where the bond should rest flaring with need. "It would help short-term, but you know that's not the solution long-term. I need both of you. Want both of you." But the thought of Drago fucking me after he's just been inside Shadow has my veins heating. The sounds I heard just moments ago echos through my head.

His eyes grow dark, his pupils expanding. He can smell me. Smell my need. His body tenses, the veins on his fore-arms pushing out as he holds himself back. A whimper escapes me. I bite my lip as I gaze at his mouth. That's all it takes. He crashes into me, the taste of Shadow's blood still potent as he sweeps his tongue into my mouth. The kiss claims me. Captures parts of my soul that feel as though they are dying and breathes new life into them.

I am consumed, my body lighting up with feral need. I move my hands up his body, gripping him hard, and wrap my legs around his waist. My core is slick with need, and I grind up against his cock, an appendage that is straining against the white towel around his waist. Visions of him fucking me flow through my brain like a movie reel.

Then he pulls off my mouth for only a moment, but that moment is enough for reality to hit me. Placing my hand on his bare chest, I push back slightly. "We can't," I say, though I'm not sure if it's to remind him or myself. Our heavy breathing echoes in the space around us.

His eyes are wild, and for a moment, I'm not sure he'll listen, and if he comes back in, I know I won't be able to say no. His body is on a hair trigger as he takes a few steps back from me, the last one putting him firmly outside the bathroom. Firmly out of reach of me. "We can't wait much longer, Ava. You know that. If he won't get his head on straight, you know what I'll have to do." His voice is stern, no give in it. The voice he uses when he's taking control.

My magic pushes up in response to my emotions turning to a raging whirlpool inside me, but I lock it down quickly. "I will never forgive you," I say through gritted teeth. "I'm never going back."

But Drago shakes his head. "I would rather have you hate me alive than be dead because our stubborn mate can't get over his demons." He doesn't wait for a response before he moves out of my sight, and I hear the bedroom door shut.

My stomach drops out, and I press the back of my hand to my mouth, desperate to contain the sob breaking through me as the overwhelming fear of being taken back home seizes my lungs. Leaving home was reckless, but it was the best thing I have ever done and going back would break me. I would choose death before that, before letting my father have any say in my life again. I allow myself to sit with the fear, allowing it to swim around in my body, before drawing a trembling breath in and pushing it back.

No. I am not that same girl. I've grown and matured. I do not have to allow anyone to dictate my life again.

Kallen was only an experiment.
One that gave us the ability to correct mistakes so we can
harness more power.
— Mori Family Grimoire

AVA

"What would you do?" I ask into the phone as I play with a piece of loose thread on the comforter.

Astrea lets out a long sigh. "I don't know. I think he needs time, Ava. He'll come around." I can hear rustling in the background, and I smile knowing it's most likely Poppy nesting. The little fox is greatly missed here. "Look, you have time to figure it out."

I wince. Astrea doesn't know who I am or what I am. Despite hearing Cordelia call me "princess" and seeing my magic, she hasn't pushed for me to tell her anything, and part of me feels awful for keeping the secret. It's the same feeling I had a few years ago that made me tell Drago and Shadow. My mouth opens to let it spill out, but a part of me worries if I vocalize it, my old life will no longer be a ghost haunting me but a poltergeist that will wreck the home I've built. "Enough about me. How are you?"

"Nice subject change," she says, and I can hear the eye roll in her voice. "But I'm okay. Ciaran and I are trying our hardest to get this magic down, but . . ." She trails off, a heavy silence filling the line.

"But?" I press.

Another long sigh comes from her. "But I worry that I'm changing. This magic . . . this magic is a lot, Ava. It feels so fucking heavy at times. Even with Ciaran's help, it feels like it's dragging me down."

I chew on my lip as I listen to her, my stomach rolling with discomfort. "What does Kallen say?"

Astrea growls. "Ciaran never should have brought her here."

I wince at the venom in her voice but push forward tentatively. "She had the magic for a long time; it might be good to get her help."

Astrea goes quiet again for a while before clearing her throat. "You are probably right. But all I see when I look at her is my dead sister. I don't know." A heavy breath escapes her. "Look, I have to go. Try to be patient with Shadow. I'll talk to you soon, Ava." She hangs up the phone before I can even say goodbye.

Throwing my phone down onto the bed, I flop over. Samhain flutters down next to me and pulls on my hair with his beak. I smile and stroke his feathers behind his neck. My cranky little familiar is the only constant I've had since coming here. During those months I was held by Alexi, he never left the outside of the prison. I heard rumors from guards that a "giant bird from hell" was killing people as they left. He did what he could to protect me, even if he couldn't rescue me. He lets out a caw, his black eyes assessing me, before he flutters back over to his perch in the corner of the room Drago has given me.

The bed sits against the far back wall facing into the room. Giant fur blankets are piled atop it spilling down onto the plush green carpet that covers the floor in its entirety. The wood-burning fireplace off to the right always emanates a light scent of smoke, even when it's not burning. With two plush armchairs in front of it, I have fallen asleep there more times than I can count. The wall-to-wall bookcases are by far the best part of the room, and the never-ending reading material makes me want to become a hermit. This room doesn't match the rest of Drago's penthouse.

Truthfully, I miss his home on the bluff. Miss the sounds and smells and the feel of it being our home. I had hoped he would bring us there, but Drago, to my knowledge, hasn't been back since I moved into The Playground. Part of me thinks he can't bear the idea of us being there again unmated.

Standing up, I make my way over to the adjoining bathroom. This one has a giant clawfoot tub in the center of it. Plants of all varieties decorate the room. Potted trees stand in the corners, and long vines sweep down from hanging baskets. Small succulents line the countertop. The chaos of it all feels oddly relaxing to me.

I fill the bath, and the hot water fills the cool room with steam that spreads the eucalyptus scent out and around. I ignore the beads of sweat that break out over my forehead as I let myself sink into the deep bath. I try to allow the hot water to ease the tension in my shoulders, but after a few moments, I realize it's a waste and pull myself back out.

Wrapping the towel around my lean body, I huff my annoyance at the fact that I apparently can't even enjoy a bath. I wipe the mist off the mirror and note the deep purple circles that have taken up permanent residence under my eyes. Clear evidence of the weight I'm carrying and the lack of connection to Hell.

Drago's threat still lingers in my mind. I have no doubt he'll figure out a way to send me home if things get bad enough. Anger briefly pulses through me at the idea, an urge to run, to show Drago he can't control me. It is a reaction that comes from years of being inhibited by my family. A reaction that is unfair for Drago to be on the receiving end of. Despite all that, I still have the itch in my skin to escape the penthouse tonight.

"Fuck it," I mutter, grabbing my makeup. I paint my eyes with kohl, the wings elegant and thin. I brush on more blush and bronzer than I should, but I need to look somewhat more alive than I currently do if I plan to leave this place tonight. I end up leaving my hair down in waves that caress my back.

I walk over to my closet, bare feet sinking into the plush carpet as I look through my options. In the end, I opt for comfort. The long black maxi dress hangs loosely off my left shoulder, and two slits expose my legs up to the hip on either side. Pulling on some gold bangles over my wrists and attaching dangling gold earrings, I assess the look in the mirror. As much as people say they like outfits that leave nothing to the imagination, I've found more people flock to me when I'm dressed like this. Simple with a hint of mystery.

Looking down at my options for shoes, I curse when I realize I don't have the energy to put on the strappy gold sandals I want and instead have to opt for my plain white slip-on sandals. While comfortable, they do nothing for the outfit. I guess I'll go barefoot tonight once I get there. Taking a deep breath, I look at myself once more in the mirror. My kohl-lined eyes stand out starkly against my skin, and despite the blush, I still look a little too pale. My blonde roots have started to peek through my pink hair, and I make a mental note to fix that. I sometimes toy with the idea of going back to blonde, but despite it making me feel connected to home, I hate that it reminds me of my time with Alexi. So, I keep the pink to remind myself I got out. To remind Shadow I got out. He got me out.

As if those thoughts summoned him into existence, I spot his tall body leaning against the door frame, his arms crossed over his muscular chest as I enter the bedroom. Drago is slung casually over a red armchair in front of the fireplace. Their contrast is sharp. Drago bleeds confidence, a danger that shimmers below the surface, whereas Shadow holds a darkness around him that is toxic and all consuming.

"Where do you think you're going?" Shadow asks, his eyes trailing over my body in a path that sets me on fire. I'm both cursing my dress choice, given how easy it would be to scent my arousal, and loving that it would be so easy, on the off chance he decides to finally give in to that need we both have.

"To work," I say. My voice is flat and leaves no room for argument. "Where have you been all afternoon?" I raise my eyebrow at him, a challenge.

"Absolutely not," Shadow says, ignoring my question.

Disbelief moves through me like a tidal wave. "I most certainly did not ask permission to go to my place of work. I'm telling you I'm going."

"It's not safe," he grinds out. I can practically taste the flames he is dying to spit out. I should stop, back down, but I can't now. I've dug my heels in and refuse to give an inch.

"It was safe enough last night, what changed?" I ask.

Neither say anything, but I have a sneaking suspicion

that Drago is pulling back, now that he knows just how depleted I am. I shoot a glare over at the bastard as he continues to silently watch our sparring match like he's at a fucking tennis game.

"The Playground is the safest place around," I argue. "Cordelia isn't going to show up there. Let's be honest, no one is getting past my magic. Besides, she knows Astrea and Ciaran aren't around."

"No, but she might look for you," Drago says. "Or someone else might be." I glare at the traitor, despite my stomach sinking at his words. "Were you planning on telling us about the two shifters who showed up last night with Kallen?"

Well, shit. "I didn't bring them. Take it up with Ciaran."

Shadow growls low. "They were Primal Knights, Ava. You should have fucking said something. And with no magic, you were unprotected."

"More reason for me to be at my own club. Like I said, nothing is getting in." I step forward, and Shadow moves to block the door. Samhain looses a warning caw at him, fluttering closer to the fray. The movement from Shadow switches something in my brain, turning the rational side off and leaving nothing but the anger I feel toward his consistent rejection of our bond. "You don't get to have a say in this. Not when you don't care otherwise," I say. "You made your choice last night, and it wasn't me." He flinches. I step closer to him. "Now. Get. Out. Of. My. Way."

"Ava," Drago says in warning, seemingly done with being a passive observer. But I ignore him, holding Shadow's glare with my own hardened one. I know it was a low blow, but my hurt and anger is boiling over.

"You can't keep me here," I say to both of them, though

my eyes stay on Shadow, locked in a standoff with him that goes beyond this moment here. We are one altercation away from coming to blows, me and Shadow. This dance we keep doing is grinding us down. His whiskey eyes are almost begging me to release him, while my own silver ones hold strong, refusing to bow. The need to have my mates feels like the worst craving imaginable. As though I'm coming off a binge on Eufori and my body is desperate for the next hit. I need him to understand what I'm going through without them, what he is choosing to put me through while he refuses to face his issues.

I hear Drago let out an exasperated sigh, his frustration evident. I think I also hear him mutter something about being cursed with bratty mates before I'm suddenly pulled tight against his body. His breath plays over my neck, and the contact sends jolts of need through me. I squeeze my thighs together, desperate for some friction, and Shadow's eyes zero in on the movement, gold flashing across them.

"If you go, one of us will always be with you. You will listen to us, obey us. No matter what," Drago says. "You will tell us if some other fucking shifters show up on our turf."

"What, so Shadow gets to fuck around, and I don't? He gets to come and go without so much as a word, but I don't tell you one thing, and suddenly I shouldn't be allowed to my own gods damn club?!"

I can't keep my eyes locked on Shadow's when I say the next words. "Don't think I didn't smell that cheap perfume on you. I hope her pussy was fucking worth it." I also can't keep the blatant hurt from my voice. I keep my gaze locked on Drago's hands splayed across my belly, focusing on the tattoos and rings instead of looking back at Shadow.

"Shadow knows he fucked up and he knows what will happen, should he do it again," Drago says in my ear, then bites out, "You will listen and obey, Ava, if we let you go tonight. You will communicate with us, no secrets."

Flames spark inside me again. I growl at him, "I don't obey anyone."

("Don't Blame Me" – Taylor Swift)

He brackets his hand against my throat, squeezing slightly, my back still flush against his front. "You obey me." His voice shoots straight to my pussy, and I have to bite my lip to keep the moan I want to let out from slipping past my lips.

I finally lift my eyes. Shadow tracks us both, not saying a word, but his body coils tighter and tighter with each moment Drago's hands are on me.

Drago lets out a small laugh. "I'm testing Shadow's patience, it seems." The hand on my stomach moves up and tweaks my hard nipple through the thin dress. This time, I let myself moan out loud.

"Mmm. You make such delicious sounds," he says into my ear before moving my hair to the side and licking up my neck. "Do you like hearing them, Shadow?" he teases as he lets his hand trail lower, until it's peeling back the maxi skirt and those ringed fingers are dancing across my lace panties, which are already embarrassingly wet. I hiss as he dips into them, touching my soft curls.

"She's so wet, so ready to be fucked," he groans as he strokes my folds, before circling my clit. The moan that leaves my mouth is nothing short of needy, and I push my hips forward, demanding more. Drago chuckles as he pushes two fingers into me, playing those cool rings against my warm core. "She's tight. So fucking tight. Can you imagine how it would feel to fuck her together?"

"Oh, fuck," I whimper. The thought makes me gush, and I feel my arousal dripping down my leg.

Drago groans, "I think she likes that idea." His cock is rock hard against my ass as he pulls his fingers out of me and offers them to Shadow.

Shadow hesitates for only a moment before leaning forward and sucking those ringed fingers into his mouth. Shadow's eyes stay locked on Drago's as he cleans them.

Drago removes his fingers from Shadow's mouth with a pop before pushing them back into me, making my eyes roll back into my head. "Shit," I mutter as I start to fuck his fingers. Drago nuzzles my neck, teeth scraping the soft skin. "Yes, Drago. Please. Please." I'm not sure what I'm begging for, but I know I'm about to cum with the image of Shadow sucking my arousal from Drago's fingers playing on repeat in my brain.

Shadow steps forward suddenly, and I stare at him in surprise, almost daring to hope. Then he says, "I'll go with her," before yanking me from Drago's hold, those thick fingers slipping from me, and shoving me out the bedroom door. I can hear Drago laughing as Shadow continues to push me down the hallway.

SHADOW

Ava whirls on me as soon as we are into the hallway. "Seriously?!" Her face is flushed and she's breathing heavily.

I shrug. "You want to go to work, right? So, let's go."

She glares at me, shooting daggers. Her peaked nipples are still on display, and her taste still coats my tongue, making my mouth water.

Mate. Mate. Mate! my dragon screams in my mind. *Take her*, it demands.

"I wasn't finished," she hisses.

"Yes. You were," I growl, grinding my teeth together.

She backs herself up against the wall, pulling back the panel of her skirt and shoving her hand down her panties. "No, I wasn't. But I'll finish now." She begins to stroke herself, resting her head on the wall behind us, those pink lips parted. "Fuck, he made me so wet. I can only imagine how it would feel to have those piercings sliding home into me." I can tell her fingers pick up speed, and her scent invades the room. My hands shake from tension. "And watching you suck his fingers? I almost came just from that."

I close my eyes, trying to avoid taking a deep breath. Avoid seeing or smelling any more of her because my ability to hold myself back is waning.

"Open your eyes," she commands. And gods help me, I do. "Watch me cum on my fingers while I think about Drago fucking me . . . while I think about you fucking me."

I lock eyes with her silver ones, as though she has me under a spell. I can't look away, can't stop my dick from hardening to a painful degree. My own hand is inching toward it to relieve pressure.

"Oh, fuck, I'm going to cum. Fuck, fuck, fuck," she screams as she fucks her own hand, her skin flushing. Her breathing is heavy as she rides her release out before finally removing her hand from her panties. She walks toward me and shoves those fingers into my mouth without hesitation. Desperate for another taste, I don't fight it.

She gives me a long, wicked smile, as I swirl my tongue around and around, refusing to leave even a drop. "Good boy. Now, we can leave." She rips her fingers out of my mouth, eliciting a small, tiny whine from me.

She knows what she is doing to me, and I can only accept the punishment. Letting my magic out, I open a portal to Ava's office, and she smiles at me once more before throwing her middle finger up at me and stepping into her office. I curse, adjusting my thick cock in my pants, willing it to go back down. But with her taste still in my mouth, it's refusing to behave.

If you would fuck her, we wouldn't be in this mess, my dragon growls.

Because of my dragon arguing with me, I don't notice that something is off until a foreign scent hits me as we step into her office. Rage clouds my vision as I see a man sitting behind Ava's desk, legs propped up on it and looking utterly at ease. His dirty-blonde hair is shaved short on the sides, longer on top. He looks like a frat boy who lost his way leaving the club. But under that appearance is something dark that has me on edge. His silver eyes track us both, like a predator stalking its prey. His fingers play across a switch blade that he keeps opening and closing.

He has silver eyes, my dragon growls.

Ava lets out a gasp, raising a hand to her mouth reflexively. A mix of emotions pour from her, moving between grief, happiness, anxiety, and fear before I can even register what my dragon is saying. Her fear is tangy on my tongue, a taste I haven't had since the prison. My dragon raises its head, and I know my eyes go gold as the flames encircle my hands and stretch up my arms.

Stepping up, I move in front of Ava, placing myself between her and the stranger and edging her back toward the portal still glowing behind us. I order her over my shoulder, "Ava, run." My voice is more animal than human when I address the stranger. "Who are you?"

He looks at me as he continues to play with his blade, before standing up and adjusting his leather jacket. When he makes a move to step around the desk, I growl again.

"Take another step near my mate, and I'll rip you apart."

He stops only to put his blade away, while glancing around my body toward Ava. "Really, Ava? Another shifter? Is this why you threw your temper tantrum and ran away? Because you wanted to play with two dragons?" I don't allow my confusion to show, don't allow him to know he has the upper hand in information. The man pulls a cigarette out before leaning against her desk. He tilts his head to the side, assessing us. "Your magic is dangerously low."

Ava is vibrating behind me, her fear slowly being replaced by anger, but her small hand clutching my shirt has me continuing to try to edge us back, regardless of her shift in emotion. I'm barely hanging on, my dragon demanding I rip him apart. Ava must feel it because she lets out a breath and moves up next to me.

"Hello, brother."

EIGHTEEN

It is with great honor that I can report I have been offered the
princess of Hell.
All the hard work over the last few years has paid off.
The Order will rise.
— Personal entry from an unknown individual in The Order
of Infernal Sin Manuscript

Three Weeks Left of the Deal

My brother, Jackson, smiles at me as he pulls another drag from the cigarette. A smile that doesn't reach his silver eyes and sends chills down my spine. He still has that boyish charm that made all the men and women of Hell swoon, but under it is a darkness that only the prince of Hell can exude. His normally clean-shaven face has a few days' worth of stubble grown out and his dirty-blonde hair is untidy in layered pieces.

"What are you doing here?" I try to keep my voice even. Steady. Ignoring his comment on why I ran.

He pushes his hand through his hair, disheveling it even more. "I wanted you to know that our father is dead."

I blink. The world is still for a moment, only to resume at rapid speed as I process the information. "Dead?" Shadow pulls me closer to his body, having extinguished his flames so he could clutch me. "How?"

Jackson shrugs. "The Order finally got what they wanted. They did us a favor, truthfully, but Mother is, however, beside herself and demands I find you immediately and 'put an end to your little vacation.'" He puts the last portion in air quotes, his voice taking on a higher pitch to mimic our mother.

"Vacation?" Shadow growls. "Your sister spent months being tortured, and you think she was on vacation?! Where the fuck were you?"

"Shadow, stop," I plead. Somehow, having my brother know what happened makes it feel worse, makes it feel like I never stopped being the little sister he needs to protect. And while I still love my brother fiercely, I don't want that role in his life anymore. I know I'm already on shaky ground; if he wants to rip me back to Hell, he'll do it, and this piece of knowledge could be the final straw for him.

Jackson blinks once, twice, and on the third, the room is plunged into darkness. His power crackles around us like electricity in blinding arcs of luminous black fractals, the only illumination besides his glowing black eyes, before he pulls his power back in. He breathes deep, cracking his neck and rolling it before looking at me, wisps of his magic still in his eyes as they fade from full black to silver again.

"Explain." His voice is deathly quiet.

Shadow growls low, his body vibrating. His control on a hair trigger.

"No," I say firmly. "It's my story, and I have no interest in sharing." I edge my body slightly in front of Shadow. His hand snakes around my middle, before he lowers his head to my neck and nuzzles into me. The move is possessive and sweet all at once, and my pussy clenches. "Now leave. You've delivered your message."

My brother growls, frustration a thick layer on his body as he starts talking, using the same voice he used when we were younger, and I was in trouble. "Ava, you have a duty to uphold. Same as me." He takes a deep breath. "You are coming home with me; I should have retrieved you long before this. And when we get there, you will tell me what the fuck happened to you up here."

My restraint snaps and anger colors my vision. "Duty? It's my duty to be bred like a prize mare?! How would you feel being told your body and womb had been purchased? And that is a direct quote from our fucking bastard father," I seethe. "You can tell Mother I'm not returning. I would rather die free up here than chained to that fucking kingdom."

The tension between Jax and Shadow could be cut with a knife; Jax is barely keeping a hold on his power, and Shadow isn't doing much better. But just as my brother moves to step forward, Drago's voice floats into the room. "I would think twice before stepping toward my mates."

Drago steps out of the darkness, hands tucked into the pockets of his black pants, and casually assesses the scene. His eyes skate from my brother to me and land on Shadow's hand still pressed to my stomach. I notice a small smile spread over his lush lips before he schools his face again. "Now, care to explain what is going on here?"

. . .

DRAGO

("Despicable" – Grandson)

The room is a tinderbox waiting to go up in flames between Shadow and Jackson, the tension palpable as the prince of Hell faces off against his sister and Shadow. Whenever I'm reminded just who Ava is, I thank the gods that Alexi never figured it out. Thankfully, he was as dumb as he was ugly. And Kallen seemed stuck on the Harbinger magic; given Ava didn't possess it, Kallen took no interest in her. Or maybe she had no idea Ava was even being held there.

"Hello, Drago. It's been a very long time," he says, his smooth voice betraying just a touch of anger directed at me. I avoid looking at Ava but don't miss her sharp intake of breath. I never told her I had contact with her brother all those years ago. A mistake that I'm sure will come back to haunt me.

"Not long enough." I shrug. "I believe I told you what would happen should you try and take what's mine." I casually walk over to my mates.

He narrows his eyes at me before shaking his head. "I didn't come to fight." He pauses to take a long drag of the cigarette, and the scent of tobacco and Eufori fill the space.

I look at Shadow, but his focus is solely on Ava, not the drugs. Pride fills me, alongside a sense of relief. My worry about him has grown exponentially over the past few months, and I fear what will happen when our three-month time limit is up in another three weeks.

"Leave, Jackson. You got your point across," Ava says again.

Jackson looks crestfallen for a moment, hurt in those

silver eyes. "You aren't safe here, Ava." He takes another drag of his cigarette. "You are a princess. You cannot stay in this city playing the part of a club owner. Not anymore."

"No," Ava says, her body locked up as she clings to Shadow. True, uncontrolled fear rolls through her. The scent makes my dragon wake up and peer out through my eyes. "I won't go back, and if you try to make me, you'll be no better than Father was."

Jackson, thankfully, manages to look embarrassed. "Father hid a lot from me. It wasn't until he died that I found out just how evil he was. Hence wishing I could thank the bastards in The Order before I roast them alive. I didn't know how life was for you."

"Arcanna told you, I know she did," Ava counters.

"Don't say her name," He growls. His body tensing.

Ava shakes her head. "I don't know what happened to you Jackson, but the brother I knew long, long ago *never* would have done the things you did. Or ignored someone he loved."

Real anger flashes over his face, but his eyes hold sadness for a moment, the silver reflecting like pools. "The fact remains, you are no longer safe here. The Order has resurfaced, and rumor has it they are in Gothic Grove." He shifts his gaze to address me. "I can only assume they are looking for Ava."

"We can keep her safe," Shadow says with such possession in his voice, it shocks even me. I glance at Ava again and find her face is white, her eyes focused on a far-off place. It's a look she had often in the early days at my penthouse, after Shadow brought her to me.

"And how do you propose to do that, dragon? You aren't mated with her. She's a sitting fucking duck," he says to

Shadow. Turning to Ava, he continues, "By your smell, I'd say one more use and you'll die."

I hold up my hand, halting the argument. "What is The Order?" I ask, actively ignoring the way his last statement made my stomach drop out and my heart stutter.

Ava lets out a long breath. "Its full name is The Order of Infernal Sin. They are a group of radicals that hate us, the royals. They feel the magic we hold would be better given to the people."

Jackson snorts. "What they really mean is better given to them. But they also believe Hell should rule Gothic Grove."

"How long have they been here, in the city?" I ask.

"A while. My contact found information that The Order has planted someone here to help bring the city down when the time comes. But they don't know who this individual is." He moves off the desk, his demeanor shifting to business as he walks toward the door that leads into the club. "You need to come home with me, Ava. At the very least, you need access to the magic."

"And who would do that Jackson? My mates are here. They are the ones who can help me. Not you. Not with no priestesses left." She counters.

He pinches the bridge of his nose, "I found one. She is still alive; I just need to bring her to the palace. So you will come home with me."

I shoot Ava a pointed look at Jackson's revelation, but Shadow's voice breaks through my stare.

"No," Shadow growls.

Hand on the doorknob, Jackson raises his eyebrows at Shadow, as if shocked someone would dare stand against him, but Ava steps forward, her back straight and eyes clear now. "I already said I won't go."

"Ava," I start.

She whips her head toward me, anger and betrayal in her silver eyes. "I'm not going. It's my choice, and I won't leave. Not yet."

Jackson sighs heavily. "Ava, if they find you, they'll take you. At best, they'll kill you. At worst . . . you know what they'll do."

"I go, and I might as well die, Jackson. You know Mother won't let me go once I'm back in Hell. I ran from that life for a reason; I have no intention of allowing it to swallow me back up," Ava argues. "And if you take me against my will, you'll have the Harbinger on your ass. And trust me when I say, you don't want to meet Buttercup."

I want to laugh at the look on Jackson's face, which goes from slight fear to utter confusion at the ridiculous name Ava gave one of the snakes. But even those of Hell know who the Harbinger is, what that magic can do. Hell got lucky during her rampage; she was stopped before she made it through their gates. King or not, Jackson isn't dumb enough to try and go against that magic alongside us.

"I don't think I want to know how you are close with the Harbinger," he mutters.

Shadow clutches Ava's hand, knuckles going white and eyes golden as he watches every move Jackson makes. The temperature in the room seems to be rising, and I know he has very little control over his dragon right now. One push, and he'll lose it entirely.

I pinch the bridge of my nose. "This is getting out of hand." I look at Jackson. "You've delivered your message; you can reach out to me to provide updates. If Ava wants to speak with you, she will reach out to you. But she won't be going with you."

He holds his hands up in mock surrender. "I won't drag

you back unwillingly, right now." The implication hangs in the air as he turns to the door again. At some point, he will drag her back.

Before he leaves, he looks back at Ava, the worry evident on his face. "You'll die, Ava," he says quietly. "I know you're mad at me, and I'll accept that. I was a shit older brother for not noticing how you were treated. But I don't want you to die."

She doesn't say anything, just keeps those cool silver eyes locked solidly on Jackson's form.

He looks first at Shadow, then at me. "I failed my sister once—don't think that will happen again." The threat is clear: if something happens to her, the king of Hell will come for us.

NINETEEN

A dragon, or wolf, that denies their mate will go mad.
We are not meant to be alone in this world.
— Rosewood Family Journal

SHADOW
("Just Pretend" – Bad Omens)

My dragon is still vibrating under my skin, despite Ava's brother being gone. My hands shake, and the need to smoke is crushing me. Those demons laugh loudly in my head. Reminding me that despite my best efforts to keep her safe, Ava is in danger. That because I am who I am, she'll die. After Jax left, Ava briefly explained that her magic has been low since saving Astrea and Ciaran, and should she deplete fully, she'll die. I curl my fists tightly and breathe deep, focusing on keeping control until I can get out of this room.

Fuck, she's going to die. That was a small piece of knowledge that Drago did not pass along to me when he told me how important it was for her not to use her magic anymore.

But she told you long ago she needed us, she needed our magic, my dragon reminds me. I'm angry at Drago for not telling me just how bad off she is, but I'm also furious he doesn't just mate her and save her. I must move up my timetable. Even if my dragon is fighting against it. Even if my heart is aligning with the beast.

The music from the club outside filters into the general quiet our group is holding. "You're a fucking asshole, Drago, you had no right to call him!" I snap my head over to Ava, who is sitting on her couch, a drink in hand. It's the first thing she's said since she explained the magic.

Drago leans against her desk, arms crossed, watching the two of us. "I had every right," he says in that deadly calm voice. "You were disappearing in on yourself, I was losing both my mates. So, I reached out to someone I hoped could help me."

She throws the wine glass she was drinking out of, and the pieces shatter just beyond Drago's form as he ducks. That red liquid runs down the wall like blood. My hand twitches at the sight. Drago looks furious at her but doesn't make a move.

Ava rarely gets angry, but when she does, she is a force to be reckoned with. She's a ball of fury at this moment, fists clenched at her sides, trembling as she holds herself back. The scent of her magic, just below her skin, fills the air. It's intoxicating. My dragon yearns for her, desperate for a taste of that scent.

"You. Had. No. Right," she says again. Then her eyes widen, and she lets out a bark of a laugh. "Holy shit. And here I was, an anxious mess about telling you both who I was, and you had already fucking talked to my gods damn brother!"

My stepbrother appears calm, but I can see how on edge his body is. His dragon is just below the surface. He drinks from the crystal tumbler in his hand, and the amber liquid disappears quickly. "The moment I discovered you were my mate was the moment I had the right. I won't apologize for that. And when were you going to mention there were no more priestesses?" Idiot. My stepbrother is a fucking idiot. Even I know this is the time to grovel.

She goes to open her mouth, but I intervene. Shaking my head, I say, "He's right, Ava. He had an obligation to protect you. And if he thought Jackson could help you, he did what he should have."

Her furious silver eyes jerk toward me, burning holes into my soul even as they flash with pain at my statement. "He knew where to find me because Drago had contacted him! What do you think would have happened if he had found me alone?" she yells. "I would have had no chance to stand against my brother's magic. You would rather he drag me back and you never see me again?"

"If it means you are safe from me? Yes," I say with conviction. The words kill me slowly as they leave my mouth.

I push off the wall and head toward the exit, desperate to get away from them. Their scents invading my nostrils making it difficult to think, to stay calm. The half-completed bond between Drago and me demands attention, alongside the one I started so long ago with Ava. The feeling is maddening. It's shoving at me constantly.

("I Love You, I'm Trying" – Grandson)

"Fine. Fucking run. I keep saying, someday, it'll be too

late. I mean that, Shadow. Someday, you are going to turn around, and I won't fucking be here," she whispers in anger, her voice cracking. I don't need to see her to know there are tears shining in those silver eyes.

I pause for only a moment, noting a sense of desperation, of anguish. But I don't say anything, I just stand frozen in the push-pull of our triadic relationship. Her body shoves past mine, her lilac scent painfully assaulting my head as she escapes the room.

Part of me wants her to turn around as I watch her leave through the door that leads to her apartment. It's screaming for her to see the broken man standing behind her, to show me I'm still worth fighting for. But she doesn't, and it cracks something open in me that spills out thick heartache. The sludge sinks into my chest, pulling me deeper and deeper into a pit of my own creation. I squeeze my eyes shut against it. It's better this way. Her hating me. It's better.

"It's not you; she lashed out because of me," Drago says from behind me. His voice sounds tired. It only adds to the feeling. The overwhelming feeling of failure. Drago has been holding us together this whole time. How much longer until he falls under the pressure?

As I reach for the door, Drago calls out, a strange rasp in his voice, "Don't do it."

As if he knows what I'm about to do. I don't stop, don't turn around, but flee out the door up to the roof instead.

———

STANDING on the roof of Ava's club, I look around the skyline as I take a long drag of the Eufori. The red haze swirls into my vision as it floods my veins with chemical relief. My hands are still, no longer shaking. But my dragon and my own inner monologue stay loud. Taunting me. Pushing me. Refusing to give me a moment's peace.

A tremor overtakes my hand again as I forcibly keep it from the blade wrapped up in my pocket. Of course, I know it would help, the satisfaction of feeling the blade, of seeing the blood, and the numbness that comes after. But I'm trying so hard to conquer at least one of my addictions. Although it doesn't really matter if I'm leaving, does it?

"My sister deserves better than someone who refuses to fight their demons." I spin around and see Jackson just behind me. "You've got one foot out the door, I can see it in your eyes." I'm not sure if he means metaphorically or in reality; either way, he's right.

I take another drag of the cigarette and wonder if holding the chemical in my lungs longer will make the reality of the situation more bearable. Or maybe the deep burn will be enough to scratch the itch crawling up my spine.

I finally blow out the smoke, and the red vapor obscures Jackson's face for a moment.

He continues to gaze out at the city below us, his blonde hair moving in the wind. "I want the name of every person who touched her. I will kill them all." This. This man right here is the king of Hell, his power radiating off him in dark waves. Even my dragon is cautious of him.

"They are dead already," I say.

A nod is all I get. "Then I owe you thanks. But that doesn't change the fact that she'll die if she stays here."

I freeze at the words, desperate to ignore them, knowing I'm to blame. Because I am always to blame for my loved ones' suffering.

"Do you know how our magic works, shifter?" he asks.

My patience is wearing thin at this point. I need out of this conversation. I need to escape reality for a while, and this is only keeping me pinned to it. So, I nod, the only confirmation I'm willing to give him.

"When Ava left, I was worried. How would she maintain her magic? She had no mates to feed from. And she hadn't gone through a ceremony prior to leaving. But why would she need magic here? I convinced myself she would be safe. No one knew who she was in Gothic Grove. And despite my father assuring everyone things were fine, I was happy she was further from The Order once things started escalating with them."

"You can imagine my surprise when Drago called me. She was sinking in on herself, and he worried she wouldn't survive. I don't think she knew he had dealings with us from Hell, or I doubt she would have stayed with him. Because he knew who she was, who I was, immediately. I was so fucking relieved when he told me about you two. She would have a way to sustain her magic, and she could live her life happy. But seeing you? I think that feeling of relief was misplaced."

He looks me up and down before continuing. "What do you hope to accomplish by leaving them?"

I don't say anything for a long moment, taking in more Eufori instead. Letting it burn me inside. "If I leave, they'll be free to mate. I'm holding them back, threatening her life by staying and refusing to mate her."

He shakes his head. "You truly think they'll forget about you? Just mate and move on?"

"Eventually. Yes." The lie feels like ash across my tongue. But I pull more Eufori in, begging the crimson drug to make me believe the lies I tell.

He shoots me a glare. "You have no idea what it's like to

lose your mate. Just because they are not with you does not mean you forget about them." A depression settles over him as he watches me. "You are a coward."

Coward. Fraud. Weak. The words bounce around in my head. My own negative self-talk, never-ending and exhausting.

The wind picks up more and the first few drops of rain begin to hit us. The transition from fall to winter in Gothic Grove is a push-pull of the two seasons. The transition to our attempted summer is even worse. Flash floods can push through the decaying streets at a moment's notice, and within the next hour, snow could be blanketing the very same streets. Right now, the city is trying to drown us.

The king of Hell and a broken dragon looking out over an equally broken city that's drowning. It's laughable, really —the two of us couldn't be further apart aside from the burden we both seem to carry. The burden of watching those we love suffer.

"I met your father once. He came to what should have been my sister's wedding. The very night she fled to this city." His deep voice breaks apart the silence. "He was a piece of shit. We all knew it, even my father. And that's saying something. I believe he had hopes of marrying Drago off to Ava, or you." He laughs. "Wouldn't that have been ironic? If my father had taken that deal, he would have inadvertently placed mates together." He chuckles to himself again before saying, "I always wondered what would make someone as powerful as you hide. Allow themselves to be taken by Alexi and used by him."

I tense as memories assault my mind, the feel of blood dripping through my claws. The ecstasy of the kill as my dragon ripped people to shreds. I shudder at the memories and the feelings that come along with them. Because no matter how much I smoke, I will never forget how much I loved the kill. It wasn't until a year into captivity that I started to realize what I had become. Started to hate it. My anger and guilt and fear had poisoned me to the point of no return.

"Even in Hell, we heard of you and your dragon. The deadliest beast, housed in a Realm Walker. Something that hadn't been seen for decades." He looks me over, those silver eyes penetrating my soul. "I think you knew what kind of evil your father was, knew what he would do if he got ahold of your dragon. So, you suffered. Even allowed yourself to be sold off like cattle." I ball my fists, not saying a word, though my mind screams for him to shut up. "But you didn't account for Alexi's brand of evil, did you? Didn't account for the bloodlust he would awaken."

I don't react. Don't allow him to see just how much I liked it. He flicks a cigarette out, lighting it and taking a deep drag before continuing. "We also heard when Ciaran took you out of his father's service, but still, you stayed close to the vampire. I assumed you were staying close to Ciaran, but now, I think it was something else. I think you stayed with Ciaran, stayed in that place, because of Ava."

I remain silent, neither confirming nor denying what he said. It feels like the silence stretches on forever.

"You protected many people from your father, but he's long dead. Alexi is dead. And there isn't any shame in enjoying the hunt or the kill. That rage you feel deep down will protect your mates. My sister needs you. And I think you need her."

"And how would you feel knowing your sister is with someone who killed his own mother? That I couldn't control the shift and ripped her to shreds in the blink of an eye?" My hands are shaking again, and I let the claws of my dragon out to dig into my palms. Grounding myself with the pain. "I'm a fucking danger to everyone around me. I hurt or even kill the people I love."

His head tilts to the side. "Who do you think asked me to talk to you? I'm certainly not up here out of my own good nature." He lets out a dark chuckle. The sound mocks me. "I couldn't care less about you; if you overdose or accidentally cut too deep, nothing changes for me. Ava would be upset, but since you aren't mated, it wouldn't kill her. However, I do care about the souls, and when one makes a request of me, I do my best to follow through with it."

I ignore how the idea of slipping away from this world feels too tempting and focus on the other part of what he said. "My mother spoke to you. How?" My voice barely whispers over the wind now whirling around us.

He shrugs. "I'm the king of Hell, I know how to find souls. Moreover, souls know how to find me." I move to open my mouth, to ask how she is, to get any piece of information I can glean about her, but he holds his hand up to stop me, letting out a long sigh as thunder rumbles in the distance. "I can't answer the questions you have about her. I'll leave you with a piece of advice, Shadow: don't make the same mistake I did. Don't let something so good walk away, because once it's gone, you'll regret it for the rest of your life."

Before I can blink, he's gone, leaving that final statement hanging in the dense air around me. The rain finally dumps down from the sky, and the feel of it makes my skin pull and itch. I drop the joint to the wet concrete and watch the embers snuff out. I want to be angry at him, but his words have sunk their claws in, and now I can't shake them loose. No matter how much I rip and tear at them, they sink further in until I start to feel the truth of them all. My dragon huffs, and I feel the fight leave me. I'm too tired to push him back, so I give in and allow him to burst forth, stretching those wings wide. A roar barrels from my throat, fighting the thunder for dominance, before I take off into the stormy night.

DRAGO

("The One That Got Away" – The Civil Wars)

My body is pulled in two different directions. My dragon, worried for Shadow, pushes to go find him, sensing his shift. The other part of me knows I cannot leave Ava right now. My family is falling apart, and deep inside, I fear I'm not enough to hold them together.

"How long did you know I was from Hell, Drago?" She spits my name out like a curse.

Ava storms in ahead of me to the penthouse, her form vibrating with the anger she is using to cover her grief around finding out her brother knew of her engagement, and something else. Ava has never withheld her emotions, she's easy to read if you know what to look for, and since our altercation with Cordelia, she's shimmered with anxiety.

I move toward the bar, pouring a drink and allowing her to slowly burn in the flames she has set herself on fire with before turning around. A storm is rolling through the city outside, the thunder rattling the windows. "The moment you opened your eyes, I knew where you were from."

Her eyes well up with tears, but I would be foolish to believe they were from sadness. No, the scent falling from her is betrayal and pure rage. "Are you fucking kidding me?" Her small body shakes, her fists clenched at her sides. "You have no idea how fucking guilty I felt, knowing you two were my mates and what that would mean for you!"

"Control yourself, Rakkaani, your magic is dangerously close to coming out." It's the wrong thing to say, but tonight, I'm living in the poor choices I've made, so why not add more?

She rushes up to me, her small hand slapping across my face hard before she lets out a scream. The sound is painful and broken, one that speaks of years of emotions held inside, now breaking free. The room vibrates with power—if she had been able to use her magic, or if she had less control, she would have leveled the penthouse with that release.

She backs away from me, her tiny body pacing back and forth in front of the windows. Her long pink hair has fallen partly free of the bun she hastily shoved it into on the way home, and her cheeks are flushed crimson from the emotional outpour. Even disheveled, she is beautiful. "Why? Why did you let me agonize over telling you? I felt awful keeping it from you."

"Hell had a long history of enslaving dragons, using us. I couldn't trust that you wouldn't do the same. So, I didn't tell you that I knew who you were, just in case. As the weeks went on and I understood who you were to me, I couldn't just let you sink in on yourself like that. When you did finally tell me, I had already reached out to Jackson." I lean against the wall, casually watching her pace. "He agreed to let you stay here if we stayed in contact. He wanted to know you were okay, so I've continued to update him. I had no idea he would show up today like he did. But I'm glad he did—if you won't take care of yourself, someone has to. And I can only worry about one mate at a time being on a self-destructive path. Don't think we won't be discussing the fact that there are no priestesses in Hell to replenish your magic. When were you planning to mention that Rakkaani."

She spins toward me. "Fuck you." The venom in those words infects the air. It seeps into my bones and my blood, dissolving any patience I had. My body moves without thought as I push her up against the windows, forcing her breath out of her in a sharp exhale. It matches my own heaving chest.

("Half God, Half Devil" – In This Moment)

I don't register her action until her spit is sliding down my face, her anger burning my hands where they hold her. My cock is unreasonably hard from the action. "Fuck. You," she seethes. "You had no right to speak with him. To tell him anything."

My teeth sharpen as I growl, "You were a shell of a person, Ava. We were losing you. What do you think Shadow would have done then? What I would have done? Hmm? Contacting your brother was the only way, in my mind at the time, to help. And Jackson wouldn't just let us keep you, he wanted updates, so he knew you were safe. He would have taken you, otherwise. We would have started a fucking war to get you back. So, yes, I allowed him to check in from time to time, but only to prevent a war that no one would have survived." A shadow of wings flash behind me in the dim room as lightning splits the sky.

I grab her throat roughly, squeezing either side. The silver rings on my fingers seem to glow in the moonlight peeking through the stormy sky. "Fuck, my hand looks good around your throat." I grind against her, and despite her anger, she lets out a tiny whimper. The scent of her arousal floods the room as she struggles superficially against my grasp. "You've been very fucking naughty. Beg me just right and I'll let you find release against these windows." I lean in close, licking up the side of her neck. "And everyone down on the street can watch it happen. Now, tell me, what is your safe word?"

Her hand jerks out, but I catch her wrist easily before it is able to smack me across the face. I tsk, squeezing her throat a little harder and notching my knee between her thighs. Her heat almost burns my leg, the wetness already seeping through the thin leggings she changed into before we left. I apply pressure with my knee and watch her eyes roll back from the friction. I lean down, scraping my teeth against her sports bra, her nipples clearly pushing through. Her moans fill the living space.

"You can take your rage out on me, but we don't keep going until I know you can tap out, should you need to. Now, what is the fucking safe word, Rakkaani?"

Her jaw is set tight, and for a moment, I worry she won't play, but then her small voice squeaks out, "Red."

"Good girl." I smile wickedly. "Mmm, you smell so good like this." I grind her down harder onto my leg, earning me another cry. "You know how to get what you want, Ava. Beg me."

But her small mouth stays stubbornly closed, fire

blazing in those pale eyes. I smirk at her defiance, relishing in this side of her. Ava has always been a brat, and I fucking love it. She's furious right now, and the wild look on her face is driving me to the edge. I move my hand from her throat to her mouth, roughly squeezing her cheeks until her mouth pops open and I can hook two fingers into it. Spit is already starting to pour out as I hold her open. My clawed hand rips through her pants, baring her glistening sex to the room.

Her scent perfumes the area as I pull the fingers from her mouth and roughly push them into her pussy, gripping her hip roughly with my other hand. Her head tilts back in a sob as I fuck her with my hand. I can feel the moment she starts to lose herself, and I pull out. The high-pitched keen she lets out has me smiling as I let her watch while I lick my fingers clean.

"You know how to end this, Ava," I say. "Beg me."

Her nostrils flare, a look on her face that says she has no interest in giving in. So, I up the stakes and drop to my knees in front of her, licking up that slit and around her clit.

"Give in, Rakkaani. I'm going to take your orgasms anyway; why are you making this so much harder for yourself?" I swirl my tongue around her again.

She growls, even as her hips push forward. "Yet, you are the one on your knees for me. Worshipping my cunt." She grips my hair hard, pulling and scratching.

Her words slam into my cock, and I have to remind myself to remain in control. Ripping my mouth from her dripping pussy, I slap her bare mound. The sound resonates through the room. "I go on my knees and worship you because I choose to. Not because you command it. Remember that. And remember that while your pretty little cunt is weeping for me, I can keep you here, on edge, for as long as I want." I lick her again before pushing two fingers into her tight heat. "I could even refuse your release and make you watch while I find my own. So, be a good girl. Fucking beg."

"Oh, fuck," she whimpers. "Fuck, fuck, fuck." Her hips buck against my mouth as she presses into me, but I pull back each time she starts getting close. After a while, I lose count of how many orgasms I've denied her, those milky legs shaking and barely holding her up, tears pouring down her face. But she never utters her safe word.

"Are you ready to give in?" Her body slumps for a moment as I pull away again. Her anger has faded, giving way to the pleasure I keep forcing into her body. My face is drenched from her, along with my fingers. I would drown in her if I could.

"P-Please," she finally whines. "Please, Drago. Please let me cum. I can't . . . I can't do this anymore."

Her broken sob gives me pause. "Do you need to tap out?"

She shakes her head frantically. "No, fuck. Please just let me cum. Fucking please."

A smile carves my face. "Who owns this pussy?"

"Fuck. You do, Drago. You do," she sobs.

"Who owns your soul?" I growl against her wet core.

She lets out a frantic sob, all rational thought gone. "You! You and Shadow!"

The satisfaction of hearing our names shoots to my chest. "Good girl. You may cum now." I swipe my tongue around her clit before sucking it into my mouth, while pumping two fingers roughly into her and stroking her inner wall.

That's all it takes before she is soaking my face, drowning me in her release. Her screams bounce off the walls of the penthouse, overpowering the sounds of the storm outside. Her never-ending release continues on and on, and I let her ride it out on my face and fingers. My cock is painful at this point, but I'll take the pain alongside the taste of her in my mouth. Because this, right here? This is my version of heaven.

———

THE CLOCK next to the bed reads 4 a.m. Lying on her back with her hair splayed out all over my pillow, this is the most relaxed I've seen her. Something has been bothering her, something beyond Shadow. But she hasn't confided in me, not even after I broke her down tonight. We have never played that hard, she's never let me edge her to the point of crying. Ava has kept control, always, until tonight.

I held her in the shower when we were finished, washing her hair and body before gathering her up and placing her in our shared bed. The tears were still coming down in silent tracks as she curled up under the covers. She never uttered a word as I held her, my hand splayed across that jagged scar, her anger long gone, faded into this quiet tempest of some unknown emotion.

Anger, I could deal with. But not this. This reminded me too much of Shadow, and history has shown me I have no idea how to help him.

I shift down into the bed next to Ava, pulling her body close to mine. Her lilac scent invades my nostrils. Her slim body curls into mine automatically, seeking my warmth. A content sigh escapes her lips as she nuzzles down even further into my arms. As if she can't get close enough to me. My dragon practically purrs with the delight of holding her in our arms; it eases the anxiety of Shadow being missing right now. I need to text Kai to find him.

Ava lets out a small moan, her brow furrowing, before she rolls again, disrupting my thoughts. Her leg moves over my hip, aligning us perfectly. I bite back a groan as her heat blankets my groin. My dick shoots to attention. Agreeing not to complete the mate bond until Shadow's ready is getting old, particularly with her scent still clinging to my face. My dragon barely held it together as we feasted on her wet cunt. I attempt to shift her a little further from me, to ease the pressure.

Like a moth to a flame, Ava follows my body until she's practically on top of me. I grind my teeth as her slim body molds itself over me, but when she lets out another content sigh, I can't make myself move again. The torture of her lilac scent in my nose and her silky skin touching my own tattoo-covered body isn't enough to ruin her sleep. And maybe that makes me a masochist, but I can't bring myself to care. So, taking a long, deep breath, I reach out through the bond to Shadow and urge him to come home.

TWENTY-ONE

SHADOW

The pain across my back feels like fire licking up my spine, every move I make another match against my skin. My dragon pushes against me, desperate to break free, to slaughter the man who continues to hurt us. But I fight him back, begging him to remain hidden, reminding him what will happen if my father knows the truth. Knows how powerful we are. How brutal.

My father's voice breaks through the haze. "Worthless piece of trash." Another slash down my back with his belt. I grit my teeth against the continued beating.

One.

Two.

Three more, and the blood is weeping from me in a cascade of penance for my failures.

Four more, and my arms give out. My naked chest hits the stone floor with a thud.

Five more, and my resolve is breaking, my ability to hold the dragon back lessening. It's pacing its cage like an angry tiger, testing the bars. Waiting for the moment it can rip free and rain down the carnage it's begging to let loose.

My father's stale breath curls around my face as he looms over me, digging his clawed hand into my shoulder. Into the fresh lashes. "You disgust me. What a poor excuse for an heir you are."

I gasp for air, coming out of the nightmare like it was drowning me. My back burns with the memory, the trauma of it imprinted on my body. My hands connect with grass and dirt, and I slowly blink away the disorientation. Overhead, the sky is cloudy, the dull gray blobs floating listlessly after last night's storm. My body is sweat-slicked and hot. Garbage and sea water invade my sense of smell upon my next intake of air, and the sounds of seagulls and ship horns invade my mind.

Fuck. The harbor. A place I never wanted to return to after the last time. When we decimated the area, killing so many innocents.

They weren't innocent if they were here, you know that. This place reeks of corruption, my dragon growls at me.

But I shake my head. Water-based witches took pride in their harbor, despite it being the main port used to traffic all manner of illicit goods. It had been beautiful before me. Before I reigned down terror and death. Now, the sea always seems to be dark and hazy. The beach and roads surrounding it collect trash, and the smell is overpowering. Shipping containers line the left side of the harbor, many long abandoned, while others house the displaced. Eufori-addicted witches, vamps, and shifters hide among the skeletal remains of this old community.

Sitting up finally, I run my hands through my hair. My body is exhausted from the shift. The whole time flying, my dragon berated me for leaving my mates, screamed that we need to finish this. The pull to turn around, to go back to the penthouse, was so strong that I'm shocked I fought it. Shocked I'm sitting in this field and not at home.

Fuck, when did I start thinking of it as home?

The last time I had a home was in my mother's arms. I will never forgive myself for killing her or allowing Ava to get hurt because I took an interest in her.

What about Ciaran? All the things he sacrificed for you?

Fucking hell, the voice in my head continues to list off the marks on my soul, the debts I owe. It's done an excellent job pushing away the little bit of hope I saw in Jackson's words. What did he say? That my mother asked him to speak to me? Why would she want me to be happy after I killed her?

We didn't.

"Then what the fuck happened?" I say out loud. My voice is carried away by the ocean breeze.

I don't know. But I hope to find out.

I grip my dark hair hard in my fists and hang my head between my knees. It feels as though I'm staring down into a dark pit and one more gust of wind will throw me into it for eternity. Ava and Drago don't understand. All my life, I've wanted someone to choose me. I thought that would fix it all. But Ciaran did choose me, and instead of helping, it made me realize I have something to lose now.

Everyone tells me I need to heal, need to let go, but no one tells you how to do that. How does one heal a lifetime of wounds that reopen daily? And that's the real question that holds me back. If I don't know how to heal, how will I be the mate they need me to be? I can barely keep myself alive.

Because no one taught us how to live.

The truth of my dragon's words slam into me, knocking the breath from my lungs.

Why would we feel worthy when our family told us otherwise?

("ARMY OF ME" – In This Moment)

Anger pushes through me, hot and fast. A lance that attempts to cauterize my heart. Tears pour down my face in an onslaught of emotion as I process the torment I've put myself through all because of my fucking father. The fact that I'm still paying for my sins, sins that just keep piling up the longer I'm alive. Sins that never would have been committed if I had been born to a different family. A broken scream tears from my throat and echoes out into the harbor behind me, and in the next moment, my dragon bursts forth from my skin, shredding my human side to pieces as he takes over. He is the conduit for all the feelings I'm unable to process. He only sees red; primal fury drives him as he rips apart the surrounding area. Lava pours from his mouth with a rage-filled cry.

The harbor quakes as he shoves off the ground, his talons leaving huge indents in the soft soil. All the while, lava continues to leave his mouth. The wind we create causes great swells of the black water to meet the lava he is leaving behind. Plumes of steam rise up as the shoreline turns into a war of fire and water. It's a visual representation of how I feel inside. Screams echo as people flee from my dragon, our shadow over the water a wraith looking for souls to reap. He moves higher and higher into the sky, and for once, we match in our feelings. Both our hearts are breaking as he carries us away from Ava and Drago.

Thank you, I say to him.

You can thank me when you allow us to return. You are in charge of us more than you believe, Shadow. And until you are well, you cannot be the mate they need. I have no interest in being the one in control, though, so I let my eyes close and tuck myself away.

TWENTY-TWO

A halfling of Hell is with Alexi.
While we counted on that—planned on it, even—we did not
anticipate his friendship with the dragon.
This could complicate things for The Order.
— Mori Family Grimoire

AVA

("The Beautiful & Damned" – G-Eazy)

The skies feel heavy, and the wind howls through the tall buildings like ghosts calling out for retribution. Gothic Grove is a city of the damned, and the souls it's claimed beg for revenge when the weather gets like this. The wind rips at my face as I exit the penthouse into the parking garage. Tucking my hands into my coat, I quickly scan the parking garage for a mode of transportation to take me to The Playground.

Spying the all-black Hellcat, I smile and skip over to it. Slipping in, I let my hands trail over the smooth leather seats as the engine purrs to life. I groan at the sound, loving how the vibration feels. I miss driving, miss the feel of the engine and the power that comes with knowing just how to read the road. In my world, there is a difference between being able to drive and actually driving. Or, at least, that's what my brother would always say before sneaking us out for the races. At least until that day when I took my freedom into my own hands.

Freedom.

The word that has motivated so many of my choices these past years. The endless search for it, only to find I'll never truly have freedom.

The radio flips onto G-Eazy, and I close my eyes for a moment, allowing the smell of leather and the lingering scent of Drago to wash over me. Leaving him sleeping upstairs was a herculean task that I'm astonished I accomplished. But I need space. I need time to cool off and ground myself. Need time to come to terms with some things that have been bothering me. And maybe I need some risk in my life right now, risk that feels controllable.

Shifting into gear, I pull the car out and begin making my way toward my home. This city never brightens, though the dark streets are illuminated by ever-burning street lamps. Most people complain about the constant cloud cover, but it feels safe to me, as though the clouds are my own personal shield against those who would drag me away. Slowly, the past is catching up to me, while the future I am desperate to avoid looms in front of me. And the future I want is slipping through my fingers.

The streets zoom past, near empty despite the hour. It's eerie and has me on edge. The Playground was my saving grace after I had escaped the prison. Drago and I started it together, and I love him for the help he offered, but I love him more for stepping away once I got my feet under me.

Sure, he visits, but he's had a hands-off approach since I took the reigns.

The Playground is, above all else, a place where people can safely explore their wants and needs. A place where you can exist in Gothic Grove that is absolutely safe—my magic is woven into the wards that keep the occupants safe from outside threats. At great cost to my magical reserve I might add. They have been tested once and only once, when I first opened. I suspected then that they had been sent by Alexi, but now I wonder if it was The Order trying to drag me back. Either way, my wards held and whoever it was failed.

My phone rings, and I see Drago's name on the screen. I let out a long sigh before hitting the button to ignore. When it rings again, I switch it off entirely. I need space. I need time. Time to figure out the emotions swirling in me. Turning the music up louder, I press the accelerator down and lose myself to the feel of the car.

DRAGO

("Judith" – A Perfect Circle)

The sound of my cell phone vibrating nonstop pulls me from my sleep. I roll over and slap my hand along the nightstand until I land on it. "What?" I grumble.

"The Order knows Ava is with you. They are coming for her," Jackson starts with no preamble. "You need to get her out of there. Now."

My hand jerks to the side of the bed Ava was on but comes up empty against the smooth, cold sheets. I glance around the room—no sign of her. Panic lodges in my chest as the reality hits me. "Shit!" I don't acknowledge Jackson in any way before I'm ending the call and dialing Ava. When it goes straight to voicemail, I try again, only to be met by the same response. "Fuck!" Next, I try Shadow, but his phone also goes straight to voicemail.

Vaulting out of bed, I slam my palm into the panic button that feeds directly to Kai, who lives in the apartment a floor down. We put it in place long ago, and it has rarely been used, but today, I'm grateful for it.

I try Shadow again but am sent straight to voicemail for the second time. "Motherfuckers, why can't anyone answer their gods damn phone!" I scramble, grabbing a T-shirt and sweats as I flee my bedroom, only to run headfirst into Kai. I know by the look on his face I'm not going to like what he has to say, but I motion for him to follow me into my home office.

"Ava was seen leaving in the Hellcat not long ago. Shadow . . ." He trails off, and I already know what he is about to say. I know because my chest hurts. It's pulling like a rubber band stretched too far.

"FUCK!" I throw my phone against the wall. The piece of titanium bounces to the floor, skittering across the hardwood.

"My men say the harbor is destroyed; he didn't leave anything standing. What wasn't burned was flooded by the waves he created," Kai says, ignoring my outburst.

I scream again, grabbing my desk and flipping it up. The wood splinters and cracks, much like how my chest feels right now. I want to deny it, but the pain in my chest tells me everything I need to know. He left us.

"Fuck, fuck, FUCK!" I can't stop pacing, can't stop moving, as I feel my world slipping away from me. The world I've tried so hard to keep together. Panic compresses my lungs, cutting off my breathing.

"Drago." He steps forward. "Breathe. We get Ava first,

then we get Shadow." Logically, I know he is right. Shadow is safer than Ava; they aren't after him. Without her magic, she is vulnerable to whoever is after her, and if they know about us, then Shadow's show at the harbor will alert them that she is unguarded by at least one dragon.

I finally manage to pull air into my lungs. First one breath, then two, then three, until my chest no longer feels constricted. My mind starts to clear again. I straighten up and smooth my hair back.

"Has anyone seen Ava since she left the parking garage?" Breathe in. Breathe out, I keep reminding myself.

He shakes his head as he sends out a text, presumably to our men.

"Get people to The Playground. If she is there, keep her there. Close the fucking club down, no one in once you have her."

He nods, sending out texts rapidly. "What are you doing?" he asks without looking up.

If he had looked up, he would have seen my shift, seen the golden eyes replace the blue, seen my hands start to turn skeletal. My dragon is no longer content with sitting back.

"I'm going hunting."

AVA

("Down With The Sickness (feat. Ai Mori)" – Violet Orlandi)

The music shifts, the sounds vibrating over the roar of the engine, as I enter the last mile or so of road before The Playground. My attention is solely on the small amount of traffic that has suddenly appeared, so I don't notice the subtle change in the air around me until the massive shadow passes over the car, causing me to slam on my brakes. The sound of tires screeching fills the air as all the vehicles on the road come to a halt.

Dread fills me as I fling the door open and spy a massive skeletal dragon clinging to the side of the nearest skyscraper. Glass and metal fold under his weight like they're paper as he crawls down the building. He's only a football field's length away from me when he lets out a great roar, black flames shooting from his maw. People scream around me, fleeing into buildings or down the road, but I stand stock-still as he slowly approaches.

"Shit . . . Drago . . ." I start, holding my hands up, palms out in surrender, expecting him to shift back.

But he doesn't. Instead, his dragon shakes his head, snapping that massive jaw. I growl at him, snapping my own dull human teeth. His golden eyes flare at my defiance. "Fine. You want to do this? Let's fucking do this." I spin on my heel and take off at a dead sprint, adrenaline pushing me forward as he lets out a devastatingly loud scream that rains glass down around me. "Fuck. Fuck, fuck, fuck," I chant as I dodge and weave through the discarded cars. Drago's dragon barrels through them, not stopping, and I realize it may have been a bad fucking idea to run from him.

DEATH DRAGON

She ran. Like a prey. And when I catch her, I'm going to fucking devour her.

AVA

Heat blasts overhead as he lets loose a volley of flames, his massive skeletal wings pushing me forward as he takes to the skies. *And how the fuck did you think this was gonna go,*

Ava? You are running from a gods damn death dragon. If I was smart, I wouldn't have fled from him. I would stop right now and submit. But the rational voice in me that says to give up is ignored and overpowered by the one that's pissed and hurt and tired of playing it safe. My magic swims up around me, but I push it back down, still clear-headed enough at least to refuse the risk.

My body screams at me as I throw myself around a corner into a dark alley. My hands scrape against the brick wall as I try to avoid falling face-first onto the dirty cement. Behind me, I hear a screech of frustration as Drago's massive body overshoots the alley I'm bolting down. A satisfied smile plays over my face, even as sweat drips down my temples. My lungs burn but I force myself to keep taking in air. Up ahead, I can see a chain-link fence separating this space and the next.

"You can do this, Ava. Go, go, go," I pant.

But Drago cuts off my escape, his black flames lighting up the fence and causing me to skid to a halt. Seamlessly shifting from dragon to human, his body drops down behind me, blocking my escape both ways. Neither of us say anything. The only sound is my uneven breathing. When I finally look at him, his eyes are golden, blazing bright like fire.

"You shouldn't have run, Ava." His voice isn't human. He may have shifted back to human form, but Drago is not in control.

DRAGO

Ava's scent hits me full force. Sweat, lilacs, and arousal. I shake my head, trying to regain some type of control. But my dragon has lost his patience with me and our mates. We push forward. Ava's eyes dart around for escape, but she has none.

"Drago—" she starts, but I lunge forward, pushing her body against the rough brick surrounding us. Her eyes go wide as I smile, my teeth still elongated.

"You smell so fucking good." I breathe in deep, eyes closing as I enjoy her scent, bask in it. My claws dig into the wall as I slide my hands down on either side of, leaving deep indents in the faded red brick, until I plant them on her hips. When I open my eyes, she's breathless, cheeks flushed a crimson shade that spreads down her neck. "Why did you run like a little rabbit? Hmm? Did you want me to hunt you? Catch you and devour you?"

She wiggles slightly, biting her lip hard. I allow my hand to slip into her clothing and down toward her core. I groan as I come in contact with her slick arousal. "Rakkaani . . . you are so wet. I want to fuck you against this wall. Claim you for my own." She whimpers at the idea. I drag my nose along her neck, stopping briefly at the mark that Shadow left. Anger pulses bright and hot through me. "He fucking left us." The words tumble from my mouth before I can yank them back.

"What?" Ava asks, her voice breathless.

I nip at the mark, careful not to bite over it but enough that I know I'll leave small indents where my teeth have pushed at it. I move to the unmarked side of her neck, my dragon in full control. "He fucking left us, left you in danger like this. I should take you right here, against the wall. Mate you without him."

Ava's small hands shove at me. "What the fuck are you talking about, Drago?" I press my full body weight into her, eliciting a gasp as I push my fingers inside her. "Stop, Drago. What do you mean, he left?"

But I don't stop, I keep slowly pumping my two fingers into her heat. "Why do you think I hunted you down?" I growl, my voice having lost all trace of being human. "He left you exposed with his little tantrum. You need magic, you need to mate. So, we do it without him." Her walls clench around my fingers.

"Drago, wait . . ." But I can't, I press my teeth into her neck and lay my own claim opposite of Shadow's.

AVA

In a dirty back alley of Gothic Grove, Drago claims me as his mate. The euphoric feeling, electric as it runs through my body, has me cuming on his fingers as they plunge deep within me. A scream rips from my mouth and is only silenced when his own mouth crashes down on me. We fumble with my clothing, ripping and tearing until my legs are wrapped around his naked body and his cock is pushing inside me. There is nothing romantic about this moment, and maybe it's better that way, given Shadow mated me in a cell. We rip at each other's flesh, my nails digging into his skin and leaving long rake marks that stand out brightly even in the dim light of the alley.

When he pulls off my neck, I know it'll look just as savage as Shadow's mark does. "Gonna fill you up, Rakkaani, going to pump you so full of me, you won't be able to forget who owns this cunt," Drago growls as he viciously fucks me into the wall. His piercings hit the perfect spot and send me reeling as another orgasm destroys me. "That's it, give it to me. Fucking give me everything."

Drago is lost to his dragon, and I'm lost to the sensation of the bond between us. My own magic pushes up toward him to complete our bond, but I shove it back, refuse to allow it to bond, refuse to allow myself to take from him. No, the first time I feed, it'll be with both my mates, and not in some fucking alley.

I feel the moment Drago starts to cum, his body locking up as he pumps his hot release into me. Our skin is flushed and slick with sweat. We fall back to earth, and the noises of the city filter back into our reality as his cock slips from me. We both stand there, his cum dripping down my thighs, his cock glistening with mine, and look at each other. He reaches out his hand to me, a peace offering, his dragon receding now.

I don't move for a full minute. I just stare at his hand. "You hunted me down." It's not a question. It's a fact.

"Yes." A pause, and then, "He left us." As if that is explanation enough, as if mating me would heal something broken in us from losing him.

I nod. My heart hurts. Drago and I knew this might happen someday, yet to realize that it is reality hurts more than I thought it would. Shadow didn't choose us. And now we have to face the reality of the situation.

DRAGO

("Tell Mama" – The Civil Wars)

It's been 3 days since I fucked Ava against that alley wall and laid my mark on her neck. Three days since my dragon laid waste to a section of Gothic Grove. And three days since Shadow disappeared. The harbor is still smoldering, the air thick with smoke even in the heart of the city. No one has seen or heard from Shadow. It's like he disappeared into thin air. The coffee in my hand turns bitter in my mouth as I touch the hole in my chest where his bond should be. Sleep has evaded me, or maybe I've refused to sleep. Either way, I can't remember the last time I closed my eyes. I need to go to bed. I know this isn't healthy.

Instead, I choose more caffeine. I can rest when he's home.

If he comes home, my dragon huffs.

He will. I respond, but I think we both know I no longer have the same conviction in that statement that I used to.

"You think he'll come home?" Ava moves up behind me, looping her arms around my stomach and burrowing her face into my bare back. My dragon preens at the contact, and I allow my eyes to close briefly. Her small fingers splay across my abs and draw tiny circles over the muscles as we stand in the large window. After the call from Jax, I moved us to my home, the one where it all started with Ava.

"If you had asked me a month ago, I would have said he would never have left to begin with. But now, I have no idea," I reply honestly. She continues to draw on my stomach, her breath leaving small puffs of warm air against my skin. "We need to make a plan, Ava."

Her movements pause for a moment but resume before she replies, "He'll come home."

"Are you trying to convince me or yourself?"

Her movements pause again, and this time, she pulls away from me. Turning, I watch her walk over to the coffee maker. "Both?" She offers a tentative smile over her shoulder.

I cross my arms and feel the sweats I have on shift a little lower on my hips. Her eyes track downward, her tiny pink tongue licking her bottom lip. "You need to feed, Ava. Complete our bond. I can't lose you, too. We've been fucking lucky so far that The Order hasn't caught up with us here."

She huffs out a breath and turns away, pouring herself some coffee and adding a pound of creamer to it.

"Jesus, Ava, could you get that coffee sweeter?"

She smiles at me, her eyes crinkling at the corners. "Probably." Moving past me, she walks over to the large leather couch and plops down, pulling the fuzzy blanket over her lap. Samhain flutters down from his perch, settling next to her. Silence descends upon the room as we each retreat into our own minds.

"He's out there alone, Drago," she says quietly after a few minutes. Her voice breaks. "He's hurting, and we can't help him."

"I know. I fucking know he is, Ava, and it kills me. But I can't control what he is doing. So, I'm choosing to focus on you. I can keep you safe," I respond as grief settles over us again.

Neither of us acknowledge what might happen if I can't keep her safe. Instead, we sit in the silence, drinking our liquid gold and hoping it'll heal that space that's so raw in our chests.

TWENTY-THREE

SHADOW

("Let It Go (with Lø Spirit)" – Chandler Leighton)

"Why the fuck do we have a dragon in our yard?" The female voice pulls me into awareness. My sight is still through my dragon, but my mind is slowly coming back online.

This is where I leave you. Figure your shit out, my dragon says before forcing the shift back and dumping my naked body in a pile at Astrea's feet. She cocks her head, assessing me as her long burgundy-and-white hair blows in the breeze. The cool air sends chills over my body.

She offers me her hand, a dark snake peeking out from her sleeve. When I hesitate, she grumbles, "Jesus, Shadow, just fucking take my hand so we can get in the house." A smile breaks my face, and I grab the outstretched hand, hauling myself to my feet. She quickly turns her back to me, allowing me some privacy. "Do not tell Ciaran I've seen you like this. I have no interest in having the conversation with him about whose dick is bigger," she mutters as she walks forward, motioning for me to follow her.

I take in what's around us as we walk. The woods are thick with evergreen and spruce trees, and the air has a chill to it that indicates mountains. Mist gathers in the air and fog billows through the trees, giving off an eerie feel. She's dressed in thick leggings and a long flannel, boots covering her feet as she walks over the frost-covered grass toward a small cabin. Not dissimilar to the one she left behind.

When she pushes open the door, the porch is flooded with warm light before I hear a hiss and the scurry of nails. "Fucking hell," I growl as Poppy flings herself out of my way, her fur standing on end. Astrea laughs, grabbing a blanket and throwing it at me. "I hate familiars," I grumble.

"The feeling is clearly mutual," she says, laughing. "Cover up. I'll grab some of Ciaran's clothing." She moves with ease through the front room into a dark hallway.

"Where is he?" I ask as I pull the thick green blanket around my shoulders. I move over toward the crackling fireplace. The hearth is large, with a fur rug in front of it. Pillows piled up around it indicate it's been used for a bed at some point. A wine glass sits on a low wooden table stationed between two large high-backed chairs. The room adjoining is a small kitchen. A pot on the stove lets off steam, and the aroma of food hangs heavy in the air.

Astrea comes back into the room holding a pile of clothing. "He's out getting supplies. He'll be home soon." She tosses the clothing at me, causing me to fumble to grab them without dropping the blanket. "Now, get dressed so you can tell me why the fuck you are here and my best friend is heartbroken in the city."

I let out a low groan as she points toward a closed door, indicating I should get changed there. I shuffle past, but just as I'm about to open the door, her voice stops me. "Shadow, I'll say this once: Ava means a lot to me. She took care of me when she could have just as easily told me to fuck off. She had my back in a fight that wasn't hers. But she also means a lot to Buttercup, and I will warn you once and only once. My magic has no interest in excuses."

When I look back, her normally green eyes are a shade closer to black, her face hard.

It's the face of the Harbinger.

———

ASTREA SHOWS me to a loft-style guest room after I've pulled on the borrowed clothing, before leaving me alone to contemplate my choices. The sounds of her cooking below are strangely soothing as I lie on the soft bed and look up at the cracked ceiling. My dragon slumbers inside, staying true to his word to leave me alone for now. I often wonder what our relationship would have been like if I hadn't been forced to hide him so long. Would we be in this same space? Would I be as broken? Would he be as feral? For so long, I've kept him locked away, kept us separate because that's what I thought I needed after everything. But maybe I shouldn't have.

The questions whirl in my mind until I'm overwhelmed, and I dig the heels of my hands into my eyes.

"Can I offer you some advice?"

I startle upward, not having heard Astrea approach up

the stairs. She's filled out since I last saw her, the curves on her body finally back. She moves into the room and sits down on the chair opposite the bed. "Go ahead," I say. "I think you're going to offer it anyway."

She lets out a laugh so unlike her. I'm envious of her, envious of the freedom she seems to have found despite being on the run. "Well, I mean, you did drop down in full-on dragon form, so I think I'm entitled to a little advice giving," she says with a wink. I watch as she pulls her hair up, looping it into a bun before tucking herself deeper into the chair.

"That wasn't my choice," I grouse.

She only rolls her eyes. "Look, you've had three months to figure your shit out, and you haven't, so now you get to listen to me. Shadow, when I say I understand how hard it is to fight your demons, I truly do understand. You pulled me from Alexi, you know what I went through, maybe even more vividly than Ciaran does. You saw me at times he didn't, cleaned me up before bringing me to him." I cringe thinking about how I found her at times. How I attempted to spare my friend from seeing her like that.

She continues talking, ignoring the ghosts that are looming over us. "I've spent most my life living in fear, that anxiety so fucking overwhelming I thought I might die from it. And at times, I honestly would rather have died. It was exhausting dealing with it, but it also seemed exhausting to try to die. So, instead, I remained in this self-inflicted purgatory. For years."

The world gutters out at those words. Words that have bounced around in my head for so long but refused to be voiced out loud.

"I also know how it feels to try to deny, or even fight, a darkness within you. This magic? It changed me. Every day,

I fight to keep control of it, but if I deny it? It finds a way out of me, and normally not in a way I enjoy." Darkness clouds those emerald eyes before she pinches the bridge of her freckled nose and shakes her head. "Do you know what helps me the most, though?"

"Gods, I hope you say me," Ciaran's deep voice sounds from the stairs. I watch him plant a kiss on Astrea's head, tugging on her bun while he does it. Their mating bond fills the air around us, the small space enveloped by it.

"Mmm. Yes, actually." She turns and looks at me. "When Ciaran pulled that piece of metal from me, my magic consumed every part of my soul—it was dark and terrifying. But Ciaran pulled me back, and our bond continues to keep me here and grounded."

I want to open my mouth, to tell her I don't deserve my mates. Not after everything I've done. I know I'm unlovable. Know that even if things had been different, I would still have a darkness in me that is untamed and wild. But I can't get the words out, can't force my mouth to open.

She leans forward, Ciaran's hand still resting on her shoulder. "You deserve the love of your mates. You deserve happiness. You may think you have too much blood and death on your hands. That you are evil because part of you enjoyed it. But, Shadow . . . you can have all those things inside you AND still deserve love. Things are not black-and-white. You saved me. You saved Ava. You are a good person AND have some darkness. I have just as much blood on my hands, and I know I still deserve this happiness."

I shake my head. "You don't know the things I've done." The statement is out before I can think twice, the words vomited into a pile in front of me. "It's my fault Ciaran had to stay under Alexi." I'm having an out-of-body experience at this point as all the words unravel out of me. "I liked killing for Alexi, enjoyed unleashing myself. The scars on my body are penance for every life I've taken, but they also served as a way to control myself so I wouldn't hurt more people. Wouldn't give into that enjoyment fully. I use Eufori to keep the voices inside back behind a glass wall." Tears slip down my face as the things I've kept locked away are pulled from me like some demonic exorcism. My soul laid bare at the feet of my brother and his mate. "I should never have survived Alexi. I wish Ciaran had let me die instead of putting himself in service to that man. I deserved that death. So many others should be alive, and yet, because of me, they aren't. My mother should be alive." The last of the confessions, the scariest one, sears my tongue before the last of my demons tumbles out. "And what if . . . what if they see that darkness and decide not to choose me, after all?"

Astrea's eyes shine with emotion, a content smile settling on her face as she watches me pull in breath after breath, sobs starting to ripple over me. Ciaran moves and gathers me into his large body, holding me through it all.

"I chose to save you," Ciaran says into my ear. "Chose to help my best friend—no, my brother escape a cage that he was put in. But I didn't realize that you would still be in a mental cage, and for that, I am sorry." He pulls back, cradles my face in his hands, and looks me straight in the eyes. "I will never regret the deal I made with him to get you out. My only regret is not understanding how much you needed reminders that you are deserving of love."

Words escape me as Ciaran says all the things I've longed to hear. All the things that I am sure Ava and Drago have been telling me, but I refused to hear. No, that's not fair. I don't think I could hear them until this moment. There is something strange about healing that no one ever tells you—something could be said a million times over, but until you are in a certain spot at a certain time, you won't absorb it.

Shadow. You and I deserve better than we've been given, my dragon echoes in my mind. *Stop punishing us. Let us have a life with our mates like we deserve.*

I'm not sure how long I sit in Ciaran's arms, but eventually, the tears dry and I'm able to pull back. Astrea is still curled up on the chair, Poppy now a fluffy ball in her arms.

"Thank you," I whisper, my voice cracking a bit.

Astrea offers me a smile before it slips from her face and she goes wholly still, her eyes tracking but not seeing, head tilting to the side.

"*Kamerat?*" Ciaran walks toward her.

"We need to go back to the city." Her voice has a far-off quality to it, infused with her power as she listens to that dark magic. "Ava is in trouble."

TWENTY-FOUR

The Order wants the princess.
They are hunting for her.
If they knew all the secrets my family has they'd come for us instead.
— Hansley Mori

AVA

"Drago, I went for a drive. I'll be back, I promise," I say into the phone as I downshift coming around the corner. The white STI takes the sharp turn beautifully. The exhaust lets out a loud rumble as I accelerate again. When I woke up this morning, it felt like I was crawling out of my skin. I knew I needed to get out of the house for a while. The urgency for freedom took control. So, with Drago still sleeping, I repeated my actions from a few days ago.

"Ava," he growls. "Do you remember the last time you left?" My pussy quivers at his voice and the memory.

"Yes, vividly. But, Drago, I'm going insane. I can't stay inside anymore; without Shadow, I'm crawling the walls.

He's out there somewhere hurting, and I can't get that out of my mind."

There's a long pause before I hear, "Am I not enough?" The way his voice breaks hurts me physically; tears form in my eyes.

"Drago, Rakkaani, of course, you are. But we both know Shadow is our person, and until he is back, I need to stay busy. So, please, just give this to me. No one knows to look for me here. I'm in a car that no one associates with any of us. I'm not going into the city. I'm staying on the back roads."

He doesn't say anything, his breathing the only indication the call is still connected. "I love you," I say. But I don't get a response before the sound of crunching metal and the screech of brakes yanks me violently from the call.

("Godly" – Tommee Profitt and Vo Williams)

The STI jerks to the side from the impact, and my head hits hard against the window. I cover my face out of instinct, releasing the wheel from my hands, as the glass breaks apart. I feel like a rag doll as my body is jerked this way and that; the only thing preventing me from actually being thrown around is the five-point harness. The airbags deploy, knocking the wind from my chest and gobbling up my screams. I think I hear Drago yelling my name, but I can't focus on it long enough before the sound is cut off and all that's left is the noise of the crash.

After what feels like hours, the car finally skids to a halt. My vision blurs with dizziness and my ears ring. My limbs feel odd as I start to pull at my harness, start to try to assess what the fuck just happened. Smoke pours from the hood of the car, obscuring my view of the street in front of me, but the scent of sulfur invades my nose, making me want to retch up the little food in my stomach.

"Fuck, fuck, fuck," I chant. I tug harder at the straps securing me to the seat, panic woven into my limbs now. I know what sulfur means. The straps finally pull apart, but the door is crumpled inward, making it next to impossible to open. I reach for my magic without care, attempting to wiggle out of the car. I'm sluggish, my magic barely able to rally enough to shove open the crumpled door until I'm finally dumped onto the concrete. My body screams at me as I go to push myself up.

Like a million spiders crawling over my skin, magic that's not my own suddenly pulls me upright off the cold ground. I grit my teeth against the feeling, but my limbs refuse to listen as I try to fight back, fight through the terror starting to grip me. Frantically, I search the area with my eyes, desperate to locate the source of the magic that holds my body prone. Before I can spot it, the mystery magic yanks me forward and drops me back onto the concrete, further from the smoldering wreckage.

This is fucking bad. So, so bad. Squeezing my eyes shut, I send a silent prayer that Drago will get here in time. That even though we have only a partial bond, he'll track me. Regret for not feeding off him courses through me.

The weight of the magic presses into my body as I try to shove myself up. When I open my eyes, I half expect to see a visible force holding me down. Then the sound of boots crunching over glass pierces the silence, and real fear pushes through me as my eyes finally come to focus on a tall man walking toward me.

"Hello, Ava." The man's voice is deathly soft and, oh, so familiar to me. "I've been looking for you. You are quite difficult to find in this shithole of a city." The man bends down toward me, cocking his head as he assesses me. A sinister smile spreads over his face.

"Oisin," I whisper. The man who was once like a brother to me looks vastly different from the last time I saw him. The scar still cuts through his left eye, the pure white of it standing out against his black hair, which hangs down in strings that partially obscure his right eye. That eye burns red, but there is no warmth in his face, no love or concern. Only poisonous malice. Confusion grips me as I try to reconcile the person I thought I once knew with the man in front of me.

He snaps his fingers, and the magic holding me raises me up, just as he comes to a stand, so I'm face-to-face with him. My body is rigid in the magic's hold, my toes barely brushing the ground. "So glad you remember me. I was worried, after you ran, that you'd forget about me."

"What is going on?" I ask, unwilling to believe that Jackson could have anything to do with this. But why would Oisin have been looking for me?

Oisin tucks his hands behind his back as he walks around my body. When he is behind me, his magic finally releases me, dropping me hard to the ground. I push up, refusing to stay where I am, despite my body screaming at me to stop moving.

He sneers down at me. "You are weak. Your magic is basically gone. We'll have to remedy that immediately." He snaps his fingers, and a woman appears. I blink a few times, trying to understand what I'm seeing. "I believe you remember Arcanna's mother." Lady Ornate smiles coolly at me, wearing long white robes stitched together with golden rope, her breasts shoved against the thin fabric. "She's my high priestess. She'll help with the initiation when we return to Hell."

Indeed, she wears the sunbeam crown many priestesses

wear, but evil seems to pour from her. "You weren't a high priestess," I growl.

She smiles at me. "True, but His Grace here allowed me to enter after my time amongst the priestesses."

Panic grips the edges of my psyche as my world tilts on its axis. I'm scrambling to catch up to the truth in front of me. "You . . . you are from The Order."

He lets out a long, deep laugh. "I am The Order." He snaps his fingers and his magic pulls me into the air as Arcanna's mother walks forward.

"Don't you fucking touch me," I scream. But she ignores my request, plunging a needle into my neck and pulling blood from me. I yelp at the feeling. Then she roughly pulls it out and walks back over to Oisin.

"I'll ready the ceremony," she says sweetly. He nods at her, snapping his fingers, and she vanishes again.

He returns his attention to me, moving his body into mine until he's so close I can see the small bead of sweat at his temple. "While I don't love what you've done with your hair, that can be fixed. After all, my wife needs to look good." He reaches out and trails a hand over my face and down to my throat. I try to pull away, but his magic holds strong. "Otherwise you are still just as tempting as you've always been."

"You're fucking insane," I growl.

A sneer pulls at his mouth, and he brings his hand up to circle my throat tightly. "You are my property. Your father sold you to me, whore. I can do whatever the fuck I want to you." He leans in closer, until his mouth is hovering next to the shell of my ear. "And I will, Ava. I will fuck you and ruin you and use up all your magic."

"My father never would have sold me to you." I counter.

Despite my father being a horrific person I'm confident in my statement.

He lets out a cruel laugh. "You should have seen the look on your father's face when I slid the knife into him and told him just who I was. That The Order was mine, and he sold you to us. It couldn't have worked out better, honestly."

He squeezes hard, and my head swims, my breath coming in short bursts now. My magic pushes desperately to the surface, what's left of the depleted well. I won't die here. And I won't be dragged back to Hell. But as my fingers tingle, a dark shape comes into view, and a smile spreads across my mouth as I take in who it is. "My mates will have something to say about that," I cough out.

He turns as Shadow's dragon slams into the ground roughly a hundred yards from us, the cement under the dragon's massive form cracking. His roar is deafening, causing rocks to tremble along the coastal highway. Molten lava drips from his mouth like burning saliva. I could cry from the relief I feel to see him, and it's not just him—atop his massive back sit Ciaran and Astrea.

("Land Of Darkness" – Rated R and CELO)

And from deep in the shadows, Drago steps out, his hands black with the veins of his power running up his forearms, a flash of skeleton wings behind him. His eyes are brilliant gold.

"You're fucked," I say in a strangled whisper despite his hand tightening around my throat.

DRAGO

Stepping from the darkness, I rein in all emotion, zeroing in on the offending hand around my mate's throat.

Shadow lets out another roar. His fury pulses down my end of the bond.

"Release her, demon," Shadow's dragon growls, lava spewing from his mouth as he does. The man doesn't bother to look worried, and it's a testament to what he's seen over his life if Shadow doesn't scare him. But he does take a second glance as Ciaran and Astrea drop off of my mate's back.

I knew he was untrustworthy. Vile. Wrong. My dragon rumbles as I take in the former confidant to the King of Hell.

"You can't win this," I snarl. "You are outnumbered."

A sly, evil grin spreads over his face as he takes in the two of them. Ciaran with his massive sword and golden magic, and Astrea with her black smoke and crackling lightning. "Oh, this is getting good." He laughs. "Do you have any idea who he is?" He nods toward Ciaran. I frown before I remind myself not to give an inch of information, but the man sees and grins widely. "This couldn't have been planned better. Do you want to tell them or should I? Brother."

The world freezes as I take in what he just said. Ciaran and Astrea, however, do not look shocked. If anything, Astrea looks bored, and Ciaran just glares at the man. "Half brother, Oisin," he responds, "and we have nothing to tell them. I want you out of my city."

Oisin sneers, "Your city? You were working to claim it for me!"

"Things change. This is our city now. Leave." He throws magic into the last word, reaching out and pushing against a barrier that I didn't notice Oisin had erected.

Shadow's dragon growls as he glances at our friends, moving away from the two of them closer to me. His eyes are wary of them as he moves, but they quickly shift back to Ava. I debate asking Ciaran what he is talking about, but my gut is telling me to get Ava first.

"Give us, Ava. We won't ask again," I growl out.

Oisin lets out a laugh, hugging Ava more tightly to him. "I would be worried about who you have as a friend there; if he is willing to betray his own brother, what makes you think he won't betray you?"

Astrea huffs out an annoyed groan and steps forward. "You currently have my best friend, so either you give her back or I'll fucking rip you to shreds, over and over, until I'm bored and then feed you to one of these dragons. I'm not fucking around with whatever this bullshit is that you're trying to sow between us all." She glances over at me. "We'll explain everything after this."

I'm not sure when it happened, but Astrea has begun to remind me of Kallen. Thinking back to my conversation with Ciaran, I wonder how much of that darkness has taken over her since we spoke. My dragon itches under my skin, furious at the situation playing out in front of us.

One thing at a time. We get Ava, then demand answers, I tell him.

Oisin grips Ava harder, evident by the wince on her face. Blood drips from a cut on her scalp, and bruises are already starting to form on her body. Walking forward, I let my power unfold around me, the black veins twisting up my arms and around my hands. Shadow moves away from me, enough to shift back into his human form, then flanks me, his own hands wreathed in flame.

Oisin's eyes narrow at Ciaran, as if the reality of the situation is finally settling in. "You've made a grave error in this, brother," he spits. "Choosing them, over me! I should have killed you all those years ago."

Ciaran, for his part, looks disgusted with his half brother. "You are weak and have no power of your own. Now, get the fuck out of my city," he commands.

Oisin smiles wickedly before dropping Ava to the ground and throwing out a powerful wave of magic. I brace for impact, but Astrea's magic meets it before it can touch us. The sound of the two colliding roars in my ears. She laughs as Oisin throws another arc of power at her. It slams into the shield again and again, unable to break it apart.

"Is that all you've got? This is fucking boring."

Oisin seethes, his face going red and his teeth grinding together in a determined scowl. "Fucking Harbinger," he spits. "I will have that magic soon."

Astrea rolls her eyes. "Many people have wanted this magic, and yet, here I stand with it still. You will be no different."

Movement behind Oisin catches my eye—Buttercup and Onyx. The two snakes moved off Astrea unnoticed at some point to join the fray. Onyx aims for Oisin, while Buttercup slowly makes her way toward Ava's small form crumpled on the pavement. As soon as Onyx is within a few feet of Oisin, he spins on the snake, but Astrea's eyes gleam and she literally mists herself from one spot to another.

"Boo!" she says, taking her daggers out and slashing at him. He stumbles back, startled by her sudden appearance, giving Buttercup enough time to curl herself protectively around Ava.

"Shadow, get them out of here," I command. He doesn't hesitate. Opening a portal, he rushes forward, grabbing both Ava and the snake, and leaps through it. Ciaran stands back and watches as his mate spars with his half brother, arms crossed across his massive chest. A pleased look on his face.

Oisin screams in rage when Astrea manages to hit him

square in the face with her fist and blood gushes from his nose. She lets out a cackle as she moves to swipe his legs out from under him. He manages to dodge the attack and whirls toward where he left Ava. He growls low when he realizes she's missing, a primal fury painted across his face.

"You won't win this! Hell and Gothic Grove belong to me, whether you work with me or not, Ciaran!" He looks toward me and adds, "And that whore, Ava, will be mine." His power lashes out before Astrea has time to throw a shield up, sending her reeling backward. Ciaran pushes forward, throwing his own golden magic out, but Oisin snaps his fingers and winks out of existence, leaving the three of us in the road.

TWENTY-FIVE

The Knights guard the royal family.
But above and beyond that, they show who has control of
Hell.
— Personal Journal of the Royal Family.

AVA

Jackson paces back and forth in front of us, his anger sparking his magic under his skin like static electricity. His eyes keep shifting from silver to black and back to silver again. He arrived the moment Shadow closed the portal behind us, just minutes before Drago, Ciaran, and Astrea came barreling into the house. Drago made a beeline for me, while the latter two hung back a bit awkwardly.

"I can't believe that motherfucker tried to take you," Jackson seethes. "I can't believe he was just using me. He was part of the fucking Order the whole gods damn time." It's on the tip of my tongue to once again remind him that

Arcanna warned him, that even I tried to point out how odd his behavior had become after his time around Oisin.

Shadow shifts next to me, his thigh brushing my own, which is still peppered with blood and bits of glass. On my other side, Drago clasps my hand in his. They haven't left my side since we returned to our home on the bluff. I can't help but feel thankful for Shadow staying, but I worry that if he leaves the room, he'll be gone for good. I have to enjoy this time while we have it. I know Drago shares the same fear. I've caught him looking at Shadow out of the corner of his eye, as if he's ready to jump on top of him to stop him from leaving if he makes one wrong move.

Oisin returning has begun to fester in my chest, the anxiety of it slowly eating away at any peace I had. He was the man in my vision, I just hadn't realized it. The vision that showed me our world ending. That showed my friends leashed to him, and my mates dead. I haven't told anyone about it, not even Astrea, and the paranoia is rapidly encroaching on me. It's like walking through a haunted house, expecting him to jump out around every corner. Expecting that future to jump out.

Fuck . . . Astrea and Ciaran.

Both have stayed out of the way of my brother but haven't left yet, putting both my mates on edge, given the revelation Oisin dropped. Half brother? Fuck. Part of me feels betrayed, worried that Ciaran and Astrea played us all. That they have been biding their time. But the rational part of my brain also knows if he had wanted to follow through with Oisin's plan, he would have the moment he saw me. My silver eyes are a dead giveaway of who I am. But he didn't, he helped Shadow and me. So, I'm willing to hear them out, hear their side of the story. Sitting between both my mates, I let their scents wash over me as exhaustion tries to pull me under. Time has no meaning at this point, and a look outside shows only heavy dark clouds, as if the seasons, too, are trying to decide who takes over next. The air is thick with anticipation.

"When was the last time you guys talked?" I ask hesitantly, trying to keep myself alert as Jackson paces back and forth in front of us.

He scrubs his face with his hand, and I notice he looks a little ragged, his facial hair starting to show. "He was with me when I met with your mate, but even then, he was distant. He stayed by my side for awhile, but he became increasingly odder in his behaviors—I should have known something was wrong. Something was off. As soon as father died Oisin was gone." He lashes out suddenly, his fist connecting with the wall nearest. "FUCK." His whole-body trembles as he tries to control himself.

Jackson will never forgive himself for this. He will hold himself responsible for something that he could never have foreseen. I want to get up and comfort him, but the thought of losing the connection to Shadow and Drago, even for a moment, is too much.

"Jax, breathe," I say calmly. His back heaves a few times as he regains control before turning around and facing us again. I frown. "Where is Arcanna, Jax?"

Grief and anger flash across my brother's face before he catches himself. "Arcanna is gone."

"What do you mean gone? Where did she go?" It's almost unbelievable that Arcanna would have willingly left my brother, particularly if I was gone. There is no way she would have left him alone. . . Right?

Jackson squeezes his hands into fists before tapping his fingers across his thigh, an anxious movement he's had since we were kids. When we were growing up, my mother and father came down hard on him for his anxiety, so he adopted movements to help manage it that they wouldn't notice. He had gotten it more under control before I left, but seeing him now, he looks fucking tired. Others may not notice, but I can see it in his eyes, the weariness that slips through every now and again. The anxiety that bleeds into his silver eyes when he thinks we aren't looking.

"She went to The Forest. She took the position of Lady of Souls." He finally manages to choke out. His face holds pure devastation as a gasp is dragged from my body and eyes flare wide. My mouth drops open but he holds up his hand to stop me from talking, "I don't want to fucking talk about it. Drop it Ava." For the first time in a long time I regret leaving, now that I see my big brother, not the king of Hell, standing in front of me. It's easy to see the loneliness he's been holding, easy to see how it's all been so heavy for him to hold alone.

"Whats going on Jax? What aren't you saying?" My eyes dart down to his movements before he quickly stops them.

His face falls even further. "Hell is not doing well . . . The Knights have left my service. And creatures of old are waking. Someone or something broke the magic keeping them contained to their corner of Hell. Whole towns have been destroyed. People are afraid to go out after nightfall, and with the Knights gone, I have very few resources. The Order, or rather Oisin I suppose, have taken over the palace with the help of the Knights. I'm surviving, barely, with the help of loyal citizens."

"Fuck." The word whooshes from me as the seriousness of this situation settles into my gut like a lead ball.

"What are the Knights?" Shadow asks.

I answer first. "The Knights of Hell are demons who

serve the ruler of Hell. It means someone of the royal family is helping him, and we all know the only one who would do that. Tell me, brother, do you know where our dear mother is?" The anger is hard to keep from my voice. Jackson has always given our mother the benefit of the doubt, but me, I've always seen her for exactly what she is: a pit viper waiting to strike.

Jackson grabs the tumbler of whiskey in front of him and shoots it back before screaming, "Fuck!" and throwing the whole glass at the wall. The glass shatters, wet shards glittering as they fall to the ground.

"You've let far too many people manipulate you." Drago says, he doesn't bother hiding the judgement in his tone. "You need to find out who is loyal to you, Jackson, build your own court now."

Shadow clears his throat, interrupting us. "We need to address the other issue. Astrea and Ciaran," he says, his voice low. Shadow has kept some part of himself constantly touching me since we returned. My head still throbs from the hit it took, and without thinking, I let it fall onto Shadow's shoulder. He stiffens under me but doesn't move. Drago squeezes the hand he still holds, and I feel myself begin to relax into the contact of both my mates.

My body is struggling with the low magic I have, starting to shut down. Judging by the way Jackson is looking at me, he knows. His eyes narrow as he goes to open his mouth, but I give a subtle shake of my head. He stops but doesn't break eye contact with me for a long moment, before taking a deep breath and shifting to look at Drago and Shadow.

"Ciaran could have taken me long ago, and he didn't," I remind them. "I don't think anything changes; they are our allies."

Drago growls, his dragon rumbling, but Shadow speaks up over it. "I agree with Ava. They didn't have to tell me Ava was in trouble; they didn't have to help us. But they did. Ciaran has been like a brother to me. They are my family. At the very least, we need to give them a chance to talk with us and explain."

"While you all argue and scheme, you are ignoring the vital issue of Ava fading fast. Maybe we should get the interrogation over with?" Astrea's voice filters in through the haze of my exhaustion. Jackson lets out a low growl that Drago echoes.

I watch Jackson look Ciaran over, as if he is attempting to see any resemblance to Oisin. He crosses his arms, leaning back against the wall. "So, start fucking talking."

DRAGO

My new mistrust for Astrea and Ciaran wars against a feeling of allegiance to Ciaran for rescuing Shadow when I could not. I know Ava feels an almost blind trust for them. Jackson clearly doesn't trust them at all, and Shadow is . . . somewhere in the middle torn between his dragon's deep-seated need to protect his mates and his allegiance to his friend. "You have to understand, my mother had no interest in The Order. Kara went to Hell for information on the Harbinger magic. That's how they met. She fled my father as soon as she knew she was pregnant. Straight into the arms of Alexi. When my powers started to manifest, my mother knew I needed guidance."

"She couldn't do that?" Shadow growls.

It's Jackson who answers, though. "No. He would have needed someone who understood Hell's magic to help him."

Ciaran nods. "She had done her best to hide what I was. A half witch, half vampire was bad enough in her eyes. She had no interest in alerting people to my ties to Hell. But she couldn't hide me for long. Not from Alexi, anyway. So, she attempted to contact my real father, but he was long dead. Instead, we got Oisin." A shudder moves through the room, coming from Jackson, but Ciaran ignores him. "I have hated Alexi my whole life, so when Oisin spoke of creating a place where Alexi didn't exist and we ruled, how could I say no? I wanted power. It felt good to have it coursing through my veins, and I wanted more. I had spent so long being at the mercy of that asshole, I couldn't say no."

"How did I never see you?" Jackson interrupts. His face is haunted, and he's continued the tapping on his leg, a motion I'm not clear he realizes he is doing.

Ciaran cuts his gaze to him. "Oisin is smart. He knew if I came around, the illusion would be shattered. But in the end, it was my mother who ended up cutting him from our lives. She took my memories and locked my magic away. Kept me safe from him."

"So, what changed?" I ask, finally finding my voice. "You obviously managed to gain your memories back and not hand over the city."

He pauses, as if trying to decide how much he should share. "My memories flooded back the moment I found the family grimore on the coven lands. Everything was unlocked, except my magic."

"But you didn't go back to him? Why?" I ask, arms crossed over my chest.

Astrea nudges him with her foot, encouraging him to keep going. He glances toward Shadow, locking eyes with my mate. He goes to open his mouth but then seems to think better of it. A long sigh echoes out of him, and Astrea wraps her arms around him.

Finally, he admits, "Shadow was why I couldn't hand over the city. He was the first real connection I had. I realized what true friendship was, what true family was. When I pulled him from the aviary that day, I knew he was my family. He was who I couldn't live without. When I first encountered Ava, I felt a tug like there was a familiarity there I couldn't place; her silver eyes itching at those locked away memories, but once everything came back in full force, I felt no allegiance to Oisin. I had my mate, my brother, and my family." He gives a nod in mine and Ava's direction, and I am reminded of the friendship Ciaran and I have built over the years.

"But you must have told him," Jackson says matter-of-factly. "about my sister."

"When my memories came back, I already knew where my allegiance lay. I have not interacted with him since my mother cut us off all those years ago. And from what I saw today, he has held onto the delusion that I will be assisting him with taking over Gothic Grove even after all these years of no contact. I truthfully do not know how he knew where to find Ava"

Ava holds her hand up. "Wait, you spoke with him about his plan all those years ago, why not use Jackson? I mean they were already together."

"He believes that if he shows Ava at his side, he will crush the last piece of resistance. He had made a plan to 'purchase' her when the time was right. Knowing that Jackson would never be free to marry as he pleased and believing the 'chaste' princess was the key to winning over the citizens" "

Ava's anxiety picks up. The scent of it is overwhelming

to my dragon, and he shifts angrily under my skin. I don't have to look at Shadow to know he feels the same, but Ciaran doesn't stop. "All those years ago, he talked about discovering ways to harness your magic; he believed the answers to be in the grimoires and planned to create a powerful binding spell that would force you to bend to his will and be his for all eternity. It was his ambition in this area that actually pushed my mom to cut him off from our lives."

The room vibrates as Shadow and I attempt to regain control of our dragons at the idea of this happening. Ava grabs our hands, squeezing tightly to keep us under control.

"Why? Why did you wait to say anything? Especially after you knew who Ava was to me?" It is Shadow's voice that cuts through the tension.

"It had been so many years ago that even after I got my memories back, I figured he had failed in his plan. I didn't want to add another layer of stress, and truthfully we've been a bit wrapped in this. . . magic. Struggling with the darkness of it" He shoots a sideways glance at his mate that weariness creeping back into his eyes.

Astrea moves forward, the tension within me snapping, and without thinking, I launch myself between her and my mates, my dragon pushing forward, teeth bared, gold eyes blazing. Astrea rolls her eyes, but Ciaran moves up closer, eyeing me with a hardness I've never seen. His comment about the darkness reverberating around me.

"I like you, Drago, but touch my mate and I will slit your throat right here," he says in a low, feral tone. The room is thick with tension as I lock eyes with him. I feel Shadow slowly easing up behind me, the conflict in him evident as he shifts from side to side.

Astrea, to her credit, doesn't move, "For fucks sake,

enough male posturing. I'm sure you all have huge dicks." She looks over at Ava. "We might have a solution to your issue of recharging your magic."

"How?" Ava whispers, simultaneous to Jackson asking the same thing.

"We have been learning a little more from my grimoire, and of course Kallen has been helping us." Ciaran says.

"You are trusting that witch?" Shadow spits. "She tried to kill you and Astrea."

I can't help but agree with Shadow, but Astrea simply shrugs. "It wasn't my first choice, but Ava talked me into it." I cut a sharp look at my mate, who smiles sheepishly at me as Astrea continues. "The fact remains, Ava is vulnerable until y'all get your shit together. Which I'm hoping, after our chat, Shadow, you will have a different view on everything."

Ava and I both look at him, startled. "That's where you were?" Ava whispers.

"My dragon took us there. I had no idea until I shifted, and he shoved me back into awareness," Shadow says.

Jackson lets out a frustrated sound. "Tell us how you think you can help my sister," he demands. He sounds like a king, his power moving under his skin like something alive. It's the first time I worry about having the Harbinger in the room with him. Because Astrea may want to help my mate, but she is still . . . off. I look at Ciaran, who watches his mate carefully, and I hearken back to our previous conversation. Is Astrea still Astrea or is she more Harbinger?

"Simple. I feed her some of my magic," Astrea says.

"And how do you plan to do that?" I ask. "You aren't her mate."

She rolls her eyes. "That's accurate. But I can still give her a little boost. A recharge, if you will. At least, it'll give her a fighting chance to survive the coming days if Oisin discovers her again."

"And he will," Ciaran pipes up. "I had my suspicions about where the missing grimoires were, hoping that they had been taken by Alexi, but after seeing him and his power today, I am confident he has the remaining grimoires. I would even go as far as to say that he is behind the necromancy that we saw in Cordelia. It is only a guess, but he may very well be siphoning the magic of the coven members for himself. I know that the magic we saw from him today is not what he has possessed in the past. I know he wants this city, and he believes the best way to get it is to have someone of royal blood at his side." He pauses as he glances at Jackson, who glares at him, those silver eyes shimmering with rage.

"Gods," Astrea groans, peering around me to Ava. "What do you say? It's up to you, after all."   Ava doesn't say anything at first, doesn't look at either of us, but keeps her eyes locked on Astrea's. "Yes."

Shadow is the first to react. "No," he growls.

She shoots him a withering look. "You left. And you've made it perfectly clear how you feel about mating. So, I'm buying us some time while you figure your shit out." Her voice has a chill and determination to it that cuts me. So unfeeling and distant as she stands up and leads Astrea out of the room without a look back at us. Astrea, however, sends a smirk over her shoulder at us.

TWENTY-SIX

Balance will always be important.
It's why we created the balance between the Harbinger and
her mate.
It would behoove people to remember that in the coming
years.
— Carmine Family Grimoire

SHADOW

My dragon rumbles, demanding I follow our mate, demanding I mate her. But Drago grips my thigh, keeping me in place. His tattooed fingers splayed across my leg, dangerously close to my cock. The need for him to take me is overwhelming, to feel his body on mine and allow him to bite me again. With Ciaran and Jackson still in the room, it's too much. My skin crawls, and I need to move. Standing up, I walk over to the small bar next to the windows in the kitchen and pour myself some whiskey.

Jackson's angry voice penetrates the haze of my brain. "Your brother is slaughtering innocent people."

Ciaran looks bored as he takes on the king of Hell. "Hell is not my problem. That's yours. You are, after all, the king."

Jackson looks like he wants to launch himself at Ciaran, but I stop him. Praying to all the gods that I'm not wrong to be putting my trust in him, I say, "I believe Ciaran and I trust him. He could have betrayed us when his memories were restored and he chose not to." I think I see Ciaran sag with relief, only a brief movement before he's straightening back up.

Drago moves up next to me. "I feel the same." He squeezes my hand as we face off against the king, but Jax only rolls his eyes and instead allows some shadows in the corner to open a portal.

Moving toward it, he pauses for a moment, as if contemplating his decision to leave. When he turns back toward us finally, his face is etched with worry. "Shadow," he starts, "you need to mate with them. Whatever recharging shit the Harbinger plans to do is dangerous. For a multitude of reasons. Please, if you care for my sister at all, help her." He looks at me and Ciaran. "I'll be in contact." And with that, he steps through, leaving the three of us alone.

———

AVA

I twist my long hair around my finger nervously. The week's—no, month's events feel like they are finally crashing down around us.

Astrea flops down next to me on the bed. "You okay?"

I don't say anything for a moment. "Nothing feels okay. My body hurts, my magic is almost gone, Shadow left us, everything you and Ciaran shared . . . nothing is okay." Tears burn the edges of my eyes as the vision flashes again in my mind. I push it down, hurriedly trying to focus on the things I can control. Like taking the help Astrea is offering.

"I get it," she says. "But I'm here. You were there for me when I felt lost, you didn't judge me or push me. So, this is me doing what you did." She startles me by pulling me into a hug, her scent wrapping around me. I melt into her hold and allow myself to let go, just for a moment, to let the anxiety and fear bleed out in my friend's arms. A throat clears behind us, and I pull back to see Drago, Shadow, and Ciaran standing in the doorway, looking at us.

Ciaran's eyes are hungry as they take us in, but my mates just look curious.

"Are you okay, Rakkaani?" Drago asks, no doubt because of the tears streaming down my face.

"No, but Astrea can help with the magic, at least for now. So, that'll help something." I can't look at Shadow as I say it, can't give life to the fact that I'm doing this because he won't mate me. Drago keeps his gaze on mine, understanding flaring in his eyes, tinged by a sadness.

"So, what's the plan?" Ciaran asks.

Astrea moves a little further from me, giving me some space to pull myself together. "Well, as we know, Ava needs to gain magic by either feeding off her mates' magic or the ceremony by the priestesses. Lucky for us, Ciaran's mother had some knowledge of the ceremony and left it in the grimoire. It's similar to the magic Ciaran used to get me out of the prison, but Ava will get to feed off my magic."

"How do you feed it to her?" Shadow asks. His voice cuts me, a longing in me warring against the hurt that he's inflicted on me.

Astrea smiles. "Sexual release."

Shadow coughs, startled by the statement. "How does that have anything to do with giving her magic?"

"Because that's how a succubus feeds," I say, still refusing to look at him. "I can't feed without that. Even the ceremony that the priestesses perform is done during their heat cycle under the full moon. A time when sexual energy is at its highest."

"You're a witch," Shadow says.

I finally raise my eyes to catch his. "I'm half witch. But every royal member is a succubus." It hurts too much to hold his whiskey eyes on mine, so I quickly look back to Astrea. "I think if we do this, it just needs to be us with one other person, to watch . . . just to make sure I don't try to take more magic than I need."

A growl echoes from one of my mates, but I don't look at them.

She smiles widely, her eyes alive and glittering. Astrea has changed—when I first met her, she was so deep in her trauma, I worried about her survival. But now she's so similar to Kallen, it's worrisome for a different reason. She reminds me too much of the Astrea in my vision.

I glance at my mates. Shadow looks at war with himself. Taking a deep breath, I open my mouth. "I can't have you here for this, Shadow, I just . . . I need more time. You left, and we haven't talked about that."

Hurt flares from deep within him, the air tangy with it. He must move to leave, but Drago has a grip on his wrist. "It's not that I don't want you, Shadow, I want you more than I can say. But we have too much to say. And I don't think you'll be able to hold back from stopping this."

"And ultimately this isn't about any of you, this is about Ava and what she needs," Astrea says. Her snakes roil over her exposed skin, coming alive suddenly and ghosting off her body. Buttercup wraps delicately around my wrist in a soothing motion, and Onyx wraps around Astrea's neck.

It takes so long for Shadow to respond that I worry I've said the wrong thing, that I've pushed him away even more. But the tension in his body finally leaves and he nods. "I understand."

Nerves rattle through me now as I take in everyone around me, all eyes on me. Drago must sense my discomfort because he releases Shadow and stalks toward me. He cups my face in his hands and says, "You don't have to do this if you don't want to. You and I can complete the bond." I hear a sharp intake of breath and sense the moment Shadow leaves the room. Drago closes his eyes briefly and opens them again with regret swimming in the depths of blue.

"I won't do that to Shadow, and I know you wouldn't want to, either. This is a temporary solution until we can all talk. Everything fucking hurts, Drago. I'm exhausted. Being that fucking vulnerable against Oisin is something that cannot happen again. With Shadow obviously still in limbo, this is the best option. You can't protect me twenty-four seven; I have to be able to do that for myself, too."

He nods and plants a soft kiss on my forehead before pulling back and looking at Astrea and Ciaran. "So, the question remains, who stays and makes sure this goes okay? Me or Ciaran?"

"I think it should be Ciaran," I say, conviction in my voice. "Shadow needs you."

Drago's dragon surges to the surface, clearly hating the idea of another male being near me.

"No," he growls.

I glare at him. No, at his dragon. "You don't get to make

this decision for me. I am in charge of this. Not you," I snap. Astrea lets out a low, impressed whistle.

Drago studies me for a moment, the tension thick, before he nods. "I'll be right outside."

With his exit from the room, I'm left with Astrea and Ciaran both looking at me expectantly. "What do we do now?"

TWENTY-SEVEN

Little known fact:
The royal family of Hell aren't just witches.
At some point in their history, a succubus appeared in the
bloodline, creating a hybrid.
Now, this has translated into how the family is able to
replenish their magic.
— Mori Family Grimoire

SHADOW

My chest feels cracked open; I vacillate between wanting to vomit up the minimal contents of my stomach to so anxious I could crawl out of my skin. Neither is a feeling I'm enjoying. I stand braced against the countertop in the kitchen, as close to the knives as I'll get. The only acceptable thing I can use if I decide to escape this feeling, now that I've given up my razors. Their corpses lie in the bottom of the harbor now, far away from me. Every single one of them, even my emergency one that I had taped under the bed. I want to heal.

Or, at least, I think I do.

I pull a deep breath in through my nose and hold it for a few moments before I push it out through my mouth. I repeat this three more times before I feel Drago move up behind me.

"You didn't stay?" My voice is hoarse, like I'm one word away from losing it entirely out of fear of saying the wrong thing. Ava hit me where I was most vulnerable today, and while I can't blame her, I also don't know how to function in this space now that I'm trying to be "sober."

Drago's hands loop around my stomach, and I feel his head press against my back. His scent surrounds me as his heat presses in through the thin black T-shirt I'm wearing. It's a moment of vulnerability for him to hold me like this. I can feel his breathing is not quite steady, not fully under control. I drape my own tattooed and scarred hand over his and fiddle with his rings as another way to ground myself to this moment. To avoid my thoughts going to that dark space.

His voice is muffled as he speaks into my back. "She commanded me out. She commanded my dragon out." There is pride in his voice.

He slowly pulls back, his hands and body leaving my own. The cold feels like it's pressing in around me now as he comes around the counter. Eyes tracking to the knives, then back to me. He doesn't say anything.

"This is my fault." My voice is quiet in the kitchen, barely audible, but he still hears me.

"Why did you run?" It's the question I knew he'd ask, but one I wanted to avoid for as long as I could.

"An excellent question." Ava's voice comes from the end of the kitchen. "I can't go through with this until I talk with you, until I hear what happened. So, talk." She doesn't come closer, doesn't move from the spot. Just steadily watches me and Drago, arms tightly hugging her own thin waist.

I push off from the countertop and move around to where Drago stands. His eyes flare in surprise for a moment as I near him but soften when I loop my body around his, burrowing my face into the space where my mark should be. We stand quiet for a moment, the only sounds our breathing.

"My dragon took matters into his own hands," I start. "I was going to run anyway; I had no intention of staying and mating Ava or you. I thought if I wasn't here, you two would give in. You'd live a happy life without me." His body tenses under me, but I keep pushing forward. "When I woke up in the harbor, I was at a loss. All these feelings I wanted to avoid piled down on top of me. So, I gave control over to him. I let myself blink out of existence for a while. I had hoped that I would stay unaware, that he would put me in a cage for everything I've done. So, you can imagine my surprise, and maybe some disappointment, when I awoke to Astrea yelling at me."

I drag in a ragged breath. "She talked to me about how she lives with her darkness. How Ciaran helps her. How she doesn't push it away but allows it to coexist with her." I pull away from his chest finally and gaze into his eyes for a moment before I continue. "They helped me see some things that I wasn't able to see."

"What things?" Drago asks. His lips have moved closer to mine, and it's hard to focus on the words that I need to say when he's this close, when his eyes look hungry. Ava, however, keeps her distance.

"That, maybe, you both were right. The way to heal, or start to heal, is to stop denying myself happiness. I can't promise I won't struggle—I mean, fuck, I was standing here trying to decide if it was worth stealing a kitchen knife and hiding in the bathroom. But I want to try. I want to live."

Ava lets out a long sigh behind us, but I still don't look at her. "That's all I needed to hear." I hear her feet shuffle away and the door open and close again. But I keep my eyes locked on Drago's blue ones.

His mouth crashes into mine, the kiss so claiming I start to doubt whether my broken-apart soul wasn't just ripped from me. I let out a long whimper of need as his hands fist into my hair, his restraint gone and replaced with feral need. My own hands grapple at his shirt buttons until I can't take it anymore and rip them apart instead so I can feel his bare skin against my hands.

"I need you," I say into the kiss. A desperate plea for absolution in our intimacy. "Please."

Drago pulls away from me, grabbing my hand and dragging me down the hallway to one of the back rooms of the house. Pushing the door open, we enter into a rather average guest room, the walls eggshell white and a pallet bed on the floor. The lines are bright white. The windows open up to the backyard, which leads to the woods. The pine trees moving in the heavy wind bring in the scent of fresh earth and clean rain.

("Miracle" – Bad Omens)

"Kneel." Drago's command pushes through me, and I drop to the hardwood floor with no hesitation. I watch as he slowly pushes his pants down, his length bobbing free in my face. "Stay," he says as he moves behind me.

I don't allow my eyes to track him; instead, I keep them locked in front of me. But I can hear him open a drawer. I feel his presence move up behind me, and one of his hands tug my black T-shirt up. "Take it all off."

I don't hesitate and scramble to remove the shirt,

followed by the pants, before returning to my knees in front of him. The press of his hand has me falling onto all fours as cool liquid dribbles down my crack toward my hole. My muscles shake as I hold completely still while he makes sure to spread the lube around, before gently pressing the tip of his thick finger in. He stays there only briefly before I feel something metal.

"Fuck," I groan as the tapered end of the plug starts to push in.

"We'll get there." Drago laughs. "But first, I want you to be a sloppy mess for me. So, you are going to keep this plug in you while we have some fun." The plug finally makes its way past the tight muscles, leaving me with a satisfying feeling of fullness. Drago leans back, no doubt enjoying his handy work. "Tell me, Rakkaani, what is the safe word? How do we stop it all?"

"Red," I cry out as the plug starts to vibrate unexpectedly.

"Good boy," Drago purrs. When he moves back in front of me, his cock is jutting out from his body, the tip glistening. I bite my lip to avoid moaning as I watch him grip his hard length and slowly fuck his own hand. He weaves his fingers through my hair and pulls, dragging my face up to his cock and pushing himself into my mouth. I groan around him as he slowly thrusts in and out, saliva starting to pool around him and drip out. He tilts his head back as he gets lost in the feeling of my mouth.

"Fuck. You are so good at that." He picks up speed, his hand still holding fast in my hair. I let my hands creep up his thighs and take his balls in one of them, slowly rolling them in my palm, applying light pressure. He hisses and rips himself from my mouth, the spray of his hot release suddenly coating my face. "That was very naughty. I wasn't ready to cum yet," he growls. "On the bed, face down."

The command has me hurrying toward the low-lying bed and flattening out, my hard cock stuck under me. The plug continues to vibrate inside me, and when Drago cracks his palm across my bare ass, I bite down hard on my cheek to keep from cuming. He leans down, body heavy on mine, his breath hot in my ear. "You are going to pay for that."

AVA

I allow Shadow's words to settle into my body, allow the truth of them to penetrate my soul, and I realize I can't go through with this. I can't take the magic from Astrea. My body may need it, but it would cross a line I don't think I would come back from. Spinning around, I head back into the room, where Astrea and Ciaran are lazily cuddling on the bed. She offers me a sad but understanding smile.

"I know. You don't have to explain," she says. I give a small nod of confirmation and exhale a long breath, the action making me wince as it pulls on my likely cracked ribs.

Ciaran frowns. "You can't survive much longer, Ava." He pauses and looks at his mate, something passing between them before he moves his gaze back to my face. "Take some of my blood. You can heal and go show your mates who's really in charge."

I shake my head. "I think it'll be okay." The lie lodges in my throat, but I let it go anyway. Because, sure, I do think we'll be okay right now, but I can't say for certain that peace will last for long.

"Girl," Astrea's sharp tone interrupts my thoughts.

"Take his blood. You need to heal physically. I'm not taking no for an answer." She leaves no room for argument.

*I often wonder if it was a mistake to give Ciaran to the
Harbinger, given where he is from.
I know his half-brother whispers in his ear.
For all that I love of my son, I see a darkness in him that I
can only blame myself for.
— Kara Carmine*

DRAGO

**("THE DEATH OF PEACE OF MIND" – Bad
Omens)**

Shadow and I stand at the kitchen bar. Music slowly
filters in through the speakers. Neither of us say anything
and instead bask in the comfort that has fallen over our
home. Outside, the air has a bite to it. I breathe deep,
inhaling the scents of both my mates now mixing in the air,
and it shoots straight to my cock. Shadow's body still shows
all the marks of our time together, bruises and bites alike.

His eyes travel over my body, still hungry for the orgasms I denied him earlier.

Taking a sip of the whiskey in my hand, I allow my arm to brush against Shadow. The shivers that move down his body are intoxicating. My eyes to trace over him, his bare chest on display and my sweatpants hanging off his hips. The deep V cuts are begging to be licked. When I drag my eyes back up to his own, I see them flare a gold that matches mine. A hunger that can't seem to be sated. I lick my lips and smile, but a low, deep growl rumbles from his chest as his eyes snag on something over my shoulder, in the hallway behind me.

Turning slowly, I spy our mate. Ava walks out like the royalty she is, the scratches healed, her skin flawless and milky. She's wearing a black lace bustier that crisscrosses up her chest into a collar of thick black satin. The bottom of the bustier connects in more straps to matching lace boy shorts that fit firmly on her small figure. Garter straps hold up sheer thigh-highs, and a long sheer skirt hangs down, covering the back. Her pink hair is done in soft curling waves to the middle of her back.

The ravenous flames within me threaten to burn me alive as I watch her saunter into the kitchen.

AVA

Drago and Shadow take me in, both with equally hungry expressions painted across their faces. And I send a silent thank you to Astrea for convincing me to take her mates blood. "Are you both in or out?" I don't clarify what I'm asking. "This is the last time I'm going to ask. I can't keep hoping and praying for something that will never happen."

"In," Drago says without hesitation.

Shadow rakes his eyes across me before finally locking onto my own. "In," he responds. Tension that I had no idea even existed releases from my shoulders when I hear that statement. He may have made amends earlier, but I still worried he would go back on what he said.

Casually, I walk over to the couch that I was laid on all those years ago to heal. The men track me, not even realizing they've both followed me over, Shadow in front and Drago on his heels. I'm like a gods damn pied piper for dragons right now.

I sit down slowly, letting my legs spread just a bit, the sheer skirt shifting. Arms splayed over the back of the dark leather I raise an eyebrow at Shadow. "Kneel," I command. He drops down in front of me, head bowed. The power I feel as he doesn't question, just trusts me in this moment, is intoxicating. "Fuck, you look good like that. Don't you agree, Drago?" Drago only chuckles behind me.

I place my hand under Shadow's chin, tilting his face up to mine. His eyes are whiskey colored, not yet golden. I sense Drago come up behind me, feel his hands move down over my shoulders until they grip my breasts firmly. I let out a low moan as Drago pulls my hair back and kisses up my neck from behind, causing my legs to part even more and giving Shadow a view of my wet core behind the lace. No doubt, the smell of my arousal invades the room.

"What will it be, Rakkaani?" Drago murmurs as he pulls off my neck, only to place his hand tightly around it. My nipples harden under the lace at the show of dominance. The question is directed at Shadow, whose eyes seem to burn into us. Drago nuzzles at my face before licking me. Shadow's eyes track the movement. "Will you take her? Take what is ours?" The way he claims me for them sends bolts of pleasure through me.

Shadow's hands curl into tight fists on his thighs, the tension in his body clear. His eyes close for a moment before they snap open again, a brilliant gold blazing.

"Good boy," I murmur.

"Now, worship our queen, Rakkaani," Drago demands.

Shadow surges forward, ripping apart the lace panties I was wearing before diving into my wet pussy. I arch off the couch, the sensation of his mouth on me overwhelming. I had forgotten the feeling of him, how he consumes me the moment he touches me. He moans as he laps at me before focusing on my clit, slowly circling it and sucking on it. The sounds coming from me echo through the room as Drago pulls on my nipple one more time with his ringed fingers before his body moves away from me. I'm about to argue, but Shadow takes that moment to push his fingers into me, and I see stars.

The combined feeling of his rough fingers and smooth tongue sends me reeling, my whole body on fire with want and need. Looking down and watching his head between my legs has me clenching, but looking over his head and seeing Drago's expression as he watches us, stroking his hard length? Fuck, that has me weeping.

"Oh, gods. Yes. Fuck, you are going to make me cum," I cry out. But Drago leans down and pulls Shadow's head from between my legs, earning a whimper from me and a deep growl from Shadow. The normally submissive Shadow is gone and in his place is the feral dragon. The one who has waited far too long to claim his mates.

("Closer" – Nine Inch Nails)

"Don't you growl at me. I'm in charge. Not you," Drago scolds. "You know the rules." Dragging Shadow up by his hair, he smashes his mouth to Shadow's, licking my arousal off his lips before pulling back. "Jesus, she tastes good on you." He releases Shadow, whose eyes are glazed over with heedy need. Drago moves around the couch until he's standing next to Shadow.

"I think our needy mate needs to show us just how much she needs this," he says. I glare up at him before thinking better of it. He raises an eyebrow at me in a clear challenge. "That was naughty."

At some point between Shadow feasting on me and now, Drago removed all his clothing, and standing this close to me, I can see the four barbells down his shaft making a perfect Jacob's ladder. My mouth waters and I must whimper, because he smiles savagely.

"Show me how much you want this, Ava, choke on my cock while Shadow eats your cunt." I scoot forward on the couch as he moves to stand over Shadow, so Shadow has better access to my dripping pussy while I swallow Drago down. Before I can take him into my mouth, he grips my hair hard. "No cuming. The first time you get off will be with my cock in your pussy and Shadow's in your ass. Understand?"

I shudder, a fresh gush of arousal leaving me at the thought, but I manage a small nod.

Slowly, he feeds me his thick cock, my jaw already hurting due to his size. When he hits the back of my throat, I gag around him.

"You look so pretty with my cock shoved in your mouth." He thrusts hard into me again. "The perfect little slut for us." I moan, those words fire in my veins, making me clench around the empty air. It's at that moment that Shadow resumes licking me. The sensations are overwhelming, and I'm close to begging to be allowed to cum.

Drago's pace is relentless as he fucks himself in my mouth. "Shadow," he commands. "Take out your cock and touch yourself while you feast on our mate. But the same rules apply. We aren't finishing until we are inside her. I want her marked outside and inside." The words send me reeling, my cunt clenching and my body ready to fall apart.

I pull off his cock. "Please, Drago. Please, I'm so close," I whimper.

"No," he says mercilessly before pushing the head of his cock past my lips again.

I keep my eyes open, trying to watch both while sucking on his length, Drago with his head thrown back in a rare moment of vulnerability, and Shadow feasting on me while he viciously grips his own cock. My pussy starts to clench, and I know that one more lick from Shadow will push me over the edge. Drago must sense the shift because after a few more thrusts, he pulls out of my mouth, spit following his cock.

"Shadow." His voice is harsh and unwavering. He sits down next to me, his cock glistening with my saliva as it juts out proudly, the silver piercings glinting in the light. "Put her on me."

"Fuck." Shadow grumbles. "Gods damn." He lets go of his own length and grabs me around the waist, lifting my small frame and hovering my opening over Drago's cock. He starts to lower me down slowly, and I throw my head back against Shadow's chest at the delicious burn of stretching around Drago.

I whimper as he continues to push in. "I can't take both of you," I pant, suddenly panicking at the thought of both their cocks in me when Drago alone feels like he might split me in half.

Shadow doesn't stop trying to impale me on Drago.

Instead, he plants soft kisses on my neck and says, "That's it, you were made to take us, Rakkaani. Such a good girl." Before I know it, I'm fully seated on Drago. He thrusts up into me slowly, letting my pussy relax around him. Shadow continues his tender assault on my neck.

"I can't stop—oh, fuck, I'm going to cum," I cry out. My body gives up the fight, and my release barrels into me like an uncontrollable freight train. I dig my nails hard into Drago's flesh, causing him to groan and hiss. Nothing matters other than the feeling of my pussy squeezing his cock.

Drago stops pumping into me and swiftly pulls me off his hard dick. I cry at the loss of movement, the loss of him inside me. "That was very naughty. I told you to wait," he growls.

I whimper, desperate to have him back inside me again. "I'm sorry," I pant. "I couldn't . . . I couldn't stop. Please, just . . . fuck, I need you inside me again. Fucking please." The words tumble from my lips without any thought as to how I sound saying them. My mind is only focused on completing the bond.

Shadow's hands push me forward so I'm flush against Drago's chest. Warm liquid is dribbled down my ass, and I feel Shadow's fingers start to probe me, slowly pushing in to open me up. His fingers feel thick and overwhelming. Drago smiles when he sees me bite my lip. "Shadow, I want you to finish the claiming mark between us." Drago's eyes don't leave mine as he says it. The fingers in my ass pause for a moment before they are removed. I see Shadow move around the couch so he can reach Drago. His movements are jerky and uncoordinated, as though he's unsure. Drago tilts his head to the side, allowing Shadow access to his neck.

"Fucking claim me so we can finish claiming her," Drago growls. Shadow's golden eyes bore into my silver ones as he hesitates only a moment longer before striking into Drago's flesh. Drago spears me back down onto him in the same moment, and I scream as he thrusts into me roughly. His hands dig into my hips hard enough I know I'll be bruised tomorrow. When Shadow finally pulls off Drago's neck, his eyes are glazed over.

"Good boy," Drago growls. "So fucking good. Now, come fuck our mate and let's finish this."

Shadow growls, his dragon still in charge.

Drago's eyes flash, his teeth elongating. "Try that again." But Shadow backs off, moving back around so he's behind me, and as I feel the head of his cock pressing into my tight channel, I cry out.

"I can't . . ." I whimper. "It's too much." But Drago swallows my cries with a kiss.

"It's not. You're made for us," Shadow says again. "Just relax." His tongue licks up and down my neck, around that mark he left years ago.

He is slow as he pumps into me, letting me adjust in a way I don't think Drago would. "Fuck, you both feel so fucking good," Shadow whispers in my ear. "Rakkaani." The word is a breathy prayer on his lips. "I've dreamed about this for so long. You felt like heaven all those years ago, you feel even better now." My body melts at the words, allowing him to ease in the rest of the way.

I can barely breathe with how full I feel once they are both in me, but it's nothing compared to the feeling of the two of them once they start moving. I'm lost in the feelings of pleasure and pain, my head thrown back in a silent scream. Drago's piercings hit spots I didn't know existed. And feeling the two rub together between that thin wall inside me? It's enough to make my vision swim. I gush around Drago's cock, my pussy pulsing as I try to hold back the tide of my release.

The feel of Drago and Shadow kissing their respective claiming marks on my neck has me crying. Tears stream down my face as my magic pushes out toward them, the room around us enveloped in the soft red glow of it as the strings of our bonds form between us. We are nothing more than marionettes for each other. It's overwhelming to the point of feeling like I'm drowning. I can hardly catch my breath, the high so intense I almost back off, almost need a moment to ground myself.

I don't realize my eyes have been closed until I feel Drago's hands on either side of my face, his golden eyes locked onto mine in understanding. But Drago has always been our anchor, the person who keeps our ships safe at sea, so it's only for a moment that he lets me see that vulnerability before he locks eyes with Shadow behind me. Checking in on him. He gives a subtle nod, and Shadow's wrist appears in front of me.

"Take his blood, make his bond complete," Drago commands me. His eyes are wide as he watches me lower my lips to Shadow's wrist. The taste of Shadow explodes in my mouth, his power slamming into me. I must have screamed, because Drago quickly claims my mouth, before I feel Shadow pump harder into me, then his release coating me. He doesn't move, though. He stays in me as Drago pulls off my mouth and tilts his neck to the side, one thin claw slicing a small cut.

"Give us one more while you claim me," Drago demands. "I want Shadow to feel you."

I nod, my sweat-slicked body barely hanging on to sanity. Someone moves their fingers to my clit and begins stroking the oversensitive nerves. The room swims as my body attempts to adjust to the mate bond with Shadow, even as I lean forward and take Drago's blood into my mouth. When I pull back, the two bonds dancing inside me, the power vibrating through my body threatens to pull me under.

"That's it, scream for us, Rakkaani," Shadow says, uncharacteristically demanding.

My magic pushes out toward their dragons. While Shadow is rage and fire, Drago is control and death. The two balance each other. Both their dragons preen as they rub against my bond, while my magic wraps around them, branding them in silvery and red light

I collapse onto Drago, eyes fluttering shut. My energy is entirely spent. I feel Shadow slip slowly out of my ass before he lifts me off Drago's cock. He sets me down on the couch opposite them without a word and takes a seat next to Drago. The two watch me with hungry golden eyes as their releases seep out of me onto the couch.

Drago's eyes zero in on my pussy as his cum leaks from me before he looks back up at my eyes. "You need our magic, Ava."

Shadow grunts in agreement.

"We can wait," I say, taking in their faces. I don't want to make this about my magic. This perfect moment. "We don't have to do it now." But they both shake their heads.

"It's okay, Rakkaani. I know you need this, and we need to do this for you," Drago says.

Letting out a long sigh, I stand up and walk over to stand in front of them. "Okay, who wants to go first?"

"Me." Shadow doesn't hesitate. My heart warms and tears fill my eyes as I sit down on his lap. Cupping his face in my hands, I bring his lips to mine in a deep kiss. I slowly

pull, and his magic starts to flood into me, the feeling eliciting a moan. The taste is exquisite. A drug that I never
want to stop tasting. His magic tastes like smoke and feels
hot down my throat. My entire body ignites with the most
delicious sensations, the type that make me want to keep
going forever. My body feels alive for the first time in what
seems like a lifetime. Drago steadily stroking my back sets
my skin on fire, and when I finally pull off Shadow, I know
my eyes are luminous in the dark room.

"Beautiful," Shadow murmurs. It strikes me that this
might be the first time I've ever seen Shadow look peaceful.

SHADOW

Silence. For the first time in my life, I don't hear
anything in my mind.

I don't think about what I deserve and what I don't
deserve.

I'm not craving drugs or blades.

I'm just here. In this moment.

And it's absolute fucking bliss.

TWENTY-NINE

DRAGO

I glare at the man in front of me, his blood splashed offensively across my knuckles. The deep red stands out against my skin. I should be in bed with my mates, the bond grinds on me to go back to them. But my phone rang shortly after they fell asleep, my security informing me they had caught someone trying to break into my penthouse. So, now, I am in the basement with this piece of shit, attempting to interrogate him.

"Here's the thing," I say as I bring over a chair to sit on. Yellow light flickers overhead, illuminating the stained concrete floors and dark walls. The brown-haired man looks at me with both a small bit of fear and a lot of defiance, rattling the chains that hold him to the other chair, his arms looped behind his back at an uncomfortable angle. "I was having a very good night before this, and now that you've interrupted it, I'm going to need you to be forthcoming with the answers so we can all be on our way."

He spits blood at me, the glob landing on my pants. I look down at it with disdain before glancing back up at him, my power now surging through my veins. "I'm not telling you shit; I know who you are. You'll kill me anyway, so you can go ahead and do it now," he says, his voice annoyingly high-pitched.

I let out a long sigh laced with boredom. He's right, he is going to die, but up until that moment, he had the opportunity to die pleasantly. "I know Oisin sent you. I just want to know why."

He lets out a barking laugh. "You're a fucking idiot if you don't already know."

"He won't gain Gothic Grove, and Hell won't fall to him," I say, counting down in my head until I can get home and watch Shadow feast on my cum seeping out of Ava. Who knew that would be something I would love? Not me. But now that I know, I need it to happen again. Only this time, I want to be fucking Shadow as he does it. "So, here is the deal, Jeffery, let's try this another way since my time is running short." I let my power flow and push my compulsion into my voice. "Tell me Oisin's plan."

Jeffery, if that's really his name, struggles for a moment before my power overtakes him and he begins to spill all his secrets. "Lord Oisin is coming for his bride. Ava will help us take down the gates separating our realms. The Order will take control of Hell, and Gothic Grove will fall next." He laughs. The frown deepens on my face. "We have all the grimoires of the families. We have everything we need."

"Ava will never help you," I reply. "How does Oisin plan on forcing that?"

"The witches gave us a spell. She will be collared and leashed to him. Forever bound to be his puppet."

Rage envelops me at the idea of Oisin getting Ava. "And what of Jackson? You plan to just ignore the fact that he is king?"

My little puppet fights the words, but in the end, they fall from his mouth at my magic's command. "Jackson has lost."

My ability to remain in control snaps and I push my death power out as I grab the man by his throat. The lights flicker overhead as my power surges around me. True fear rushes through the man I hold at last as the shadow of my bone wings flashes behind me and he sees me, wide-eyed, for what I truly am. I feel my features turning animalistic, the fingers gripping his throat morphing into skeletal claw-tipped hands.

I lean in close to him. "People seem to forget what I am and what I can do because I live in this human suit all day. You think I'm afraid of Oisin? Or The Order? The magic they have is nothing compared to me. Shadow isn't the monster they should have worried about. I am." I snap his neck with a satisfying crunch and drop his lifeless body at my feet.

"Well, that was quick." Jackson's voice comes from behind me. "I thought for sure you'd last longer with him."

A growl erupts from me. "Didn't you hear him?"

"Yes. But I would have liked some more information from him before you killed him." He has a hardness in his voice as he looks at the corpse. I note a splash of dark blood on the white T-shirt tucked under his leather jacket. His hands, too, seem to be stained with the same blood. He's been busy.

"And the grimoires? Astrea's will be an issue."

A smile spreads over his face. "Let them try to use those. They can see what real magic looks like."

It's not the first time I wonder what Jackson might be capable of.

———

I SLIP BACK into bed in the wee hours of the morning. A smile ghosts over my face—Shadow and Ava are wrapped tightly around each other, a look of peace on Shadow's face that seems to have stuck around since the mating and Ava feeding on his magic. Allowing my body to curl around his massive one, I nuzzle into his neck, breathing in his deep aroma. He shifts slightly, rubbing his ass against my dick. I have to bite my lip to keep the moan from escaping.

"You smell like blood," he says, still clutching Ava.

A deep sigh comes out of me. "There was an issue. But it's been taken care of."

He tenses. "What kind of issue?"

I stroke the chiseled panes of his stomach before pushing my hand down and grabbing his hard cock.

"Don't try to distract me," he grunts, but he pushes his ass out harder into me. I kiss and nip along his shoulder and lick over my claiming mark on his neck, feeling his cock jerk in my hand at the sensation. "Fuck," he hisses.

"Mmm, it seems like you don't mind being distracted." I play my thumb over his slit, grabbing precum before continuing to move my hand up and down. "How quiet can you be, hmm? Can you avoid waking up our pretty mate while you fuck my hand?"

His hips buck into my hand, and I feel his body tremble as he resists the urge to cry out. I pick up my pace as I stroke him, continuing to lick and suck his neck. "That's it, Rakkaani, take your pleasure in my hand. Such a good boy for me."

He whines and begins to fuck my hand harder.

"Do you want to cum?" I ask. He moans and nods, but I bite down hard on his neck. "Use your words," I demand.

"Fuck, yes, Drago. Please, I want to cum so bad." His voice is no longer a whisper, and I have no doubt Ava is wide awake at this point, given the scent that is coming off her.

"Cum for me," I command. I feel the hot spurts of his release covering his stomach and my fist. Once I feel him start to relax, I pull my hand off him and bring it to my mouth to lick his salty cum off my fingers. "Fuck, you taste so gods damn good," I moan. "Ava, would you like to watch Shadow swallow my cock down his throat?"

I see her pink-haired head pop up over Shadow's body, her eyes glazed over with arousal and the last remnants of sleep. Her plump bottom lip is pulled between her teeth, and she nods frantically. I smile at her, and Shadow shifts his massive body up as I lie back on the bed. My cock juts out proudly from my body, and Shadow's stare is hungry.

"Be a good boy and show Ava how well you suck dick," I demand. Shadow doesn't hesitate as he envelops me with his mouth. I fist his hair in my hands and almost cry out at the feel of his tongue across my piercings. "Fuck, your mouth is sent straight from heaven." I thrust upward, hitting the back of his throat. The gagging sound he makes is music to my ears.

Glancing over at Ava, I see her slowly slipping her hand between her legs, but I shake my head. "Did I say you could touch yourself?" She whimpers. "Keep your hand away from that tight cunt. Come sit on my face."

Her eyes widen before she is scurrying into action, throwing her leg over me while her hands grip the headboard above. "Ride my face until you drown me."

"Oh, gods," she moans out at the first feel of my tongue on her wet velvet. "Oh, fuck. Drago." She begins to thrust her hips, and I alternate between pushing my tongue deep inside her and playing with her clitoris. I'm in absolute bliss as Shadow sucks me and Ava grinds on my face, the three of us lost in the sensation. Shadow's fingers start to creep downward, inching toward my hole. I shift my hips up slightly to give him better access and groan at the first brush.

I pull Ava slightly up off me. "You have until I cum to get off. And if you can't, you'll be waiting all day with that wet pussy begging to be filled." She begins to fuck my face with renewed vigor, my chin dripping from her enthusiasm. I push a finger inside her, gathering some of her wetness before I spread her ass cheeks and slowly probe with my fingertip. The tight ring of muscles gives way, and I finger-fuck her with slow, measured movements. I feel her muscles clench right before she floods my face and screams my name. My own release is not far behind, and pump after pump fills Shadow's mouth.

Ava slumps to the side, removing her delicious pussy from my face, and Shadow pulls my now soft cock from his mouth. The three of us lie panting, covered in sweat and cum, and utterly blissed out.

It's easy to forget that my mate isn't safe when we are like this.

———

SHADOW

"Shadow, you have to go to her." Ciaran's voice sounds pained as he begs. But I keep shaking my head no, the words failing to come out. It's been weeks since I last saw Ava, and my skin feels like it's crawling. As if tiny bugs are making their home directly under my skin, or searching for a way out. Ciaran shoves me into the wall, plaster cracking from the force of it. "She's your fucking mate, and you're leaving her to rot in my father's prison. You are killing her." His voice takes on a sinister tone before it begins to morph into one I know well.

"Worthless boy." My father's form replaces my best friend. "End this now. The world is better off without you." He pushes the blade into the palm of my hand, and sweat breaks out across my temples. My hand shakes as he continues to describe how terrible I am. How worthless. All the things that I already know and feel.

"Stop," I beg. "Please." The words tumble from my mouth even as I bring the blade closer to my arm.

("Gasoline" – Halsey)

My body shoots up from the bed, the dark room around me suddenly suffocating as I try to ascertain reality from the nightmare. My breath is heavy and feels too loud in my ears. The sheets that were once comfortable are now a jumbled mess around my body, mistaken for ropes tying me down in the darkness. I push my body off the bed, almost falling out of it as I rush to the bathroom. I barely make it in time for the contents of my stomach to end up in the toilet. I don't stop until it's only bile and my body shakes from the effort of trying to expel something that no longer exists.

They say drugs are harder to walk away from—that's a fucking lie. The Eufori withdrawals lasted a week, and since that time, I haven't wanted the drug. Sure, it's been tempting, but the thought of my mates in my bed has helped. But the craving to hurt? To see blood? That is something I can't seem to pull away from. Even in my dreams, the urge stalks me relentlessly. My palms itch and arms shake whenever my anxiety starts to take hold. Or when those memories sink their poisonous talons into my mind.

Eyeing the drawer to the left, I am trembling head to toe. My hand moves without permission, as if someone has taken control of my body, and I watch as it lifts the hidden blade, wrapped in tissue paper, out of the drawer. I had forgotten about this one, missed it when I purged the rest of the house.

With it firmly in hand, I flee to the one place I haven't been since this all started: the empty apartment Drago gave me. My portal opens to it, and stale air hits me square in the face. The air feels oppressive as I step in and drop to the ground.

Pushing back, I sit against the wall opposite where the fissures formed the last time I was here. I brace one hand on the cool tile floor as my body attempts to return to a normal temperature. The other is still holding the piece of metal relief I've been fighting against using. I eye it hungrily, the desire creeping into every pore of my body.

Just one. You can do one or even two and no one would know. Easily hidden or explained away.

"Fuck," I groan, dropping my head back against the wall and closing my eyes for a moment. The temptation is too great. I've never been good at resisting.

Drago and Ava have moved into their roles flawlessly, as if the past no longer exists and it's just us now. But I can't let go of the past. I remember every time I failed them, every time I chose to run to drugs or just run away in general. My mind refuses to allow me to forget the poisonous words that bled from me onto Ava and Drago all the times I tried to push them away. And no matter what I do, I can never forget the feel of my mother's body in my arms as she died.

No matter what Jackson says of her ghost, I cannot allow myself to forget or forgive the mistakes I made. Her blood is on my hands, the first kill my dragon and I ever made, and it wasn't the last. When I die, I know I will face a tribunal of angry souls whose lives I took gleefully. Whatever punishment they deem fit will be the price I pay for this life.

"Are you okay?" The sudden interruption startles me, and I look up to find Ava standing in front of me. Her eyes briefly land on my hand before they go back to my face. She doesn't wait for an answer before she invades my space, sliding down the wall next to me. "I mean, I suppose that is a dumb question. You're here at four a.m. having just puked your guts up. And you're holding onto that as if it's the only way you'll stay alive. So, a better one is, what is going on in your head?"

"How did you get here?" My voice sounds too loud in my ears.

"Ah, benefit of our bond, it appears," she replies as if that's enough. She rolls her eyes, "We share magic now, whatever you can do I can do to some extent. It's how the bond works between us."

For a moment, I don't speak, I just close my eyes and allow us to be in the same space together. "I was horrible to you."

Silence descends between us again before I hear her breathe out a long sigh. "Yes. You were. You pushed me away, and because of that, I got hurt." I wince at her words, but she holds up her hand, stopping me from saying anything. "I got hurt because you refused to mate me. I'm not talking about the physical wound, that wasn't on you. That was on Alexi. I'm talking about the fact that you claimed me on a dirty-ass mattress and then refused to bond to me fully. That is the hurt I'm talking about."

The look on her face is broken, a type of grief you can only know when you've experienced heartbreak of this magnitude. I have no words for her, no apologies I can give that will make amends. She blinks her silver eyes, clearing the emotion. "Shadow, I'm not going to punish you. You've done that enough yourself. I'm not an idiot; I see the scars under those tattoos. I watched you spiral. Whatever you did to yourself is worse than anything I could do right now." She scoots a little closer, her hand now resting over the tissue-wrapped blade. "Our past will always be here; triggers will always exist."

"So, how do we move on?" *How do I stop this cycle?*

She slowly slips the blade from my hand. "Shadow, you aren't walking through a minefield alone anymore. You have us. You aren't the same person you were days, weeks, months, years ago, as you dealt with all this shit. Cravings aren't going to go away, but cravings don't have to have the same power they used to." She pushes to stand, a halo of light appearing around her. "This thing only has power the longer you sit with those thoughts. The more you feed it, the bigger it gets. So, next time you feel like this? Come to us, first off, but second, acknowledge its existence, but don't dwell."

I shake my head, not understanding. *How do I acknowledge something but not dwell on it?* It's a monster in the closet, stalking me from behind the closed door whether I say it's there or not.

She smiles warmly at me, her eyes alight with love and understanding. "Imagine a leaf floating down a river. You see it, you know it's there, but you don't stop it. You let it float by. You aren't ignoring it. But you also aren't allowing it to build up and clog the river." She bends down and plants a kiss on my head, the move so tender it brings tears to my eyes. "Remind yourself of the times you didn't give in, like right now. Never forget the battles you've won." Her lilac scent wafts by me as she exits the apartment, leaving me alone again.

AVA

My hand shakes as I drop the blade into the trash can of our bedroom. My breathing is barely contained; I don't have to wonder what would have happened if I had walked into that bathroom a moment later. Guilt ravages me as I think about what will happen to Shadow if I execute my plan to stop my vision. I bite my lip hard to avoid the broken sob that wants to wrench itself from my throat. The metallic taste of blood floods my mouth.

The kitchen is barely lit by the early morning light, but I can make out the coffee pot regardless. The liquid is still piping hot from Drago having made some for his workout. I can't remember a time he's been in bed when I've awoken. He's either at the club or at the gym. Shadow, however, is normally always with me since we mated. Which was what made this morning so strange and had me rushing to the bathroom when I realized he wasn't coming back to bed.

Samhain flutters down to my shoulder, his beak pushing through my hair as he nuzzles into me. I scratch the soft feathers behind his head, closing my eyes and soaking up the calming effect he has on me. As I settle onto the couch, he flutters down next to me. I clutch the warm coffee mug like a lifeline, as if I'll suddenly be thrown into a typhoon of emotions if I set it down.

I know what I need to do now that I have my magic again. The idea came to me in the wee hours of the morning after we mated. But I can't bring myself to ruin the bliss we've created here. We've been mated for such a short time, I don't want to throw a grenade into it. I want us all to enjoy this peace. Yet, I know the longer I wait, the worse it'll be when it all comes crumbling down.

Setting the mug down, I stand and spy my cell phone where it lies discarded on the countertop. I grab it and scroll down to my brother's name, then take a deep, grounding breath before I hit send and bring the phone to my ear.

"Ava?" his deep voice rumbles, sleep coating it. I can imagine him lying in bed, hair messy, as he holds the phone.

"Jax, I need your help."

THIRTY

My Loves,
I know if you find this letter, I've called in my favor to my
brother.
I also know you may never forgive me for that.
— Ava

DRAGO

("SWEET DREAMS" – HANZO)

From the dark recess above the crowd, I hold court. Partially hidden behind black velvet curtains, I sit on my leather couch, legs splayed open and both arms thrown over the back of it. I look at ease with my surroundings. My white shirt is thrown open, revealing my tattooed midsection and the defined muscles from years of fighting. My white hair hangs untidy in my face.

I keep my eyes scanning the crowd, on alert for issues but also looking out for my mates. Ava and Shadow are down there someplace, one enjoying the fray while the other is most likely cursing our tiny hellion for wanting to be in the crowd. It wasn't my first choice to have her out on the floor, but something has been off about her, an anxious energy that keeps pulsing down the bond. So, I couldn't say no to her tonight. And Shadow would rather brave the crowds than allow someone to touch what is ours.

The movement of the curtains blocking the stairway pulls my gaze away from the congested dance floor, and I find my head of security walking up to me. Kai doesn't look imposing to the naked eye, but there is a reason he's managed to work his way up to being one of my most-trusted men. His dark hair and luminous yellow eyes give him an edge. I look him up and down. His black suit is pristine.

"The weather is getting worse; it's bringing more people in," he says in his typical flat voice.

I nod. "Make sure anyone who needs to get home is able to. I don't want my people in danger because of this fucking storm," I say, before taking a long drag of liquid from the tumbler in my hand. Outside the weather clashes, wind and rain pelting the streets in a maelstrom.

He nods, already sending out a text from the phone in his hand. "We have one more issue," he says, his voice uncharacteristically unsure.

I pinch the bridge of my nose. If it's flustering Kai, it can't be good. "What now?"

He rocks on his heels, as though he wants to be anywhere but here, delivering me this information. "It's Ava. Tren saw her take something from the stash. I, uh . . . I don't think she's sober."

("Promises (Skrillex and Nero Remix)" – Nero)

A long sigh escapes my mouth as I lean forward on my knees before standing and walking to the edge of the railed balcony. Looking down, it only takes a second for me to find

Ava—crawling up into one of the cages on the mainstage. She's wearing a black mesh bodysuit. Save for the patterns of dark snakes that curve over the most sensitive parts of her body, it's entirely transparent. Her pink hair is pulled up into two buns, one on either side of her head, and even from here, I can see the obscene amount of glitter she's plastered on her body. Cheers erupt from the crowd as they see her take the stage. But instead of entering the cage, she stays in front of the DJ booth, her hands suddenly producing flames that match Shadows.

"Shit," I mutter as she starts to dance in a sultry way, those flames licking over her body like a lover's tongue. The crowd goes wild as she dips and spins around, her ass on full display in the tiny bodysuit. Off to the side, I can see Shadow seething, his own flames practically spilling off him. She continues to run her hands up and down her body, those flames following her obediently. The DJ is living for it—he continues to pick up the beat of the song, throwing his hands in the air as the crowd screams. I continue to track her body as the song draws to a close, and when she meets my eyes, I know she sees the small tilt of my head.

"Get them up here."

SHADOW

("Movement" – Hozier)

Ava stumbles down off the stage to the cheers of the crowd, her face plastered with a giant smile as the flames, my flames, snuff out on her. Her eyes are glazed over from whatever she took before I hunted her down. She throws her arms around me before smashing her mouth into mine, and her taste is intoxicating now that it's mixed with the smoky taste of my flames. When she pulls off, I can see her pupils are blown wide and sweat is beading down her face.

"Drago wants us," she whispers before wrapping her legs around my torso, as though we are alone in our own world, and locking her lips on mine again. I manage to pull away for a moment, long enough to see Garrett open the side door for us to go through the back hallways up to Drago. Ava continues to kiss my neck, causing my cock to strain against my tight jeans as I maneuver the dark hallway.

Drago's scent hits me as soon as I enter his balcony. The scent used to physically hurt; now it feels like coming home. Ava giggles before she bites down on my neck, not hard enough to draw blood, but it still draws the attention of Drago.

"What the fuck did she take?" he asks as he takes in our tiny mate climbing me like a tree. Her body is warm against mine, her tongue tracing over the bite mark she just put on me.

"I don't know. By the time I found her tonight, she was already high." Moving to the couch, I peel Ava off me before placing her on the cushioned seat. Her eyes take a moment to focus before they lock onto Drago. A brief moment of realization flashes across her face when she suddenly understands how fucked she really is, given what she's done, but as quickly as it's there, it's gone again, replaced by a sultry smile.

"Hello, boys," she purrs, her hands now wandering over her body.

Slowly stepping into her space, Drago looks her over, his eyes calculating and assessing. "Hello, Rakkaani. Care to tell us what's going on?"

She has been acting strange for a while. It got worse

after our conversation in the bathroom the other morning. When she thinks we're not paying attention, she lets her mask drop, and you can see the worry on her face. Our dragons can smell the fear rolling off her in those moments, fear that we can't place to a specific danger. Her getting high only amplifies the suspicious behavior.

Flopping onto her back dramatically, she lets out a long sigh before a fit of giggles invades her small body. "I'm just getting to live. I mean, I've spent so long not living, I don't want to move on without actually living. You know?"

I frown, catching Drago's eyes. He looks just as confused as I feel. "Ava, what are you talking about?" I ask as I lean down, eye level with her.

Another dramatic sigh whooshes from her before she sits back up, eyes blinking a slow pattern. "I just wanted to know what it was like to be free. Truly free. It's why you do it, isn't it, Shadow?"

I blink once, twice, and then realize what it is she's on. "Eufori," I say. Drago nods as though he figured. "She must have popped it and not smoked it; otherwise, I would have smelled it on her." Drago only sells what you can smoke, but some people have put it in pill form and sell it illegally behind his back. It isn't safe in that form, often mixed with whatever back-alley drug they could find to keep the price of production down. While slower to get you high, it lasts much longer. Ava has never shown an interest in the drug; in all the years we've known each other, I have never seen her do anything more than drink occasionally.

Drago snaps his fingers, and Kai walks in. "Tren said he saw her take it from us? She took a pill—find out who put that in our stash and bring them to the basement." Kai only nods.

Standing back up next to Drago, I try to ignore the small

craving that weasels its way into me as I watch her high. That could be us. We could enjoy this together. Imagine how it would feel to fuck together while high. I try to breathe through the voice, breathe through the way my muscles tense and my airway starts to feel constricted. The cool hand of my mate squeezing the back of my neck wipes away the thoughts. The squeeze brings me back into this moment, brings my focus back to the one in front of me, who needs me.

"We should get her home," I say, watching as she taps out the beat of the song with her eyes closed. This close, I can see the glittering freckles she's painted on her face, the matching glitter in her hair. She looks almost angelic, until you take in the dark bodysuit that clings to her. Her pale skin glows—even when stuck in the prison, she glowed. Tonight, she looks ethereal.

Drago leans forward and scoops her up. She nuzzles into his neck, nibbling and licking up and down as he moves toward the lifts to bring us up to the penthouse.

"Are you two going to fuck me? I could use some dragon cocks in me," she slurs.

I snort. "The only thing you're getting tonight is a hot shower and water."

The pout on her face would be adorable if she weren't high out of her mind.

"Promise me," she whispers.

"Promise what, Rakkaani?" I ask, catching Drago's eyes.

"Promise me you'll forgive me."

DRAGO

As we step into the lift, Ava shifts in my arms and sends a devastating pout toward Shadow. I'm shaking with anger at this point, anger that she put Shadow in a position to be triggered, anger that someone gave her Eufori, but mostly anger that something drove her to get high and she won't share with us. But when she asks for forgiveness, the anger in me falters and I worry that the forgiveness she is asking for isn't just for tonight.

The doors ping, sliding open to reveal the penthouse. My feet move on autopilot toward the bathroom, but Shadow stops me and takes Ava from my arms, jerking his head toward the living room.

"Go. I'll get her in bed. She's not going to give us answers tonight," he says.

Ava is clearly going through something, and it's not fair to try to interrogate her now. So, I nod and watch the two disappear into the bathroom. The sound of the shower coming on followed by Ava's tiny yelp at getting dumped in has me smiling. Standing at the window, I look out over the city. My dragon huffs out an annoyed breath; it wants to stretch its wings. It's been a long time since it was allowed out to play.

"She's down." Shadow's voice pulls me from the window. Turning around to face him, I find him standing in a pair of gray sweats with no shirt, his dark hair still wet from the shower. "She's going to have one hell of a hangover tomorrow." He crosses his arms over his chest, those muscles rippling under his tattoos. The deep V cuts into his abs and dips down below those sweats, tempting me, oh, so much.

But instead of ripping those sweats down so I can lick his cock, I let out a long sigh. "Something is going on with her."

"That's obvious. The question is, what? She's never been this closed-off before. I'm worried," Shadow says as he walks over to me. Looping his arms around my body, he drops his head to my chest. The feeling is comforting, and the tension in my muscles melts away. "I'm supposed to be the mess. Not her," he says, quietly laughing to mask his anxiety.

My fingers dance over his back, tracing the raised scars under his tattoos. "You aren't a mess."

"Why was she asking for forgiveness?" he asks.

I don't answer him. The silence elongates as we hold each other tight, as if we are afraid letting go means the momentary peace we found in mating will be shattered and the world will crash down around us.

THIRTY-ONE

Shadow,
What I'm going to ask is incredibly unfair.
And I am so sorry for that, given how hard you've worked to
heal.
How hard you are still working to heal.
– Ava

AVA

("Exile" – Taylor Swift)

When sleep finally leaves me the next morning, my head is cracked in two. I barely make it to the bathroom before the contents of my stomach are heaved up into the toilet. I wait a few moments before slowly standing and grabbing the mouthwash. I don't bother looking at myself in the mirror. In the distance, I hear the coffee start up. Taking a deep breath, I make my way out to the kitchen, ready for my interrogation. Only, it's not Shadow or Drago standing there.

Astrea's long hair hangs loosely down her back, the waves messy and uncontrolled. Her curvy body is dressed in a sweatshirt and leggings. I watch as she rolls up the sleeves of her sweatshirt before turning around and offering me a smile. "I was wondering if I would have to drag you out of bed or if coffee would summon you."

I chuckle. "Coffee can summon me from even the deepest pit of Hell." She slides a steaming mug toward me. "What are you doing here, Astrea?"

She grabs her own mug and motions to the couch, where she sits down with her feet tucked under her. "Our mates were seemingly worried about us and thought some girl time was needed." It's the first time I notice that she looks exhausted, her dark circles matching mine. A heavy sigh flows out of her body before she takes a sip of the coffee.

"What's going on?" I ask, folding myself up in the chair opposite her. It hasn't been that long since we last saw each other.

It takes her a while before she responds, her eyes distant, looking out the large window across from us. "I think our families underestimated what it would mean for this power to wake." She pulls her green eyes to me. "They greatly underestimated it, Ava. The more I train with it, the more it takes hold, and I know Ciaran sees it. I'm worried it's going to take hold of me fully one day."

I don't say anything, because truly, what can I? That dark magic that flows through her isn't something any of us truly understand, aside from maybe Kallen. So, instead, I put my mug down on the coffee table and lean forward. "It sounds like we need a girls' day of movies and pizza."

She smiles sadly but nods in agreement. "You aren't going to tell me what's going on with you?" My heart breaks a little, desperate to let her in on why I'm so upset but knowing nothing good can come from sharing. "You know,

Hansley used to get like that, when she saw something. Something that scared her." I stay quiet, my eyes trained on the floor so she can't take anything from them. "Ava, in the end, that killed her. Don't make my sister's mistake. We can help, if you'll let us."

"Your sister was a Seer, so you above all should know and understand just why I can't say anything. One wrong word, one wrong conversation, and it can all go up in flames," I try to explain.

She shakes her head sadly. "If we can change it for the bad, why can't we change it the way we want it to go?"

"It doesn't work that way, Astrea, you know that. Please, please, don't push me on this. I'm already barely hanging on. I don't want to keep denying you this information. So, please, stop asking." My voice cracks, tight with tears threatening to pour over.

For a moment, I worry she won't let it drop, but in the end, she gathers me up in her arms for a hug and a promise that she won't push. For the rest of the night, she gives me what I've desperately needed: a moment's rest to forget what is hunting us.

———

AFTER THE EUFORI INCIDENT, we fall into a strange routine of fucking, working, and cuddling. But my anxiety is always there, clawing at me, demanding a way out. Astrea's words are also haunting me now. It's eating me alive, and I know I don't have long before I lose my mind trying to keep it all at bay. I can see why Shadow used drugs to deal with his emotions; it's easier than sitting in them all the time. Drowning in them.

Shadow and Drago rotate who is with me whenever I

work at the club, despite the assurance from my brother that the wards will hold. Drago doesn't let me return to his club, though he disappears often at night, coming home with cracked knuckles and blood that isn't his own. Shadow is always the one to go to him first, taking care of him alone. It's time I often wish I could intrude on, if only to spend the precious few moments I have left with them in their presence.

Drago must have left this morning only a few hours after he got in, the side of his bed long cold by the time I roll over and reach for him. Shadow pulls me against his bare chest instead, and I enjoy the warmth. It's these moments that make me endlessly thankful for how Shadow has evolved during our time together. He has developed a softer side, a side that he refused to have prior to our mating. Cuddling was something he never allowed before, and now, he can't keep his hands off me. This will make it so much worse when it all happens.

Tears threaten to spill as the intrusive thought pushes its way into my happy moment. It makes me angry, that my mind is refusing to shut the fuck up. Refusing to give me this. I'm giving up everything else, fucking give me this.

"You got tense, what's wrong?" Shadow's voice breaks through my thoughts. I go to open my mouth to pour out some excuse, but he covers it with his tattooed hand instead. "I don't want a lie, so if you aren't ready to tell me, don't say anything."

The breath whooshes out of me and I only nod. Neither of us say another word, and I can appreciate that. Because if he had asked me again, I don't think I could have held back.

THIRTY-TWO

Kallen,
Fuck, I hope this finds you. I instructed Samhain to give it to
you, but I can't be sure it made it.
I never thought I would be looking to you as someone to help
my family.
But here we are. I'm trusting you.
— Ava

AVA

("Dangerous Hands" – Austin Giorgio)

When we wake up the next morning, I slip quietly from the blankets, my skin feeling tight. I stand looking out over the city. I wrap my arms around my body, fingers digging into my sides. When Shadow's presence moves up behind me, my need to feel him overpowers me.

I spin toward him. "I need you." It's all I have to say. His eyes go gold as he drops to his knees. "You look beautiful on your knees for me," I whisper, my voice sounding like smoke. He licks his lips but doesn't say anything. I step back from him, dropping my satin robe so my naked body is silhouetted against the city landscape.

I watch the hunger flit across Shadow's face as he sees my sex bared to him. His eyes rake over my naked body, snagging for only a moment on that brutal scar before meeting my eyes. I back toward the couch until it hits the backs of my knees, then drop down on the edge of it. Beckoning him forward with two fingers, I spread my legs in invitation. "Crawl."

He has no hesitation as he follows my instructions until he is directly between my spread thighs. I lift his chin with my fingers. His eyes are still blazing golden. "In here, I am in charge. That means you do nothing without my permission. If I tell you to do something and you don't understand, you ask me." I stroke his black hair as I talk. "Do you understand?"

"Yes," he breathes.

I cock my eyebrow. "Yes, what?"

"Mistress."

A wide smile splits my face. "Good boy. And how do we stop if you need to?"

"I don't need that," he growls.

"You might not, but I do. I feed from your magic, Shadow. If things become too much, I need to know," I explain. "And if you can't do this, we won't ever be able to be alone. And I want time alone with both my mates. So, please. For me."

Shadow still has little to no regard for his own safety and self-preservation. I worry that part of him hopes I'll feed a little too deeply and he won't walk away from it. I know he isn't using Eufori anymore, nor is he doing self-harm, but coping skills like those do not go away overnight. He still talks in his sleep, still cries out for the mother he lost, still holds onto that blame like a scarlet letter.

The silence stretches on, those golden eyes never leaving my silver ones, an array of emotions passing over them.

"Okay," he says. "Red."

"And if you can't speak?"

He growls low. "My dragon won't let it get to that point," he says with conviction.

Narrowing my eyes, I debate on if I want to argue the point, but instead, I just nod. "Strip," I command. He does so without question, shucking his shirt off quickly.

"May I stand, mistress?" he asks.

I smile widely. "Good boy, asking. Yes. Stand and take your pants off. After that, kneel again." He moves without hesitation. His thick cock bobs out, and I salivate at the sight. Before he can kneel, I stop him with my hand splayed across the rippled muscles of his abdomen before taking his thick cock into my mouth. The salty taste permeates my senses. He groans low but keeps his hands at his sides as I take him in and out of my mouth lazily, fingers creeping up before I grip his hips hard and pick up the pace, fucking his length with my mouth.

"Fuck. Av—I mean, mistress, please. Please." He's begging so quickly, coming undone so rapidly. This Shadow is new to me, vulnerable and needy.

I pull off briefly. "What do you need?"

I watch his hands flex and realize he's holding back from fisting my hair. He wants to touch me. The bond in my chest purrs against his dragon. "Tell me, Rakkaani. What do you need right now?" I ask again, adding force to my tone.

"I need to cum down your throat, please. I need to fuck

myself in your face. Please, please, please." His begging is my undoing. My pussy is flooding down my legs.

"Yes. Take it, Shadow, you have permission."

His nostrils flare, no doubt smelling how turned on I am, and he fists my pink hair in his hand and shoves his length back into my mouth. His pace is relentless. Spit and tears streak down my face as I gag on him repeatedly. The whole time, I'm dying to taste his release. It doesn't take long before I feel him tense, but instead of cuming down my throat, he pulls out and covers my face in his release. While it was hot as fuck, he broke a rule, and the smile I give him is nothing short of savage.

SHADOW

I knew I was fucked the moment I made the choice to cum on her face. But I need the punishment I know will come. Since I stopped self-harming, I need something else to scratch that itch. And I'm running out of space to be tattooed. This feels healthier, like a way to get what I need while still facing what I've been running from. At least, that's what the therapist I've been seeing keeps saying. She calls it "harm reduction," a replacement of one behavior with another. Both might be slightly destructive, but one is less dangerous than the other.

She probably didn't mean allowing my mate to punish me with a crop, but I think I'm allowed to take some liberties with my healing.

"That was naughty," Ava says as she stands up. Despite the arousal I can smell dripping down her legs, her tone is harsh. She lashes out with her hand and squeezes my throat, pushing me back to the ground in front of her. For such a small person, she commands a room. She would have been a fierce queen, maybe even a better ruler than Jackson if she had been allowed. She squeezes slightly, her little nails digging into my neck. My eyes roll back in my head at the feeling.

She lets go and moves away from me; I don't track her with my eyes. Her presence comes back up behind me, and the soft feel of leather skates over my bare back. "Face down on the bed. Now." The command has me scrambling up, my limbs not moving quickly enough for me. Anticipation zips down my spine like electricity. The feelings war within me, the need to submit and the need to fight back pushing and pulling against each other. Like waves crashing against the shore.

"Remind me of your safe word," she purrs. I can hear her soft feet padding around the bed, pacing back and forth. If I could see her silver eyes, I know they would be predatory in nature. She's a lioness stalking her prey right now, and I offer myself up on that altar gladly.

"Red," I say, forcefully ejecting the air from my lungs as I eagerly give her what she is looking for.

"Good boy. Now count to ten." It's the only warning I get before the crop flies across my back, the burning sensation overpowering. Ava has two methods of punishment: edging or the crop. I've watched her in the club using the crop on people, not that she knew that, and every time, I wished it was me.

"One," I grunt. She levels another, her precision excellent. After four, I feel the familiar sting of abused flesh and the scent of iron. If my needs were the ocean waves, my blood is the tributary. My mind can get lost in this feeling.

Cock twitching and painfully hard, I must forget to

count because Ava is suddenly in my face, her eyes searching mine. "Check in." She strokes my hair gently, those luminous silver eyes full of concern and love.

"I'm good," I pant, desperate for her to continue. The sweet bliss that is floating away was in my grasp before she stopped, and I want it back. She pauses for a moment longer before nodding.

"You were at eight. Keep going."

By the tenth, my eyes are rolled back in my head, the sting making me grit my teeth.

She drops the crop on the floor and comes back into view. "You did so well, Shadow. Such a good boy, taking your punishment." I think I smile, but I can't be sure. My whole body feels light, everything floating and hazy. I don't even care that I haven't cum yet, my cock still trapped under my body. "Check in," she utters as her mouth moves to the shell of my ear.

"I'm good." The words slur from my mouth. Her hand stroking my hair has my eyes struggling to stay open, fluttering closed and back open again and again.

"I love you," she whispers.

"You two are certainly having fun." Drago's voice filters through the haze, but I don't move. My body feels boneless, and I don't want to lose this feeling, the one I constantly search for through pain.

DRAGO

("I Walk the Line" – Halsey)

The scent of Shadow's blood has me panicking for a moment when I enter our home. Years of finding Shadow on the floor in his own blood flash before my eyes. I rush down the hall, expecting to find him a mess, only to be hit with the scent of Ava's arousal, and his. Walking into the bedroom, I see Shadow face down, back covered in welts, Ava applying salve to soothe the red skin. His face is absolute bliss as she checks in with him. I can already tell he's lost and won't be coming down for a while. She strokes his hair gingerly as she whispers in his ear.

"Ava," I say. Her head whips to face me, eyes glazed with hunger. "Did you get what you need?"

She shrugs. "Yes. I wanted him to feel good. I achieved that." Lies. Such lies pouring from her pretty little mouth.

I stalk forward, slowly rolling each sleeve of my shirt up my arms, until I'm standing in front of her naked body. "You should know how I feel about lying, Rakkaani. Now, shall we try that again?"

Shadow slowly rolls over so he can watch us. Catching Ava's face in my hands, I pull her mouth to my own, devouring her in a kiss that can only be described as starving. She moans loudly. Her own arms encircle me, dragging me even closer. I feel the slow sip of her pulling from my power. It's an intoxicating feeling, it being pulled from me. Her body shivers as she attempts to hold back, trying to remain in control of the situation.

Pulling away from her, I step back and pull my pants down, taking my cock out and sitting down on the bed next to Shadow. "Ride me and feed. Now."

She closes her eyes, and I can see her trying to turn her brain off, to switch into a submissive role. After an eternity of watching her, those silvery pools open and she launches herself at me. Feeling my cock slip into her tight heat has me digging my hands into the sheets to hold back from cuming too soon. She rocks her hips and groans before dropping down to my mouth, and the moment she latches onto my magic with her own, I'm a goner. The room fades away to nothing and the only thing I can feel is her tight cunt wrapped around me and the pulsing pleasure of her drawing from me.

Shadow moves in next to us, hands running over my body as he slips one between us to rub her clit. She lets out a long moan, pulling off my mouth to say, "Oh, fuck me. Just like that." Her hips pick up speed.

"That's it, Rakkaani, fuck my hard cock," I tell her, and she opens her eyes, the silver now pools of starlight. She grabs Shadow's head and pulls his lips to hers, latching onto his mouth and pulling his magic into her. I feel her pussy convulse and her orgasm shatter through her, the hot liquid gushing from her and onto me. "You're soaking me," I groan as she rides out her release. After a few more thrusts, I let myself go and drive up hard into her until I'm filling her up with my own release.

But she doesn't stop feeding off Shadow. Instead, she lets my cock slide from her so she can straddle him. Sitting up, I push my dragon forward slightly and pull her head from his, separating them. Her silver eyes whip to mine, a savage energy swimming in them. She hisses at me like a feral cat, almost launching herself back at Shadow, who slumps back onto the bed.

I loop my arm around her waist so she can't move. "You're done," I say, my voice taking on my compulsion. Immediately, she shakes her head, looking dazed like she's waking from a dream. Then she quickly moves over to Shadow.

"Check in," she whispers.

"I'm good," he says. "You didn't take too much."

She seems to breathe out a sigh of relief and allows

herself to curl her body against him, and his arm wraps around her. Looking at the two of them, I'm hit with a deep foreboding. Because I realize now that if I ever lost either of them, I wouldn't be able to pull myself back from the edge of oblivion. And I'm absolutely positive I would take this whole city down with me. Maybe even Hell.

THIRTY-THREE

> *Drago,*
> *This will be the hardest on you.*
> *I know that.*
> *And I wish I could make it easier. Help you understand.*
> *All I ask—no, beg, is please don't kill my brother.*
> *He only did what he thought was best for our home.*
> *— Ava*

SHADOW

("The Grey" – Bad Omens)

I watch Ava shovel the food that Drago brought us into her mouth. Every time I move, my back pulls a little, sending jolts through my body again. Drago watches me with careful eyes. I just sip on the drink in my hand before taking one of the french fries in front of me and popping it into my mouth. He has taken his role of protector seriously, and while he worries about us, I worry about him. He's thrown his whole existence into protecting us, and I know exactly what that mentality can lead to. The all-or-nothing toxicity. I go to take another bite when Ava's drink slips from her hand, spilling onto the carpet as her silver eyes jerk to the corner of the room.

A shimmer of magic erupts into the room, and the scent of a Hellbeast invades my nostrils. My dragon pushes to the surface and fire wreaths my hands as I step away from Ava, putting my body between the beast and my mates. Drago lets out a growl, and I don't need to look to know those black veins are spreading up his arms.

The massive beast steps out of a shimmering portal, not unlike my own, a growl rumbling from its muzzle. I move forward to intercept it.

"Wait!" Ava shrieks, suddenly pushing out from between us before I can grab her. She moves up toward the beast, who lowers its head, dropping a thick envelope before it sits down on its hind legs. Its massive tongue, dripping that green saliva, lulls out like it's a fucking golden retriever.

"Ava," I growl. But she waves her hand dismissively as she reaches up and pats the great beast's head. Its black fur shines in the light, clean of gore and filth. Nothing like the beast that showed up at the apartment to take Astrea and Ciaran that day. That one had been a feral creature. Or maybe they are all feral, because its yellow eyes have a hint of savagery in them as they track our movements over my mate's head.

"Look at you, being such a good puppy, bringing us a message," she coos. I can't take my eyes from the dark green saliva in the beast's mouth, so close to my mate. That poison almost killed Astrea; without Ciaran, it would have. My body is coiled, ready to spring at it.

Drago lets out a long sigh next to me. "Ava, please don't make friends with any more dangerous animals."

She turns toward him and frowns. "I mean, it's not my fault Buttercup loves me." That is putting it simply. Ever since she was almost taken, Buttercup has shown up at random, the snake's smoky body appearing out of thin air. The last time, it happened while I was fucking her from behind in the shower. I did not appreciate that interruption and sent Astrea an angry text message about it after. All she did was laugh.

"What's in the letter, Ava?" I ask. Having the creature that close to her unnerves me and is putting my dragon on edge.

She pulls it open. "It's from Kallen." Neither of us say a word because it feels obvious, given she's the only witch or person we know who controls Hellbeasts. Ava's face goes ashen as she reads it. Fear trickles down the bond, followed by despair, before I'm cut off completely from her for a moment.

"What is it?" Drago asks, stepping toward her. "Ava?"

She takes a deep breath. "She's warning us."

I frown. "Of what, Ava?"

She nervously plays with her shirt as she looks at the letter, refusing to meet our eyes.

"What aren't you telling us?"

Drago moves in beside me, resting his hand on my low back as if to ground me here, as if he can see the nervous energy rippling through me.

AVA

My mates look at me with worry and an edge that tells me they won't allow me to walk away from this without giving them something. It's true, Kara showed Kallen the same vision I saw, but that future changed the moment I decided to call Jax. Or, at least, that's my hope.

"It's about Astrea . . ." I say and start to read that portion of the letter:

> Astrea is not doing well with the magic, and Ciaran is less and less concerned about it. I saw the future, Ava, I know what happens. We are barreling toward it every moment. I know what The Order has planned. I'm bringing Ciaran and Astrea back to pack lands. I hate to admit that we need to stay as a group. Particularly if we are going to avoid what the future holds. Drago will know where my mate's lands are; he is president of the Primal Knights MC.

SILENCE COMPRESSES the air around me before Drago's voice breaks through. "And what exactly is this future you've been hiding from us?"

THIRTY-FOUR

My Mates,
I love you.
I want to say more, but it's all falling apart as I sit here and try to push words out.
I know after today, you'll probably hate me.
But as long as you are alive, I don't really give a shit.
— Ava

AVA

Drago and Shadow spring into action, readying us to go to the pack lands as soon as I share a small amount of the future I saw. Drago makes sure Kai will have control of the club while he is away. Shadow refuses to leave me alone, as if he can sense the plan that has formed in my head. Knows what is coming next, and that him being constantly near me will make it all the more difficult for me to carry it out. None of this has helped the ever-present anxiety that continues to encroach on my soul. It's like a stain you can't get out of a white shirt. No matter how much I try to wash it away, it's still there.

Before Kallen's beast leaves, I send another letter with it, hoping she can pull off what I'm asking. I send a desperate text to Jax, asking for help distracting my mates, but his response is less than helpful. He says the best he can do is send a text to Drago to meet up, but he cannot leave Hell. He is hunting down the beasts of old. Elkers have begun to wake, creatures straight out of the nightmares of those of us who are from Hell. The Order has summoned them. I shiver at the thought, the screams I heard as a young child when my father banished them still a core memory.

———

IT'S BEEN two days since Jackson sent the text asking to meet up with both Shadow and Drago. Two days of chewing on my fingers and trying to disguise my anxiety and fear. I pace around my apartment, which they shut me in at Jax's suggestion, having been convinced that it was safer to leave me in these wards while they are away.

Samhain watches with his dark eyes as I pace back and forth, the judgment thick in his black gaze. "It's the only way," I grumble. He puffs his feathers up before shaking his head.

My pacing halts as Drago and Shadow enter the room.

"We'll be back soon," Drago says, planting a soft kiss on me. I breathe in his scent, knowing it's the last time I will. Tears prick at my eyes, but I shove them away, reminding myself I am doing this for them. It's the only way, the only way to save them all.

Drago pulls away, and Shadow moves in next, his eyes seeing much more than I want them to. "You'll stay here." It's a question and a command. I don't respond and instead plant a kiss on him, wrapping my arms around his solid body.

"I love you both," I say into his shirt. I can't look at them. I know Shadow will see through me if I do. So, when I pull away, I keep my face hidden in my hair and turn to flee down the hallway to my bedroom. When I'm in the doorway, I finally look back at them. The fake smile plastered on my face is one I used so often in Hell. "Come back soon so we can play!"

"We love you," Drago says as he turns to leave.

But Shadow holds my gaze, a frown forming. I blink rapidly and wave to him before shutting myself in my bedroom.

I give myself a count of five before I let the sobs rip through my body and I break apart, sliding to the floor of my bedroom. The anxiety and guilt that's been eating away at me for months is finally breaking free as the end draws near. The sounds of my cries echo through the room as I curl in on myself, desperate to catch my breath. I allow it all to flow out of me as I send my magic outward, slowly taking down the wards I have kept up for so long. Bit by bit, the magic cracks and fades away until nothing is left of the safety I've held so dear since getting out of the prison.

Taking one final breath, I let it go and stand up, my tears drying, spine straight. I move with purpose through my room, changing into leather pants and a crop top. My fingers are quick to braid my hair back and away from my face. As I finish tying it off, I sense the presence of magic and feel the rumble of the building.

I close my eyes, steeling my spine before taking a deep breath, summoning my magic up around me, and walking out toward the stairs to the club above. "Go to Drago and Shadow," I say in a low whisper to Samhain. He looks like he is going to refuse for a moment. "I can't let Oisin harm you, please." With a soft caw, he shoots off out the window high in the wall, just as I see the dark figure of Oisin meandering down the stairs.

My vision flashes before my eyes, reminding me why I'm doing this. I take another cleansing breath, clearing my mind of anything and everything that might give me away at this moment, and sending out a prayer that my mates will forgive me, that I'll see them again to beg their forgiveness.

("The Fighter" – In This Moment)

Through the darkened hallway, I see the broad figure of Oisin strolling in, casual and unbothered. "Hello, Ava," his dark voice purrs. "This is such a lovely club you have here." His black suit blends in with the inky shadows that shroud the hallway. He pauses across the floor from me, hands in his pockets, that one crimson eye assessing me. "You dropped your wards."

Please forgive me. I send the prayer out, then take another breath, closing my eyes briefly and shutting the Ava that is mated to Drago and Shadow behind a door in my mind. "I did," I say.

"Giving up so easily?" He moves a few inches closer, looking around my home. "I'm disappointed the dragons aren't here."

"I sent them away." The words taste sour in my mouth, and bile rises in my throat. "I wanted to talk with you, without them."

He narrows his eyes at me. "Why?"

I shrug, my best attempt at appearing nonchalant despite the action feeling wrong. "I'm tired of being locked up like a pretty little pet of theirs. Since you attacked, I've barely been outside." I move closer to him, closing the distance. I'm standing almost toe to toe with him now. So close, I can see his throat bob as he swallows.

"So, you called me?" he asks quietly as his eye tracks over my chest, my breasts dangerously close to spilling out of the top I'm wearing.

My heart hurts as I stand here. "Yes."

"I don't believe you." His voice is dangerous. Infused with the promise of pain.

Another shrug. "Is it so hard to believe I want power? My father had no interest in giving it to me. Jax is the exact same. You grew up with me, you know how it was. I don't want to be powerless anymore. Bring me with you, and I'll help you take down the gates and hand you Gothic Grove."

His eyes narrow again, head tilting. "Why? Why would I do this deal when I can just take what I want?"

"I'm a princess of Hell. You don't think I know things? Those grimoires you stole, that Cordelia provided you, they may be powerful, but they aren't me. You have me, and you get the Harbinger and your brother back. I am destined to be more than what those dragons want me to be, more than what my worthless father thought I should be. You are my best bet at achieving that."

He lets out a low chuckle, the sound radiating evil. "With me, you'll be a fucking queen."

He slams his mouth into mine, destroying what little soul I kept when I pushed the bond away. He pulls away from me, assessing me. Seemingly satisfied with what he sees, he snaps his fingers, and Cordelia appears. Her skin has a gray hue to it and the makeup she has on is doing little to cover the cracks in her skin as it flakes away. Necromancy is a dangerous business and not something that lasts long. I glare at her as Oisin runs his hand up and down my arm.

Lady Ornate steps out next to Cordelia. She looks smug until she sees the placement of Oisin's hands. It's easy to see she did not foresee me coming willingly.

Oisin's voice pulls my attention from her. "Ladies, bring your queen to her chambers."

He steps back and swings his arm toward the portal where the two women stand, bidding me to move forward. One more breath of my mates' scents, and I send strength up my spine as I walk back into Hell.

SHADOW

"Something isn't right. Something was wrong with her; we never should have left her alone," I say, my chest pulling tight. I rub my hand on it absently, back and forth, in time with my dragon pacing inside me. I shake my head. "This is wrong," I mutter.

Drago goes to open his mouth, when I hear the distinct caw of Samhain. Spinning around, I see his massive body looms in the distance—not his normal, small raven body but his truly massive size, only slightly smaller than my dragon. Panic bleeds off the familiar as he lets out screams that no longer sound like caws. No, they sound like a warning of death.

"Ava!" Drago yells, fear and panic in his voice, because we both know Samhain wouldn't leave her alone, wouldn't be searching us out, unless she was in danger.

I move to shift, but before I can, I'm hit with excruciating pain and fear. It drops me to my knees, stomach heaving and head spinning. Drago is somehow still standing, though barely, but breathing rapidly, his eyes dilated and his face ashen.

I am reminded why it is so costly to love someone this deeply. Because in my heart, in my soul, I know we've just lost our mate.

PART THREE

Into the belly of the beast.

There are many individuals who control death.
—Priestess Codex

AVA

Hell is almost exactly as I remember it, and yet entirely different. When I left here, I was young, naive, and all I wanted was to live in freedom. Now, I'm not sure who I am as I return.

Cordelia and Arcanna's mother dropped me unceremoniously into a spare bedroom as soon as the portal had shut. The room itself is bland, the only thing standing out against the dull creams of the wall is the grand four-post bed in the center of the room made of whirls of black steel, the ends coming up in jagged points that look sharp enough to kill. It's the most dangerous thing in here, and something tells me that is by design.

A fire crackles in the hearth on the other side of the room, illuminating a dark oak desk with two sitting chairs.

One or two books lay atop the desk, giving it the illusion that someone could study there. I move toward the armoire stationed next to what I can only assume is my bathroom, but with the door to it locked, I have no way of knowing. I guess they think I won't ever need to pee. Opening the armoire, I find nothing but slinky dresses and lacy garments that have me rolling my eyes to suppress the vomit threatening to come up. As I'm shutting the wardrobe, Oisin strides in, followed by two young women.

"Is the room to your liking?" he asks. His voice feels like oil on my skin as he surveys me from head to toe. That red eye gleaming with hunger and cunning.

I plaster on the fake smile I've learned to wear so well. "It's a little plain, to be honest," I reply, folding myself down into one of the chairs.

He lets out a laugh. "You always did have extravagant taste. Don't worry, after our wedding, you'll be moved into my wing, but for the sake of the kingdom, we need to uphold the idea that you are still a virgin. No need for them to learn that their queen is a whore."

The fact that Oisin believes that means he never knew me. Anger pulses through me, but I say nothing, playing the obedient pet. A role I've played well most of my life. I smile pleasantly but offer no comment.

Oisin seems pleased with my lack of response. He snaps his fingers, and another person moves into the room. "This is Harrowlena. She is a priestess in training, but for now, she'll be your handmaiden."

I hold back a gasp as I take in the young woman standing in front of me. Covering from the bridge of her nose down to her chin and halfway up her cheeks is a metal mask. Crafted to appear as lace, the contraption is held to her jaw via brass-looking screws. Her silver hair is bound back in a simple ponytail, revealing the device in its fullest. Her eyes remain locked on the floor in front of her bare feet.

Utilizing my distractedness as I look on in horror, Oisin plants a firm kiss on me that my entire body wants to revolt against. It's all I can do to contain my shudder of disgust, but he pulls back with a smile. "My staff will attend to you. You'll be dressed for dinner this evening to meet my subjects. They'll want to know their queen has returned."

He turns from me and calls, "Harrowlena." The young girl moves up next to him cautiously, her violet eyes finally connecting with my own as Oisin pets the top of her head. "Tonight needs to be perfect; make sure it goes off without a hitch."

She gives a nod of her head, those haunted eyes cast back to the ground as Oisin lets his hand slip down her waist before he moves away. The other two women stand in a row, silent. "These two will be at your disposal as well; anything Harrowlena cannot help you with, they will. They will come to me with updates on how you're settling in," he adds. The subtext is easy enough to read: These are my spies and you would do well to remember that.

"The young priestess will be more than enough," I counter.

But he gives me a patronizing smile and shakes his head. "No, no, only the finest for our queen. I'll see you tonight, my dear!" And with a final wave, he exits out the door he came through. It's not lost on me that the lock engages the moment he is out the door. He doesn't trust me, which is fair, but it will make my time here more difficult. I need to find those grimoires and get the fuck out of here. If I manage to kill Oisin, that will be a bonus.

I turn toward the silver-haired woman. "Harrowlena, is it?" I ask the priestess. She nods. The women behind her unlock the bathroom, and one begins to draw a bath while the other busies herself with cleaning and readying various cosmetics for the evening. I tilt my head in question at the priestess, my eyebrow raised. "And does that mask come off?"

"Your Grace," one of the women says behind me, "Harrowlena is not allowed to remove the mask unless his lordship allows it. She is a danger to herself and others without it."

I glance between the maid and the priestess, curiosity tugging at me. "And why is she dangerous?" I ask, not missing the way those violet eyes flash with a profound rage. Too quick for anyone else to notice, but the contrast between how meek she was with Oisin and that anger makes me think she is not as compliant as these women.

The other maid clears her throat as she exits the bathroom, the cloying smell of roses now seeping out amongst the steam escaping the room, immediately making me long for Drago's scent. "She is a banshee, Your Grace. Now, if you please, we must get you bathed and ready."

My eyes widen a fraction. Banshees are rare women, their powers passed down through a very select line. Stories of the power they hold claim they have the ability to level entire civilizations with one scream. It's why the kings of old hunted them down and destroyed most of them. I have certainly never met one before, nor to my knowledge has Jackson. I keep my eyes trained on hers before I offer her a small smile.

Before I can make a move to head toward the bathroom, an older woman with graying hair pulled up in a high bun walks in. The two young maids suddenly snap to attention. All of them wear the same uniform dress, simple black with a white apron around the waist. Each of the younger two has their brown hair pulled low in a bun at the nape of her neck. The picture of modesty.

The eldest clucks at me in what only can be described as pity.

"Oh, sweet dear." She delicately places her arm around my shoulders in a motherly fashion, pushing me toward the open bathroom. "I know how scary this is. Master Oisin told us what's happened, but don't worry, he'll fix you right up."

I clear my throat, unsure of the story he's given the staff. "What do you mean?"

She looks at me with sadness plastered on her face. "Those dragons took you. Your brother is trying to steal the throne. Lord Oisin told us how scared you were when it first happened. He was heartbroken when he found you and realized they had brainwashed you. But he'll fix it. As we speak, he's working with the Fairmore witch to counteract it." She pauses for a moment as she looks over at the younger girls.

So, that's the story he is giving, that I was kidnapped and brainwashed? A storm is brewing under my skin as she continues to talk. A storm that makes me want to rip Oisin's heart out of his chest and feed it to Shadow. Visions of my hands turning black as I feed him my mate's death magic penetrate my mind before I'm pulled back out of them by the older woman's annoying voice.

"My name is Pearl, and this is Ada." She points to the youngest one, who told me Harrowlena is dangerous. She has brown eyes to match her plain brown hair. She curtsies but otherwise ignores me and goes about tidying the already pristine room. "We'll be attending to you from here on out. Master wants to make sure you get to know us, so you feel comfortable. Oh, and of course, you met dear Harrowlena."

It takes every fiber of my being to avoid lashing out at

her. "And the other girl?" I bob my head toward the one still preparing for my bath. "What's her name?"

"My name is Elspeth," she says as she walks in with a pile of towels, back straight as if she's got a rod pushed through her. Unlike her counterpart, her eyes are a bright aqua blue that stand out against the brown hair.

"Your bath is ready, milady," she says briskly. The two girls move to strip me, but I bat their hands away with a hiss.

"I've got it," I say before I can think better of it. The smell of roses is starting to make my head pound relentlessly. All I've smelled is Shadow and Drago over the past few months, their scents grounding and calming. The roses make me want to throw up. I quickly begin to disrobe with the sole intent of dunking myself in the bath before fleeing, when I hear the sharp intake of breath.

Glancing up, the violet eyes of Harrowlena are locked onto the wicked scar that spans my belly. Her eyes flash up to mine, a strange look moving over her face before she schools it again.

Pearl moves in behind her, pushing the priestess to the side. "Those animals," she says, disgust woven into her voice.

"It wasn't them," I growl without thinking. *Fuck, fuck, fuck, I need to play this part better if I'm going to make this plan work.*

"Oh, dear. I know you believe that." She pats me on the shoulder before gently shoving me toward the bath. "That tattoo is atrocious, too. Oisin will hopefully get that removed."

I almost ask her what tattoo but look down before opening my mouth, and curling around my right thigh is the tattooed form of Buttercup.

THE WOMEN SPEND hours scrubbing and polishing every portion of my body. My patience is running thin as they chatter around me like gossiping birds. They remind me of my mother's help. I never hated my attending ladies at the palace, but they had never been mine. They were my mother's, first and foremost, meaning anything that happened was brought back to her. These women are no different, they just report to a different jailer.

When they remove the pink from my hair, returning it to the blonde I had as a child, it takes everything in me to hold back the tears. Whatever magic they've used has also forced the side-cut to grow out to match the length of the rest of the hair. The person in the mirror looking back at me is one I had hoped to avoid, golden hair wrapped up in intricate braids atop her head, a small golden crown tucked into it. It gleams with a red jewel in the center. My only saving grace is Buttercup on my body. She's kept the panic at bay. Though I have no memory of her planting herself on me, I can't help but let my finger stroke over her every so often in thanks.

Pulling my attention back from Buttercup, the older woman walks in with a blood-red dress. The younger girls rip the towel from my body despite my shout of protest and shove me into a red thong before they wrap me in the sheer tank-top dress. It flows long, down around my ankles and outward into a pool of red behind me. Next, they fix a golden collar around my neck, a leash attached.

"He cannot possibly mean for me to walk out like this," I say, taking in the sheer dress. Nothing is left to the imagination, my tits on full display, that golden leash hanging down between them. Ada walks over, holding a black lace cinch that she positions over me from behind, the boned piece of fabric covering my breasts and stomach. I can barely breathe in it once she is done lacing it up. "Ah, so he just expects me to suffocate for all of dinner," I mutter under my breath.

While the other women coo at "how beautiful" I look, I watch Harrowlena. She fidgets with her linen pants. All priestesses in training wear loose linen pants, with a bandeau wrap around their breasts and a long linen jacket over it. She is wearing cream, marking her position as high priestess in training. At some point, she put her own crown on, a golden sunburst similar to my own, and her long silver hair is unbound in loose curls. Her pale, almost translucent skin is unblemished in the areas that are exposed. But I would bet money she is hiding bruises and scars under those clothing articles.

She clears her throat in awkward response to my gaze, and I quickly school my features, returning my attention to the other women.

"Tonight, you'll be introduced to the court," Pearl begins. "You'll sit with His Grace and greet those he wishes you to. After that, you'll be brought back here. I'll be here waiting for you and will attend to you overnight."

"I don't need anyone overnight," I grumble, but she waves me off. I glance at Harrowlena. "Why can't she attend to me?"

Harrowlena blanches at my tone. But Pearl explains, "As a priestess, she is readying for the full-moon ceremony."

I frown at them. Despite not knowing the girl, there's something about the priestess that makes me see a kindred spirit in her. It makes me think I can trust her, and I would rather have her with me than one of Oisin's little spies.

"She'll ascend to high priestess once her first cycle

happens," Elspeth says. "She receives her instructions at night." My stomach sours and white-hot rage pushes through me at the implication. Harrowlena averts her eyes from mine, cheeks turning a deep crimson.

"Ladies, go ahead. I wish to speak with Harrowlena alone," I say, channeling my mother's voice and father's confidence. The three maids look uneasy, obviously stuck between my orders and Oisin's. "Do not make me ask again," I growl, allowing a little wisp of my power to push out. They scurry out, leaving me with the priestess.

I pick up the length of my skirt to keep from tripping over it as I head toward the door, pushing it firmly shut behind them. I don't turn toward the young woman as I start talking. "I'm going to take a calculated risk here and trust you. Trust that maybe we are on the same side. And maybe it's because you've got a fucking metal mask on your face and I'm in a collar. Or maybe it's because it's being insinuated that my soon-to-be husband is fucking you. But either way, I want you to know that I will do everything in my power to protect you." I finally turn and face her. "My brother talked about a priestess that he knew, one that was trapped in the palace. I think he was talking about you."

The girl's violet eyes take me in, raking over my body in a strange way before finally locking back on my own. She gives a small nod. The only confirmation I need.

"Now, let's go raise some Hell."

*We are the life blood of the young royals while they are
without mates.
Without us, the royal magic cannot be replenished.
Even with the Well, the rituals are unknown to all but us.
– Priestess Codex*

("FATE BRINGER" – In This Moment)

BEING the king of Hell should come with perks. It should be filled with parties, plenty of drugs and alcohol, and most importantly, beautiful individuals to keep you warm at night. It should most certainly not include being covered in fucking demon blood that smells like a rotting corpse. It also should not mean walking around in these gods forsaken sewers below my own damn kingdom. Although, truth be told, I think I prefer this to managing the politics that come with ruling.

Another Carnargion demon slinks from the shadows, its body barely formed before it's shooting out at me. Carnargion are the cockroaches of our city. They have little brains

and care only for their next source of food, which unfortunately seems to be me right now. I slash out with my sword,
allowing the black blade to pierce the demon in front of me.
Its shrill shriek of pain no doubt summons others toward us.

"Fucking Hell," I grumble. I need to get back above
ground. Reaver told me not to come down here alone, to
meet my contact anywhere else. Even went so far as to say
he would come with. His bulky six-foot frame of thick
muscle was intimidating enough even without his magic.
Reaver's rich toffee skin gives him away for being from the
southern part of my kingdom. He is powerful, the most
powerful of his kind. We met shortly after my sister fled and
Oisin disappeared, when he pulled me out of a bar fight and
refused to leave my side after.

An annoyingly handsome, tattooed, black-haired man
who is now the only family I have left. But did I listen to
my friend? To his insistence on coming with me? No. Of
course not, because I always have to be fucking stubborn.
Before I ran into all these demon scum, my plan was to look
around and then meet my contact, who's placed in the
palace right now, to alert her of my sister's impending
arrival.

When Ava told me her plan, including her vision, I
didn't want to agree. But in the end, she reminded me she
would go with or without my help. If I'm stubborn, my sister
is an unyielding mountain when she makes a plan. Now, I'll
have two people in the palace I need to fucking worry
about.

The shrill call of another Carnargion demon summons
my attention toward it, away from my anxiety around my
sister being subjected to Oisin. "Fuck this," I growl. I slip
my sword into its holder straight down my spine. My wings,
still tucked tightly against my body, under a glamor, brush

against the cool blade. You learn early on wings don't belong in a battle that is close quarters.

My magic pulses at my fingertips, crackling black lightning echoing over my body. A low thrum vibrates through the tunnel as I unleash myself. My power pulses through the inky blackness, liquifying everything it touches. Screams are cut short, the very essence of each being eradicated from all realms in a blink. In a matter of seconds, the tunnel goes silent, save for my heavy breathing. I wince as I feel my magic drain a little more.

A crack behind me has me whirling, pulling my sword from its sheath, my vision blurring at the quick movement after the drain on my magic. Through the darkness, a light shines, pure white light. The closer it gets, the brighter it gets, causing me to shield my eyes until it dims to a point that I can drop my hand.

I breathe a sigh of relief as I take in the familiar silver hair and violet eyes peeking out from the dark, hooded cloak pulled tight around the newcomer. Her slender hand holds a small ball of light tucked into the palm. It's been so long since I laid eyes on her, since she stumbled into the street races wide eyed and overwhelmed It had taken her awhile to warm up to me, and just when I had felt like I earned her trust she was whisked away again. It was a risk asking her to meet me today, but I had to try. Had to hope the start of our friendship had meant something.

She doesn't say anything, doesn't move to take off the cloak, and instead just stares.

Dropping the tension from my shoulders, I offer a smile and take a step forward. "I can't tell you how happy I am that you took the risk to meet with me," Her violet eyes track me as she gives me a slight nod. The only sounds between us are the drips of water and my echoing voice.

"My sister, she's coming into the palace. If she's not already there." When her eyes flare wide, I know she's already met Ava. "Please help her, help me. I know it's been a long time since we've spoken but my sister is good. She is everything I'm not."

I pause, breathing deeply. Waiting for her to either refuse or agree. Those violet eyes feel haunting as though she is stripping my very core away. Fuck, do I hate the position that she's in. Hate that she isn't out and free like she should be, I'll never forgive myself for not attempting to rescue her. She deserves so much more; deserves the freedom she was never granted.

The silence stretches on. That hood pulled tightly around her face only exposing those eyes. Taking a step forward, closer to her. I cock my head in question at what is going on?"

She shakes her head at me, still keeping silent. Dread pools in my gut alongside suspicion. "Drop the cloak," I command. She shakes her head, the movement drawing some loose hair into her face. "Drop. The. Cloak."

Still, she doesn't. Closing the distance between us in a move too quick to perceive, I'm in her face, my hand pulling at the fabric. A muffled shout of protest comes from her throat, but it's too late. I zero in on the torturous device affixed over her mouth. Crude brass bolts are screwed into her jaw, holding the piece of metal in place. There is no way for the mask to open. For her to talk or eat or drink.

Panic bleeds into my body as I look her over. As if sensing my alarm, she holds out her hand, pointing to a vein as if to show me this is where she gets hydration. I also see a very small hole in the mask at the base that would barely fit a straw. "I should have come for you," I say. My voice shakes, my power rumbles and skips over my skin. "I never should have listened to Oisin. I should have rescued you."

For a moment she seems to falter, eyes swimming with a strange emotion. Before she steps backward, away from me and the words I've spilled into the air. Pulling the hood of her cloak back up, she gives me a subtle nod, as if to confirm that she will watch over Ava for me. She backs away slowly until her body fades into the deepen darkness and I'm left alone with only my thoughts.

I stay in the tunnel long after she leaves, before I finally explode, and it all goes dark.

THIRTY-SEVEN

When the High Priestess comes of age she will learn the
magic to survive her heat cycle.
It will be passed to her from the previous High Priestess.
- Priestess Codex

AVA

I scan the crowd that has gathered in front of the dais that Oisin has us seated upon, all nobles that swore allegiance to my family at one time or another. They seem to believe whatever bullshit lies Oisin has been spreading. The first evening he introduced us, I hoped I would find an ally in the crowd, but no one has given any indication they see me as anything other than their new queen. I commit all of them to memory so when this is over, I can help my brother hunt them down.

Oisin stole our ancestral home in the heart of the city. The palace never truly felt like home, but now it feels even worse. The room we currently sit in is considered a VIP room, at the end of a lengthy corridor that leaves no space for threats to hide. Even if someone got down the hallway with ill intent, no one is allowed to leave before Oisin deems it appropriate. The first night he brought me out, I watched a young performer try to sneak away. Her body was incinerated the second she touched the wards.

Those are courtesy of the Mori grimoire.

Harrowlena is my only support, a silent presence that gives me reassurance whenever I start to forget why I'm here. But she's been missing for a few days now. Instead, I've been stuck with Pearl and the others. None of whom care to tell me where the young priestess is. After two weeks of being here, I can't bring myself to enjoy their company any more than I could the very first day.

I stare out blank-faced. Oisin sitting next to me is ever the picture of a devoted fiancé as he holds my hand. Acrobats dangle from the ceiling on silks, servers pass around food and drinks, people dance and sing and laugh. They seem willing to live in the bliss of being favored by Oisin as opposed to remaining loyal to my brother. A numbness has settled over me since coming here, and I fear the longer I stay here, the longer I'm away from my mates, the worse this feeling will become. Mates are not meant to be separated this long. Particularly mates of dragons.

I've slipped into the role of the pretty little doll so seamlessly next to him, not unlike what I did for my father all those years ago. Tonight, I've been dressed in a white wrap dress. The material crisscrosses over my breasts before it wraps down into a long, flowing skirt with slits up the side. My scar is on full display, painting a story of the savage nature of the dragons. It's a narrative I've been forced to sell.

"I can't believe what they did to you," a noblewoman

says as she sips her drink in front of us, her husband deep in conversation with Oisin, who keeps his grip tight on my hand.

"Mhmm," I murmur, bringing my other hand up to itch under the golden collar I wear. Once it was locked onto my neck that first night, Pearl refused to remove it. I can't help but picture my vision, and the collars my friends wore. When I questioned Oisin about it, he simply said it was his version of a wedding ring. The golden leash is always within reach of him. It's humiliating and uncomfortable.

"Ava." His voice is like oil and makes me feel sick. I look over at him in question as he pats his lap. "Come sit."

I pause for a moment, wrapping my head around the part I need to keep playing, before I stand and move over to him. I lower myself onto his lap slowly. His one hand splays against my bare midriff, while the other traces up and down my arm, his arousal growing with every moment.

"She really is beautiful," the lord in front of us says.

"And she can hear you," I snap. Oisin tenses, but only for a moment before he chuckles and plants a kiss on my shoulder. The lord looks outraged. After all, little dolls don't use their pretty little mouths to talk back.

"She is correct, she can hear you," he purrs. "My fiancée certainly has a tongue on her that I will enjoy putting to good use." The two laugh, and while I'm ready to rip him apart, I can only smile sweetly and lean back further into his touch. My stomach rolls with every moment his hands are on me, and as he continues to kiss my exposed skin, I have to keep swallowing the vomit down. They'll forgive me. I will get out of here, and they will forgive me.

"I don't know how you've waited," the other man sneers as his gaze roams over my body, pulling me from the mantra that feels more like a silent prayer now.

Oisin runs his fingers up and down my arm, a gesture that I loved from Drago. From Oisin, it makes me want to snap his fingers. "I have someone who keeps me company at night," he replies. Guilt moves over me at being thankful it's not me, because I'm certain it's Harrowlena he speaks of.

"Your Grace," a light-sounding voice sweeps in, disrupting his lips from polluting my skin.

Lady Ornate comes into view. Her white dress covers her from neck to ankle and flows out behind her. Her shoulders are decorated with gold embroidery and the long sleeves cling to her arms, coming into golden cuffs at her wrists. Atop her blonde hair, she wears a crown of golden whirls that has a mask attached to cover her eyes. If she were a true high priestess, she would lower the mask when she receives a vision.

She bows low in front of us. "Ah, Lady Ornate, thank you for joining us." Oisin motions for her to get up. Her eyes track him hungrily before sweeping to me, still perched on his lap. Disdain flashes across her features before she controls them. It's the first time I've seen her since she and Cordelia brought me to Hell.

"Of course, we wouldn't miss it." She steps aside and motions for Harrowlena to come forward. They've dressed her down to try and hide her beauty, but even in the plain beige dress and metal mask, she is radiant. Her violet eyes grab mine, and I try my best to convey my worry over not seeing her. I hope she is okay.

"Harrowlena agreed to accompany me tonight as well. As you know, her time is coming near, so I will be keeping a very close watch on her," she says as she keeps her eyes glued to Oisin. His eyes, however, shift directly to the young girl and seem to light up in wicked delight.

"Of course." He pushes me up and out of his lap,

forcing me to sit back in my own chair. "Come up here for a moment."

The girl doesn't move, her body frozen until Lady Ornate pushes her forward. She stumbles up toward Oisin, and from my seat, I can see her body trembling, as if she is holding herself back. Oisin drags a finger up her arm before he lands on her chin, tipping her face up to meet his eyes. "Yes, I can smell how it is near. Are you ready to receive the great honor of becoming my high priestess?" Oisin smiles. "I look forward to having you in my service fully." He gestures back to me. "Ava will, of course, be present to witness and participate, should I require it."

My entire body is vibrating with rage, so much so that I can feel Buttercup shift slightly on my leg. As if the snake is debating bursting off my body. "Tell me," I start, "how will she be doing all this with that contraption on her face? Surely, you can remove it."

The high priestess shoots me a withering look, but Oisin, as smooth as ever, smiles at me. "Harrowlena learned a very long time ago she cannot be trusted with the mask off. Should I need a warm mouth, you've already shown tonight you are more than equipped to handle it." The implication is clear as day. Around us, people shift and laugh at his bold statement. I can do nothing but sip on the sweet drink that a server handed to me.

Harrowlena bows and backs away from Oisin and me, her eyes catching mine again briefly. I hope I convey how sorry I am that she is in this position.

Oisin claps his hands. "So glad we are all getting along. Now that the high priestess has returned, we can move forward with the wedding." He rises to stand. "Friends! Family!" His voice booms across the great ballroom. "I want to thank you for coming to celebrate the return of my lovely fiancée these past weeks. It's been difficult these past few years not knowing where she was." Murmurs of understanding and sympathy ripple through the crowd.

Weeks without Drago or Shadow. I can feel my sanity slipping further from me every day I'm here. And I only have myself to blame, given I freely walked into this. To save them. To save Astrea and Ciaran. To save them all.

Oisin's drawling voice pushes back into my head as he grips my hand and pulls me to stand beside him. "But now that she is returned, we don't want to waste a precious moment in starting our new life together." He squeezes my hand tightly. "After all, we want to get a move on making an heir to the throne." Laughter bubbles through the crowd as if it's an inside joke.

Panic lodges in my chest at the words. Panic that I won't get out in time. I drink down more of the wine, hoping it'll ease the urge to vomit all over the dais. The liquid is strangely bitter now that I've reached the bottom.

"The invitations have gone out; in two weeks, we will wed. In front of all of you. What better way to celebrate her return to me and her family!"

Oisin steps back and grips me overly hard by the back of my neck, smashing his face into mine, his tongue worming its way into my mouth. Cheers from the crowd go up, and the wine threatens to come up from my stomach.

He pulls away, his hands lingering on my body. "But an early wedding gift for my lovely bride!" he shouts out across the cheers.

Someone moves up toward us as he turns back to the crowd, and shock ripples through my body as I take in my mother's face. She looks the exact same as when I left all those years ago, plus a few more wrinkles. Her ash-blonde hair is pulled up tight on her head, silver eyes mirroring mine above the sneer painted across her face, but only I can see it before she turns around and addresses the crowd with a smile.

"My sweet Ava has finally been returned. Now, we can work on joining our two families and place the one true king on the throne." If anyone had doubts about Oisin, they wouldn't with the backing of the former queen. I never should have come here alone. "Oisin has been the son I always wanted to have; he has been a steady hand in these dark times. The betrayal of Jackson murdering my husband took a heavy toll on me." Her eyes mist over, and I want to laugh at the audacity she has. "This will finally be over once Oisin marries Ava. Once she carries the next line. How lucky we are that she came home to us so willingly."

She looks at me with that last line, a wicked, cruel, knowing smile spreading over her thin face. My mother may be evil incarnate, but she is smart, she can read people, and judging by how she is looking at me, I know she can see how tense I am. My jig is up. There is no way she hasn't told Oisin I'm lying.

Terror moves through me, pushing me to run. As if sensing it, Oisin pulls me to his side, hands digging into my hips as he holds me slightly in front of him. "If everyone would please head out to the gardens, my soon-to-be wife and I will retire for the evening." He places a lingering kiss on my neck before licking the mating claim that Drago left. "After all, we need to rest up for a busy wedding night." The crowd cheers again, laughter echoing at his joke, and I see my own mother clapping and smiling along with them.

My head swims, and I stumble, the golden leash pulling taut as the party whirls in front of me. My mother moves forward, blocking me from the crowd as my body wobbles again. My limbs feel heavy and uncoordinated.

"What's happening?" I slur, my tongue and mouth refusing to cooperate. I can't seem to keep myself standing upright, and suddenly, I'm on my back on the cool marble floor.

"Oh, Ava. You never were bright. You really should learn to detect magic within things. A lesson neither you nor your brother ever truly learned did you?" Her wicked smile is the last thing I see before the world goes dark.

———

SHADOW

("I Would Die for You" – In This Moment)

Weeks. That's how long it's been since Ava was taken. Weeks of torment, feeling her down that bond until last night, when she was suddenly cut off from us, the feeling like a rusted piece of metal stabbing me in the heart. But that was nothing compared to the agonized scream of Drago as he collapsed to the ground, finally succumbing to all the feelings he had been trying to keep locked down. Whereas I've felt too much my whole life and tried to numb it out, Drago has always locked his emotions away, and the sudden cut off from Ava cracked that box wide open, flooding him with everything.

I push my hand into my pocket, feeling the crumpled-up piece of paper I've carried around with me ever since I found it, addressed to me. She knew what would happen if she was taken, and yet, she still let it happen. She knew how Drago would fall apart, and how it would be up to me to keep us afloat. Even if Ava hadn't left us those fucking letters, making me promise to watch over Drago, I still would be.

I look over to him where he stands in the frost-covered forest next to Astrea and Ciaran. His hair is a mess since he can't seem to stop pushing his hands through it. His normal dress pants and shirt have been discarded for sweats and a hooded sweatshirt. He looks beautifully wrecked, and it shatters my already broken heart.

We will get her back, my dragon growls. No argument in his tone.

I know.

Because there is no alternative for Drago and me. We either get her back or die trying. We won't be leaving Hell without her. Which is exactly why we find ourselves standing outside in the freezing morning air as we wait for Jackson to portal in. Drago had been hesitant to involve Astrea and Ciaran, but we don't stand a chance without them, which I reminded him of. He isn't happy about it.

Glancing over at the two, I can't blame him entirely. They are both different, their energy has shifted, even outside the fact that Ciaran hid being from Hell.

Samhain lets out a caw as he flutters down onto my shoulder, the familiar suddenly attached to me now that Ava is gone. Another caw echoes through the woods, which have gone eerily quiet. A warning. We all go on high alert, each pulling our magic up and at the ready.

The air shimmers as a portal opens in front of us, and I see familiar blonde hair come into view. Jackson is followed closely by another man with rich toffee skin covered in whirls of tattoos, and when his blue and green eyes lock onto me, I let out a hiss.

"*El Dador de la Muerte.* The Giver of Death," Drago

rumbles, and I don't have to look to see that he's starting to shift slowly.

A soft chuckle comes from the newcomer. "Hola, Drago." He nods toward me. "Shadow."

"What are you doing here, Dios?" I ask, my eyes bouncing between the two men. They seem oddly familiar with one another. Dios, or as most know him, *El Dador de la Muerte*, is part of the Primal Knights MC. Last we heard, he was Demon's sergeant at arms. What he's doing with the king of Hell is a worrying mystery to me.

Jackson steps forward, angling his body almost in front of Dios. "He's with me."

Astrea moves forward, Onyx snaking around her in his shadow form. Ciaran moves to grab her, but she brushes him off. "How do you two know each other?" She may not know who Dios is, but like calls to like. Her power would recognize someone similar.

Dios offers her a chilling grin, but it's Jackson who answers. "It doesn't matter. And he is helping us for now."

"Helping us with what?" Drago asks. His voice is low, but the fury and grief are thick within it. My heart breaks a little more as I watch my normally stoic mate finally start to crumble.

"Rescuing my sister," Jackson starts. "And getting my gods damn kingdom back."

"You're lucky we don't gut you right here," Drago says.

Jackson looks us over, cocking his head to the side. "Ah. Did she tell you, then?"

Drago lets out a snarl that is more animal than man and has me stepping forward without thought. "Drago." I cut him a sharp look, angling my body between him and Ava's brother before focusing back on Dios and the king. "She didn't tell us anything except that we couldn't kill you.

Which, as you can see, is testing the limit of control that we have."

I watch his fingers start to tap his leg before he shakes out his hand in a quick motion. Dios's eyes track the movement, too, and I watch the shifter lean in and whisper something. Jackson flushes and clears his throat. "Look, nothing changes. We need to get her out. That's all that matters—but to do that, we need to get you all into Hell."

———

AVA

("How Villains Are Made" – Madalen Duke)

Slowly, consciousness begins to take hold of my hazy brain, and I blink open heavy lids to see the canopy of my bed above me. I try to push up, but my body is having a difficult time responding. It feels heavy and sluggish. Almost as if I have strings attached to each limb, and they are pulled taut around me. Unease creeps through me. Once I'm finally seated and my head stops spinning, I look down at my body. No longer in the clothing I passed out in, I find my breasts are banded with white cloth and my legs are covered with a similar white cloth. I feel around my neck and meet the thick band of that golden collar, the cool metal smooth against my fingertips. The leash . . . I follow it with my eyes and see the end of it is now tethered to the bedpost.

"What the fuck?" I murmur. I move to get up, but my body still feels too heavy, still feels attached to something else I'm not seeing. As if I'm trying to push through water while the tide is trying to drag me out.

"Ah, you're awake. Finally." The dark voice comes from my left as the large door swings open.

Oisin saunters into the room, a smile across his face and

his one red eye gleaming. His long hair is slicked back, exposing the jagged scar through his eye. Despite all that, he is still objectively beautiful. Behind him, Harrowlena follows, her head bowed low, eyes focused on the carpet. Cordelia Fairmore comes in last, her body clearly rotting and hanging on by a thread. Her skin is mottled and gray, her once fine hair hanging in wisps around her scalp.

Instinct has me moving to stand, but my body still won't work, and my vision swims, making me slouch back down against the pillows behind me.

Oisin comes to a stop in front of the bed. "Ah, yes, the drugs might still be in your system. I did tell Cordelia not to overdo it, but . . ." He shrugs. "She doesn't always mind. You should be fine by this evening."

"What have you done to me?" I growl. "You drug and chain up your fiancée? I came to you willingly, and this is how you treat me?"

He keeps his hands in his pockets, smiling at me. "I was truly hoping you would come to me willingly. But your mother knows you best and doesn't seem to think you're here with altruistic intentions."

Stepping forward, he unchains the leash from the bed. The minute his hand touches it, my body responds, as if I have no control over what I'm doing, and that collar tightens around my throat. His lips pull up into a smile, the scar through his eye looking brutal in this light. My magic roars to the surface, toward him, along with the remnants of Drago's and Shadow's magic. His eyes roll back in his head, pleasure seeming to swim over his body.

"What the fuck is this?" Dread pools in my belly.

He plays with the chain in his hand before wrapping it around his fist. "It's truly remarkable, really. This little piece of jewelry will allow me to control you, including how you use your magic. The Mori grimoire offers so many fun little spells, this one in particular. So, you see, I don't need you willing. In fact," he adds wickedly, leaning down close, "I would rather you weren't. It's my magic now."

I command my body to rebel, to fight, but he continues to pull from me undisturbed. "The wine. You drugged it with this magic. It activated the collar," I say as it all clicks into place. My body goes cold, like all my blood has turned to ice water. *This is bad. This is really fucking bad.*

"Fuck, your magic feels good," he pants. I can see it now, shimmering around him in a red haze. His pupils are blown wide, and he bites down on his lower lip as his gaze travels over me. "I always had to be so careful with your brother when I drank from him. But you? Oh, Ava, we are going to have so much fun together."

"They'll stop you," I wheeze as my body weakens. "They won't let you open the gates."

He lets out a laugh, yanking me into his body. "While I would love Gothic Grove, that was merely a distraction. Keep my brother and his pesky witch occupied while I go in search of what I truly want. What you'll help me find."

The reality of the situation guts me as I understand just how fucked I truly am. "The Well," I whisper, eyes widening. "You're after the Well."

His grin widens. "Ah, you finally understand. With you, I'll have the magic to access it. And with your dragons, I'll have the means to keep away anyone who would want to stop me."

He drags his nose up my cheek, and I cringe inwardly, his touch burning. "They won't help you. They'll kill you."

"They'll help me because you'll ask them to. You'll demand they help your new husband. Demand that if they wish to stay with you, they'll bow to me. Serve me."

A low growl rumbles through my chest. "They'll know I'm not here willingly. You may have my magic, but they'll fucking know."

He lets out a laugh, pulling on the leash again, and my body responds. I have no control. "I think you'll find the performance very convincing." When he presses his lips against my own, I can't help but respond, my body betraying me to whatever magic is within this fucking collar.

*While most priestesses are simply witches,
every few generations, there is one born who is more
powerful.
— Priestess Codex*

(California Dreamin – Sia)

STEPPING into Hell is like walking into a disjointed time capsule. Horse-drawn carriages roll next to motorcycles. Cobblestones line the streets while electric lights buzz overhead. Signs flash, attempting to draw people into the casinos and clubs that line the streets. Individuals stand on balconies beckoning others into pleasure houses next to steampunk-style buildings. I can barely take everything in.

While Gothic Grove abstains from any color, it seems Hell is bursting with it. The sky overhead is a deep shade of red split with light hues of orange. Dusk is upon us, the time of day right before the sky transitions into a burgundy star-freckled oasis. The streets of Hell are abuzz with people and beastly creatures being walked by demons, witches, and cacodemons. All manner of individuals are busy in preparation for the upcoming nuptials.

I have to give it to Jackson, he dressed us well. We each have our part to play to blend in. Unfortunately, my part is the most uncomfortable.

Shadow and Drago wear matching black linen pants that are tight to their bodies. On top, each has a white button-down shirt with a dark button-down vest over it. Both their faces are covered by plague-doctor masks. Power rolls off them in waves, uncontained. It's intoxicating to be around. It also keeps people out of our bubble—citizens skirt around us the moment they hit that wall of power.

Glancing at Ciaran, I see him swipe his hand down the black shirt he has on before rolling up the sleeves. He doesn't wear a plague mask but instead has his face painted, black makeup streaked over his eyes and dripping downward. His blonde hair is pulled back in a braid, those runes shining bright. He is unrecognizable from his usual self, but looks the most comfortable out of all of us.

He would have been a good ruler, Onyx whispers.

I grumble as I pull a sheer black veil over my face, longer panels of it flowing down my back. The bodice is rippled leather that molds to my supple frame and has two thick straps holding it up. The skirt is multi-layered sheer black material that flows out long, covering the twin blades always strapped to my thighs. Onyx remains hidden under the skirts.

"I hate that I'm in a dress," I whine as Ciaran drags me into his body.

"You look good, kamerat," he whispers, sending shivers

down my spine and straight to my core. "Remind me to have you dress in this when we are home."

He plants a kiss on my temple before backing off and taking his place at my side, as a guard would.

"Let's get a move on," Drago grumbles, his muscular body pushing forward.

THIRTY-NINE

I worry for us.
The Order is coming, and they will not allow us to run.
— Priestess Codex

DRAGO

"Could they be any fucking louder?" Astrea grumbles with her arms crossed over her chest. She's changed into one of Ciaran's sweatshirts and a pair of black leggings. Her hair is now a mixture of black, red, and white, thrown into two messy space buns, one on either side of her head. It's a style Ava would wear. Fuck. Even thinking about her sends a jolt of pain through my chest, like a lance of fire burning in my heart. I rub at the spot, aware of Shadow tracking the movement.

The room at the safe house we arrived at is tiny, the four of us barely fitting into it but unwilling to separate. Ciaran nuzzles Astrea's neck. "Jealous, kamerat?" She blushes a deep burgundy, and he only huffs out a laugh. Astrea is a walking contradiction. At times, you can see that destructive magic rolling under her skin in thick waves, her eyes glazing over to the power, and at others, she is like this. Quiet, almost shy. More sounds echo upstairs from Jackson and Dios, making her roll her eyes.

"Do we have a plan?" Shadow asks the room, his voice attempting to cover up the sounds of Dios and Jackson next door. That had come as a shock, to realize the king of Hell and Dios were fucking. An odd pairing, but judging from the noises, one that seems to work well. "Or are we just winging it?"

Ciaran snorts. "I think we need to talk to Jackson and Dios; they are going to be a huge part of this. It seems pointless to plan without them."

I watch Astrea chew on her nail before her head tilts to the side, as if she's listening to something. Her eyes widen before she suddenly sucks in air as if she hadn't been breathing at all.

"Astrea?" Ciaran looks at her in alarm. She quickly fumbles with her sweatshirt, ripping it off to reveal her scarred body—along with not one but two snake tattoos.

"Buttercup," she murmurs, worry lacing her voice and fear decorating her face. "Ava sent Buttercup back."

Shadow surges forward. "What?!" Ciaran puts his body between the two out of pure instinct. I have to bite down my own rising panic as I clutch Shadow, pulling his body into mine.

"Is she okay?" I ask.

Astrea tilts her head toward some invisible voice again. "Ava went of her own accord, to prevent a future she saw. Jackson helped coordinate it. But . . ." She pauses again, listening. "Oisin was able to obtain a spell from the grimoire. He has placed a collar on her. When holding the leash, he has full control over her body and magic; he's draining her and is looking for something called The Well.

She was worried Buttercup would be controlled as well and didn't want to risk that."

My body is vibrating with rage. Her eyes look far off as she continues to listen to whatever that dark magic whispers to her. "Ava asked Buttercup to return while she knew she still had the ability to. She knew we would need her help." Astrea's face pales. "She believes he has other collars that he plans to use, but she has been unable to locate them, given she is now under his control."

The room goes quiet. Everything in me slams to a halt. Shadow grips my hand hard. "We need to get her out, now," he growls.

Astrea shakes her. "Buttercup says to wait. That until the wedding, she needs to stay in hopes she can find the grimoires."

"Bullshit!" I yell. "We are pulling her now. I don't give a fuck what she wants. That motherfucker has my gods damn mate and he's using her in whatever way he sees fit!" A plethora of intrusive thoughts ravage my brain. Image after image of all the things he could do to her play through in a slideshow of horror.

The words are barely out of my mouth before I lose control, then I'm nothing but a mist of shadow and darkness stepping into the bedroom where the king of Hell is lounging as Dios casually sucks his cock.

We will not allow them to gain access to the Well.
We will protect this secret at all costs.
Even at the cost of our own lives.
– Priestess Codex

CIARAN

"Stay here," I growl, despite knowing Astrea has zero interest in remaining behind.

Throwing myself out of the bedroom, I follow Shadow out into the hallway to come face-to-face with Dios squaring off against a half-shifted Drago. Darkness flows up Drago's skeletal hands and his face, partially shifted, looks like a macabre drawing. Behind them, Jackson's wings are flared wide, lightning crackling over his form as his eyes move from silver to black. As Shadow moves to intercept Jax from breaking up Drago and Dios, the entire room halts as I feel my mate's magic pulse over everyone.

"I've had about enough of this," she grumbles, stepping

forward. "Honestly, you are a bunch of children. This isn't helping Ava. Now, who wants to start talking so we can hurry this along and rescue my friend?"

No one says a word. Silence so thick you could cut it with a sword descends upon the townhome. My mate grumbles something that sounds like, "Fucking alpha asshats," before she and Onyx walk into the center of it all, Buttercup still tattooed on her body.

"Astrea," I warn.

She cuts me a withering look that communicates just what she thinks of the caution I want her to embody. "Ava has been placed under some magical hold. They managed to use a spell out of my grimoire so Oisin can siphon her magic and is in complete control of her through a collar," she says to the room. "That's what we discovered upon Buttercup's return, so now, who wants to go next?"

When Jackson doesn't say anything, I cock an eyebrow at him. "We know you helped her get in."

His bravado falters for a moment, and I watch Dios move closer to him, as if drawn in by the emotions he's casting out. He tucks his wings back into whatever invisible place they normally are and runs his hands through his hair. A low rumble from Drago has me eyeing him in the corner. "I said no at first. I didn't want her anywhere near this, particularly given she was what he was looking for. But she told me what she saw, and it was enough to change my mind."

Shadow crosses his arms over his chest. "What did she see?"

"The same thing my mother showed Kallen, I would imagine," I respond.

Astrea closes her eyes and sighs heavily. "I knew she was hiding something, but she wouldn't tell me. Most who have visions don't share them with anyone for fear of it either coming true or changing drastically. But fuck, I wish she had given us something." She looks to Jackson again. "She also said Oisin is searching for something called the Well."

Jackson goes deathly still, his power freezing on his body for a split second before he takes a shuddering breath to pull it back in. His tan face pales as if all the blood has drained from it.

"What is it?" I ask.

He casts a glance at Dios, the two seeming to communicate something silently before he looks back to us. "I'll get in touch with my contact, get us into one of the parties tonight. At least to get eyes on her. We can't just rush the palace; even with the considerable magic we hold in this room, that wouldn't go well." He looks toward Shadow and Drago. "It can't be you two going in to see her. I'm not having you do something idiotic that gets my sister killed. It's got to be Astrea, and just Astrea. He'll recognize the rest of us."

"We are getting her out tonight," Drago growls at the same time I yell, "Fuck that."

Astrea steps forward into Drago's space. "Look, I know you want your mate out. I get it. But if we do this wrong, we won't just be losing the opportunity to rescue her, we'll lose everything. Oisin will win, there is no question. I may not know the vision, but I know that much." She turns toward me. "And you can't go with me because he'll know you. If I go in, there is no way he'll have any idea who I am if I'm alone."

"That's a huge risk. He could know what you look like; plenty of witches do. Or what if Ava recognizes you and says something to him? You don't know how much control she has over herself at this point," I counter. Fear weaves through my body at the idea of sending her in alone, not because she isn't powerful enough to level that whole palace, but because I know if push comes to shove, she'll trade places with Ava in a heartbeat.

Shadow steps in, shoulder to shoulder with Drago. "We trust you, Astrea."

It's clear Shadow means it, but Drago pushes away from his mate, storming out of the room.

I just shake my head, feeling at a loss. "This is an awful idea."

"And it's the only one we got," she responds before turning back to Jackson and Dios. "Tell me what to do."

ASTREA

(Wicked (feat. Royal and the Serpent) – Tommee Profitt)

Standing in the security line of the royal palace, I keep my face as passive as I can without inviting anyone to try and strike up a conversation with me. I tuck my hands in the pockets of my high-waisted black pants, a gold belt clasped in the front. My dark jacket is casually resting on my shoulders over the sheer bodysuit I have on. Onyx and Buttercup have woven themselves into the bodysuit, each resting a head on my chest, covering my tits. All round me, people are in dresses of every variety, but I am tired of being caught in fights with a dress on, so on the off chance I must fight tonight, I wanted to be able to have full range.

"Name?" the man at the door asks, breaking into my thoughts. I plaster on a seductive smile, batting my eyelashes and twirling the ends of my long straight hair. His eyes travel over my body, and I see hunger flare in them.

Gotcha. Ever so slowly, I pull the invitation out from my jacket, making sure to brush it across my chest before handing it to him and purposefully allowing my jacket to slip off my shoulders, fully exposing my bare arms and the plunging V of the body suit.

"I believe you'll find everything you need in that," I purr.

He gulps and licks his lips before opening the invite. To anyone else, the small poof of dust from the envelope would look like nothing, but the moment he breathes it in, the magical compound swarms him. A wicked, devious smile steals across my red-painted lips.

"Am I free to pass?" I ask my new puppet. He nods, mindlessly. "Good boy," I murmur and pat my hand on his chest. "Walk with me, will you?"

I slip my arm through his as he whistles to another guard to take his spot checking people in. "Now, my little friend, what's your name?" I ask as he leads me toward the entrance.

"Kyle," he says blandly.

"Well, that won't do—it's, oh, so boring. How about Bartholomew?" He grunts his acceptance. Leaning in to avoid being overheard, I press my mouth to his ear. "Now, my dear Bartholomew, I would just love to meet the future queen. Do you think you can get me to her?" He nods, a groan escaping him at our close contact. "Wonderful! And if you are an extra good boy for me, I'll make sure to reward you."

Bart winds us through the outside of the crowd that has gathered in the grand entrance of the palace. Unlike Alexi's compound, this looks more like a nightclub than a palace. The room to the right is built like a casino: card tables and electronic machines attract all types of people as they are tempted to try their luck. A thick layer of smoke hanging over the entire room creates an enticing haze for people who might want to hide their devious actions. Another room holds a dance floor, lasers skillfully decorating the air above those dancing. Bodies gyrate in cages and on platform stages. And on every wall, there seems to be a bar offering up any number of libations.

I watch as a man does a line of white powder off the chest of a small female. Just beyond them, I watch a couple pass crimson smoke between their lips as they kiss. People laugh loudly as they push by, spilling champagne from their overfilled cups. It's the picture of hedonism.

We move up into the thick crowd that's attempting to move through the magic and metal detectors. "Bartholomew, I would prefer not to go through those. Be a gem and get us around that." He doesn't answer but gives a curt nod. He walks to the edge of the room, bringing me along with him, still on his arm, and flashes his badge when we reach the velvet ropes that keep people in line and security able to control the crowd.

"Need to pass," he says. The man who reads his badge looks between us, and I make a show of pressing my chest against Bart's arm. A bashful smile is all I have to give, and it's easy for the other workers to believe he's bringing me back here to fuck. The man in front of us smirks and jerks his head for us to move through.

"Hey, baby." He grabs my arm, pulling us up short. "Maybe after he's done, you come find me."

I take a deep breath in a desperate attempt to restrain myself from unleashing on him. I am once again reminded how men feel entitled to everything and anyone. Not trusting myself to speak, I simply smile and give him a wink before Bart drags me forward, bypassing the security that would surely have detected my daggers, hidden tonight against my lower back.

(Shadowboxer – Fiona Apple)

Bart pushes past the loudest areas until we are walking down a long corridor that has more cameras and security than I've ever seen in my entire life. Gods, Alexi didn't even have this much in his prison. It's not lost on me that if something happens, there is no plausible way I'm escaping back down this hallway. The path toward the VIP room is decorated with windows every other step. Some have people behind them, some have animals. It's disgusting. Every single one of them looks either high or deeply unhappy. The floor is a dark red marble that produces an eerie glow in the low light cast by golden chandeliers. In its entirety, it's unnerving and feels as if I've just fallen down a rabbit hole.

"VIP guests are brought in early. No one is allowed in or out until the end of the party once it begins." Taking a deep breath, I can barely scent the warding layered into the architecture around us. It's clever spell work, and now that I'm over the threshold, I'm trapped in its web.

Fuck. This was not part of the fucking plan.

Bart leads us through two giant golden doors that stretch from floor to ceiling. The scent of Eufori hits me immediately when I step into the giant room. My senses are overwhelmed as I take it all in. On the edges of the room, platforms stand just above the crowd with women dancing with fire, and every few moments, one blows a giant fireball. Coming down from the ceiling are acrobats who swing on silks and hoops, drawing the eyes of the crowd when they do something particularly daring. People are laughing and dancing, drinking, and smoking. In the dark corners, I think I even see some people fucking. It's everything one would think of the city of sin. And there, directly at the end of the long path we are standing on, sits Ava atop Oisin's lap.

("The Tradition" – Halsey)

I release Bart's arm so I don't drop him with the power surge as I see my friend with that gods damn collar around her neck. One of Oisin's hands wanders while the other is lodged firmly under her skirt. Her eyes hold a vacancy, the silver dull and lifeless. Her once pink hair is a muted blonde, the limp strands contrasting the vibrant hair of my memory.

"Miss?" Bart taps me on the shoulder. "Will you be needing anything else?"

Ripping my eyes away from the scene, I focus my attention on him. "When is this over?"

He shrugs. "When His Grace says it is." That was not what I wanted to hear.

"Okay, thank you, Bart. You can go back to your post, but remember not to tell anyone I'm here, okay?" I say sweetly. He gives a curt nod and leaves.

Taking another breath, I move toward the outside of the crowd. There is no way I can walk directly up to Ava, but I can at least get close enough to try to catch her eye. Ciaran had been against her seeing me, but I had promised Shadow I would do what I could to see how she was doing before I left, so I am taking a risk. A very fucking calculated risk.

Onyx and Buttercup vibrate against my body as if they, too, can sense just how risky this endeavor has suddenly become. Weaving through couples and groups, I finally land off to the corner of the great dais Oisin erected to hold the massive thrones. Casually, I grab a drink from a waiter passing by and push my free hand into my pocket. Taking a sip, I walk out of the shadows, allowing my eyes to move up to catch Ava's.

Her vacant expression guts me to the core. My once vivid friend looks as if her life has been sucked from her. Dark circles pop out against her skin at this proximity. The sheer dress they've put her in shows how much weight she's lost. Oisin is currently peppering her shoulder with sloppy kisses. I want to vomit and impale him on one of my daggers. Her silver eyes scan the room and when they land on me, it's the first flare of life I've seen. True fear passes through them. I hold her gaze for a moment, then two, before she leans in and whispers to Oisin.

"Ah, Harbinger, I was hoping you'd come." Without even looking at me, Oisin stops the whole room in one single sentence.

———

CIARAN

I watch the glittering lights of the palace from the rooftop Drago, Shadow, and I are perched on. My anxiety presses in harder every moment Astrea is gone past when she was supposed to check in. The plan was simple. She was to get in and out. No more than an hour. Certainly not for the two hours that have slowly ticked by. Jackson and Dios left after an hour, saying something about attempting to contact the person he has stationed within the palace. But it's doing nothing to help my fear.

"We shouldn't have agreed to this," Drago grumbles, all but ripping his hair out as he paces. "We should have just fucking stormed that place and burned it to the ground. Dealt with the aftermath later."

The clicking of a lighter pulls my attention toward Shadow. The zippo opens and closes every few seconds, as if to quell whatever is pushing through his system. I turn my back on them and walk back to the edge, peering down at the crowds that haven't dissipated.

"She should have been out by now," I growl.

A deep sense of dread fills me, choking the air from my lungs and turning my stomach repeatedly. I can't help but feel like we made a colossal error allowing her into that place with Ava.

FORTY-ONE

We met with the Lady of Souls today.
She was not provided the ritual, but she knows enough that
should they take one of the young, she could help her.
It kills me to write this, to know one of our own will be
without support.
— Priestess Codex

AVA

("Iris" – Tommee Profitt and Ruelle)

The world around me feels as though I'm interacting with it underwater. I'm aware of what's happening and yet unable to stop it. As though I've been severed from my physical form, I'm watching my body move without my permission. I miss Buttercup now; the desire to send her away was truly out of preservation for her. With the collar around me, I had no guarantee Oisin couldn't use her, or worse, access all of Astrea's magic through her. Sending her away was what needed to happen, but now I am well and truly alone.

I am their puppet, controlled by a golden leash, its influence leeching my will away with each pull of my magic. Oisin has pushed the limits of what he can do, and my body has bent to his every whim. It's as though I'm permanently in a state of dissociation. Apathy washes over me like thick oil coating a surface. I'm not sure I'll return from this. The fantasy of falling from the high window of my room flits through my mind regularly. I suddenly have more understanding of Shadow after these past few days. Frowning, I realize I don't know if it's been weeks or months since I last saw my mates. Even the grief of losing them has been cut off from me, drowning in that thick oil on the other side of that glass wall between my halves.

All around me, people laugh and smile, and I can't remember what that feels like at this point. My eyes move over the crowd robotically, until they catch a familiar head of hair, for just a moment. My heart skips a beat, causing the smallest of fissures in the glass, and feelings suddenly begin seeping through from that glass room they've been shoved into. It can't be. I drag my attention back to Oisin, who is allowing his hand to roam freely. Everywhere those fingers go becomes the path of a sickly fever burning its way through me.

Shifting on his lap, I feel the bone of my corset bite into my ribs. The gown I am dressed in tonight is objectively beautiful: the corset bodice is whirls of white lace with rose-gold patterns under it that bleed down into the white tulle skirt. A gold chain goes from the center of the breastplate up to a neck piece that covers the collar fully and flares out over my shoulders. The gold chain jets out across the chest to attach to the shoulder pieces, and off the arms flows more white tulle.

Tonight is our engagement party; we are to wed tomorrow. Fear, real fear, pools deep in me as it slowly trickles out of that small fissure in the glass wall that holds my true self back. Because despite attempting to change the future, I've still ended up here. Ended up dooming us all because Oisin now has my magic. And if I could, I would scream in agony, knowing what happens at the end of it all. Because no matter how hard I fought taking the path unknown, I am somehow still barreling toward an ending that will break us all.

When I turn to reach for my champagne, I see two green eyes looking at me, fear and anger and sadness swimming in them. More emotion pushes through that fissure, making it a full crack now as I take in my friend. Astrea. Relief courses through me, followed swiftly by deep, horrifying fear that the Harbinger has walked right into this place.

I feel it the moment he takes control, my body snapping up to attention, a puppet being pulled by its master. My mouth moves to his ear without permission. He sips off my magic like one would sip off a fine wine, before he lets out a low laugh. "Ah, Harbinger, I was hoping you would come."

("Shattered Dreams (feat. VE)" – Hidden Citizens)

The room goes silent, everyone turning to look at my friend, who has kept her eyes firmly locked on me. She looks sad, as if she knows I had no choice but to betray her. I want to scream, tell her to run, but my voice is locked down now; Oisin has me firmly under his control.

Astrea's magic unfolds around her, those two snakes

ghosting from her body to form next to her. "Give me my friend back." Her voice is hard, no waver, no fear.

Oisin smiles, shifting me off his lap. "You are in over your head, Harbinger. You are alone here."

Astrea laughs, the sound echoing through the room. "If you think I need my mate to help take you down, you're sadly mistaken." Her dark magic is all around her, dark mist weaving through her fingers. "So, this is your last chance. Give me my friend back."

The pull from my magic is instant as Oisin sends it out toward Astrea, and a cry is yanked from me as I physically feel the drain. It smashes into a shield of Astrea's magic, but Oisin just takes more and more from me, pummeling magic into the shield around my friend, trying to break through.

"You'll kill me if you keep going," I manage to say between gasps of breath. "I don't have enough magic." The glass wall cracks a little more, my true self pushing harder against it.

Astrea darts out from behind her shield, those two blades now in her hands, taking down anyone who crosses her path, as Onyx and Buttercup cut their own path of death through the crowd. At some point between when I last saw my friend fight and now, she's grown into something incredibly lethal that I'm not even sure my magic can stop.

An agony akin to starvation grips me, and I cry out. My magic rips through me near constantly now, emptying the space it should hold in my body. "Oisin! You'll fucking kill me!" But he ignores me, his sole focus on getting to Astrea, even as I collapse to the ground.

———

SHADOW

("(I Just) Died In Your Arms Tonight" – Hidden Citizens)

The air explodes with the scent of magic, both Ava's and Astrea's. A cold wave of dread moves through the three of us as we see people come running from the palace, and guards pushing to gain entry through the massive crowd.

"Astrea is using her magic. I can feel the pull," Ciaran says. "We need to fucking get in there right now." His eyes flare red.

I glance at Drago, who nods. His power pulses through the air as his shift starts. "You two go in and get them. I'll take care of anything out here," Drago growls.

"I love you," I say. "Don't do something stupid."

"I love you, too." His eyes turn gold, and his skeletal dragon breaks free, pushing from the rooftop and letting out a massive ball of black flames into the air before his roar rattles the very foundation of the rooftop we are on.

*I often wonder if things would have been different if I never
had visions.
If being a seer wasn't my destiny.
-Hansley Mori*

("The Devil Wears a Suit and Tie" – Colter Wall)

I STARE out over the crowd that's amassed outside what was once my home, eyes shifting uneasily. Since this fucking usurper invaded, it no longer looks like the space I grew up in. What was once vast and sprawling forest and gardens has been replaced by huge walls to keep people out . . . or to keep people in, it's unclear. Oisin has created a separation between the citizens and the royals that even my monster of a father never had. The wind shifts, blowing my hair into my face and bringing the scent of magic with it. The sky overhead crackles as if it knows powers are about to clash.

Somewhere in the crowd are our companions, anxiously

awaiting the return of the Harbinger witch. And even deeper in the crowd are the two that I brought in as back up.

Dios moves up next to me, the wolf shifter silent even on two feet. I allow my eyes to pull toward him briefly. "You got them settled?"

"*Si.*"

I let out a sigh. "I need your help with something."

He raises his eyebrow at me. "What is it you need?" His voice is rich and feels smooth running over my body.

"There is a woman. I need her out and unharmed when all this goes down," I reply without looking at him.

He moves closer, his scent washing over me. Bergamot. He sets me aflame with things I never knew I wanted or needed. All my life, I have been the dutiful prince, something I was happy to do, honestly, never questioning what my own personal wants and needs were. At least until meeting Dios. Until I realized what it might do to me to say goodbye to him. And I will have to say goodbye soon. He cannot stay here with me. For so many fucking reasons, he cannot stay here with me.

"Sending me in will deliver a message," he says simply, cutting off my train of thought.

I put a cigarette to my lips and light the end, watching the flame flare before disappearing, leaving nothing but the smoldering ember that I pull from. The smoke curls around us in a haze, clinging to us both. I want nothing more than to pull us back into that townhouse and get lost in his body again. I want to pretend that after today, nothing will change, and we will go back to this forbidden affair we have begun. That I won't have to be a king, and he won't have to be . . . what he is.

"*Mi cielo?*"

My heart stutters at the pet name he's come to use for

me. "I don't give a fuck what kind of message it sends. Let them understand what they've done siding with that fuck."

He lets out a deep, rumbling chuckle. Not one that inspires warmth but one that sends chills through my entire body. He's right, it'll send a huge fucking message when he's seen walking through those halls. I know I should care, should worry what it'll say about my reign as king. But truthfully, I'm not confident we'll survive the fucking night, so that will be tomorrow's problem.

"Who is this girl to you?" He pulls the cigarette from my mouth between his thumb and pointer finger and places it in his own, drawing the smoke deep into his lungs. His mismatched eyes glow as he looks at me.

Taking a deep breath, I pause, trying to decide how much to tell him. "Someone who I should have rescued long ago."

He looks at me pensively before giving a shrug. "How will I know her?"

"She'll have her mouth bound by a mask. You won't miss her. Trust me on that." Anger still radiates through me at what Oisin has done to her. Nothing survived in a five-block radius after she left me. My power incinerated everyone and everything before I managed to pull myself together. I had promised to keep her safe. That very first night I had promised, and I let her get dragged back to them, let them brutalize her into the female she is now.

"And if I encounter anyone?"

I know what he is asking. "If they aren't with us, kill them. Paint the fucking halls red."

Another wicked chuckle escapes him before he passes the cigarette back to me and stuffs his hands in his pockets. "See you on the other side, *mi cielo.*"

I watch as I send a devil of a different kind into a den of vipers, before dropping off the roof to the ground below.

FORTY-THREE

The Lady of Souls is a position of great importance.
And it is incredibly lonely.
-Priestess Codex

DRAGO

Rage flows through my bones. My dragon does not care who gets in the way.

We set the city on fire with our black flame.

Our skeletal wings push buildings over and our roar shatters glass.

Our goal is simple: Bring this city down. Make it impossible for any reinforcements to gain entry.

———

AVA

("Me and the Devil" – Soap&Skin)

The walls of the palace shake, the cold glass almost

cracking as a roar deafens us. A roar that I would know anywhere. *Drago. My mate.*

Screams can be heard echoing throughout the halls. Astrea has left a trail of bodies in her wake as she has held her own against Oisin, against me. But I can see her energy waning, see that she is holding onto her mind the best she can.

"You can't keep this up forever!" Oisin yells.

"We can't, either," I mutter as he drains more and more of my magic.

Astrea grits her teeth. "I don't have to." She dodges a guard's sword before gracefully stabbing her dagger through his armor. "I only have to hold out long enough to kill you. And I will kill you, make no mistake." But even from here, I can see the sweat beading on her brow, and with each wave of that black mist she sends out, her body sags a little more.

"Tell me, Harbinger, is it the madness you are avoiding? Or do you truly just not know how to wield your magic?" He jumps off the dais, dragging me with him by the arm. The release of the leash gives me a moment's peace, my body sagging and my mind rapidly trying to make sense of everything that's happened.

"Oisin!" My mother's voice cuts through the room, the sound of her high heels suddenly piercing my ears. Oisin turns to look at her. "We are ready!"

"Finally," Oisin drawls, his voice laden with annoyance.

That's when I see Lady Ornate, Cordelia, and a few other witches appear beside my mother. All of the witches are decaying and smell of death. Oisin didn't just reanimate Cordelia, he reanimated the whole damn coven. The thought slams into me with the sudden understanding of just how deeply Oisin has gone into magic he never should have touched. When one of the witches shifts, my eyes meet the Mori grimoire held tightly in her decaying hands.

"No," I breathe out as the magic starts to snap in place. I push against the control over me, forcing my mouth open. "Astrea, run!" I scream. Oisin turns, red eye flaring with rage as he grabs hold of the leash, silencing me again.

For a second, I think I gave her enough time to run, but I see vines of golden magic start to pepper the ground around her. When one attaches to her leg, she screams in agony before sending her magic slicing through another that was attempting to latch to her arm. Vine after vine appears until they manage to tether both legs and both arms.

More of her magic flares out as she fights off the containment, while Onyx and Buttercup attempt to intercept the witches crowding around her. Then another loop appears around Astrea's throat, and the two snakes instantly mist away and reappear solid on her body again. I watch as my best friend thrashes against the spelled vines to no avail, and my heart drops to the floor when I realize we are losing.

———

SHADOW

("Voices" – Hidden Citizens)

Ciaran walks forward, toward the back entrance Jackson directed us to. Off to the side and covered by shrubs, the gate has been all but forgotten, only used now as a way for servants to send trash in and out. Even from here, I can feel the wards rolling, black eels alive and well. Ciaran lifts his hand, his gold magic wrapping around them, and the magic drops out, our path suddenly clear.

As we move to walk forward, Ciaran stumbles, clutching his chest.

"Ciaran?"

He growls. "It's Astrea. Something is wrong." For a beat, he holds his chest, before righting himself. "We need to hurry." He pulls his sword off his back, and flames wreath my hand as we walk in. The halls are quiet compared to the screams outside. The passage has low light, cool stone and marble lining the walkway. Shimmering torchlike lamps hang low, giving an eerie feel. Our footsteps are loud, echoing off the walls as we push forward.

"The passage lets out in a closet, he said," Ciaran repeats to me, as if I hadn't been there when he told us. "Just a little further. We can make it."

I'm not sure who he is trying to convince, me or himself.

FORTY-FOUR

We will return.
-Mori Family Grimoire

AVA

("This Is Where It Ends" – Hidden Citizens)
Oisin circles Astrea. My own exhausted body lies in a pile next to the thrones he created. His voice seems distant as he talks with my mother and the decaying coven. My eyes stay locked on my friend, an apology hopefully evident in them. Oisin erected a shield of my creation around the palace, blocking Drago out and presumably Shadow, and he seems confident that the magic will hold against my mates. The way I feel right now, I am hopeful that confidence is misplaced.

I hope Shadow is safe. My heart stutters at the reasons Shadow wouldn't be with Drago.

No. Just because you haven't heard him or heard anyone

talk about another dragon doesn't mean something bad has happened to him. If Ciaran and Astrea are here, he is to.

Cordelia's reentrance to the room stops the conversations. My mouth goes dry at what she holds in her hands. The same golden collar that I have on. They are going to collar Astrea. Her eyes flare wide at the same moment the realization hits me. Rage and fear are painted across my friend's face.

It all happens in slow motion, Cordelia nearing Astrea, Oisin smiling in victory, and the door bursting open to reveal Ciaran and Shadow.

SHADOW

("Don't Speak" – Hidden Citizens)

I zero in on Ava's crumpled form near the gaudy thrones of gold. Nothing else exists as I see her pale body, shoved into that wedding dress. I don't hear anything other than her broken sob of relief as she locks eyes with me. Relief unfurls in my chest, too, but at the same time, I'm consumed with rage.

"Astrea!" Ciaran bellows, pulling my gaze from my mate to my friend's mate, who is bound in the center of the room.

Astrea thrashes against those magical bindings, her own gaze pulled to us and those green eyes seeming to switch from black to green and back to black all in the span of a second. Her dark magic flickers like a candle flame as the magic holding her tightens its hold, drawing her body closer to the ground.

"Ciaran, go! Get Ava and go!" she screams. "He's got more collars!"

Oisin's cackling laughter echoes in the room. "Hello,

brother. I was hoping you would come. It's so lovely to finally have you home."

Ciaran growls, and his golden magic snaps at Oisin. "I will fucking gut you, brother." The magic slams into the wards erected between us and them. Oisin's face pales slightly, the smile sliding from it as the wards seem to falter under the strain of Ciaran's magic.

AVA

I laugh in shocked delight as hope fills me.

In the blink of an eye, Oisin's in front of me, hand wrapped around the chain again. My magic flows out against my will in a glittering expansion. I want to scream, but I can only stand there as he plays with his pretty puppet.

"Time to show them where your allegiance lies," he whispers into my ear.

I cringe as my will is drained back out of me and the strings are pulled taut once again. Shadow lunges forward, even as Ciaran continues to break down the wards. Flames meet the transparent barrier as my mate fights with everything he has to get to me.

"Get that fucking collar on her," Oisin screams at my mother and Lady Ornate, who have taken the job from Cordelia. The zombie-witch is looking rapidly through the grimoire, no doubt for something to help Oisin. The two women seem hesitant to approach Astrea, whose eyes have gone wholly black now, and the golden vines are smoldering. Holy gods, she is going to break through the magic. If I can stall this for a little longer, she could break free. We could win.

Oisin's voice pulls me away from her and back to

Shadow and Ciaran as he addresses them. "I would like to introduce you to my new wife." He walks us forward, my body following him like a loyal puppy. Shadow's flames and Ciaran's magic cut off, neither willing to risk hurting me. "She looks beautiful, doesn't she? Tell them, my dear, tell them all about our time together."

Whether it's true or not, Oisin forces my mouth open, and half-truths and lies pour from me like an avalanche. Shadow's devastated look would gut me if I could feel anything. Oisin commands the words, and I repeat them. Ciaran looks furious, the runes burning brightly across his head.

"We will kill you," Ciaran vows, his knuckles white as they hold his sword.

("Paint It Black" – Hidden Citizens)

A scream from Astrea has me glancing back to her, only to see her magic faltering again, and the golden collar being placed around her pale neck. The pieces suddenly form together in my memory. This—this is how my vision starts. The realization is enough for me to push through the small fissure in that wall holding my will back. Tears silently track down my face as I realize this is the end. That despite it all, we are still losing.

Oisin drags me forward, the train of my white dress dragging behind me. Shadow is screaming my name. Ciaran's eyes are locked on my mother as she firmly locks the collar around Astrea. I need to fight this. I need to get them out.

I pull against the inner chains binding me. I hit that small fracture, cracking it wider and wider until it splits open and I'm breaking through the magic. My purpose is clear. It's my magic holding Shadow and Ciaran back. My magic they cannot breach in time. I might not be able to access it with this collar, but I can sure as hell cut Oisin off from it. A strange sense of calm washes over me like a gentle ocean wave pushes over a rock. There is strength in the knowledge that you know how something will end. Even if it's terrifying.

My magic wanes as Oisin pulls and pulls, taking more than he should, before he finally releases me and allows my body to drop to the floor near Astrea, but not close enough to touch her. He blasts a wave into Ciaran and Shadow, sending them flying backward. Shadow manages to land on his hands and knees, but Ciaran hits the back wall with a resounding crack.

"CIARAN!" Astrea's broken scream cuts through the room as she sees her mate's limp body crumpled on the floor.

"This is working out better than I planned. Not only will I have two dragons, but I'll have the Harbinger as well." He sneers at Shadow as he grabs me by my hair, pulling me back to my feet. "I'm going to keep you alive, dragon. You will have a matching collar to the one she wears; you'll be at my service, whether you want to be or not. You thought the prison Alexi kept you in was bad? Mine will be so much worse."

My sobs echo around the room as I think of what that will do to him. My chest cracks in two like the land on a fault line during an earthquake.

Oisin glances back to Astrea. "She'll look beautiful tethered to me. A matching set, if you will." His eyes are hungry.

The palace shakes, and plaster starts to fall from the ceiling. Outside, screams and shrieks echo through the air amid the sounds of Elkers and other hellish beasts that should never have been set loose. But it's the roar in the distance that I focus on the most. Drago is not far; I can taste his magic. In a matter of moments, he'll be here, and my gut tells me that will be the nail in the coffin. I close my eyes, steeling my spine, and give another shove against the magic of the collar.

Shadow lifts his head, eyes full of fear and panic as I give him a sad smile. One that I hope conveys how much I wish we could have had longer together, that this isn't his fault, it's just our fate. He opens his mouth to yell, but I shake my head as I manage to pull control from the leash for just a moment.

"Oisin," I say. He jerks his head toward me as I yank myself out of his embrace. I pull the crown from my head, the spikes atop it brutally sharp. I walk backward, away from him and my family. "Let's see if you can keep that magic with its source gone." My voice is hard, anger strengthening it.

I shift my eyes to Shadow, ignoring the pounding of my heart. "I love you. Please take care of Drago." Oisin lunges at me, but I'm too quick as I drive the crown's spikes across my throat in one brutal slash.

The last thing I see is Shadow unleashed, his dragon roaring to life as he rushes toward me. Astrea's pained screams echo in my ears; my name being wrenched from her in a sob is the last thing I hear.

DRAGO

("Bigger Than the Whole Sky" – Taylor Swift)

It's the fear from Shadow that stops me in my tracks first, followed by agony and anger from Ava. Then a sharp pain, and she's just gone. My chest cracks open, raw as I finally break through the magic that has held me out. No, I don't break through—the magic itself is gone. Only remnants of it remain in the wind. My dragon fades away as I drop back into my human form. The space next to Shadow's bond is empty now.

A portal opens for me, Shadow seeking me out without realizing it, and I step through with no hesitation, searching for visual confirmation that the missing bond is a lie. My eyes snag on Ciaran's crumpled body off to the side of the room, before finding Astrea bound in the middle of the room by vines of gold magic. I go to take another step toward her, but her magic explodes out of her, releasing her from whatever they were attempting to bind her with.

"You," Astrea screams. I watch her eyes go fully black as they narrow on Oisin, who is backing away from us. "I am going to make you suffer."

Her black, smoky magic fills the room alongside her snakes. Oisin has the decency to look utterly terrified. His eyes dart around, and before I can tell her to grab him, he mists out of the room. She lets out a scream of frustration, before our attention is pulled toward two women who are attempting to scurry from the room. One I recognize as Ava's mother, and the other is the half-rotten corpse of the reanimated Cordelia Fairmore.

"We will kill them all," Astrea hisses, her voice no longer one I recognize. She ghosts out of whatever was holding her and moves toward the two women. I watch, almost mesmerized, as she appears behind Cordelia, snapping the dead woman's neck with a smile across her tear-streaked face. Buttercup moves up behind her and swallows the witch's corpse in one bite. Ava's mother looks terrified as she has the full attention of the Harbinger now on her.

"Please! You cannot kill me! I can help you!" she begs.

"Like you helped your daughter? You did nothing, and now, she's gone. I hope wherever you end up, she can torment you," Astrea says. She puts herself directly behind Ava's mother, dragging one of those blades across the woman's milky skin, a wicked smile painted across her red lips.

She looks at Ciaran, who has managed to push himself up to a seated position. "Let's go hunt your fucking brother." He gives her a nod, but I see the hesitation in his eyes. Astrea unleashes her power, death and destruction pouring out of her in waves that drown us all, as she goes in search of revenge. The two move out of the room, Ciaran casting a look filled with grief back toward me, so much fucking grief that it almost brings me to my knees.

When my eyes finally connect with my mate's, I know before I even reach them that Ava is gone. I know that space in my chest is truly empty, nothing but hollow pain and desperation. A void that will never be filled. I run toward them but pull up short when I see Ava's white skin splashed with red. Tears cascade down my face as I fall to my knees, fists tearing at my hair. Shadow screams, rage and grief pulsing out of him in a tsunami that overtakes everything.

The world around us dims, and I can only see the broken body of my mate, only the failure of not reaching them in time. Shadow meets my eyes, and I know we won't recover from this. I don't deserve to recover from this. The failure is mine and mine alone. Shadow sobs into Ava's body, her name a prayer on his lips as he begs whatever gods we have to bring her back.

I'm not sure how long I sit on my knees, a broken shell of a man, watching my mate hold our heart in his hands. I throw my head back, and the sound I emit is nothing short of a broken cry as I shift back to my dragon, the pain too great to stay in my human form.

Shadows gaze cuts to mine. "Don't you dare leave me, too," he growls. He stands, cradling Ava's limp form in his arms, as if my shift has galvanized movement. "Let's go." His broken voice echoes in my head. He opens a portal and steps through before I follow him, still in dragon form.

*There are creatures in our world that dream walk from one
realm to another.
Often seeking their mates without knowing.*
-Priestess Codex

JACKSON

Cleaning up Hell and the mess Oisin has left in his wake after fleeing is taking more time than I care to admit. His mockery of a palace and the city around it is nothing more than a refugee camp at this point. Bodies are still being uncovered, an endless amount of death discovered everyday as rubble is moved and cleaned.

I pinch the bridge of my nose as another tension headache begins to form. Clearly, Dios did not fuck the tension from me like he said he would.

The death god surprised me by not only remaining at my side even after the battle was done but following to the lake house we are currently at. I had assumed he would return to his club, but thus far, he has made no indication that he has any intent on leaving. Which is good because if I'm alone long enough, my anxiety might just finally take me under. Since the battle, and truthfully even before that, my anxiety has begun to take on a life of its own again. My nervous tapping is now a constant movement.

The long sigh from Kallen interrupts my thoughts.

"Yes?" I ask from behind the large oak desk. This nuisance arrived shortly after the dragons disappeared with my sister, wolf-shifter mate in tow. Both covered in gore and presenting an Elker head as a prize. Dios and Harrow had arrived only moments before, the latter with her mask ripped free of her face.

"Are we going to talk about the plan moving forward?" Kallen asks, her voice taking on a hint of boredom. It takes everything in me to keep from organizing the papers strewn about on the desk in front me just to give my hands something to do.

"Astrea and Ciaran are back in Gothic Grove," I say. After the hunt for his brother and Lady Ornate failed, he rapidly pulled his mate back to the city. I can't fault him; he almost lost her. I would have done the same thing.

"The Harbinger cannot be brought back into this." Kallen's voice is deadly quiet. "She will lose herself to that darkness, and we do not want what will awaken from that. Let them run the city, but do not allow her back in Hell." Her mate looks at her with a look that I can't quite place as he grips her uninjured shoulder. The fact that this witch defeated an Elker, that they both walked away from it, is astounding. Not many people can claim to have done that. So, her saying she's worried about what will happen if Astrea comes back into my realm is enough to have me heeding her advice.

"Astrea and Ciaran will take over The Playground, for now," I say.

"You seem awfully cavalier about them taking over your sister's place. Are you going to tell us why you aren't grieving your sister and her mates?" Demon asks. The shifter's blue eyes appraise me, his wolf just beneath the surface.

I shrug. "This is Hell. Death isn't the same here." It's the least complicated answer I can give. And it's technically the truth. Death doesn't exist here the same way it does in Gothic Grove. So, while I worry about my sister's soul, I'm not distressed. The distressing part is her mates. Having two dragons loose in Hell won't end well for anyone. Particularly those two dragons.

Kallen stands up. "Well, that's not cryptic or anything." Walking over to the bar, she grabs the open bottle of wine atop it and takes a long swig, forgoing a glass. "Now, we should talk about the plan surrounding Oisin. Do we know what he wants? Where would the little weasel hide?"

As I move to open my mouth, the door to the room swings open. It's the scent that hits me first, the first rain of the season overlaid with sandalwood, and I don't need to look up to know who I'll be staring at. My heart drops to my stomach, and my chest pinches tightly. I clench my fingers into a tight fist.

"Your fucking ex-boyfriend is in my Forest." Her voice sends shivers through my body. I slowly raise my eyes off the wood surface of the desk and lock them onto a pair of storm-gray eyes framed by long black hair. She crosses her arms over the cropped white tank top she has covering her chest, the gold bangles on her wrist ringing through the room as they hit each other. The long, smooth green skirt she wears settles around her, brushing the ground, but not before I catch a glimpse of her toned leg peeking through the slit that goes up to her hip. She's grown up.

"Arcanna," I mutter, unable to keep her name from spilling from my lips

Her eyes are hard when I reach them again, having drank my fill of her body. "Lady of Souls to you," she spits at me.

I don't let it show that my heart cracks a little hearing that. Late into the night, we would lie in my bed talking about everything and anything, until the night we took things too far, made promises we never should have, and in the end, it ruined everything.

I open my mouth, to say what, I'm not sure, but anything feels better than the silence choking me. But she raises her hand. "I don't want to hear it, Jackson, I have no interest in whatever excuse you were about to try to soothe me with. I'm here on business only."

"And what would that be?" Kallen asks. As if Arcanna is just now realizing other people are in the room, she turns and looks at them. Kallen smiles at her, a curling of her lips that looks slightly unhinged.

Demon curses, noticing it. "Kallen, what have we talked about?"

She rolls her eyes. "Yes, yes, 'try to keep the crazy contained.'" She looks at Arcanna again. "Apparently, my smile makes people uncomfortable."

Arcanna only shrugs. "Men seem to get uncomfortable very easily in the presence of a powerful woman, don't they?"

Kallen cackles. "I like you!"

"Jesus Christ, there are two of them," I mutter, which only brings Arcanna's cold eyes back to me.

"I'm here because we need to stop Oisin. As you are the king here, I expect you to help."

"Who's watching the Forest while you're here?" I ask, leaning against the desk.

She shrugs. "I have help." A growl echoes out of me as I think about who could be helping her. Is there someone warming her bed at home?

As if she knows where my mind went, she gives me a wicked smile. "I have a lot of help."

All I can hear is Kallen cackling as rage pours through me. But I tamp it down, pinching the bridge of my nose and taking a deep breath. "Good. I'm glad."

It's the wrong move, because her face turns even colder, the temperature in the room dropping with it as ice seems to form around us. And for a moment, I wonder if she even realizes her powers are creeping out. Her breath puffs out in a cool cloud that turns to ice and falls to the ground, and the sound of it shattering is what pulls her magic back into her. She shakes her head as if to clear it before dropping her hands from her chest to wipe ice crystals from that green skirt.

"You'll be helping me, Jackson, and I won't be leaving without you. So, either you make this easy or I'll fucking drag you out of here." She whirls around and storms back out of the room in a rage. "I'll be in my room—if that jackass left it alone, that is. Come find me when you're ready to leave," she yells over her shoulder before leaving us alone in silence once again.

Demon clears his throat awkwardly. "Who was that?"

"That, Demon, was my fucking mate."

EPILOGUE

("Marjorie" – Taylor Swift)

TO MOST HUMANS, death is scary. We fear the unknown and what might become of our immortal souls. But to those of us raised in Hell, or raised in Death's embrace, we do not fear it. We know the peace that can come with it. We know that death isn't truly the end, it's simply the next step. Death is peaceful, when your soul is finally freed, and when you arrive in this Forest, you are finally home.

"I didn't not expect to see you here." The voice behind me brings tears to my eyes as I turn around and take in the beautiful Lady before me.

"I did not expect to be here like this," I reply. She raises an eyebrow at me, and I shrug. "Okay, maybe I did, but I had hoped it wouldn't be this way."

She nods in understanding. She moves up next to me, her dark form glowing in the evening. Almost as if she is the moon and the woods are her sky, with each of our souls the stars that move around her. We both look out over the once lush, green forest, but now, portions of it seem to be rotting away, as if they are being taken by the mountain range that separates this place from the Land of the Damned. While the Forest is a place of healing, the city within the Land is something else entirely.

In the distance, where the gates are located to this sacred space, comes a roar shattering the peace within the air followed by another.

She glances towards the sounds raising her eyebrow. "What will you do if I allow them here with you?" she asks, her voice soothing.

A smile spreads over my face. "We will help you restore the Forest."

"How?"

The peaceful smile I had turns slightly wicked. "We have a personal vendetta against the ones doing this." Her black hair shifts in the wind, those stormy eyes twinkling as she nods, then she snaps her fingers. She turns to me, planting a kiss on my forehead, as my body seems to materialize. Suddenly whole again.

"You will remain here and take care of things while I gather reinforcements," she says as I smooth my hands over my body as though it might disappear again.

I look up at her, holding those storm-gray eyes for a moment, and take her in fully. Her hair is long, wild even, and the black eats up the night sky around us. She's dressed in linen overalls, a white tank top underneath, and her feet are bare on the forest floor. If she weren't holding the massive glaive in her hands, she could be confused for a simple gardener. But it's the overwhelming sadness that stands out the most.

"He missed you," I whisper.

She cuts me a hard look. "Then he should have come for me."

A frown paints my lips. And she cuts me off as I go to open my mouth, to ask her what she means. "You should meet them at the gates. I don't want the little remaining forest to be burned down because they don't know how to get to you."

She snaps her fingers, and a portal opens to the lake house, the scent wafting through and carving out a well of homesickness that lodges in my throat. I watch her step through, her body disappearing as the portal shuts and cuts off the place I once loved. I let out a long huff as another keening sounds enters the air and from the corner of my eye, I see black flames shoot into the sky.

"Impatient dragons. . ." I mutter as I speed off towards the gates.

OISIN BONUS SCENE

Four Years Ago

Straddling the king I smile wildly with my knife pressed to his throat, the look of shock in his eyes shooting straight to my cock. "Didn't see this coming, did you?" I muse with deep satisfaction.

"How dare you!" He growls. His body remains rigid, the paralytic agent I slipped into his drink earlier doing wonders to keep him prone on the bed. "I gave you my daughter!"

I shake my head, "You gave me the promise of her and yet you never delivered. She's gone. Fled from the city. And now I have nothing."

"Jax—-" he starts to sputter but I press the knife in harder, blood now welling against the sliver blade.

"Jackson isn't Ava. I needed a queen, not just a hole to fuck." I let out a long, dramatic sigh. "I want you to know that your kingdom is mine now. I will find your daughter; I will tether her to me until I drain every last drop of magic from her and The Well and then I will toss her into the shallow pit of a grave I intend to throw you into." His eyes widen and the fear that wafts off of him is delicious.

"Jackson will never allow it."

A laugh huffs free of me, and I lean in a bit closer to his face, now covered in a light sheen of sweat. "Jackson will be so far gone in my manipulation he'll never know what hit him until it's too late. Trust me, your son is the least of my fucking concerns." I press the blade in harder now, his skin giving way. "I'm the one who burned the forest. Killed the priestesses. It's always been me. I have everything I need now to take this kingdom down. I hope you enjoy watching it from your place in the afterlife."

Outside the wind whips against the windows of the royal palace, the sand kicking up and pelting the glass windows. It covers the sounds of gurgles pulled from the king as the blade cuts through one final time and his blood spills free. I watch until the last bit of life leaves his eyes before pushing free of him. I wipe the blade clean on the bed before tucking it away in its sheath. Whistling I clean myself up before meandering down to Jackson's bedroom. When I push the door open I find the prince sprawled naked on his bed, the moonlight peaking through at just the right moment to bathe him in its glow.

When I envelope his cock in my mouth I enjoy knowing that the hands holding him now stole the life of his father only moments ago; my little puppet's cock swells to the swirl of my tongue and I work my own hardened length as I relish in my flawless execution. I'm the true fucking king here.

THANK YOU FOR READING!

Thank you for taking the time to read about Ava, Drago and Shadow. I promise they will be back. I am a firm beilever in HEA and I would never not give my sweet babies a happy ending after all they've been through. All they ask is you leave a review for them on the good ol' Zon and Goodreads. It's truly the lifeblood of indie authors!

Pre-Order for Ruined Kingdom (coming Jan 2025) is up right now! Preorder here

---

Need more?

Make sure to join my newsletter for extra special, spooky and spicy fun! Subscribers get sneak peaks on upcoming projects, bonus content and occasionally free kindle versions of new books. You also get early preorder access for any of the physical books that cannot be found on the zon. All books include sprayed edges and NSFW formatting. Join here!

TRANSLATIONS

Kamerat – "mate" (Norwegian)
Rakkaani – "my beloved" (Finnish)
Mi cielo- "my sky" (Spanish)

<u>Astrea Mori and Ciaran Helvig</u>
Witch and Vampire/Witch Hybrid
Mates
Holds Harbinger magic

<u>Kallen</u>
Witch
Original holder of Harbinger magic
Currently, her soul is possessing the body of Reem Mori
Glamour, Realm Walker, Elemental, Mind Control and other unknown powers

<u>Jameson "Demon" Knight</u>
Preseident of Primal Knights MC
Alpha wolf shifter
Mate to Kallen

<u>Shadow</u>
Stepbrother to Drago and mate
Dragon shifter

Fire affinity and Realm Walker

<u>Drago</u>
Stepbrother to Shadow and mate
Dragon shifter
Death affinity

<u>Ava Daemonium</u>
Magic unknown
Mate to Drago and Shadow
Princess of Hell

<u>Jackson Daemonium</u>
Ava's brother
Magic unknown
King of Hell

<u>Oisin</u>
Leader of The Order of Infernal Sin

<u>Other</u>
Arcanna Ornate
Harrowlena
Dios
Reaver

ACKNOWLEDGMENTS

Okay, this is going to be a long one, you guys. Because this book really wouldn't have happened without so many people. This was a tough one to write. It really pushed me and pulled things from those boxes in the attic we all like to ignore. It tested me in ways I wasn't expecting (looking at you, Drago). But it also forced me to face some shame I had around my own history with self-harm. So, I have to send deep gratitude to my sweet baby Shadow for allowing me to heal through his story.

I want to start by thanking my wonderful partner, my husby, my human in all things, for sitting with me through this process without even knowing how he was helping. Whether it was making new spicy content to write about, playing with the kids while I wrote, or just a simple hug, it all made such a huge difference to me.

Also, to my found family: Chelsea, Serena, Courtney, Jordan, Sam, and Kristin. You guys all supported me in so many ways, through the nights that I was forcing myself to write and on the days when I was celebrating all the wins in writing. You all kept me going and filled my cup. Truly, I wouldn't be here without you.

I need to give a nod to my fellow authors who have helped me so much. You are beautiful humans inside and out. Corrine, thank you for the help with figuring out random things like, "Hey, how do you print your NSFW art?" Lark Taylor, Alethea Faust, and Cora Rose, your books have helped me de-stress and become reinspired when I'm struggling.

The Smut Collective: Edie, Blake, Mads, Kelsey, and Kenan. I don't even know what to say. Our group chat keeps me going. From the TikToks to the book discussions to what new toys we should buy, the conversations are irreplaceable.

My beta and alpha readers. You guys were so beyond valuable. You read the hot mess that this book started as, along with dealing with all the changes that I kept making. Sam (both of you), Serena, Courtney, Adrienne, Tara, Celeste, and Morgan. While some of you I've known forever, many of you are new to me, but I can't imagine doing this without any of y'all.

The Gothic Grove HOA. You know who you are. But for those that don't . . . they are my hype team. My ARC readers. My street team. The people who have made this book possible and have kept me writing, even when I saw bad reviews and questioned what I was doing. The ones who blow up the Discord channel in excitement.

A very special nod to Lem for doing amazing artwork to bring the books to life. Seriously. Love you for never questioning me when I'm like, "Hey, so I know you just gave me a piece, but I have another idea." You have a true talent.

My editor, Paisley. Thank you so much for working with me and all my back-and-forth. This was a hard one to give up because I wanted it "perfect" before handing it over.

Mads thank you for continuing to exceed my expectations with formatting, I'm so excited to see what you do for the rest of the series. You have grown so much and I'm so proud of you for following you're dreams. Sam, thank you for the cover. You continue to leave me in awe at the ability you have to create something so magical.

And finally, to my readers. Without you, Gothic Grove

wouldn't be a thing in general. But even more so, without you, I'm not sure I would have moved forward with Shadow, Drago, and Ava's story. The resounding excitement around these characters gave me the continued push I needed to portray their story in its entirety. Bookstagram and Booktok have showed up for me even outside of this book, and I will forever be indebted to this community.

ABOUT THE AUTHOR

JA George is a spooky, hearth witch living in the PNW with her two goblins and husby. She has three fur babies who provide endless support. She loves all things smutty and dark. She believes Halloween should be all year long and thrives in the wind and rain.